The Gilded King

Sovereign: Book One

Josie Jaffrey

By Josie Jaffrey

The Solis Invicti Series

A Bargain in Silver
The Price of Silver
Bound in Silver
The Silver Bullet

The Sovereign Series

The Gilded King

Short Stories

Living Underground

1

Julia's world was blue.

Blue was everything. Blue was safe. Blue was home.

How she longed to see red.

She could just glimpse it from the alley in which she crouched. The forests of the Red were ever present, cradling and encroaching on stone and blue paint. The tops of the trees danced over the stuccoed walls of the buildings that formed the Blue: the last city on earth.

'They're coming out,' Claudia whispered.

Julia looked away from the tree line that marked the edge of her world and turned to follow her friend's gaze. The doors of the temple were swinging open, soundless and majestic. Their silence left a vacuum where there should have been noise. She wanted to scream into it, to fill the void. Instead, she wrestled another weed from between the paving stones and threw it hard into the trug.

Claudia's fingers clasped at Julia's arm in excitement, her eyes fixed on the doors across the square. 'Here they come,' she said.

'You see them every day, Claud. They're just people.'

'Not like this though. It's Inauguration Day. Why aren't you excited?'

Julia couldn't have cared less about it, because it had nothing to do with her.

She wrapped her fist around the leaves of a dandelion and pulled, leaning back to put her body weight behind it, but she'd been too rough. She fell onto her backside as the leaves snapped off in her fingers, leaving the roots in the ground and a feeling of tight impotence in her chest.

The procession spilled out into the square as Julia brushed the leaves from her hands. The new Candidates followed the priestess like little ducklings following their mother, crowding close with small, shuffling steps in their eagerness. There were only seven girls this year. Julia recognised all of them; the Blue wasn't that big.

'There she is,' Claudia sighed.

She didn't have to point, because they both knew whom she meant: Marcella. The girl was so shockingly beautiful that anyone would think she was already a Noble. No one had been surprised when she was chosen as a Candidate. Her skin was smooth and flint-black, illuminated so perfectly by the sunshine that it was as though it were worshipping her with its rays. She was average in height, but proportioned like a taller woman, with long, delicate limbs and a graceful neck. Her hair seemed to crown her head in a riot of dark curls.

All of the girls were dressed in their best clothing, showing off swathes of skin dripping in jewels. Most of them seemed weighed down by their decoration, as though they had been subsumed into it, but Marcella wore it lightly. Nothing could make her any more or less stunning than she already was.

'Look at Diana's hair,' Claudia whispered. 'Isn't it gorgeous?'

The girl was taller than the others, nearly as tall as the priestess herself. Her blonde hair was teased into a fountain on the top of her head so it spilled in tumbles down the sides of her face. Combined with her jewelled orange dress, Julia thought it made her look like a wilted carrot.

'It's stupid,' she said.

'You think everything's stupid.'

'Only things that aren't real. This is real,' Julia said, pushing her fingernails between the paving slabs as she sought out the elusive dandelion root. 'Dirt is real. Earth is real. Work is real. All that glitter out there in the square is just make believe.'

Claudia sat back on her heels and stared at the girls as the priestess led them towards their new lodgings. They would be housed in the grander buildings now, the ones whose gardens and kitchens Julia and Claudia were too lowly to tend.

'That's not what you really think,' Claudia said. 'You weren't like this last year.'

'Yeah, well, last year I was stupid too.'

'Because you thought you might be one of them.'

Julia shook her head with a bitter laugh. 'I never thought that,' she said, but it wasn't entirely true.

It was too late for them both now. They'd been assigned to their rank months ago, and with it went Julia's hopes for a better life. They'd never be anything other than Servers, from now until the day they died. Cleaning, cooking, gardening, laundering and waiting on the Nobles would take up the rest of their lives. And feeding, of course, but Julia wasn't even good enough for that, apparently. It was a matter of taste, they said, and she had too little delicacy about her.

'This is the last morning we'll spend together,' Claudia said quietly.

'I know.'

'Then don't ruin it.'

'I'm sorry. I just…'

'I know,' Claudia said, 'you wanted to be a Candidate.'

She was dead wrong. What Julia wanted, what her heart screamed for, was the freedom she imagined to exist in the Red. That wasn't a desire she could show to anyone, not even Claudia. In a city of many taboos, a human leaving the Blue was the biggest. They said it was dangerous, and that no humans had ever returned alive. But if they did survive out there, then why would they come back?

If it hadn't been for Claudia, Julia would have left without a backward glance. She was nothing here, and she would always be nothing if she stayed.

But she wasn't ready to risk death for the faint possibility of liberty. Not yet.

Her eyes strayed back towards the treetops as she rose to her feet and wiped her muddy fingers on the front of her cloak. Clouds were being blown across the sky by a wind that began to batter the edges of the forest. She pulled the sides of her hood tighter around her face, suddenly cold.

'Are you thinking about them again?' Claudia asked.

'Do you think about yours?'

'Sometimes,' she said, picking up the trug as she stood. 'I wonder what my father was thinking. He just can't have loved me that much, I guess.'

'Or he loved your mother too much.'

'Maybe.' Claudia fiddled with the weeds they'd collected. 'Either way, they're gone now.'

'Well, at least your parents weren't traitors,' Julia said.

Claudia met her eye with a wry smile. 'Not both of them, anyway,' she said, 'but one was bad enough to make me a Server.'

'The other was good enough to make you an Attendant.'

Despite herself, Claudia smiled at the reminder of her recent preferment.

If there had been any justice then she would have been a Candidate. They both knew it. She was sweet in nature and appearance: the perfect combination. It still hadn't allowed her to follow in her mother's footsteps, but if she couldn't be a Candidate, then an Attendant was the next best thing. She would remain a Server, but of a higher class, assigned to one of the Nobles as their own.

It seemed the worst of both worlds to Julia - still being a Server, just with even greater scrutiny - but Claudia was delighted. Julia didn't want to spoil this for her.

'I wonder if he'll be handsome,' Claudia said, her voice wispy and soft. 'Maybe we'll fall in love. Maybe he'll love me so much that he'll insist the Empress makes me a Candidate, so we can be together forever.'

Trust Claud to view her new servitude as romantic.

'How do you even know he'll be a he?' Julia said.

'That's what they said when they told me it was happening. They even gave me his name: Rufus.'

'Latin,' Julia said.

'Yep, just like us.'

'He was born here, then?'

'It sounds like it, doesn't it? I wonder how old that makes him. He must be young.'

'The Blue's been here for hundreds of years, Claud.'

'Fine, *relatively* young then.'

'Yes,' Julia said, unable to resist teasing her, 'but he might not look it.'

Age wasn't simple in the Blue. These days every Candidate was under thirty, but admission to the ranks of immortality hadn't always been so controlled. Most of the Nobles were frozen in their prime, but some were as gnarled as the old woman who ran the kitchen.

Claudia's face screwed up in distaste. 'I hadn't considered that.'

'I'm sure he'll be wonderful.'

'And handsome,' Claudia said, smiling winsomely.

'I'm sure.'

And heartless, Julia thought, *just like they all are.*

They spent the afternoon in the kitchen, speaking in whispers as they scrubbed vegetables. The room around them was filled with quiet industry as Servers worked together to prepare dinner. Everything was scoured, peeled and scorched until the life had been pummelled out of it, just in case. Gnarled old Livia said there was only danger in things that bled, and even then only if they came from the Red, but you could never be too sure.

Blood could give life in the Blue, but in the Red it was death.

The beds of Julia's nails were already sore from prying weeds out of the concrete, but still she scrubbed. It mattered that her work was done well. Children in the Blue were raised on cautionary tales that shaped their fears: maidens poisoned with apples tainted by a drop of robin's blood, or heroes conquering great beasts, only to die alongside them as monstrous gore - pure contamination - washed into their wounds. Julia lived in the shadow of those stories.

'Are you alright?' Claudia whispered.

'Of course.' Julia forced a smile for her.

'I'm sorry. I shouldn't have brought up your parents.'

'It's fine, Claud, really.' She put a clean parsnip on the pile and reached for another to wash. 'But…'

'What?'

'They must be dead. I mean, if they were alive, wouldn't they have come back for me?'

Claudia didn't reply. She was avoiding Julia's eyes.

'You do think they're dead,' Julia said.

'It's not that.' Claudia's voice was gentle. 'They left you, Jules. They walked out into the Red and left you behind. If they're dead - which yes, I'm sorry, I think they are - then do you really care?'

Julia dug her aching fingernails into the vegetable in her hand. The pain radiated up her arm through the tendons, burning off the irritation that had been tickling under her skin.

'I suppose not,' she said.

It made no difference. She didn't want them anymore. She didn't want to follow them into the Red so she could find them, like she'd wanted when she was a child. Now she wanted to follow them simply to see what they had found, because she hoped desperately that what was out there might be better than what was in here.

She didn't know, though, and that was what fixed her feet at the boundary line every time she thought of running.

'Anyway,' Julia said, 'do you know when you're meeting him?'

'Sunset.'

Julia stifled a snort. 'Of course. How dramatic.'

'Oh, don't be like that.'

'Alright, so you meet him. Then what?'

Claudia nudged her with an elbow. 'You know what.'

'Yes, but do you?' Julia nudged back.

'There *is* training, you know. I know what I'm doing, thank you very much.'

They both jumped as Livia tossed another bag of roots onto the table beside them.

'Come on, you two,' she said. 'At this rate, we'll be serving up dinner for breakfast tomorrow.'

'No one can tell the difference anyway,' Julia murmured, earning herself a gentle clip around the ear. The blow was deliberately soft; Livia might be old, but she was far from feeble.

'With that mouth,' she said, 'it's no wonder you weren't picked for Attendant.' Her words were not without love. 'Maybe next year,' she added.

'I hope not.'

'Me neither,' Livia said with a smile. 'I'd hate to lose you both.'

'You'll still have me in the afternoons,' Claudia said.

Livia took the scrubbing brush from Claudia's hands and rubbed her fingers between her own. 'Not for this work,' she said, her voice pitched low. 'There'll be no dirt under your nails, not when you're serving a gentleman. You make sure you clean them up nicely when you're done.'

'He won't care about my nails.'

'Is that what you think? You'll soon find they care about the wrapping as much as they do what's inside. You can trust me on that.'

Someone called Livia's name from the other side of the kitchen and she left them to their scrubbing. Julia watched her go before leaning close to Claudia's ear.

'I heard she was Attendant to the Empress,' Julia whispered.

'No!'

'It's true. One of the gardeners told me.'

Claudia looked over her shoulder and studied the old woman more closely.

'It would certainly explain a lot,' she said.

'Her rooms upstairs,' Julia added.

'For one. That necklace she wears as well. I wonder whether the Empress loved her.'

'I doubt it, or she wouldn't be here.'

Claudia shrugged. 'She's old.'

And that was the end of it as far as Claudia was concerned: Livia's age alone made her worthy of being discarded, even if the Empress had feelings for her. It was the way the Nobles thought. Claudia really should have been a Candidate, because if she stayed human there was no way she was going to cope with the changes time would work on her body as she aged.

How strange it must have been for Livia to grow old while those she knew, maybe even cared about, stayed the same. Although Julia was too young to have experienced that incongruity firsthand, the fact of it didn't sit well with her. It seemed distasteful for the elite of the Blue to stay eternally young and shiny while their Servers slid into decrepitude around them, piece by broken piece. There was an arrogance to it that troubled her, although she couldn't deny that such arrogance seemed justified.

'Well,' Claudia said, 'I fully intend that my Noble will fall head over heels for me.' Her tone was playful, but Julia couldn't tell whether she was joking or not. She fervently hoped that she was.

'You'd better go and get ready then. I'll finish these off.'

Claudia needed little encouragement. She rushed back to their room to clean and primp herself, leaving Julia alone at the sink. She supposed she had better get used to it. Without Claudia, Livia was the only Server in the kitchen who would talk to her. She was marked by her parents' treachery, and none of the others would risk censure by association.

She'd be scrubbing alone from now on.

Julia was already in bed by the time Claudia returned to the room they shared in the cellar. It was mattress from wall to wall. Their garments hung from pegs behind the door and a small shelf held a few treasured possessions: a pocket knife, some ribbons, a brush and a plastic ornament a boy had once found in the earth and given to Claudia. It was precious not just because most plastic had degraded now, but because the boy was gone too.

Space was so tight that the door thunked into the mattress as Claudia squeezed into the room.

'How was it?' Julia asked.

'Okay.'

Claudia didn't take off her cloak before sitting down on the edge of the bed. Meagre moonlight leaked from the single high window, but it wasn't bright enough for Julia to be able to pick out her friend's features.

'Claud?'

She looked away.

Julia threw off her blanket and shuffled closer. 'Are you alright?' she asked softly.

'I'm fine. It was fine. I just… It wasn't how I expected it to be.'

'In what way?'

She finally turned towards Julia. The moonlight caught the shine of moisture in her eyes.

'It hurt,' she whispered in a voice that was strangled by emotion. 'I expected it to hurt a bit, but Jules, I was screaming. And there was so much blood.'

'Already?'

Maybe she'd been naive to think he'd wait. It was what the Attendants were for, after all.

'Every day,' Claudia was saying, her words worryingly distant. 'I'm going to have to let him do it every day. I'll never stop bleeding.'

Julia took Claudia's hands in her own. 'Show me,' she said.

There was a long pause before Claudia raised her shaking hands to her hood and pulled it down, baring her neck. The jagged wound glistened.

'It burns,' she said.

It was like no wound Julia had ever seen. She'd imagined that blood was taken from Attendants with needles and knives, not with teeth.

Naive was definitely the word.

'He just... bit you?' Julia asked.

'They told me he might. I thought it would feel, you know, good. Doesn't everyone say it feels good?' Desperation was creeping into her voice now.

Julia didn't know what to say, but she knew what had to be done.

'Stay here,' she said as she stood and grabbed her cloak from the back of the door. 'I'll be back in a moment.'

She slipped from the room, her bare feet padding soundlessly on the cold stones as she made her way back up to the kitchen. It was warmer there. The fire always smouldered through the night, and it wasn't yet late enough for the flames to have died down completely.

Livia was slumbering in her chair in front of the hearth. She stirred as Julia struggled to extricate a bowl from a cupboard.

'Ah,' the woman said. 'Claudia's returned?'

'Yes.' Julia took a clean towel from the pile by the sink and made her way towards the back door. There was a small courtyard beyond, with a pump well that fed the buildings surrounding it.

'No need,' Livia said, calling Julia back as she pushed herself up from the chair. 'I have hot water ready here. Needle and thread too, if she needs it. She'll want something to eat, too.'

Livia bustled around the kitchen, making up a tray with a candle, medicine, and precious tea with a few biscuits that she must have pilfered from the tins of the Nobles. She smiled when she saw Julia's surprise at the sweet confection.

'Just this once,' she said. 'They owe it to her, don't you think?'

'You knew,' Julia said.

'I had an inkling. Here, you fill up your bowl and I'll carry the tray down for you.'

'How?' Julia asked as she lifted the kettle from the hearth. 'How did you know? If this is what happens, then how did we not know it? Why did no one tell her?'

Julia jerked the kettle around as she spoke, her movements erratic in her agitation. Water sloshed out of the spout to steam on the flagstones.

Livia gently took it from her hand and used it to fill the bowl.

'He hurt her?' she asked.

'He bit her.'

'They're not always the same thing, my girl. You can take it

9

from me.'

'Well, this time they were.'

Livia shook her head. 'He's young. Those ones, sometimes they like to make their mark. Does she need stitching?'

Julia looked at the needle Livia had set on the tray and imagined pushing it through the skin of Claudia's neck. The thought made her dizzy. She couldn't understand how Livia was so calm.

'I don't know,' she said, putting her hand on the counter to steady herself. 'I could only see blood.' She could feel her hairline prickling with sweat.

Livia took her arm and guided her back towards the fire. 'Come sit in my chair for a moment.'

'No, I've been away too long already. I need to get back to her.'

She would do whatever she needed to do, because it was for Claud.

'Alright then,' Livia said, picking up the tray. 'I'm right behind you.'

Claudia was waiting exactly where Julia had left her. Livia struggled for a moment to get the door open wide enough to pass in the tray, then she left them to it.

Julia sat down next to her friend, the bowl and towel in her lap.

'How are you feeling?' she asked, passing over the mug of tea. It had been made with used leaves, the Nobles' scraps, so it was weak, but at least it was hot.

Claudia cradled it in her hands. They were less shaky now, but she was still pale.

'I'm sorry,' she said. 'I overreacted.'

'No, you didn't. Can you tip your head back?'

Even when she brought the candle closer, all Julia could see was blood staining Claudia's throat, seeping into the top of her dress. She helped her shrug out of the cloak then set to cleaning the wound. It must have been painful, but Claudia held perfectly still as she wiped the mess from her skin. She could see his teeth now, stamped into the flesh. It had mostly stopped bleeding, but a few deep gashes still seeped.

'I'm going to have to sew it closed,' Julia whispered.

Claudia ate the biscuits and washed them down with her tea while Julia prepared the needle. It was sharp, but still it needed to be forced through the skin. Julia hadn't expected that. She'd thought it would slip through smoothly, but instead it felt like she was perpetuating Rufus's violation.

Claudia screwed up her face against the pain, but she didn't flinch.

After four difficult stitches and some careful bandaging, they curled up beneath the blankets and tried to sleep. Julia held Claudia close for a while, but it wasn't long before the girl rolled away from her. The mattress shook with the misery of her silent tears.

Julia was lonely without her. She had woken that morning to find that Claudia had already gone back to Rufus. Julia was left alone to her weeding, finishing off the alley where they had been working the previous day.

It was a pretty spot. She could imagine it might have been nice, once upon a time. Dainty stone staircases ran up the sides of the buildings to upper floors and down into recessed basement doors. There were bare colonnades built to support trellises and awnings that had long since rotted away. She could even see the remains of different coloured paints in the layers of cracking stucco: pinks, yellows and oranges. These days, there was only blue.

Today, it was the boys' turn to have their Inauguration Day. There were more new male Candidates than female - Julia counted twelve - but she'd be surprised if any of them made it to the Casting. It was unusual for them to be selected for the honour in the year of their inauguration, and even those chosen to participate were rarely successful. There had been only one new ennoblement in Julia's lifetime, a statistic so dire that she wondered why anyone would risk their life by accepting the rank of Candidate.

Still, she couldn't say for certain that she wouldn't once have taken that risk herself, had the opportunity been offered to her. For some, even the slim chance of becoming Noble was worth it. Perhaps others hoped never to be selected for the Casting at all, but simply to live a comfortable life with the greater privileges the rank of Candidate afforded them. Either way, Julia was glad she had no friends amongst the boys who were now following the priest to their new homes. After what she'd seen last night, she wanted nothing to do with the Nobles.

Unfortunately, that was out of her control.

By the time she got back to the kitchen, Claudia had returned, all smiles. Julia might have thought she had hallucinated the events of the previous night, were it not for the bandage on Claudia's neck and the way that she carefully avoided looking at Julia.

'So, is he handsome?' one of the younger girls asked.

'You wouldn't believe how handsome he is!' came the reply. 'He's got these gorgeous blue eyes, and dark hair that's sort of messy but perfect, and the prettiest mouth you've ever seen.'

Julia set the edible weeds she had collected onto the sideboard and started towards the back door to fill her scrubbing bowl from the well.

'Is it true that he's favoured by the Empress?' another asked.

'That's what they say. And this morning, he gave me this.'

Julia looked over her shoulder to see Claudia showing off a choker she wore around her neck. The black lace stood out against the bandage at her throat.

'He's a complete gentleman,' she went on.

Livia caught Julia's eye while the other girls sighed over the gift. Julia knew the price Claudia had paid for it.

She didn't want to hear any more. She pushed her way out into the courtyard and put her bowl down on the ground, leaning against the pump as her mind threw up unwelcome memories of the needle piercing Claudia's skin, the thread pulling her broken flesh back together.

'You know she doesn't believe a word of it,' Livia said.

Julia hadn't realised that the woman had followed her out.

'It's just what she has to tell them, and herself,' she went on, 'because she's ashamed of the truth.'

'It's all she ever wanted,' Julia said as she filled up the bowl. 'After they didn't make her a Candidate, it was all she ever talked about.'

Livia stepped towards her. 'Leave that,' she said, taking the bowl from her hands.

'No, I'll feel better if I just get on with scrubbing the vegetables.'

But Livia wouldn't let it go.

'Livia?'

'It wasn't what you wanted, though, was it?' the woman asked her. 'You never wanted to be an Attendant.' There was a rueful note in her voice that made Julia wary.

'What?'

'The priestess came by earlier.' Her tone was so soft it was practically a whisper. 'One of the Nobles is pregnant, and with

Quintus missing they're already down one Attendant so their reserve is spoken for. They need another.'

'Now?'

Livia nodded, and Julia's stomach dropped. The ranks had already been finalised. Julia had assumed she was safe, that her lack of delicacy had saved her.

'They can't want me,' she said.

'They won't take anyone else. You're the best option, the priestess said, for the Noble who needs attending.'

'A pregnant woman?'

An indecipherable expression crossed Livia's face. It could have been regret or anger on Julia's behalf, but it might also have been guilt.

'No,' she said. 'They've moved one of the other Attendants to care for her, so you'll be caring for, well, someone else. A man.'

'One of the young ones?'

'Yes.'

The unspoken words hung between them: one of the young ones who liked to make their mark, just like Rufus had on Claudia. Soon Julia would be the one who needed to be sewn up by candlelight.

'When?' she asked.

'Tomorrow, at sunset. Wait at the temple steps, and he'll find you.'

'So soon? With no training?' Her voice sounded strained. She couldn't believe this was happening.

'The priestess will talk to you in the morning. I'm sorry, Julia.'

Livia gave her a look filled with sympathy, then carried the bowl of water back into the kitchen as though it were just a normal afternoon.

Julia couldn't make sense of it. There was no reason for the priestess to pick her, particularly not for a young male Noble. She wasn't poised or pretty or disciplined. She had none of the qualities that made Claudia so prized. There was nothing they could want from her. Was she being punished? Was *he* being punished?

She'd thought she was safe, but there was no true safety in the Blue.

Julia stopped only to collect her pocket knife and a spare cloak before making her way towards the boundary fence. She moved quickly and quietly, keeping to alleys where she could, until the buildings started to drop away into rubble on either side of her. These outer reaches of the Blue were so neglected that she had to clamber in places, hauling herself over tumbledown masonry and under fallen trees.

They felt more oppressive here, like sentinels at the fence.

The trees were always present in the Blue, crowding in from the forests of the Red that surrounded them, but here they hung heavily over the divide between the two worlds, cradling the city in their boughs. Their branches draped over the boundary line as their roots burrowed under it, as though they might crush the fence between the two.

Julia stroked one of the wooden posts with her fingers, feeling the texture of the weathered grain. It wasn't an impressive fence. It only came up to her shoulders here, but it wasn't designed to keep people in, just to keep out what few animals remained in the Red. After all, the most effective barriers against the humans were the ones in their minds, and the rulers of the Blue had built them well. There was no point in building a boundary wall too when fear alone would keep them contained.

That fear was with her now. It told her she would die the moment she set foot outside the Blue, or if not then the apples she ate would be poisonous, the beasts she met would be monstrous and any blood that touched her would prove fatal.

Were the monsters of the Red any worse than the one who awaited her in the Blue? She didn't have the measure of either, and it was that uncertainty that had brought her to this threshold. If she didn't leave the Blue now, she never would.

She took a deep breath and gripped the top of the fence. It was time to find out.

There was a flash of red between the trees. It was too bright to be a deer or fox, and too fast to be natural. Julia wondered for a moment whether she had imagined it, but then she glimpsed it again. It moved like nothing she'd ever seen, with a strange percussive noise.

Thu-thu-thhhwump.

It was then that she noticed the silence. There were no bird calls here, just the sound of the breeze moving lightly amongst the leaves, and the thudding movement of the red figure.

Thhhwump-chk.

Even the woodland's ubiquitous squirrels were absent. The red creature was the only living thing here with her.

An inhuman cry cut through the forest. It was plaintive and feral, but distorted into something twisted as the figure strobed between the trees. It chilled her blood.

There was something out there that she didn't want to meet.

Her fingers clenched against the wood for a second longer before she finally let go and ran back to the alleys she knew without a backward glance.

She was staying in the Blue.

For now.

2

Cameron's world was red.

He'd spent weeks there this time, most of them without blood, and all for nothing. He'd left it too long, and he was on his knees.

It was time to go home. For one night, he promised himself, but no more.

He rarely stayed long in the Blue these days. He couldn't stand to look at the others when they all knew this was his fault, though they were careful not to blame him. Still, he blamed himself. The passing centuries might not have aged him, but his guilt had, hardening his enthusiasm into determination.

He'd never forgive himself for what had happened to his friend. He'd never stop searching either, even though he was starting to think she was truly gone.

He yelled his frustration into the trees, using the last of his strength to pummel his fists into their bark. It didn't help. The outburst just made him feel puerile and helpless. It also opened up the skin over his knuckles, which then refused to heal. It had been too long since he'd had any blood.

The lack dulled his senses, but not so much that he didn't hear the footsteps rushing away in the direction of the Blue. He was closer to the city than he'd thought, too close to be throwing punches into the trees at hyper speed.

'Nice one, idiot,' he muttered to himself. 'Really fucking stealthy.'

He clenched his fists, splitting wide the skin so the blood poured freely.

It still didn't help.

'Cam? You're finally home!' Viv had spotted him in the square. She pulled him into a welcome hug, but he shrugged free after a second. Affection no longer came easily to him.

'Hey,' he said. 'Where are the others?'

There weren't many of the Solis Invicti left, but those who remained stuck close together. The Empress used them as her elite military and bodyguard, a role they were used to filling, although not for her. The Blue was so peaceful that it had been a long while since they were last needed, so she didn't object to Cam's frequent absences. He didn't much care even if she did. She knew why he searched.

'They were up at the palace for the new Candidate introductions this afternoon,' Viv said, 'but they should be back in the bunkhouse by now.'

'It's that time of year already?'

She smiled. 'You've been gone a long time, kid.'

'I'm over a thousand years old. When are you going to stop calling me that?'

'When you're older than I am, you young whippersnapper.'

He groaned.

'Come on,' she said. 'Let's go celebrate with the others. They'll be pleased to see you home safe.'

It wasn't far to the building they occupied. It sat between the temple and the palace, a little way back from the northeast corner of the square. The civic face of the Empress's rule dominated the space, while the military provided back up. It was neat, but it meant that they were always a little too close to the centre of things for Cam's tastes. He'd enjoyed that, once. Now he liked the quiet of the woods.

A wide flight of steps ran up to the front doors, which were standing open despite the cool weather.

'Hey Secundus,' Viv called up, 'look who's home.'

'Well, it's about bloody time.' The man who greeted them could never have been mistaken for anything other than what he was: a soldier. 'Where the hell have you been?' he said, but despite his gruff tone, his eyes were kind.

'Nice to see you too, Tommy.'

'Come on, man,' he said, putting his arm around Cam as he

joined them on the steps. 'You're just in time for dinner.'

They made their way to the lounge, where Cam was greeted, hugged and had his back thumped by his friends. The pleasantries were shorter this time, as they were every time he returned. It made them feel awkward, he thought, to watch him obsess. He made them uncomfortable.

'Darius, Aaron, Tiberius,' he said, greeting them each in turn. There was little hope in their eyes, just relief.

At first, they'd searched with him. For the first hundred years or so, all of the Solis Invicti had scoured the Red as far as they could go, searching for any trace of her. Tommy, who was their leader, the Secundus, had mapped it all. He'd meticulously marked off the sectors and plotted new targets, but eventually Cam had been searching alone. When he came back, they no longer asked him whether he'd found her. They just held him, fed him and made him sleep for as long as they could before he slipped away again.

Only Tiberius's greeting held any hint of excitement, but even that was reserved. He was the youngest of them, smiling and bubbly, and always willing to sit and listen to Cam's stories of his time spent in the Red.

Cam had been like him once. He couldn't remember when he'd last looked at the world with that kind of joy.

It wasn't long before even Tiberius vacated the room, leaving him alone with Viv and Tommy.

'I covered F24 and G24,' he said.

'Shit, Cam,' Tommy said. 'No wonder you were away so long. We said one sector at a time.'

'It's too slow.'

The lounge wasn't glamorous, but they had some comfy sofas stuffed with wool and horsehair. Cam could smell the familiar tang of the lanolin. He threw off his dark cloak and sprawled into an armchair, his gangly limbs spilling over its edges. Unfortunately, the action drew attention to his bleeding knuckles.

'Viv,' Tommy said, 'fetch him some blood, would you?'

'I'm fine,' Cam protested.

'No you're not.' As Viv left the room, Tommy took a seat in the chair next to his. 'What happened?'

He cringed. 'Yeah, about that. I think a human might have seen me speeding in the trees.'

Tommy dragged a hand down his face. 'Cam…'

'I know, and I'm sorry, I just didn't realise how close I was.'

'And you were wearing that shirt?'

Cam looked down, noticing the brightness of its colour for the first time. He'd picked it up on his way back, desperate for some clean clothes, and hadn't given it another thought. So long away from home had made him forgetful. No wonder the watcher at the boundary had run.

To the humans of the Blue, red was the colour of monsters.

'Shit,' he said. 'I'm sorry. I'm such a fuck up.'

'I suppose I should just be grateful that you put on your cloak before walking through the square.'

Viv returned then, handing a cup to Cam. 'You would've caused a riot,' she said. 'That might have been fun.'

'Missing the action?' Tommy asked her.

'I never would have guessed that life would be so boring with Laila as Empress. I mean, seriously, could you have imagined this?'

Tommy shrugged. 'I suppose the Revelation changed her.'

'No,' Cam said, 'Emmy changed her.'

There was a moment of awkward silence. Cam sipped at his drink, lost in guilt while the others shared an anxious glance. In the end, it was Viv who spoke first.

'We've got a pregnancy,' she said brightly. 'So that's good news.'

'We're still down five percent this year,' Tommy grumbled. Viv slapped him lightly on the arm.

Cam gulped down the rest of the cup. 'We're dying out,' he said. 'Ed's gone, Carrie's gone, Drew's gone. Sol and Emmy may as well be gone. Soon we'll all be gone too.'

Tommy shook his head. 'It's only five percent.'

'Yeah, but if you take away five percent every year then eventually you end up with none. We're done for, Tommy. The fucking Weeper vaccine will be the end of us, and I'm not so sure that's a bad thing.'

'You don't believe that.'

'Don't I?' Cam put his empty mug on the table and got to his feet. He'd been alone too long, and now the company of his friends made him too anxious to relax. It itched his nerves like the dried sweat itched his skin.

'You don't see what I see out there,' he said, making for the door. 'They're better off without us.'

'You could help if you stayed,' Viv said, catching his hand in hers.

He laughed; a hollow sound. 'What, by settling down with one of Laila's Candidates? By trying to fall in love with a teenager? I'm a hundred times their age, Viv, so a hundred times: no.'

She didn't let go of him. 'That's not what we're asking.'

'I want you to think about becoming Tertius,' Tommy said. He was offering him second-in-command of the Solis Invicti. It was a staggering proposal.

'What about you?' Cam asked Viv, his brow wrinkling in confusion. She was, and had always been, Tommy's right hand.

She smiled. 'Well, that's the thing,' she said, releasing Cam so she could take Tommy's hand. 'I'm the one who's pregnant.'

Cam sat back down.

'Wow,' he said. 'I mean, congratulations. Just, wow. So, um, when did this,' he waggled a finger between the two of them, 'happen?'

'About a decade ago,' Viv said.

Cam's mouth dropped open. Love was nearly as rare among their kind as pregnancy. He couldn't believe he hadn't noticed.

'You've been away,' she added. 'There's a lot you've missed.'

'I guess so.'

'Promise that you'll think about our offer.'

It was supposed to be an honour, he knew that, but how could he give up on Emmy? He couldn't just stop looking.

'You know I can't.'

'It's been centuries,' Tommy said. 'We, well mostly you, have covered practically every inch of the continent.'

'I'm not going to stop now. I'm not going to stop until I find her.'

'Cam,' Viv said, leaning towards him as though to soften her words, 'you can't be sure she's even still alive.'

'Of course I can. Sol's still alive, so she must be too. If she'd died, he'd have, you know…' He made an explosive gesture with his hands.

'And if he were dead, how would you know it?' she asked gently. 'The Primus hasn't moved for centuries, Cam. Maybe he's already gone, and maybe she's gone too. Maybe she's been gone a long time.'

It was a possibility Cam wasn't willing to entertain. This was why he never stayed here. They'd all given up already, and they wanted him to do the same.

He pushed himself to his feet again and, with another murmur of, 'Congratulations', made his way up to his room.

Laila asked to see him the next morning. The messenger was waiting for him when he got back from the showers. He'd known she would request his attendance sooner or later, but he usually managed to be in and out of the Blue before she realised he was there. Someone must have ratted him out, and he was willing to bet that someone was Tommy.

He ambled into her audience chamber without waiting for an invitation, a careless presumption that would have been more easily pardoned if he were still his jovial former self. Everyone had loved him when he'd smiled.

The room wasn't big, and the tapestries that lined its walls made it feel even more intimate. As well as being decorative, they muffled the sound from within so it wouldn't carry.

There were two women sitting at a low table furnished with fruit, nuts and pastries. Even if he hadn't known her for centuries, Cam would have guessed which of them was the Empress. She was dressed richly in bright fabrics, elaborately embroidered and jewelled, and she was holding the wrist of the other woman to her dark lips.

He'd caught her in the middle of breakfast.

'You summoned me?' he said, effecting a mock bow.

Licking the blood from her lips, she waved away her Attendant, then waited until they were alone before speaking.

'I'm surprised you came at all.'

'I didn't realise I had a choice. My brothers seem to have turned against me.'

Laila looked supremely unconcerned. 'Petulance doesn't suit you,' she said.

'Decadence apparently suits you.'

'I always hoped it would.' She gestured to the cushion beside her. 'Sit.'

'I don't have time for this.'

'Cameron, sit.'

He did as he was told, his long legs spreading awkwardly across the floor. Where he was tall and loose-limbed, the Empress was petite and composed. Every movement she made was precise and delicate, yet fluid at the same time, as though she were moving to a rhythm only she could hear.

'You're wasting your time,' he said. 'I'm not going to stop looking.'

'Did I say you should? I'm fairly certain I said no such thing.'

'But you want me to stop, don't you? You wouldn't have any of this if they were here,' he waved a hand around the room, taking in the tapestries and wall carvings, shining with precious stones and metals.

'You mean all this luxury?' Laila laughed, a melodic rill that was almost blithe enough to belie the steel beneath it. 'A palace where we have no electricity or running water, and where blood is so scarce we have to ration it? Yes, decadence indeed,' she scoffed. 'This unheated hellhole is precisely what I dreamed of back when I used to bathe in warm blood while drinking champagne and watching satellite television.'

'And what would you have if I brought Emmy back?'

She gave him an even look. 'You're going to make me fucking say it, aren't you?' she said. 'You know how I loathe sentimentality.'

'No, really? You shock me.'

'I searched for her too, or do you not remember that?'

They'd all searched in those first few years, Laila longer than most. She and Emmy had been close, or as close as Laila got to anyone, but it had been so long ago.

'We're suffocating here,' she continued. 'Our last death was a suicide. We're all stuck in the arse-end of nowhere: the only place we can get uncontaminated blood, and the only place we can never show people what we really are. I don't just want you to find her, Cameron. I need you to find her.'

'Then why am I here?'

Laila studied him for a moment. 'I wonder if she'd even recognise you.'

'What?'

'You're not the puppy dog she'll remember. The Red's changed you. You're harder.'

He thought of the hunger, the exhaustion, the nights he'd spent sleeping in the snow until his fingers turned blue and black. Blood might regrow his flesh, but he still felt the pain.

'We're all hard,' he said. 'We're Silver.'

Her mouth shaped a delicate moue of reproach. 'You know we don't use that word in the city.'

'Fine, we're *Nobles*,' he said, pouring scorn into the euphemism.

The Empress said nothing.

'You do think she's still alive, then?' he asked.

Laila rose gracefully to her feet with poise Cam could only dream of and opened a bureau in the corner of the room. When she came back to the table, she was holding a single sheet of paper.

'You're here for this,' she said, offering it to him.

He stared at it, trying to make sense of the marks on its surface.

'Directions?' he asked. 'Is this up beyond the mountains?'

'That's right. One of the roamers heard about a settlement up on the coast, in what used to be Germany.'

Cam shook his head. 'We've searched there already.'

'Recently?'

He tried to think back. That was the problem, of course: Emmy wasn't necessarily staying in the same place. They couldn't search everywhere at the same time, not when they had to move at human speed, and things were so much slower now that he was working alone. He couldn't remember the last time he'd been up that way.

'Shit,' he said. 'Do you know where on the coast this is?' He waved the map.

'The roamer got the sketch from a trading caravan, who got it from another. They'd never been there themselves. That beach,' she pointed to a mark on the paper, 'could be anywhere.'

Determination hardened Cam's jaw. 'I'll find it. Did he say anything else?'

'Only that they knew what he was. He wasn't masking the silver in his eyes, and they recognised it.'

It was the feature that defined their race. They had been called the Silver once, named for the colour of the shining filaments that threaded through the whites of their eyes. They could hide it so they appeared human, and they took care to ensure it was always hidden in the Blue. They didn't need to be so careful in the Red.

Cam thought it through. If there were others of his kind living out there, then they must have found uncontaminated humans from whom to feed.

'Wait,' he said, 'are you saying what I think you're saying?'

'I think she's alive, Cameron.'

It was the first good lead they'd had in years.

He got to his feet with some difficulty, scattering the cushions beneath him.

'Thank you for this,' he said, holding up the map. After a moment's hesitation, he leaned down and kissed her cheek.

Her expression was halfway between a smile and a grimace. 'Just find her, alright?'

'I'll come back with her,' he promised, 'or not at all.'

It didn't take him long to pack: he just threw some clean clothes into a bag. He'd pick up some food and blood on his way out. Tommy preferred the Solis Invicti not to use Attendants - they were a security risk, he said - so there were always plenty of bottles in the cellar. There was no point in taking more than a couple, though. It wouldn't stay fresh for long.

He was fetching some cheese and bread from the pantry when Tommy tracked him down. Cam had hoped he might get out of the Blue without bumping into him again, but he hadn't been fast enough.

'Hey,' Tommy said, 'where do you think you're going?'

'Do you really need me to answer that question?' he replied, stowing a couple of water skins in his bag.

'Are you not even going to consider my offer?'

'Nothing ever happens in this place. You don't need me here.'

'And if we want you to stay?'

'You know why I can't,' he said, fastening the straps.

Tommy put his hand on Cam's arm.

Cam barely resisted the urge to flinch away. He just wanted to leave, to get out of the oppressive atmosphere of the Blue. He could feel the Invicti looking at him and worrying. The problem was that they cared too much, and that got in the way of what he needed to do.

'You just got back,' Tommy was saying, 'and you haven't eaten, have you? You haven't even started to recover from your last trip. What's so urgent that you can't stay another night?'

'I'm following up a lead.'

'Which sector?'

Cam swung the bag onto his shoulders. 'Not sure,' he said.

'Somewhere between A15 and A21.'

He knew the grid like the back of his hand now. When he closed his eyes he could see it so clearly that it may as well have been etched on the insides of his eyelids. He could picture the coastline, with its bays and promontories, and pick any one of twenty locations that might match the beach on the sketch.

'That's a lot of ground to cover on your own,' Tommy said.

'I've covered more.'

Tommy was quiet for a moment, then said, 'Will you give me an hour?'

'I don't have time to hang around. I want to be out the other side of the forest by dusk.'

'You will be. I've got an idea that will help.' Tommy's voice was coloured by his excitement. 'Just give me an hour, okay?'

He wouldn't leave the kitchen until Cam had reluctantly agreed to wait.

With Tommy gone, Cam was alone in the bunkhouse, bags packed and nowhere to go. He paced in the lounge, too agitated to sit. There wasn't even a clock to help him track the passing of time.

'I thought you'd have left by now.'

'Lorelei,' Cam said, turning to greet her. 'I wondered where you were.'

'I was on watch when you got in. Didn't see me when you crossed the boundary though, did you?'

'Wasn't looking for you. I didn't even realise you still bothered with the watches.'

'I'm not sure why we do.'

She threw herself down on the sofa and put her feet up on the table. The soles of her boots were caked with mud, but the bunkhouse wasn't the kind of place where caring about dirt made you popular.

'Nothing ever happens here,' she went on, pushing her auburn hair out of her face. 'You're the scariest thing that's walked across the boundary in the past decade.'

'I'm not sure that's a compliment.'

'Hey, grab us a couple of bottles, would you? I've just got off duty.'

He obliged her by ducking down into the cellar and returning with enough blood for both of them. There was no refrigeration, but the cellar was cool enough to keep it good for weeks sometimes, depending on the weather.

'Thanks,' Lorelei said as he handed her a bottle.

He took a seat next to her and opened his own.

'Funny, isn't it?' she said, holding her bottle up to the light. 'With all the artificial shit that's broken down, all the plastic and metal gizmos, glass is the thing that lasts. Fragile as all hell, but it lasts.'

'I guess,' Cam said. 'It's not much use in pieces, though.'

'I'm making a metaphor, dickhead,' she said, swigging from the bottle. 'We're Silver, so we're metal, right? As a race, we're strong, but we corrode. The humans, they're glass. They're so breakable. They shatter, but the thing is, even fractured, they're the ones who'll survive for millennia, not us.'

There was a pause that Cam imagined was supposed to be filled with poignancy, but he hadn't just come off a twenty-four hour shift, so he wasn't feeling quite as philosophical as Lorelei.

'I see where you're coming from,' he said, 'only silver's a noble metal, so it doesn't corrode very quickly, if at all.'

It was Ed's knowledge, not his. All those years in London, rambling around their attic rooms with his crucibles and alembics. Cam had never been interested in the experiments himself, but the facts had crept into his memory nonetheless.

Ed had been in Cam's thoughts a lot recently, smiling in the dark corners of his nights. Cam could try to forget about him and Carrie, but then some borrowed nugget of information would float to the top of his mind, and it would transport him back to their old garret, filled with noxious fumes and regret.

But they were both gone now, and there was no rescuing them from the fate they had chosen.

'Fine then,' Lorelei said, dragging him back to the present, 'we're fucking aluminium. Whatever. The point is, the humans are going to outlast us, and you know why?'

He suppressed a sigh. Why did he always get stuck in conversations like this when he was home?

'Because,' she went on, 'we're tarnished.'

That was clearly supposed to be the big climax to her speech, but Cam didn't follow.

'Erm, okay?' he said. He wished Tommy would hurry up. He felt like he was trapped in the kitchen with the drunkest girl at the party.

'Things are wrong here,' she said. 'You can feel it, right? We can all feel it.'

'What do you mean?'

'You're old enough to remember what things were like before the Revelation. Everything since then has just been downhill all the way, and now we're stuck in this shithole. We should be finding a way to counteract the vaccine. If we don't, then pretty soon we'll all be living and dying human lives.'

This was starting to sound like a familiar refrain, but Cam knew that not all of their kind feared that end. Some of them chose it.

'I know you feel the same,' she went on. 'Verity heard you talking to Tommy last night.'

'Then she can't have heard much.'

'What?'

'I'm all for humanity, Lori. As long as I can find Emmy first, then you can sign me up.'

She gaped at him. 'You're not serious.'

'As death,' he said. 'You're right: humans are the future. Us? We're just a mistake.'

She blinked at him, and he guessed it wasn't what she had hoped to hear. He couldn't have cared less.

'Well, shit,' she said.

He drained his bottle and grabbed his pack, feeling like he'd outstayed his welcome.

Fuck Tommy. It was time for him to make a move.

He didn't get away easily. Tommy caught up with him just as he was heading out of the square, and he wasn't happy.

'I said an hour.'

'It's been an hour.'

'It's been forty minutes.'

'Well,' Cam grumbled, 'it felt like a fucking hour.'

He couldn't wait to get out of the city. The day was unusually gloomy for the time of year, which meant that he was losing daylight, and the last thing he wanted to do was spend the night trekking through the forest. If he left now, at least he'd make it out of the trees in time to reach his first camp by sunset.

'I swear,' Tommy said, 'the more time you spend out there, the worse you get. It's not good for you, being on your own.'

'Well, this time I won't be,' he said, hitching the bag up on his shoulder, 'because I'm going to find her, and I'm not coming back until I do.'

Tommy looked at him with more pity than he thought was warranted.

'Cam-'

'I mean it. She was my partner, and as long as she's in the Red, I will be too.'

Tommy trailed behind him as Cam started to walk away from the square.

'And what about the people you're leaving behind?' he said. 'We don't want you to throw your life away like this. We cared about her too, you know, but we don't want to lose you.'

'You care about her,' Cam said.

'What?'

He turned to face Tommy. 'You mean you *care* about her, not *cared*. She's still alive.'

'And what if she's not?'

Cam was so sick of hearing those words. It was as though everyone was looking for an excuse to write her off, so they could get on with their lives guilt-free and just let her slip away.

'Shit, Tommy,' he said. 'I never thought the day would come when Laila would agree with me instead of you.'

That gave him pause.

'What does she have to do with this?' Tommy said.

'Who do you think gave me the lead? She still believes Emmy's out there, so why don't you? Why have you given up?'

Tommy raised his hands in surrender.

Typical.

'Fine,' he said, 'go if you have to, but I promised you something to help with your journey. At least let me give it to you.'

'Fine.' Cam held his hand out palm-up to take whatever it was, but Tommy had already turned and started walking away, back across the square.

'Follow me,' he called.

'Tommy.' There was a warning in Cam's tone.

'Trust me,' he replied. 'Come on, it's not far.'

Cam cursed him under his breath, but did as he was asked.

True to his word, Tommy led the way around the back of the bunkhouse, where Viv was waiting with a friend.

'Ta da!' she said.

It was an enormous thoroughbred stallion, easily seventeen hands high, with a coat the colour of midnight.

'Are you sure you can spare him?' Cam asked.

They never took horses out into the Red, because once they had crossed the boundary it wasn't safe to bring them back. If one became contaminated, then it might compromise the entire stable, and they didn't have so many that they could afford to just send them away.

'You spend all your time out there,' Tommy said, 'so we can justify it. We've got some new foals anyway, and you could do with the company.'

'Besides,' Viv said, handing Cam the reins, 'he's such a bastard that no one else will ride him.'

'Oh, great, thanks,' Cam said. 'A horse who'll throw me at the first sign of danger is exactly what I need in the Red.'

'He won't do that. He's totally fearless.' After a second's thought, she added, 'He might bite you, though, and step on your feet. Rather a lot, I'm afraid.'

As though to demonstrate, the horse leaned into Cam and lifted a hoof into the air. Cam only just managed to get his feet out of the way before it slammed back down into the paving.

'Like I said,' Viv grimaced, 'he's a bastard. His name's Hades.'

'You're kidding.'

Tommy grinned. 'He pushed Lorelei over last week and tried to trample her.'

'I'm amazed he's still alive.' Cam said.

'I think she was impressed, actually,' Viv said. 'We all were.'

'And something about his behaviour made you think that he was the perfect horse for me?' Cam was a good rider, but it sounded like managing Hades might be beyond him.

'Take him or leave him,' Tommy said. 'Your choice.'

Hades swung his head towards Cam, but Cam ducked out of the way. On the backswing, the horse bit his shoulder. His snorting whinny sounded like a snicker.

Cam narrowed his eyes at the beast. The challenge had been issued.

'I'll take him.'

3

It was almost dark by the time Julia arrived at the temple. She'd left it until the last possible moment, because she really didn't want to do this. Livia was right: she'd never wanted to be an Attendant.

She was angry. Angry that this choice had been made for her, angry that Claudia was ignoring her, and angry that her attempt to leave the Blue had been thwarted by her fear.

But the more she'd dwelt on it, the more her anger had cooled into something like shame.

She was a coward.

She hadn't even tried to investigate the noises in the Red. She'd just run.

But the burn went deeper still, because in the midst of her escape she hadn't once thought of Claudia. Something was up with her friend, and instead of trying to help, Julia had almost abandoned her.

She'd been selfish. A selfish coward.

Her burning cheeks were the only warm part of her as she climbed the steps barefoot. The wind had dropped, but it was still chilly in the shadow of the temple's entablature. The braziers between the pillars were unlit, the only light coming from the dim glow that slipped through the crack between the temple doors.

It was too dark for her to see him coming.

'Julia?'

The voice was soft, but it still made her jump.

She nodded at the dark shape, attempting to use the gesture to cover her fright, then realised that if she couldn't see him, he might not be able to see her. She would have to speak her answer.

'Yes, Master,' she said, as she had been taught.

There was a momentary pause, in which Julia felt uncomfortably as though she were being assessed.

'Follow me,' he said.

The priestess had told her that she would be taken to his rooms, so she had been expecting this command, but still her legs were unsteady as she made her way back down the steps behind him. She could feel her pulse hammering at the back of her throat.

She remembered the thread pulling Claudia's skin closed, and nearly missed her footing.

Her fear and shame bundled together.

Colours writhed dully in her vision, and the gentle noise of the square at dusk barely penetrated her ears. Her senses were so overwhelmed with panic that she felt dizzied by them.

When he reached the flagstones, the Noble paused and waited for Julia to join him.

In this light, he was nothing but a shadow.

Like her, he was wearing a full-length cloak with the hood pulled over his head, so she could see nothing of his physical features save that he was tall. She couldn't see the shape of his face, or the colour of his hair, or the width of his build.

She didn't even know his name.

'This way,' he said, setting off across the square.

The voice didn't seem unkind, but neither did it seem friendly. It betrayed no desire for conversation or company.

The weight of silence grew between them as they reached a tall building at the far end of the square, opposite the palace. It appeared sturdy and comfortable, almost grand, at least until the Noble led her up the stuccoed staircase attached to its side. Their destination was the room at the back of the building on the fourth and final floor. The plaster was crumbling away from the bricks here, and Julia could see where damp was seeping in through the walls. He had to kick at the bottom of the door to release it from the frame.

The inside wasn't much better. The space was ten times larger than the cellar room she shared with Claudia, but no less sparsely furnished. At least her room was waterproof, which was more than she could say for this one. Even in the feeble light, it was clear that there was a hole in the ceiling in the far corner, and one of the window shutters was broken beyond repair. The space smelled faintly of dirt and mould.

'Sit if you like,' the Noble said as he lit a candle from the lantern that was already burning on the other side of the room.

There were no chairs, only a pallet with an uncomfortable-looking mattress. The sheets were neatly folded, but it was bleak. Julia stayed standing.

The Noble pulled his hood down, and she got her first glimpse of his face. He was young, around twenty, she guessed, or at least he appeared to be. His skin was pale, but everything else about him was dark: hair, eyes, expression, even the shadows that stained the skin under his lashes. The only highlights were the two small dots of brightness contained within one of his earlobes, two silver studs stroked by the locks that clustered there.

'So,' he said as he took off his cloak. The motion wafted a fresh scent in her direction, almost like the mint that grew in Livia's garden. It was unexpected given her dank surroundings.

Julia waited for him to continue, but apparently he had nothing else to say. He shifted from foot to foot, the set of his shoulders awkward, as though he were just as uncomfortable as she was.

She scrambled to assemble words into an acceptable pleasantry to break the silence. She couldn't ask questions, because she'd been told that would be impertinent. She couldn't comment on his home, because that would be presumptuous. She probably shouldn't even speak without being asked to do so.

Inarticulacy coated Julia's mouth so thickly that she was chewing on it.

'It's cold tonight,' she said finally, at the same time as he asked, 'Will you take down your hood?'

There was to be no delay, then.

He needed her neck bare, so he could drink. So he could bite.

The flickering candlelight drew unpleasant shapes across his face, pooling in his eye sockets.

Julia's fingers trembled as she pushed the material from her head. It pulled her hair loose as it fell, a second layer of defence, but she gathered it to one side and tipped her chin to bare her throat. There was no point in prolonging what she knew was to come.

She could feel her skin tingling, as though it were bracing itself for the shock.

But there was no bite.

'Are you alright?' he asked, taking a step towards her.

'Yes, Master,' she said. 'I was told…' She gestured to her neck, letting her body indicate the offer that she refused to put into words.

'Oh,' the Noble said. 'No, that's… well, yes, but not like that. I thought we could talk?'

She nodded, hiding her relief behind the curtain of her hair as she dropped it back into place.

He looked at her for a moment then sighed. 'This isn't going very well, is it?'

Julia simply returned his look. She remembered too late that her eyes were supposed to be downcast, as the priestess had instructed.

Was he angry with her? She moved her gaze quickly to the wooden floor.

'I know it's not very nice in here,' the Noble continued. 'I spend most of my time upstairs. Would you like to see it?'

Upstairs? Julia was sure that this had been the top floor of the building.

Her eyes crept up from the ground as he moved across the room towards the far corner, and she saw that the hole in the roof was in fact a hatch, accessed by a ladder that was propped against the wall.

He was halfway up before he realised that she wasn't following.

'I promise it's safe,' he said.

As if the promise of a Noble meant anything to Julia. In the end, her curiosity was enough to coax her up the ladder, not to mention her fear of what might happen were she to disobey.

She had to tuck the bottom of her cloak into her belt to avoid stepping on it as she climbed, but her bare feet found a firm hold on the ladder rungs. When she got to the top, the Noble was waiting with his hand outstretched.

This was all wrong. Nobles didn't help Servers.

Unease rolled in Julia's stomach, warning her to tread carefully. She hesitated, pausing just long enough that he withdrew, stepping out of sight as she clambered up and got her first glimpse of the view.

It was breathtaking.

The city was laid out before her, inky buildings cutting geometric shapes in the dusk. A dark tincture coloured the air, the faint glow of lanterns throwing the streets into sharper relief where pockets of human industry and Noble pleasure continued into the night.

Light flared beside her and she turned to see that the Noble had kindled a fire in a brick structure at the roof's centre, raised a foot or so from the concrete floor. The fire illuminated the rest of the scene, and here Julia saw the comfort that the room below had lacked. He had constructed a shelter next to the fire pit: a low, three-sided building filled with bedding, bottles, boxes and books. Wide benches lined the other edges of the fire, although their surfaces were mostly cluttered with pots and pans. It didn't look as though guests were often invited to join him here.

Every other part of the roof was covered with a forest of plant life. There were pots of herbs and fruit bushes, trunks filled with what looked like root vegetables, stands of beans, bowls of strawberry plants and even a few glass-topped hot frames holding peppers and tomatoes.

It was so unexpected that Julia's mouth dropped open.

'Have you eaten?' the Noble said to her.

She shook her head.

'Alright then.'

The Noble worked quietly, smiling to himself as he chose and harvested the vegetables he wanted. They made a beautiful crop, washed with water he collected from a rainwater tank on the corner of the roof, but they weren't what held Julia's attention. Instead, her eyes kept drifting back to his face, which was transformed by turns with concentration and pleasure.

Julia knew what the Nobles were, and this was not it. They were distant and ancient, their actions dictated by the accrual of respect and benefit rather than by the simple enjoyment to be found in human work. Their company was not supposed to be restful.

But she was finding it difficult not to relax with this one.

She told herself that it was the setting that had eased her tension, so removed from the city that surrounded it. From where she sat on one of the benches, soaking in the scent of fresh plants and earth, it felt like a sanctuary. It was easy to feel free in the open air.

Still, her eyes were on him constantly. He must have known that she was watching, although her gaze hit the ground as soon as he looked her way, but she couldn't stop herself.

That smile. Surely Nobles weren't supposed to smile like that. She had seen them laughing before, haughtily and cruelly, but that gentle contentment was something she had never expected to see from one of his kind.

He was happy, and his mood was infectious.

A pan sizzled over the fire, filled with onions, garlic, tomatoes, peppers and some eggs that had been squirrelled away in the hut. A handful of herbs went in too, and some dried ingredients that Julia couldn't identify, but that smelled decadently rich. The Noble's movements were smooth and practised, as though this were something he did every day, as though it were normal for someone in his position to make his own meals.

Why? she wondered, suspicion tingling along her skin.

Everything he needed was right here in this self-sufficient empire.

Everything except blood. He couldn't grow that.

Well, not in soil, at least. It was why she was here: to serve him.

She had never heard of a Noble serving his Attendant, though.

'No plates, I'm afraid,' he said, setting the pan down on the bench next to Julia. He handed her a spoon and some bread.

She kept her eyes on her lap.

'Will you have wine?' he asked.

Julia had never drunk wine before. The Blue only produced enough for the Nobles, and in any case Servers weren't allowed to drink alcohol, although that didn't stop Livia from brewing up some potent concoctions of her own in the cellar. She administered small doses on occasion, for medicinal purposes, but Julia and Claudia sometimes sneaked extra for themselves.

It helped, on the bad days. It made things feel less real.

'It's forbidden, Master,' she said, because it was what she was supposed to say.

'It's Lucas,' he said, pouring out two glasses.

'Master?'

'My name. Please call me Lucas.'

He was asking her to breach one of the most fundamental tenets of the Blue. To address someone by their name was to claim equality with them, or to claim superiority over them. A Server would never address a Candidate by name, let alone a Noble.

'It's forbidden-'

'Here,' he said, holding out a glass.

Her unease returned threefold.

Was this some sort of trick? Was he testing her, trying to make her fail? If he reported her to the temple, they'd imprison her without hesitation. She'd be a forced donor for the rest of her life.

'It's forbidden,' she said again, raising her eyes for a moment so she could watch for his reaction.

Disappointment, but tinged with sadness, not anger. There was no frustration in his expression, none of the irritation she would have expected from someone who hoped to lure her into disobedience.

'Very well,' he said, and some of the joy he'd gathered while preparing their meal went out of his eyes.

This man was nothing like she'd thought he would be.

She reached out quickly and took the glass.

'Thank you,' she said.

He smiled, returning the glow of pleasure to his features, then sat down on the other side of the pan.

With the food this close, the appetising scent was distracting. The eggs were perfectly cooked, nestled in a rich red sauce that looked darkly tempting in the firelight.

Julia's mouth began to water, but she hesitated, turning her bread in her hand. He was so close that if she leaned over to eat, her cheek might brush his own. In the meantime, he had ripped open his own roll and spooned the hot mixture onto the bread, releasing fresh and enticing scents in a cloud of steam.

'Dig in,' he said, waving at the meal with his spoon.

The intimacy of it was disconcerting.

When she still didn't move, he sat back and looked at her anxiously.

'Did I do something wrong?' he asked, putting his bread down in his lap.

Julia shook her head, glancing away. Now she was just making a fool of herself.

'Are you not hungry? Or is there something you don't like? I'm sorry, I should have asked.'

'No,' she said, slightly bewildered by his question. She always ate what she was given, regardless of whether she liked it or not. The concept that someone might reject food simply because they didn't enjoy the taste was completely alien.

'No,' she went on, 'I apologise, it's just that you, I mean, this is… not how I thought it would be.'

She looked around at the profusion of plants that cocooned them as they sat in the dark by the fire, and at the cosy nook he had made for himself in the hut to the side. Despite the chill in the air, everything about this place felt warm.

Ritual and detachment and teeth in her skin, that was what she had anticipated.

The priestess had talked her through it: how the Noble would first taste her blood to determine whether he wanted her as his Attendant, then indicate his acceptance with a ritual gesture, and finally cut a lock of her hair to symbolise his ownership.

'I'm sorry about that,' he said. 'I hope you're not disappointed.'

He wasn't accepting her, then.

The beginnings of a feeling she hadn't yet acknowledged crumpled into nothingness in her chest.

It wasn't a surprise. Julia knew that she was plain, with colouring as exciting as mud and a figure built for labour rather than leisure, but she was irked nonetheless, which was ludicrous because she'd never wanted to be indentured to a Noble in the first place.

'You are rejecting me as your Attendant,' she said, carefully modulating her tone to make the words a statement rather than a question.

He seemed upset by her response. 'No, that's not it at all. I meant I hope you're not disappointed with me. I know what they say about me. I know I'm not the assignment you all hope for.'

'Master-'

'Lucas.'

She still couldn't bring herself to say his name.

'I was a regular Server until this morning,' she said. 'I didn't train with the other Attendants. I don't know what they say.'

'Oh.' His voice was quiet, as though he regretted his disclosure. 'Then will you eat with me?'

She wondered then whether there was something that would have stopped the other Attendants from sharing his meal. Eating from the same dish felt too close, presuming a deeper relationship than the acquaintance they shared, but Julia could see no other reason to refuse food that was fast becoming irresistible to her empty stomach.

She picked up her spoon.

The mixture was as sweet as it smelled, bursting with flavours she couldn't recognise, and soon she was having to hold herself back to avoid eating at an indecent speed.

'You like it?' he asked.

She nodded as she swallowed.

They ate quietly until the last trace of sauce had been wiped up with hunks of fresh bread, and in that time their silence had become almost comfortable. Julia couldn't remember the last time she'd been so full, or so relaxed.

Where had her fear gone?

'You don't look at me,' he said.

Julia quelled her impulse to look at his face.

'Attendants do not look at their masters,' she said, surprised that she had to explain this to him.

He looked embarrassed.

'I didn't know,' he said. 'I don't really know about any of this.'

Julia said nothing, but she was confused. Why would he comment on behaviour that his previous Attendant must also have displayed?

He sighed. 'I know it's strange. You must have questions.'

'Attendants do not ask their masters questions.' She had to stifle an unexpected smile that was twitching the edges of her lips.

'Are you teasing me?' Something in his voice told her he wouldn't be unhappy if she was.

'Attendants are instructed to keep their eyes downcast,' she said, 'to refrain from questioning their masters, and to behave demurely at all times.'

'Then why are you smiling?'

'I think I may not be a very good Attendant.'

He put the remains of the meal under the bench, leaving no barrier between them, and reached over gently to take her hand. His fingers were as rough as hers, calloused from labour.

That feeling in her chest was back, not crumpled away after all. It was slowly unveiling itself, petal by petal.

'Julia,' he said. 'You can look at me. You can ask me questions. You can be yourself, and I won't complain.'

This time, the insistence in his voice made her certain he wasn't just testing her.

'Please,' he said.

His hand moved to her chin, slowly raising her face until she was looking into his eyes, his hair shading them from the firelight.

She looked. Her first transgression.

She hadn't expected him to look at her with anything other than hunger. There was something else there in his eyes though, a softening around their edges, something like curiosity.

'Ask me whatever you want,' he said.

The petals unfurled.

'Alright then,' she whispered.

'Good.' He dropped his hand from her chin, sitting back so there was space between them once more.

The absence of his touch left her skin feeling cold, giving her an unwelcome impulse to close the distance. She covered her discomfort by picking up her wineglass and raising it to her lips.

Wine. Her second transgression.

The flavour was less aggressive than the burn she had come to expect from Livia's bucket brews. It was actually quite enjoyable.

Lucas smiled again.

The corners of Julia's mouth tweaked in sympathy, but she couldn't let herself reflect his expression, and her failure dimmed his smile.

He turned towards the fire, and that was when she saw it: something glinting in the whites of his eyes. As she leaned closer, she saw it shine again.

'What?' he said.

She shook her head and looked away.

'No,' he said, 'tell me. Ask whatever you like.'

She looked into his eyes, focussing on the bright tendrils that had caught her attention, and saw unhappy comprehension dawning on his face.

'There's something…' she started, then determined to take the plunge. 'Why are they shining?'

A question. Her third transgression.

He looked away. 'That, I can't tell you.'

'Is it forbidden?' she asked, looking meaningfully at the wine in her hand.

He laughed. 'Yes, something like that.'

She wasn't going to push her luck by asking again, but he hadn't finished yet.

'It's only fair, I suppose,' he said. 'But this is a secret they really care about keeping.'

'They?'

'The Nobles.'

One of her eyebrows started to rise. She pulled it back down where it belonged.

'You're a Noble,' she said.

'Only just,' he joked, but this time his laugh was hollow. 'I'll tell you if you want, but it's a dangerous thing to know. Are you sure you want to hear it?'

Julia considered for a second, but it was a very brief second. Her curiosity had been piqued, and there was no turning away from it now.

'I won't tell,' she said.

He looked at her again, tilting his head to the light so she could look. Where she would have expected to see blood vessels in the whites of his eyes, there was instead a tracery of silver, gossamer-fine.

'All of the Nobles have them,' he said, 'but most of them can mask the silver and pass for human.'

'And you?' Julia asked.

'Too young,' he said. 'So I stay out of sight.'

So that was the reason he had created this little oasis. He was hiding here, but not by choice.

'Now,' he went on, 'will you answer me a question?'

She considered, and decided that she probably owed him for his revelation.

She nodded.

'What did you do to deserve being assigned to me, the pariah of the Blue?' His tone pretended lightheartedness, but there was chagrin in it.

'I don't know,' she said. She turned the wineglass in her hands, remembering now what she had thought when Livia had first told her the news.

'They told me I was the best option the priestess had,' she went on, 'but I think maybe they're punishing me.'

'Punishing you?'

Was that pain in his eyes?

'I didn't want to be an Attendant,' she whispered.

He looked away, his eyes shadowed and unreadable. When he got to his feet, he took the empty pan with him and carried it to the other side of the fire. He was the one avoiding eye contact now.

'You should have said something,' he said.

'It's not my place, Master.'

'I'm not your master!' The pan clanged to the floor, the spoons spinning against the fire-pit bricks with a tinkling that chimed out into the night. Julia shrank back, pulling her cloak around her.

'I'm sorry,' she said quickly. Anything to calm him down.

It had only taken a few smiles to make her forget what he was. The priestess's rules existed for a reason, and she wouldn't be in this situation if she had simply followed them.

No eye contact, no questions, no names.

She wouldn't forget again.

'No, I'm sorry,' he said. He pushed his fingers through his hair, clasping the dark strands at the nape of his neck. 'Perhaps you'd better go.'

She didn't wait for him to ask again. Leaving her transgressive wine on the bench, she slipped down the ladder, through his room and out into the night. She didn't stop moving until she was home.

'You were gone a long time,' Claudia muttered on her return, in the tones of someone who resented having to break her silence in order to satisfy her curiosity.

Julia was feeling too shaken to respond.

The room was dark, so dark that she struggled to hang her cloak on the back of the door. It was later than she had realised.

'Livia told me about it,' Claudia said. 'She told me you've been made an Attendant.'

'Yes,' Julia said, sitting down on the edge of the mattress. She expected jealousy perhaps, or rivalry, but Claudia's next words were filled only with understanding.

'Tonight was your first meeting?' she said.

'Yes.'

'Are you alright?'

'I'm fine, ' Julia said. She tried to make her voice sound cheerful. She had nothing to complain about, after all. Tonight had been nothing like Claudia's first night with Rufus.

'He didn't do anything,' she went on. 'He didn't even perform the ritual.'

'What?' There was outrage in Claudia's voice now, on Julia's behalf, and just like that their quarrel was forgotten. 'Don't tell me he rejected you. I know he's supposed to be the bottom of the barrel, but I didn't realise he'd be bloody blind.'

'Bottom of the barrel?'

'Some of the other girls mentioned him while we were training. Something wrong with him apparently.'

'What?' Julia asked, shuffling her way under the blankets.

'Don't know,' Claudia said.

Julia could feel her shrug, shifting the bedding. She pulled it tighter around her shoulders, shutting out the draught.

'They wouldn't talk to me, obviously,' Claudia went on, 'so I was eavesdropping. No one wanted to be assigned to him.'

'Hmm.'

'Rufus mentioned him too,' Claudia said after a moment.

'Oh?'

'Doesn't think much of him, I'm afraid. Was he awful?'

Julia thought back through the evening. Right up until that final moment, she had almost been enjoying herself. His moment of anger was not enough to eclipse the kindnesses he had shown her throughout the evening: the dinner, the wine, the confessions, his touch on her skin...

'He wasn't what I expected,' she said finally.

Claudia chuckled, a little bitterly.

'They aren't, are they?' she said. 'Was he handsome?'

'I suppose so.'

Dark hair, dark lashes, and dark eyes surrounded by shining silver. He was beautiful enough to make Julia feel even more plain than she usually did, and then there was that smile.

'But you won't be going back?' Claudia asked gently.

'I don't know.'

'But he didn't complete the ritual.' The tone of Claudia's voice made it clear she thought that was the end of it.

'But he didn't reject me either, Claud. So do I go back, or not?'

'Did he say anything?'

I'm not your master!

The sharp crash of metal on concrete.

'Not about tomorrow,' Julia said.

'You could ask at the temple?' Claudia suggested.

'Maybe,' Julia whispered into the darkness, but she remembered her training too vividly to be willing to face the priestess. If she gave any hint of what had transpired at her meeting with Lucas, her transgressions would be totted up and she could say goodbye to what little remained of her freedom.

'Anyway,' Julia said, 'how was your day?'

What she really wanted to ask was whether Claudia's experience with Rufus had improved, but after the horror of two nights ago, she didn't know how to broach the subject.

'It was a very good day,' Claudia said, with a determinedness that made it sound as though she were deciding that it had been, rather than remembering it that way.

They lay together in silence for a moment before Claudia spoke again, whispering the words, as she often did when she had something important to say.

'He didn't bite you then?'

'He barely touched me,' Julia whispered back, rolling over so she was facing Claudia, inches away across the pillows. 'He didn't even taste my blood, Claud.'

This revelation required another pause, and then it was Julia's turn to ask a question.

'What do you do when you're with Rufus?'

Claudia shifted under the sheets, as though she were reluctant to reply, and Julia worried that she might not want to hear the answer. She'd heard rumours of the ways that the Nobles used their Attendants. The stories were so common that they were practically clichéd.

'You know what happens,' Claudia said eventually. 'He drinks my blood.'

'Yes,' Julia said, 'but what about when he's not doing that?'

'What do you mean?' Claudia asked.

Julia propped herself up on one elbow, resting her head in her hand.

'Well,' she said, 'it takes him five minutes. What do you do the rest of the time?'

'I wait,' Claudia said, as though it were obvious.

Julia hoped that her relief wasn't audible. The answer could have been so much worse.

'Why, what did you do tonight?' Claudia asked.

'The same,' Julia replied, because she didn't know how to feel about the difference in their experiences.

Claudia's Noble had bitten her so badly that her skin was stitched shut, and now he made her wait on his pleasure like, well, a Server. Julia's Noble had made her dinner.

Her unease forced a confession she might otherwise not have made.

'I didn't want to go,' she said. 'I nearly ran away. I nearly followed them.'

'No,' Claudia said, sitting up. 'When?'

'Yesterday. I got as far as the fence. I'm sorry.'

'Because of me?'

'No, Claud,' Julia said, tugging her friend back down onto the mattress. 'Because of him. Because I didn't want to be an Attendant. But I'm not going anywhere. It was just…'

There were footsteps in the corridor outside their room: Livia's familiar shuffle. She was probably fetching a nightcap from her stash. They waited until she was back upstairs before speaking again.

'Do you think that's what happened to Quintus?' Claudia whispered.

The boy had been missing for days now. He'd been made an Attendant last year, promoted for the beauty of his face, and Julia had seen little of him since then. She supposed it was possible that he had been unhappy enough to leave the Blue, but it was also possible that the Noble whom he attended had let herself get carried away.

Julia didn't want Claudia to reflect on how regularly Attendants met their ends that way, so instead she just said, 'I don't know, Claud.'

'The other girls say there are creatures out beyond the fence,' Claudia said, 'and that if the earth doesn't poison you, the animals will.'

'And you believe that?'

'You don't?'

'They're just fairytales,' Julia said, but a wave of fear raised the hairs across her arms as she remembered red strobing between the trees.

Thhhwump-chk.

Like the thud of flesh against bone.

4

Hades was not an easy travelling companion. Cam had made it to the cabin in time for nightfall, but that was despite the horse rather than because of him.

He really was a bastard.

They'd made good progress when Cam could urge Hades into a canter, but in the thick forest they rarely managed more than a walk. At any speed from a trot down, the horse jerked his head around in an attempt to chew on Cam's feet, and when Cam moved them out of range, Hades just gnashed after them in circles like a giant dog chasing its tail.

It had not been a restful trip.

The worst thing was that Hades wasn't just a bastard, he was a *clever* bastard. When they'd finally arrived at the cabin, he had waited patiently until Cam had groomed him, cleaned his hooves and fed him before kicking him clear across the campsite. It wouldn't have been a problem if Cam had been prepared for the blow, but he'd been lulled into complacency by Hades's bout of good behaviour so it caught him by surprise. To compound the offence, Cam was certain that Hades had snickered as he rebounded off a tree, cracking his ribs.

In summary: Cam had travelled no further on horseback than he would have done on foot, he was down one bottle of blood from repairing his broken bones, and he was angry as hell.

Stupid fucking horse.

He was halfway tempted to go back to the city and leave Hades there, but of course it was too late. He'd made his decision, and they wouldn't take the horse back now. He was stuck with him for every day of what was likely to be an eight-week round trip.

Never again, he vowed.

Hades had now settled for the night in a lean-to at the back of the cabin, keeping him away from the fire while Cam made his dinner. It wasn't that Hades was bothered by the flames, it was more that Cam was worried the bastard would steal his food or kick cinders at the cabin or stamp on Cam's supplies or do any number of infuriatingly disruptive things. In the lean-to, the horse would be comfortable and warm and, most importantly, out of Cam's way until tomorrow.

Oh god. Tomorrow.

They'd reach the ferry tomorrow. The thought of the havoc that one hundred stones of horse could cause on a floating vehicle was enough to thoroughly obliterate Cam's good humour.

As if it wasn't already compromised enough.

Things were always worse for him at night. In the dark, he could see it all happening over again in his mind's eye. He hadn't even been able to sit by the campfires for the first few months, not until the memory of the flames had started to die away. It was easier now, but some evenings were still filled with memories of Delphi.

There had been a camp there, hundreds of years ago. After the Revelation, after the Weeper virus had swept across the globe, there had been little pockets of habitation scattered all over Europe in strange corners. It was the older places that seemed to call to people, places that had been chosen thousands of years previously for their defensible locations, natural resources and sheltered geography. The Ancient Greek ruins at Delphi offered some of those things, but not enough to explain their appeal, or the size of the shanty town that grew around them.

The truth was that people, humans, wanted to believe that there was something mystical about the site of the ancient oracle. They thirsted for the magic, until it was more vital to them than the tiny spring that sustained their growing population. They saw the Revelation as only confirming the existence of the paranormal world that they craved, and the race that were then called the Silver epitomised it.

Humanity had been looking for a god, and they found one.

By the time Cam and Emmy arrived, it was already too late.

But they'd tried.

The vaccine had been so widespread by then that there were very few humans who had not been inoculated. It made them resistant to the Weeper virus, but contaminated their blood so that the Silver could no longer drink it.

The settlement in Delphi was different. There had been no virus there and no vaccine, and a rogue Silver had decided to make it his personal blood bank.

Cam and Emmy hadn't been expecting to walk into that. They hadn't expected the shanty town to go up in flames like roman candles along the hillside. They hadn't expected the devotion of the humans, that they would be prepared to die for the Silver who was masquerading as their god. They hadn't expected to know his face.

Emmy had suffered for that ignorance, but mostly she'd suffered for Cam's mistake.

The campfire spat a cinder onto his arm. He sat and watched it burn to blackness, remembering the smell of cooking flesh.

The next morning's journey was a quiet one. Even Hades was subdued in the cold stillness of the forest. His attempts to chew on his rider were halfhearted, and by the time they arrived at the shore he had stopped trying entirely. Cam should have been relieved, but instead the horse's silence only increased his own anxiety.

He hated it here. Out on the continent things were different, in the Red proper, but in this small slice of it, on the wooded slopes that ringed the Blue down to the shore, it felt as empty as death. Not even the wind moved in this place. There was no life on the edges of this island. No people, no animals, just a few birds passing through on their way to better things.

It was necessary, of course. They had to keep wild animals out so their blood didn't contaminate the humans, but the bleakness their absence created just felt wrong. It was unnatural, and every cell in Cam's body could sense it.

What his kind were doing here was wrong.

They clung to their superhumanity and bricked themselves away in this hollow place to preserve it. Cam had spent so much time in the Red that he no longer understood what they were trying to save. The city felt like a tomb.

Better to live a human life in the sunshine than an immortal life in the grey vacuum of the Blue.

The noise of the world started to come back when they finally broke through the trees onto the stony shore. The water here was rich and salty, filled with life that washed through a narrow inlet from the Black Sea into the salt lake. There were birds in profusion here, feasting on the spoils of the tideline, and their squabbling cries were a relief. They popped the quiet bubble of the forest.

The ferry was right where Cam had left it, pulled up to the landing stage that projected from the rocks. The boat was a simple platform that followed a line slung from beach to beach, the direction kept true by poles sunk deep into the silt. Salt had bleached its wooden deck, which was starting to show its age. It wouldn't be long before he'd have to replace it again.

Hades remained docile as Cam led him onto the ferry and pushed off from the shore, heaving on the line to drag them forwards. It wasn't until he had pulled them halfway across the lake that the horse regained his usual demeanour and nudged Cam sharply off the edge of the raft and into the water. He should have been ready for it, but at least the gloom of the island had lifted.

Hades nickered happily at him, but after a few playful stomps aimed at Cam's fingers he allowed him to flop back on board in a spluttering puddle.

'Bloody horse,' Cam muttered, but there was no venom in it.

The day was now bright, the water cool, and Cam had plenty of spare clothes. It was difficult not to enjoy the breeze across the water, blowing away the oppressive funk of the island. The sharp air filled his sinuses and cleared his head. With a few hauls on the line, the dry fibres pinching his hands, the Red-ringed Blue fell away from them.

This hadn't always been water. When they'd first settled the Blue, the city had sat on the mainland. Soon, it was surrounded by tidal flats, becoming a headland, then a peninsula, until finally it became the island it was today. It made things easier for them: it was easier to protect, and easier to avoid contaminants, but the price of its isolation was isolation itself.

They no longer knew how many others of their race were out in the Red, or how many humans thrived, because they received few visitors and Cam was the only one of their own group who still wandered any distance. Without the roamers, no one would even remember that the Blue existed. That was the way Laila liked it, but from the looks of things, it wasn't going to last.

Cam could see the tracks when he reached the far shore, the edge of the continent. They hadn't bothered to be subtle. He tied up the boat and vaulted straight into the saddle, riding Hades onto the beach to limit the damage to the ground, but even from his high vantage point the marks of their passage were clear. This hadn't been just a single roamer. There were tens of tracks here, all converging on the ferry crossing.

They'd stopped here, but they hadn't crossed.

A hundred feet up from the beach on a wooded incline, he found their camp. The ground was littered with hoof prints, and cart wheels had churned up the mud beneath the trees. Whatever its destination, the caravan wasn't travelling light.

Flattened areas of undergrowth betrayed the footprints of tents for twenty. The fire pit was big enough to roast a pig, with stacks of animal bones tossed in the ashes.

If this was a human group, then they were doubtless contaminated. If it was Silver, then it was the biggest gathering Cam had seen outside of the Blue. From the nature of the tracks, it looked to be a mixture of the two.

What were they doing all the way out here? There was nothing this side of the mountains. Nothing, that is, except the Blue.

Hades stopped at the edge of the camp and would walk no further. This wasn't his usual recalcitrance. The horse's muscles were tensed and hard, his eyes wide, and his ears pricked in a way that spoke of fear rather than mischief. Cam slid from the saddle, stroking Hades's neck as he did so, and the horse leaned in to his touch.

He must be terrified, Cam thought. It was the first time he'd shown his rider the slightest bit of affection.

Moving carefully, Cam walked towards the fire pit. After two more steps the smell hit him, and he knew what had unsettled Hades.

Blood. Rotting blood, a few days old at least.

He should have scented it sooner. It had been wrapped up with the odour of meat and bones in the ashes, but that wasn't its origin. There was a darker circle in the leaf litter on the other side of the pit where the ground was soaked deep with the stuff.

It was human, and there was a lot of it.

'Shit,' he said.

Hades snorted and stamped at the ground in response, clearly keen to get out of the miasma of death.

His own kind wouldn't waste blood unless it was contaminated, so why spill it? Cam's gaze was drawn irresistibly to the remains of the fire, and to the cracked and ashy bones that poked up from its coals.

Hades snorted again as Cam approached the pile, but he had to know. He didn't want to sift through it with his hands, but kicking at the dust would have felt like disrespect. He had no choice.

His fingers recognised the shape of the teeth before he pulled them from the ashes, fixed loosely in the remains of a human jawbone. There were tool marks across its surface.

These travellers didn't want blood. All they had wanted was the meat.

Cam and Hades spent the next four nights sleeping under the stars, moving steadily northwest towards the far coast of the continent. They weren't the only ones who were travelling in that direction. Cartwheel ruts regularly crossed their tracks, these more recent than the ones they had seen at the shore, but Cam never seemed to gain much ground on them. The caravan was moving quickly, too quickly for them to be traders.

Cam followed them through through forests that had grown up through concrete, so dense now that towns were half-buried in soil and foliage. More than once he came across the remains of the caravan's camps, often pitched in the shells of moss-covered buildings, but there was no more blood spilled.

Cam thought about it often, that deliberate drenching of the earth, and wondered what it might symbolise. He'd seen its like before in his long millennia, and it smacked of religious motives that he struggled to understand given the ritual's proximity to the Blue.

Was the blood supposed to be an offering? The more he followed, the more Cam was unsure that he wanted to learn the truth.

Their paths diverged as the terrain became rougher. Hades was sure-footed enough to carry Cam up the winding paths that led to the mountains, but the carts would have to take the long way around. Cam would likely reach the plains at the same time as the caravan. He hadn't yet decided whether or not that was an encounter he should avoid.

Both Cam and Hades remained uneasy about their fellow travellers, but that had resulted in a slow detente between the two of them. Now that he was far from his familiar pastures, some of Hades's malice had dissipated. Instead of constantly delaying, he had become miraculously obedient while saddled, as long as Cam was forceful. Once Cam was on foot it was a different story. Then he was fair game for being bitten, stamped, kicked and, on one occasion that Cam would rather forget, pissed on. He just counted himself lucky that he'd escaped without any more broken bones.

The sixth day brought them into Transylvania, to their first respite, and their first human contact.

Cam had been here before, to the clear lake that nestled in the crook of the Carpathians, and he knew its people. He'd known their parents, their grandparents, and their ancestors, all the way back to the first post-Revelation settlement by the icy waters.

They were a people who had dug in for the long haul, and it was paying off. As Cam rode down out of the pass, he had time to appreciate the scope of what they had achieved here. The crags were thick with sheep and goats, who grazed widely on their grassy peaks, and a patchwork of crops grew in the fertile plains of the valley. There were buildings here of stone and wood, enough to accommodate every family, with some larger structures for gatherings. Cam could see children playing in the fields and swimming in the lake while their parents washed and fished.

They had everything here that they needed, everything that there was in the Blue, only here it wasn't tainted by racial hierarchy.

It was the most perfect place he knew.

He saw a few arms pointing in his direction as he approached, and by the time he reached the town his welcome party had already been assembled.

Vasile waited until Cam had dismounted before greeting him.

'Domnul Cameron,' he said, clasping his hand in his own. 'It's been a long time.'

'Domnul Vasile, Doamna Ana,' Cam replied, greeting Vasile and his wife. 'You're both well, I hope?'

The couple were elderly now, grey but still strong. He had visited them once every few years, a frequency that only emphasised the passing of time. At this end of their lives, he could track the slip of pigment from hair, skin from muscle and muscle from bone. Each time he came, he had the odd sensation of having skipped a few pages ahead from the point at which he had left off.

He should have been used to it after his long years, but these days his agelessness felt more and more like inertia. They moved and changed and grew, but Cam was a flatline constant.

'You will stay with us tonight?' Ana asked.

'If it wouldn't be inconvenient.'

'Of course not! Domnul Cameron is always welcome here.'

She turned to lead him to the same hut in which he usually stayed during his visits. It was slightly removed from the others, on the edge of the settlement that backed onto the crags, but he couldn't blame them for wanting to keep him away from their own homes. Their folktales had memories long enough to tell them what he was. He might be harmless to them, but he was still a strigoi mort.

'You have a new companion,' Vasile said, nodding at Hades.

'A badly behaved one, I'm afraid. If you can find room to stable him I'd be grateful, but I should probably see to him myself.' Cam didn't want to compound the imposition by letting Hades injure his hosts.

'You'll find the end stall is free,' Ana said, nodding towards the small barn on the other side of the settlement. 'And once you are comfortable, you will join us for dinner in the hall, yes?'

'I'd be honoured,' Cam replied with a little bow that made Ana flush with pleasure. At least, he hoped it was pleasure.

It didn't take long for him to get Hades settled. The horse was so overwhelmed by the sight of fresh apples and carrots that he entirely neglected to kick Cam on his way out of the stall.

Cam found his reception in the hall to be exactly as it always was: warm and heartfelt, but reserved. There were more people than ever dining with them tonight, a factor of the passing years. The more the population grew, the more people had parents or grandparents who had known the strigoi mort, or had received some gift from him, and the more people wished to dine with him so they could tell their children that they had once done the same.

It gave Cam an unpleasant feeling of celebrity. It was the fact of his existence that was of interest, not what he achieved with it.

Vasile led him to a seat near the head of the long table over which he and Ana presided. It was already heaped high with breads and cold salads, but now some younger members of the settlement were carrying in pots of hot, rich-smelling stews. Cam had a pot of his own, individually cooked and placed reverently in front of him by a man he recognised as Ana and Vasile's son.

He could remember Ana and Vasile as children, skimming stones across the top of the lake. Now they were the closest that the settlement had to rulers. When guidance was needed it was to Vasile, Ana and their contemporaries that the people of the lake would turn, but the power they held was gently wielded and born from respect for their accrued knowledge rather than violence.

The climate could be harsh in this remote place, but the settlement was kind and beautiful nonetheless.

There was a moment of quiet anticipation, the only noise coming from the fire crackling in the centre of the hall. It sent its smoke lazily up through the hole in the roof, scenting the air with the sweetness of burning sap.

'*Pofta buna*,' Ana declared to the room at large, the signal for everyone to dig in. The pronouncement was met with cheers.

'This looks delicious,' Cam said, taking a chunk of bread to dip into his stew.

'No meat,' Vasile said, 'as always.' There was a question in his voice, one that often arose during Cam's visit, but it was never posed directly. The answer was not one that Cam was prepared to offer.

He smiled instead, then set about filling his empty belly.

The truth was that the vaccine was in the blood.

The vaccine was the cure.

The cure was in the blood.

Still, after all of these centuries, the concoction that had wiped out the Weeper virus, that would turn him human, lived in the bloodstreams of the creatures of the Red. If meat was well cooked then the cure would be rendered inert, but how could he be sure that every part was burned away? It was a pointless risk to take and so here, for Vasile and Ana's people, he was vegetarian.

The humans had forgotten about the vaccine.

In those first years, blood had become a weapon. Cure one of the Silver, and they were just as mortal as anyone else. The humans had massacred them, and in turn the remaining Silver had massacred any humans who knew the ulterior use of the vaccine.

Eventually, the certainty of the cure had been replaced with

53

ambiguity: the contaminated humans only remembered that they were safe from the Silver because their blood was impure. They didn't remember its power.

Cam changed the subject, denying Vasile the truth. He had no choice.

'I'm going northwest, up to the coast,' he volunteered. 'Is there anything I can bring for you on my return?'

'Oh no,' Ana assured him with a smile. 'We have everything we need.'

'Are you certain? I can bring beer or wine up from the plains, or salt if your store is running low.' Cam knew he would have to fight to get them to accept anything, but he also knew that they expected him to do so. It was the way they traded here.

'No, no,' Ana assured him. 'I'm sure you will have enough to carry.'

'It really is no trouble, Doamna Ana. It's the least I can do to repay your hospitality.'

'Well, if you insist…'

Cam smiled his relief. 'I do.'

'Some salt would be very welcome, and perhaps some needles, if you can find them.'

'You shall have them,' Cam replied. *And some new knives*, he thought, taking note of the scant few that were being passed from hand to hand along the table.

Once their transaction was settled, Ana gave Cam the news of their people from the last few years: deaths, births and marriages. He met new arrivals, congratulated new couples and commiserated with the mourners. His joy and grief were real because he knew these people, he knew the rhythm and colour of their lives, but his emotions lacked intensity because he knew them as a whole rather than individually. They were a bunch of flowers rather than single blossoms, and together their scents were dulled into uniformity.

Eventually, they finished the meal with mugs of a clear spirit that tasted like vodka and burned like battery acid. Everyone partook, but none of them lingered.

Soon Cam and Vasile were alone by the fire.

'Do you ever tire of life, Domnul Cameron?' Vasile was drunk now, slurring his words, and had become more direct than was the habit of his people. 'After so many years, do you feel that you have seen enough?'

'It's a matter of perspective, Domnul Vasile. The older I get, the less clear things become.'

'How so?'

Cam allowed Vasile to fill his mug.

'When I was young,' Cam said, 'I'd look at situations through the lens of one experience. When I'd lived five lifetimes, I had five experiences, and five lenses laid on top of one another through which to view the world. They distort each other, and so everything blurs. Eventually, there's no right or wrong anymore, only choices.'

'And?'

Cam downed the contents of his mug. 'I'm tired of making choices.'

Through the warmth of the liquor, he could admit to himself that he had been looking for too long. He had searched for Emmy because it was easier to carry on than it was to admit that she was gone. Admitting that would mean that he would have to find something else to do with his life after everyone he loved was dead.

Laila was humouring him with this last lead, he realised that now.

'There is a choice that I have made, Domnul Cameron,' Vasile said.

'Oh?'

'I will not be here when you return.'

Cam's focus sharpened on the man, pulling him out of his reverie. 'What are you telling me, Domnul Vasile?'

'I have not been well, my friend. It has been a long time coming, in the chest, and I think it will not be long now.'

Cam listened to the old man's breathing, and heard now what the noise of the banquet had eclipsed. The air rasped through his lungs, constricted and thick. The dense wools that he wore had hidden the worst of it, but it was clear from the shadows sunken into his face that he had lost weight.

'I'm sorry,' Cam said.

'I have no wish to live out the end of my days in pain, you understand?'

Cam nodded, an unwelcome shock of sobriety chasing through him. Was this really a better way, to live and die in sixty short years?

'I will see you in the morning, then,' Vasile said, handing him the rest of the bottle as he pushed himself painfully to his feet. 'Then we can say our farewells.'

Cam took the bottle back to his hut. He rarely drank alcohol these days, but tonight felt like a good time to make an exception.

He was wrong.

The inside of the hut was comfortable, but there was no fire here to warm the air. Thick blankets protected against draughts and dampened the sting of the cold, but the building was designed to be heated by the congregation of bodies rather than by coals. In the huts a little way off from his own, he could hear the soft concerts of breath as families slumbered in the arms of the people they loved.

Cam was alone.

Alone with his bottle.

His nights sleeping in the open air had been better than this. At least he'd had Hades to grumble at.

The isolation was not assisted by the alcohol. The more he drank, the more he remembered the people he had lost.

His first memory was always of that night in the bar back in London, just after the Revelation, the first time the four of them had drunk together: Cam, Ed, Carrie and Emmy. It had been the first of many. The four of them had downed vodka until even Cam had been falling over.

Those were the early days, the worst days, but the ones that burned brightest and deepest.

That was the snapshot his mind loved to rub in his face. He could see them so clearly, even centuries on. Every one of them smiled too widely and laughed too loudly, throwing emotion at him as though there were a bottomless font of happiness in the world. As though it wouldn't soon be emptied out entirely.

He thought of the person he had been then, all smiles, hugs and easy affection.

Laila was right: if he ever did find Emmy, she wouldn't recognise the cipher he had become.

5

Julia didn't recognise the person she was becoming. It was as though someone had taken away her brain and replaced it with that of a girl of the wet blanket persuasion.

The problem was that Julia had always thought of herself as being different from the girls who romanticised the Nobles, who thought they were dashing and exciting and handsome. She knew the Nobles were nothing more than leeching bullies, and she wanted nothing to do with them.

She'd never wanted to be an Attendant. She told herself she'd never even wanted to be a Candidate. She wasn't like the other girls. It wasn't that she was better than them, it was just that she was, well, more grounded. More sensible. She loved Claudia more than anyone in the world, but secretly, in her heart of hearts, she'd always thought her friend was a bit silly.

Julia was decidedly not silly, and so it irritated her to be plagued by silly thoughts. She tried to remind herself of those last seconds she had spent with Lucas, of his yell and the crash of the pan as it fell to the ground, but all she could see in her mind was his quiet smile as he tended his garden.

What was wrong with her?

She might not be able to control her thoughts, but she could control her actions, so she hadn't gone back to the temple that week, nor had she returned to the Noble's home. It was reckless; someone at the temple was bound to notice she was neglecting her duty sooner or later, even if Lucas didn't come for her himself.

She'd spent the first day in the kitchen, convinced that he would arrive at any minute to drag her away from her scrubbing, but he'd never showed. She'd sighed when she'd retired to bed that night, with relief, she told herself.

On the fifth day she was comfortable enough to return to her weeding in the alleys surrounding the square, although she kept out of sight of his building. He never mingled with humans, she remembered, so she was safe from him in daytime streets filled with the bustle of Servers rushing from task to task. At night she remembered the crackle of the fire and the reflections its light traced across the silver filaments of his eyes.

By the tenth day she was starting to think that she had made good her escape, and tried to feel pleased about it. She didn't bother to keep away from his building anymore, which was just as well since its central position made it hard to avoid. Every day she was creeping closer to it, until now she worked practically in its shadow.

The weather was warmer, and the flagstones beneath her knees were reflecting heat from the afternoon sun. Between the pale pavement and the light blue stucco walls, the alley she was clearing had become enough of a heat trap that she stripped off her cloak, her shoulders bared to the sunshine by the shift she wore underneath. Sweat dried and tightened on her skin, a clean and salty scent on the breeze, and she couldn't help her eyes from drifting upwards.

It was a perfect day for gardening. She wondered if he was there, behind the bulk of the water tank she could see perched on the edge of the roof.

A gong rang out across the square and she startled, thinking for an irrational moment that she had been found out, but it soon became apparent that she was not the human who needed to be concerned.

'There you are!' Claudia barrelled up the alley behind Julia.

'What's going on?'

Claudia's face was grim as she pulled Julia to her feet and dragged her out into the square.

'They found Quintus,' she said.

It had been a week and a half now that he had been gone, but something in Claudia's tone told Julia that his return was not a cause for celebration.

'Where?' Julia asked.

'In the Red.'

A crowd was gathering at the far end of the square, in front of the palace. As they hurried closer, Julia could see that the Empress was standing on the palace steps with two members of her guard at her side. They held between them the struggling figure of a human dressed in muddy hues.

The gong rang again, struck by a Server who stood at the door to the palace.

'Who is it they're holding?' Julia said as they joined the back of the crowd. 'Is that Quintus?'

'No,' Claudia said, her eyes locked ahead. She was taller than Julia and could see through the hundreds-deep audience that separated them from the palace.

'Claud?'

The gong rang out for the third and final time, and hush descended across the square, now packed with Servers from across the city.

Two more of the Empress's guard stepped up beside their gold-draped mistress then crouched down below Julia's line of sight. When they stood again, they were carrying a stretcher between them. The body that lay on it was barely recognisable.

'That's Quintus,' Claudia whispered, and there was no colour left in her rosy cheeks.

The Empress raised her staff then thudded it down onto the stone steps, silencing the whispered gasps that had raced through the crowd as they saw what was left of the boy.

'I have been petitioned by the Noble who was attended by this boy,' the Empress said. 'She has asked me to pass judgement on the human whom she claims is responsible for his death.'

She turned to her guards, who pushed forward the human they held. He stumbled to his knees, but quickly jumped back, apparently fearing more from the crowd than from the Nobles at his back.

Julia could understand his fear. Fingers reached up towards him, grasping to snatch at his skin. He was enveloped with jeers and hissing as the slaves of the Blue parroted their obedience.

'State your name,' demanded one of the guards. She was dressed in rough clothing that was bound around her arms and legs with leather thongs. Her hair was the brightest thing about her: red and orange and blonde.

The man closed his eyes, but from this distance Julia struggled to discern his precise expression.

'Marcus,' he said after a moment. His voice carried across the crowd's anticipation despite its softness.

'And the particulars of the charge?' the Empress asked.

The redheaded guard was the one who replied. 'This man is charged with murdering Quintus, then dragging the body into the Red in an attempt to conceal his crime.'

'No!' Marcus shouted. 'He was my friend! I would never-'

The redhead backhanded him across the face, drawing blood from his mouth.

'You will speak when addressed,' she said.

'Motive?' the Empress asked.

'I suspect jealousy,' the redhead answered. 'Quintus was a valued Attendant, and this man hoped to take his place.' The sneer in her voice made it clear how likely she thought that was to happen, and Julia realised that the redhead must have been Quintus's Noble. This trial had been called at her request.

The man just stood silently, shaking his head gently from side to side as blood dripped down his face.

'And the proof?' the Empress asked.

'He was found over the body, the knife in his hand.'

'In the Red?'

The redhead nodded.

'Then his guilt or innocence is irrelevant,' the Empress said, turning to Marcus. 'Human, whether or not you committed this murder, you have contaminated yourself by breaching the boundary. You are exiled to the Red. Should you attempt to return to the city, you will be killed on sight. Understood?'

Marcus nodded, but kept his gaze on the ground.

'Hear me well,' the Empress said, sending her voice out over the crowd. 'If you abandon the protection of the Blue then I will abandon you to the death that waits for you in the Red.'

'Thank you, Your Majesty,' the guard said, reaching out towards the Empress.

She batted the proffered hand away. 'You can clear up the blood,' she said, then turned her back on the redhead. The gesture was full of irritation and disdain.

It made Julia wonder.

The crowd didn't begin to disperse until the Empress had

returned to the palace. The stretcher was carried away while Quintus was dragged off by the second guard, leaving the redhead alone on the steps. She didn't look happy about it.

'Did you know him?' Julia said softly as Claudia's fingers intertwined with her own, leading her gently away from the palace.

'No,' Claudia said. 'He wasn't an Attendant, I know that much.'

'So you think it's true? You think he really murdered Quintus to take his place?'

'It wouldn't surprise me.'

But it surprised Julia. Marcus hadn't seemed like a killer. He'd seemed harmless, although next to the redhead she thought anyone probably would.

What surprised her even more was the idea that Marcus would have chosen to leave the city. The Blue wasn't densely populated, and there were any number of hidden holes that could have concealed the body without requiring him to strike out into the Red.

It didn't make sense.

'Would you go out into the Red just to hide a body?' Julia said.

'Why? Did you have one in mind?' Claudia chuckled, but Julia was too tied up in logic for humour.

'I mean, doesn't it seem strange to you?' she insisted. 'Isn't it weird that he'd risk it?'

'I don't know, Jules,' Claudia replied, the levity gone from her tone. 'You're the expert on leaving the Blue.'

'Claud, please.'

She'd forgiven Julia for nearly leaving, just as Julia had forgiven her for her silent treatment after the incident with Rufus, but they hadn't spoken about either event since. They were still as close as sisters, but there were new barbs in their relationship that only time could blunt.

Claudia sighed. 'I've got to go and see Livia,' she said. 'Do you want to come, or are you going back to your gardening?'

'I should finish off that section,' Julia said, nodding towards where she had left her trug. The alley was close to Lucas's building, and as she turned her head she caught a glint of something on the roof amongst the foliage, just to the side of the water tank. As she watched, it flickered in the sunshine then disappeared, blinking out into nothingness.

'See you this evening, then,' Claudia said, pulling Julia into a hug.

'Yes,' Julia said, watching the rooftop over her friend's shoulder. 'This evening.'

It only took an hour or so for Julia to finish clearing the alley, and then she had no excuse to linger, but there was time yet until dusk, time yet until she would be expected by Claudia.

She looked up at Lucas's building, searching for the reflection she had seen from the other side of the square, but it never returned. Her eyes dropped back to the pavement. There were no weeds left here to clear, but in the next alley, in the alley where the crumbling staircase climbed up to his room, she knew there were plenty.

That would keep her occupied until dinner.

She was just starting on the wall opposite the staircase when she heard footsteps behind her. She knew it was what the silly part of her had hoped for, that he would want to speak to her, but she still wasn't entirely sure whether the thumping in her chest was from excitement or fear.

She dropped her handful of weeds into her trug and stood, turning to face him without lifting her eyes from the ground.

'Julia?'

Her eyes flicked upwards to the face of the man standing opposite her, then quickly glued back to the ground.

It wasn't him. It wasn't Lucas. The man who stood in front of her was taller by a couple of inches, with lighter hair and tanned cheeks pinked with bonhomie or wine. Probably both, by the look of him.

'Yes, Master,' she said, confused.

How did he know her name?

'You're Claudia's friend, yes?'

Julia nodded.

'I saw you with her earlier,' he said. 'I'm Rufus.'

Claudia's Noble.

He took a step towards her, reaching out to touch her cheek. Julia's pulse raced, but this was not the ambivalent excitement that Lucas elicited from her, tugging at her curiosity. This was undiluted fear. This was the man who had scarred Claudia's neck with his teeth to leave his mark.

She knew Rufus by his deeds.

'You lack her beauty,' he said, his breath sharp with wine.

She had to stop herself from edging away, because though she longed to run from him, she knew that she had no hope of escaping. If he wanted to touch her then he would, and she'd only make it worse by making him chase her, cat and mouse.

He's just pushing you, she told herself. *Show him no fear and he'll lose interest.*

His fingers trailed down her cheek, soft as a whisper, but unwelcome enough to leave an ache of violation on her skin. She wanted to rub it away, but she kept her hands by her sides.

How she wished she could run from him.

'Why are you touching my Attendant?'

Empress be praised.

Lucas's voice was the sweetest interruption. Julia used the opportunity of his arrival to slip away from Rufus's grasp under the guise of collecting her trug and cloak from the ground.

'She's yours, is she?' Rufus said, eyebrow raising as he turned to face Lucas. 'Well, how was I to know that when there isn't a mark on her?'

'We don't all maul our Attendants like animals.'

'Maybe not, but they're not much use if you don't drink from them at all. Wasteful is what it is. If you're not using her then why shouldn't I?'

'Who said I wasn't?' Lucas replied, his tone unconcerned.

Rufus shrugged. 'Your mark's not on her.'

'Yet. Julia, go upstairs please.'

His words made Julia apprehensive, but not so much that she considered disobeying them. If the choice was feeding Lucas or Rufus, she knew in her gut which was the better option.

She hurried up the staircase, her trug clacking against the stucco as she went.

'See you again, I hope,' Rufus called after her. 'My rooms are here on the ground floor if you every get tired of hanging out in the attic.'

'Really, Rufus?' Lucas said. 'How far are you going to push this?'

'What? Still bitter that I got the best digs in the city?'

'With no view.'

'What do I want a view for?' Rufus's laughter followed Julia up the stairs. 'I've got a garden, five heated rooms and a private wine cellar.'

'Is that what you sold your integrity for? A hole in the ground?'

'Better than a hole in the ceiling.'

They were still bickering in the alley below when Julia forced open the door to Lucas's room, leaning her full weight against the jamb to dislodge it from the frame.

The space was as bleak as she had remembered, but less tidy. Clothes were piled on the bed, which didn't seem to have been slept in, and buckets of soil now sat in a line along the wall. The air smelled even mouldier than it had on her last visit, and as she approached the buckets she realised why: Lucas was growing mushrooms. The scant light from the open roof hatch picked up the first tiny caps pushing through the wet compost.

Unwilling to linger in the darkness, Julia left her trug behind and climbed up through the hatch into Lucas's garden. The fire was crackling in the pit as a pan sizzled on the grate above it, onions and garlic burning to its sides.

Lucas had forgotten his dinner.

She wrapped her cloak around her hands and used it to pull the pan from the heat, but the contents were already blackened beyond redemption.

'Too late?' Lucas asked as he joined her. Julia hadn't heard him approach.

'I'm sorry,' she said, setting down the pan on one of the benches.

'It's my own fault. I should have taken it off the fire before…'

Rufus.

Lucas had abandoned his dinner to intervene. Julia wasn't sure whether she'd been rescued or captured, but there was no doubt that she'd rather be up in this terraced retreat with Lucas than trapped in an alley with the alternative.

'Thank you,' she said.

'I wasn't expecting you to come back.' There was an edge of irritation in his voice.

'I didn't,' she said, feeling compelled to defend herself. 'I was working.'

It wasn't exactly a lie, but nonetheless she knew it wasn't the truth. Perhaps it had been curiosity driving her, or maybe she was just as silly as the other girls, but she had put herself in his way. She had wanted to see him.

Still, it was true that she had never expected to return to this place, with its crisp leaves, its warm bricks, and its dark tenant. It was different at this time of day, divorced from the intimacy that came with the night. In the afternoon sunshine his world was exposed, and she could see the damage in it: the broken pots, the sun-bleached wood and the dirt that covered everything.

He didn't want her here.

She shouldn't have come.

'I'm sorry,' she said, gathering her cloak around her shoulders, but he caught her as she made her way back to the hatch.

She froze.

'I can't let you go now,' he said, his words quiet but firm.

Julia looked down at where his fingers circled around her wrist. She could feel her pulse thudding against his grip.

'You should have stayed away,' Lucas said.

He reached into his pocket and produced a small penknife, flicking it open while he turned her hand palm-up. She had barely registered the threat before the point was in her finger, drawing a drop of blood that Lucas raised to his lips on the blade.

She should have been scared, but there was nothing in his eyes that frightened her. There was no violence in them, just hunger.

He drew her finger to his mouth, and then all she could feel was the aching pull in her veins as he ran his tongue over her skin.

'You told me you didn't want to be an Attendant,' he said as he withdrew.

She didn't reply. She wasn't sure she could.

'Well, I hope you've changed your mind, because if I don't mark you then Rufus will do it his way.'

He ran his hand over her neck, pulling her closer as he looked into her eyes. His gaze was intense and demanding, as though he wanted to make certain that she understood.

She did. She remembered the stitches in Claudia's neck and prayed that Lucas would be more gentle.

He wrapped her against him, his fingers threading through her hair as he tilted back her head. She let him, closing her eyes, waiting for the pain.

Instead, his lips touched hers.

Her eyes opened in surprise.

He had kissed her.

They looked at each other for a moment, their faces a whisper apart, and something changed. Julia could feel it in the quickening of her pulse and in the tension that melted down her throat until it hit her stomach, warm and seductive.

Her palms were pressed against his chest, but not to push him away. The cloth under her fingers, as coarse as her own dress, moved over his muscles as his chest rose and fell, his breath coming as fast as her own.

'Julia?' he whispered.

He was so close that she felt enveloped in his scent, fresh mint and honey filling her head until there was nothing but him: his dark eyes on hers, his hand around her waist, his lips so close that they brushed her own as he spoke.

She kissed him.

She shouldn't have done it. If it was forbidden to call him by his name then she was certain that it would be forbidden to kiss him, but he had started it. She didn't care either way. She was wrapped in his arms, wrapped in the feel and the taste and the smell of him, and for those few moments he was all there was in the world.

They ended abruptly with a soft tearing sound by her ear.

They fell apart.

Lucas took a step away, one hand holding the knife and the other clasped around a lock of long, brown hair.

Julia's hands flew to her scalp, searching until she found the place at the back of her neck where the strands were missing.

'My hair,' she murmured, and then she realised what a fool she'd been.

'For the ritual,' Lucas said, coiling the hair carefully around his finger. 'I accept you as my Attendant.'

It had been as the priestess had said it would be. He had tasted her blood, indicated his acceptance and then cut a lock of her hair to symbolise his ownership. She just hadn't expected his acceptance to be quite so enthusiastic.

'It's part of the ritual,' Lucas said, his eyes trailing down to her mouth. Her fingers were touching her lips, although she couldn't remember putting them there. She dropped her hand.

'Of course,' she murmured.

'It's one way of leaving a mark, a scent mark,' he said, talking quickly and with a forced cheerfulness that spoke of his discomfort. He wasn't meeting her eye.

An unwelcome misery stole through her.

'The other way is the one that Rufus prefers,' he went on. 'But don't worry, the scent mark only lasts for a day or so, so it will be gone by tomorrow night.'

Her nerves buzzed with exciting possibilities.

'So,' she whispered, 'we'll have to... do it every day?'

'Oh, no,' he said with a laugh, hollow and sharp. 'No, once is enough. Don't worry about that. Now that I have this,' he raised the finger that was twined with her hair, 'no one will challenge my claim. You're safe.'

So it had all been a ruse to protect her from Rufus's teeth. Julia tried not to feel disappointed, but it was difficult not to be hurt by Lucas's words.

Once is enough.

Had it really been so bad? It had probably been the best kiss of Julia's life, but once was enough for him.

'I'm afraid you will have to come here every day though,' Lucas said, looking at his hands as he fiddled with the penknife. 'You know, as my Attendant.'

She would have to serve him every day. She would have to face him every day, and feel his lips on her skin every day as he took her blood, pulling sensation through her every day while he felt nothing but awkwardness.

She disdained the Nobles. She'd never wanted anything to do with them. She'd never wanted to be an Attendant.

But... perhaps she could have tolerated being his.

Her blood felt like it was frenzying in her chest, battering to the rapid beating of her heart. Then it broke. Feelings she didn't know she'd had were spilling out of her, leaving her insides cold and empty.

She might have wanted to be *his* Attendant.

Not like this, though. She didn't want him to do this out of some twisted sense of duty.

She couldn't stand in front of him, this man who had somehow forced a contradiction in the most fundamental aspect of Julia's self esteem, and bear his pity.

She needed to go.

'I'm late for dinner,' she said.

'I'll see you at dusk tomorrow, then,' he said briskly, turning his back on her as he walked over to the water tank.

He was picking vegetables for his own meal as she left.

She didn't say goodbye.

Claudia met her as she was skirting the edge of the square, making her way from Lucas's building to their own.

'You had me worried sick,' Claudia said. 'Dinner was ready ages ago.'

Claudia took the trug and wrapped an arm around Julia, banishing the twilight chill from her shoulders.

'Sorry, Claud.'

Julia meant to explain, but was interrupted by a heavy thud as the doors of the guardhouse were thrown open across the square. She tugged Claudia into the nearest alley and they crouched there together as they watched, hidden by the sunset shadows.

Two of the Empress's guard were marching a man between them.

'Marcus?' Claudia whispered, her voice so quiet that Julia only picked up the word because it was what she had expected to hear.

Julia shrugged in response, a redundant gesture in the darkness.

The trio marched silently past their hiding place and out of the other side of the square. Julia guessed that they were heading for the boundary fence, the point at which she had almost left the Blue herself.

'Come on,' she whispered, abandoning her trug as she stood to follow the guards.

Claudia hesitated for a moment, but apparently she was just as curious as Julia because she needed no encouragement to join her.

They could hear the boots of the guards echoing in the streets ahead of them, but their own bare feet were almost inaudible on the slabs. Servers were meant to be as invisible as they were silent, and Julia and Claudia had trained to excel at both skills. They tracked the group through the paved streets, over the dilapidated cobbles that circled the centre of their world, and finally into the broken ground that marked its edge.

They were a little to the east of the point at which Julia had planned her own escape. There was a gate set into the fence here, closed with a simple latch that one of the guards was lifting aside.

Claudia pulled Julia behind the carcass of an fallen tree so ancient that the width of its trunk almost equalled their height. They curled into the protection of its unanchored roots, picking their footing carefully in the moonlight, and waited.

The guards stepped clear of the open gateway.

'Go on then,' one said, a man.

'It wasn't me.' There was desperation in the voice, so that must have been Marcus. He had his back to them, but it was clear that he didn't want to cross the line into the Red.

'Look, you heard the Empress.' This new voice was feminine, the second guard. They were both so tall that Julia would never have guessed that one of them was female.

Why was everyone taller than her?

'It wasn't me, I swear,' Marcus said.

'You've been out in the Red before,' - this was the male guard again - 'so what's the big deal?'

'No, I haven't!' Marcus's voice was pleading now, cracking through a tight throat. 'I was never in the Red!'

'So you're saying Philo's a liar? You're saying he didn't find you with the body?'

'That's exactly what I'm saying. It's a mistake! It wasn't me!'

'And you expect us to believe you over a Noble? Are you fucking kidding me? Just get out.'

Marcus spread his arms and clung to the sides of the gateway as the guards moved to push him through. He teetered for a moment on the edge, fighting with all his might to keep his toes out of the Red, but it was a pointless gesture.

There was a crack as one of the guards brought his hand down on Marcus's arm, and his strength went with the break. Julia could hear his cry pitching down through the gateway.

'You heard the Empress,' the female guard said. 'If we see you again, then we'll kill you.'

The gate slammed shut, the latch returned to its place. The boundary fence would be easy enough to climb if Marcus was determined to break back into the Blue, but the threats of the guards would keep him away. It was too late for him anyway, now that he had crossed the line into the land of poisoned fruit.

Julia drew Claudia further into their hiding spot, wrapping her arms around the other girl's shoulders as the guards turned back towards the city.

'Is it just me,' the male guard said to his companion, 'or was that a bit odd?'

'Don't tell me you believe him,' she said.

'Of course not.' There was a pause. 'Well, I don't know. I mean, could Philo have mistaken him for someone else?'

'Don't be an idiot, Jens. That Server was always hanging around Lorelei's Attendant. Philo saw him all the time. Of course he'd recognise him.'

'Ah,' said the guard called Jens.

But Julia couldn't help but feel that there was something wrong with their logic.

If Marcus really had been out in the Red before, then why would he fight so hard to avoid crossing the line? He would already be contaminated, and the threshold would be insignificant. She supposed he could have been faking it, but to resist so hard that the guards broke his arm... it didn't make sense.

They waited until the guards were out of sight before emerging from their cover.

'He didn't do it, did he?' Claudia whispered.

'I don't know.'

Julia looked over at the gate, almost expecting to see Marcus making his way back into the Blue.

He wasn't. He wouldn't. He'd risk bringing the blight with him, and that was unthinkable.

As unthinkable as it was for him to go out into the Red to hide a body.

Julia hesitated a moment longer, torn between her will to help him and her knowledge that there was nothing she could do, then she gently led Claudia away, back towards the city, towards their cellar and to Livia's secret still.

They both knew that Marcus would be dead by morning.

6

Cam was jolted awake by a sound in the trees behind him.

No, not a sound, but the absence of sound. Stagnancy pooled around the smouldering campfire. It was like being back in the Blue again: no movement, no animal sounds.

Only people.

Hades had been sprawled out on the ground behind him when Cam had gone to sleep, perfectly positioned to kick him in the back during the night, but there was no sign of him now. Cam had secured the horse's halter to a nearby tree root before settling down, but that too was gone. It hadn't been broken or frayed, either. It had been untied.

Someone had stolen his bloody horse, and not just that. His pack was missing, as were the weapons that had been attached to Hades's saddle. Which, of course, was also gone.

If he hadn't been pushing himself so hard these past few days then it would have woken him, but he had been running from the memory of Vasile's farewell. He'd taken some of the mountain lake's alcohol with him, and it had warmed him by the fire the previous night.

It seemed he'd let himself get a little too warm.

'Shit,' he muttered, pushing himself unsteadily to his feet.

He shouldn't have been this drunk, but then he had been spinning out his blood rations. He only had a single bottle left, which was in his pack, which was… gone.

Cam groaned and pulled his cloak around his shoulders, the only possession that they had left him. He might have been tempted to let the thieves take Hades off his hands, but he couldn't lose the last of his blood. He was going to have to track them.

The silence in the forest was coming from the south, so that's where he headed. He had left the dense conifers of the mountains behind him several days ago, and the trees that surrounded him now were all deciduous. The smell of the leaf litter was lighter too, more fruit and less spice.

Even moving at human speed, it took barely ten minutes to catch up with the bandits. There were only two of them, both slight enough that Hades could have carried them together without any trouble, but apparently he had objected to doing so on grounds of principle rather than inability. Both men lay in the undergrowth where Hades had thrown them, and they were now scrambling around in a desperate attempt to avoid the horse's thundering hooves.

'Hades,' Cam called or, more accurately, slurred. 'C'mere.'

Hades looked at him, holding his gaze for a second before deciding that he was having more fun tormenting his new friends. His feet harpooned into the ground, chasing fingers and soft vulnerabilities.

'Hades!' Cam shouted.

The horse stamped once more before nickering softly and abandoning the chase.

The thieves rose carefully to their feet, never taking their eyes off Hades.

'Gentlemen,' Cam said to them. 'I'll be taking back my belongings now, if you please.'

One of them nodded towards a nearby tree, his eyes still wide with fear, and Cam saw the pack and saddle discarded there. He scooped them up along with Hades's halter, then started to make his way back the way he had come.

'You don't want to go that way,' one of them called after him in bastardised Hungarian.

'Oh?' Cam said, intrigued by the man's motives.

'Izcacus that way,' he replied.

Blood drinker.

They thought Cam was human. They might have tried to steal everything he owned, but they still had enough solidarity to try to warn him about vampires.

'Where?' Cam asked. He wondered if this might be the start of the trail he needed to follow to the coast, to the settlement Laila had told him about.

'Everywhere,' the second man said. His voice was so quiet it was almost a whisper. 'They come in carts in the night, and leave blood and bones behind.'

The description sounded eerily like the campsite he had found by the salt lake. Cam had seen no sign of the caravan's tracks this side of the mountains, and had started to think that they had turned back to the Blue.

'When did they come through here last?' Cam asked.

But the men had already gone, disappearing between the trees. Cam couldn't muster the energy to follow them.

He sighed.

'And what about you?' he said to Hades. 'You wake me up to chew on my boots, but you can't make one sound to let me know you're being stolen?'

The horse didn't acknowledge Cam, but there was a smug look in his eyes. Apparently his violent tendencies were sated for the time being, because he allowed Cam into the saddle with no objections.

'Come on,' he said. 'Let's see if we can find this Izcacus.'

Traces of human habitation proliferated through the forest. Some of them were hundreds of years old, the straight edges of half-buried masonry betraying the sites of ancient towns, but nowhere had they successfully resisted the wilderness. The woods were the cities here. There were trees so entwined with buildings that their growth had reshaped walls and bent metal around them, producing strange hybrid sculptures topped with canopies of spring leaves.

Those few structures that retained their roofs were strewn with the detritus of recent transients. Blackened concrete spoke of endless campfires, and the floors were so well-used that moss no longer covered them entirely. Where there were no ruins to inhabit, the forest floor was pockmarked with circles of burned stones.

And yet Cam saw no one.

He travelled on horseback until dusk, fording streams and climbing from lush valley to even lusher valley, but still he saw nothing more than the fire pits left behind by the people who lived here.

The following day, after a night under the stars, he found a campfire whose ashes were still warm, but that was the closest he came to human contact.

He was starting get the feeling that the inhabitants of this place were avoiding him.

On the third day he found the remains of the Izcacus camp, but it wasn't what Cam had expected. It couldn't belong to the same caravan as the one that had visited the lake by the Blue, because it was huge. The space had been cleared of enough undergrowth to accommodate a hundred tents. There were six separate campfires, each of which was stacked with bones, although there was less blood in the earth here.

What did it mean?

It had puzzled Cam ever since he had found the first camp. Why would these Silver waste the blood if it wasn't contaminated? And if it was impure, why would they risk eating the flesh?

He had no answers, and this new camp simply raised more questions.

Cam dismounted so he could examine the ground more closely. There were regular sets of holes, deep and wide, and they'd been moved more than once. Tent poles, he guessed. It could only mean that the caravan hadn't just passed through here; this was a place to which it returned.

He stopped in the middle of the camp, stroking Hades's neck to quiet him.

There was something…

A noise just on the edge of his hearing, a scent so subtle he could only catch it with a favourable breeze: nutmeg and blood.

There was someone else here.

No. He paused, scenting the air. *Two someones.*

One was nutmeg. The other was blood, with laboured breathing.

Cam walked towards the sound, slowly at first, but he broke into a run as he identified its source. The blood was smeared on the bark of an oak tree at the foot of a small rise. The low-hanging branches hid the figure well, but Cam could still see the darker spot against the crown of the tree where there should have been only grey bark and greenery.

'Stay away,' the figure rasped as he approached. The voice was breaking on its ragged breaths.

Human, and male, not young.

'I'm not going to hurt you,' Cam said.

'Of course, Izcacus,' the man replied, rattling out a coughing laugh. 'This is what you all say, for otherwise we would stay in our trees.'

The man made a good point. Cam had drawn close under the branches, so he could look up into his face. He was old indeed, perhaps seventy, a ripe old age for this lawless stretch of the continent. His scraggly beard was matted with blood.

'What happened here?' Cam asked.

'What always happens when you find us. People died.' The words were blunt, but his face was creased with grief.

'And you?'

He shook his head. 'Contaminated. No good.'

'The others?'

'You saw their bones, Izcacus.' The word was hissed like a curse, but Cam didn't mind the insult. His attention was fixed on puzzling out the implications of what the man had said.

The Silver in this camp must have found uncontaminated humans. They were feeding from humans whose blood didn't carry the cure, out here in the middle of the Red.

Was this the group he was looking for?

'Where did they go?' he asked.

'Away, for now.'

'To?'

The old man smiled. 'They left you behind.'

'I'm not one of them,' Cam said.

'But you are, Izcacus. I've lived enough to recognise it in those old eyes of yours.'

Cam smiled back. 'I don't deny that I'm an Izcacus, *Öreg*, but they aren't my people. I come from the southeast, over the mountains.'

'Then you aren't the Izcacus named Cameron, who visited this place in my childhood?'

Cam stared, trying to strip the years from the man's features and remember his face. There had been so many faces though, and so many years.

'You knew them back then,' the old man said, and then he would say no more. He wouldn't come down from the tree either, so Cam left some of his own food at its base and hoped that the man's injuries weren't too severe for him to make his way out of the valley unaided.

He paused to taste the air again before he moved on, but there was no more nutmeg on the breeze.

For the first time in years, Cam's campfire felt lonely that night. He wanted to puzzle things out with someone, to pick apart the clues he had collected until they made sense. It wasn't something he was good at doing alone, not when there was so much to unravel.

Even Hades was no use as a companion. They'd ridden hard through the afternoon, and the horse had crashed out the moment they'd made camp.

Cam had never known a creature so undignified in its sleep, all straggling limbs and drool. It was enough to lull him into a false sense of security. Cam would start to think of Hades as though he were a dog, one of the big and stupid breeds full of enthusiasm and goodwill, but then he'd reveal himself as the crafty bugger he was by pinning Cam up against a tree so he could nose through his pack for apples. Between that attrition and the food Cam had left behind with the old man in the valley, his stores were becoming worryingly low.

He wished he could remember the old man's face.

He had passed this way regularly at that time, sixty-odd years previously. The Invicti had been searching along the coast, section by section, trekking through these valleys month after month as they travelled between the Blue and the north.

But there had been no Silver here then. There had been only a few clusters of civilisation, long-since disbanded, filled with vaccinated humans who were prepared to trade food for trinkets the Invicti brought them. The villages that had stood here had been small but, like the people of the mountain lake, they'd had their hierarchy. Cam had dealt with their leaders when he passed through in the same way that he did now with Vasile and Ana.

The old man's words tugged at the edges of his memory.

You knew them back then.

There had been no tribes of Izcacus moving their caravans around the Red, stripping flesh from human bones and soaking the earth with blood.

But yes, he had known the people who had once lived here. They'd been swallowed up by the valleys over the years, but apparently something else had been spat back out.

Something had arisen in these woods, something that was unlike anything he had seen before, and it was on the move.

When Cam finally slept, his dreams were not restful. He blamed the nightmares for what happened when he woke, them and the hard riding and the horrors of the Izcacus camps, although those influences still did not excuse it.

He wasn't sure that anything could excuse it.

A hand on his shoulder woke him from his rest, and his instincts kicked in. It was the second time he had allowed himself to become so impaired that someone was able to sneak up on him as he slept, although this time it was the fault of exhaustion rather than vodka.

He jumped to his feet, ducking to slide out of the grasp of his attacker, and then his hand was wrapped around the man's throat. He recognised him a split-second too late, a fraction of a moment before his neck cracked in Cam's hand.

His beard was now a brilliant white, washed clean of blood. A blood-soaked bandana bandaged his throat, but otherwise he looked to be in perfect health.

Except that he was dead now.

Cam could still hear the snapping of the bones in his head, that sickly crunch. The sound reverberated through his memory, raising sweat across his shoulders.

He lowered the body to the ground, laying him out beside the remains of the fire. It wasn't yet dawn, but it wasn't far off either, and there was little warmth to be had from the embers.

He must have travelled straight through the night to catch up.

But why?

Why had he chosen to follow him, after showing such reticence back in the valley? Why did he have to creep up on Cam while he was sleeping? How was Cam supposed to know it would be him?

But the old man was not the one to blame.

His eyes were open but vacant while Cam untied the bandana from his throat to bare the wound: a bite. He'd said he was contaminated. Had that been a lie, or was there a newly-human Silver somewhere in these woods? There was no way for Cam to tell without risking his own immortality.

It didn't seem like such a bad exchange, all things considered, and Cam contemplated it. He clearly couldn't be trusted with the strength of his own hands. After all these hundreds of years, he was finally starting to lose control.

If it hadn't been for Emmy, he might have done it, he might have spun the wheel and tasted the blood. It would be useful, if it would prove that there were uncontaminated humans this far into the Red. If the old man had been telling the truth, if he really was contaminated with the cure, then at least Cam would be neutered.

But there was still the lead. He still had an obligation to Emmy, for one last time. If it hadn't been for her...

Chasing her had kept him sane for centuries, but nonetheless this was what he had become: crazed, and a murderer.

This was what they all became, in the end.

It was a good thing that he'd never find Emmy, because she'd hate him for this, almost as much as he hated himself.

Cam found the old man's horse hitched to a nearby tree, a bay mare with saddlebags filled to bursting. Feeling guilty as all hell, he poked through them. They were stuffed with food and drink, not just the packages that Cam had left behind for the old man, but other supplies as well. There was some kind of jerky, along with dried fruits, nuts, pies and biscuits.

The man couldn't have been an itinerant. These were foods made by a population who had access to ovens, smokers and livestock, but Cam had seen no traces of a settlement that sophisticated. All he had found were the tracks of people moving through the forest in small groups, roaming ahead of the carts of the Izcacus.

So where had the man come from?

Cam was refastening the bags when he caught the scent on the air again: nutmeg. Nutmeg was a tropical plant, far too delicate for the chill of the continent, so the smell couldn't be coming from the trees that surrounded him. It was sweet, like a perfume, the scent of warm spice.

Someone was watching him.

He left both of the horses and followed the traces of the scent among the trees, finally tracking it to a tall oak. Hoisting himself into its branches, he found the air was thick with the warm richness of skin. Someone had been sitting in the crook of the branches, body heat passing through wool-covered limbs into the wood. Whoever it was had sat there long enough to warm the sap under the bark, releasing its resinous odour along with the nutmeg burn that was the human's own scent.

Cam dropped from the branches and turned, trying to catch the trail. It was difficult to pick out from the flood of nutmeg at the base of the tree. He tracked out in circles, patiently looking for the nasal hook, but by the time he found the right direction it had started to rain, and the final traces were drowned into the earth.

At least it had given him another clue. It was the second time in as many days that he had found a human watching him from the trees. That couldn't just be a coincidence.

And whoever had evaded him had doubtless seen Cam kill the old man. He would know that Cam was an Izcacus, because only they would have the strength to kill so carelessly.

Cam had made himself a target. He needed to get moving.

He travelled faster with two horses, switching between them. Hades seemed almost affronted that Cam would prefer the mare over him, but Cam had to admit that she was easier company. She hadn't once tried to bite him, or step on his feet, although she did seem subdued. He wondered whether she was mourning her previous rider.

Cam was.

He remembered a crunch, as though he had squeezed the bones deliberately rather than snapped them accidentally, and each time he relived it he convinced himself a little more of his guilt. Every time the leather of the mare's reins rubbed against themselves in his hand, he felt the fracture. He could feel the ghosts of the vertebrae grinding together in his palm.

Despite the nature of the Silver, he had never been hardened to killing. He had killed in self defence, or in defence of others, but this was different. To have taken a life, a human life, by mistake…

If it had been a mistake at all. He had thought over the incident so many times that he could no longer tell the difference between memory and fantasy.

He heard steps from time to time. Not hoofbeats, but the steps of people, too fast to be human, running alongside his path through the trees. There was more than one, more than two, and in his weakened state Cam knew he couldn't risk confronting them. They obviously had access to enough blood to waste its energy in fast running, while Cam only had his emergency bottle left.

He wished he knew more about them, but in the circumstances what he already knew was enough. He knew to stay out of their way, and they didn't try to approach. It was as though there were tracking him out of their territory, seeing him clear to its edge.

The runners dropped away as he broke through the tree line, pushing out of the woods onto a plain where wild horses matched the mare's stride. If Hades hadn't been tethered to her saddle, Cam had no doubt that he would have run off to terrorise the locals.

There were people in the meadows, too. Cam had come out of the forest at the top of a hill that sloped down for half a mile or so before it disappeared into more trees. At the bottom of the slope, figures were gathered around campfires close to where a stream trickled through the grasses, and a small collection of tents and wagons was discernible just under the woodland canopy behind them.

The figures seemed to be human. There was no blood on the air, only the heavy scent of rich stews and unwashed bodies. Laughter and singing drifted up towards him. This was not the caravan of blood and bones that he had feared.

The mare nickered as she saw them, and started tugging at the reins to pull in that direction, but Cam was uneasy. It was nearly dark, and he wanted to be across the plain and into the forests at the other side before night fell. It would be easier to hide there.

He weighed up the options for a moment before deciding that he could spare the time to visit the camp briefly. The mare's interest was worth investigating.

Calls sounded from the gathering as he approached down the hill, but what had initially been cries of welcome turned to suspicion as he drew nearer. They had recognised the mare, but he was not the man they had expected to be riding her.

Silence fell over the camp.

'Halt there!' a voice called out when Cam was twenty feet away. 'Where is Peterke? Why do you have his horse?'

'He's dead,' Cam replied.

There was a gasping sob from the back of the crowd. Of the thirty-odd people in the camp, every one of them was affected enough by the news that Cam could imagine they had all known him personally.

What had he done?

'Bitten?' the spokesman asked.

'Yes,' Cam replied, truthfully but not honestly. The bite was not what had killed the man.

'Then at least he took one of the Izcacus with him.' That
answered one question, at least. 'You saw them?' the man went on.

'No,' Cam said, 'but I think they were following me through the
forest.'

'Then come.' He waved Cam into the camp.

As Cam dismounted, one of the other men came forwards and
took possession of the mare. Cam didn't feel he was in a position
to argue her ownership. Hades was carrying her saddlebags, so
Cam still had the supplies in any case. He would have surrendered
them too, particularly the jerky since he couldn't use that himself,
but he had so little left to get him through the next six weeks. He
wouldn't have been able to explain why he didn't need the meat
without raising suspicions, and he didn't want to upset these
people further.

What was he doing here?

He needed to gather what information he could, then move on.

'What's your name, traveller?' the man asked him as they joined
the circle of people sitting around the nearest fire.

'Cameron.' He spoke without thinking, before he remembered
that it was a name the old man had known, but a quick survey of
the faces around the fire reassured him that none of the others were
old enough to remember the last time he had passed through this
part of the world.

'I'm Gergo. Peterke was my wife's uncle.'

Guilt writhed in Cam's chest. 'I'm sorry,' he said, meaning the
apology more deeply than Gergo could tell.

'He was a stubborn old bastard,' Gergo said with a chuckle, to a
chorus of rueful smiles from the others around the fire. 'He never
would listen to us when we warned him not to wander off.'

'What was he doing out there?' Cam asked.

'Where did you find him?'

'A day or so's travel southeast. There was a camp there, bones
in the fire. Blood.'

Gergo shook his head, disbelieving. 'I told him not to go that
way. Stubborn bastard.'

'He was the only survivor, he said. What is that place?'

Gergo's gaze snapped to Cam's face. 'He was still alive when
you found him?'

Shit. Cam was too tired to deal with this.

'He wasn't killed until this morning.'

'What happened?'

Cam took a deep breath, frantically trying to piece together a story that wouldn't make him a monster. Gergo misinterpreted the gesture as emotion and offered Cam a drink.

'No, thank you,' he said, holding up his palm. Alcohol had caused him enough trouble on this trip already. What he needed right now was clarity.

'The camp was empty, but I found Peterke hiding in a tree.'

Gergo nodded, as though it were normal for the elderly to climb trees. Perhaps it was amongst these people.

'We exchanged a few words, but parted ways. I didn't realise that we had travelled in the same direction until I found the body.'

The lie sat uncomfortably in Cam's chest.

'Where?' Gergo asked.

He should have brought the body with him. If he'd known, then he would have brought Peterke back to his people.

'It was a day's ride southeast,' Cam said, 'by a campsite in the forest.'

Gergo's face wrinkled into a frown. 'Peterke wouldn't have lit a fire,' he said. 'None of us light fires in the trees. It just attracts the Izcacus.'

Cam thought of all the campsites he had found on his journey this side of the mountains. He hoped it was just Gergo's people who took such precautions, because those fire pits couldn't all have been left by the Silver. There couldn't be that many of them out here.

'Do you know what they're doing?' Cam asked, keen to move attention along from Peterke's death.

'You're not from these parts,' Gergo said.

'No. I've travelled up from the south.'

'For what purpose? Why would you risk this journey?'

'To find a lost friend. My people heard that she might have come this way.'

Gergo nodded, apparently satisfied with this answer. 'We all risk our lives for love,' he said. 'It's a noble thing you do, I think.'

Cam didn't correct him. He did love Emmy, of course, but not like that. Things had never been that way between them.

'It used to be that it was just us in these valleys,' Gergo continued. 'We had our families, our homes, our animals, and our lives uninterrupted. Then, about twenty years ago now, it changed.

There were new people, riders, burning our villages in their search.'

'For?'

'A baby, they said. A baby boy. They took our son, took all of our sons, and we never saw them again.'

The woman who sat next to Gergo entwined her fingers with his, squeezing his hand until the flesh turned white.

Their son.

'How old are you, Cameron?' the woman asked him.

There was no way he could answer that question truthfully, so he told her how old he had been when he had turned Silver, the age he still appeared to be.

'Twenty-one,' he said.

She nodded. 'He would have been your age now.'

Cam hated to intrude on their grief, but he needed to know more.

'Do they still raid your homes?' he said.

'Now the Izcacus own the forests,' Gergo said, wiping his eyes. 'We have no homes left, and so we travel. Mostly they let us be, but not all times. Sometimes they take from us, or they take our people, and then they're gone, like our boys.'

'Take them where? What do they do with them?'

But Gergo had no more answers to offer.

He tried to persuade Cam to stay with them in the camp overnight, saying that it was safer out of the trees in the darkness, but Cam made his excuses and led Hades away from the fire.

'You be careful out there, son,' Gergo called to him as he mounted Hades. 'You're the right age, and they'll take you if they can.'

'They'll have to find me first,' Cam called back, and then the wind was in his hair, blowing tears from his eyes as Hades blazed across the plain, black on black, disappearing into the night.

It was full dark when Cam reached the shelter of the trees on the other side of the meadows. He was grateful for it, because the rain had started again when he was out on the plain, thick spatters that drenched his hair and rolled down his neck to soak in under his cloak. Even some distance into the woods the canopy thudded gently with the weight of the water, pouring streams of collected raindrops into the spaces between the leaves.

Hades was not pleased. He was strangely prissy for such a large beast, and he wouldn't walk far before he halted immovably. Cam didn't have the will or energy to argue with him, but the horse still wouldn't leave Cam alone until he was stripped of the wet saddle, rubbed down and settled on a patch of drier leaves in the cover of a dense beech tree.

Thankfully, Hades had picked a perfect spot. There was an old campfire here, ringed with chunks of masonry that would have made a solid base for a spit, if Cam had had anything to roast. There was enough cover that he thought he should be able to get a fire going, and though he wouldn't be able to eat any meat in the Red, he could probably make something hot from the contents of Peterke's saddlebags. Maybe there would even be some bread he could toast on the fire.

He had only a second of pleasant anticipation before the guilt overwhelmed him once more. He had killed the man and stolen his food. What right did he have to enjoy it?

Hades interrupted him with a snort, shaking his head so his mane scattered water droplets all over Cam. He'd thought he'd been as wet as he could get, but apparently not. Assuming it was Hades's way of demanding his dinner, Cam gave him a nosebag and went to find some wood for the fire. It was a good thing Cam could see in the dark.

Everything was soaked, of course. Hades seemed to have identified the only tree within a mile radius whose foliage was thick enough to keep the ground dry, and there had been no firewood at its base. Cam was on the verge of returning to the camp empty-handed when he spotted a large branch in the undergrowth between a cluster of birch trees.

His attention was so fixed on the prize that he didn't notice the suspicious regularity of the shrubberies that surrounded it.

When he was two paces away, the ground gave way beneath his feet. He had been too long without blood, and his reactions were too slow to save him from pitching backwards into the pit that opened under him. His last sight was of the branch racing towards his face before his head hit something sharp at the bottom of the pit.

The grayscale of his vision dimmed into darkness.

7

It was dark on the terrace. Julia sat quietly on the bench as she waited for Lucas to dismiss her, hoping that this would be the day he would finally let her stay.

It had been the same all week. Julia would arrive at dusk, as instructed, and make her way up to the roof. The fire would already be burning, casting hypnotic shadows on the angles of Lucas's face as he sat on the other side of the flames.

He would nod a greeting, then start to prepare his dinner, but as soon as he placed the pan on the grate to begin cooking, he would say the words she had come to hate:

Until dusk tomorrow, then.

He never asked her to join him in his meal, not anymore. He never looked at her, always avoiding her eye. He never took her blood. He never spoke to her, except for those four damned words.

But she'd had enough of being ignored. Tonight, she wasn't going to let him send her away.

He lowered the pan towards the fire.

'Until dusk-'

'You shouldn't have done it,' Julia interrupted.

He looked so startled that Julia wondered if he had forgotten that she could speak.

'Done what?' Lucas asked.

'Accepted me. You shouldn't have accepted me if you didn't want to.'

The last thing Julia wanted was for him to reject her, but she'd rather break their relationship utterly than let it limp along in this odd approximation of civility.

Lucas took the pan away from the fire, putting it down on the bench behind him.

'Who says I didn't want to?' he said.

'You didn't need to say it. I can tell.'

He hesitated for a moment before walking around the fire to join her on the bench, a respectable gap between them. It felt like miles.

There was a quiet moment in which Julia could see him collecting his thoughts, leaning forwards with his elbows resting on his knees. He still didn't look at her.

'You didn't want to be an Attendant,' he said. 'You told me as much.'

His eyes flicked to hers briefly, resting on her face only for as long as it took her to nod her agreement.

'With Rufus there,' he said, 'I had no other choice. I'm sorry that it was necessary, but it was for the best, and I'm not sorry I did it. But I'm trying to make this easier for you. I know the ritual is a bit intense, and I'm trying to give you some space.'

Julia tried to find some deeper meaning behind the words, but there was nothing there. He'd done her a favour, and that was all there was to it.

'Well, you don't have to give me this much space. You must need blood,' she said, and as she spoke she could see how tired he was. The shadows under his eyes were darker than usual, and everything in his posture spoke of exhaustion.

How long could the Nobles go without blood anyway? She suspected that was knowledge they guarded carefully. They didn't like to broadcast their weaknesses, which made it all the more surprising that Lucas was prepared to let himself become so impaired.

'I thought it might be a bit much,' he said, 'after the ritual. I didn't want to make you... uncomfortable.'

Oh Empress. He knew. He knew what his touch had done to her. Of course he did.

He was trying to spare her feelings.

This was pity.

Julia forced a laugh. 'I'm not like Claudia,' she lied. 'I'm not one of those girls who dreams of becoming an Attendant because she has some fanciful notion that a Noble will fall in love with her.'

Lucas looked at her, his eyes finally lingering on hers, at the moment when she least wanted his scrutiny.

'I'm not stupid,' she said. 'I don't believe in fairytales. I'm here to do a job.'

In that second she would have said anything to distract him from his examination of her, anything to cement her conviction that she was who she had always imagined herself to be.

She was not a girl who dreamed in jewel tones and kisses. She was not weak. She didn't need to covet the constructs of the Nobles.

And one day she would leave this place behind, just like her parents had done.

'Alright then,' Lucas said as his eyes finished their search of her own. Julia couldn't tell whether he believed her or not.

'Alright,' she said. 'So, blood?'

'If you wouldn't mind.'

'Of course not.'

She tried to ignore the heat she could feel creeping up her cheeks. She remembered his lips on her fingertip, and the stroke of his tongue.

No! Don't think about it!

Lucas stopped in the middle of pulling out his penknife, his brow creased in concern, almost as though he could follow the direction of her thoughts.

She tried to distract herself by thinking about other things: breaking the ice on the water buckets in winter, her fingertips sticking to the frost on the pump in the courtyard, snow so cold it gathered in a thick blanket then froze with a crust along its top.

'You're sure?' he asked.

She nodded, not trusting her words, and held out her hand.

He looked at her for a moment, and Julia thought he might pull back, but something overrode the hesitation in his eyes. The blade was at her wrist this time, a tiny cut to the vein, and then his mouth was covering the delicate skin.

She tried not to groan.

It shouldn't have been pleasurable. From everything that Claudia had told her, and from everything she had overheard since in Livia's kitchen, she knew that she should be in pain, but all she could feel was the gentle pressure of his lips on her skin, and the warmth of his mouth.

She could feel it igniting something inside her that left her feeling light-headed and breathless. His touch, his scent, the heat of him.

It was too much. After barely a minute, she was intoxicated by it.

Lucas caught her as she slumped against him.

'Empress's blood,' he cursed, taking her face in his hands. 'Are you alright?'

'Mmm fine,' she murmured, but her head was spinning. Everything was sugar and mint and Lucas's arms.

'Let me look at the cut.'

It had already stopped bleeding, but Lucas pulled a handkerchief from his pocket and bound it up nonetheless.

'I didn't take much,' he said, looking at her with concern. 'Have you eaten today?'

She had, quite well by Server standards, but she grabbed onto the excuse.

'Not much,' she said.

'No wonder, then. Come on, let's get you comfortable.'

He settled her into the nest of blankets he'd created in his little hut and then, for the first time since the night they'd met, he made dinner for two.

'Who's Claudia?' he asked.

It was cosy in the hut with the two of them. They sat at opposite ends of it, backs propped against the boarded sides and cushioned with thick woollen rugs while they cradled their empty bowls in their laps. Lucas had made a vegetable stew, thick and rich and packed with potatoes.

Julia's stomach was gloriously full.

She hoped Claudia's was too, and that she wasn't waiting for Julia to come back. Julia had asked her not to.

'We share a room,' she said. 'She's sort of my best friend.'

'And she thinks she's going to fall in love with a Noble?'

'Not anymore, I don't think,' she said.

Julia remembered the stitches. Even now they had been removed, the scars left behind by Rufus's teeth were still red and angry on Claudia's pale skin. Her hood wouldn't hide it, which was the whole point, of course. She'd been marked by him, a toy he could break as he wished because she belonged to him.

The injustice of it burned in Julia's stomach.

She remembered how Claudia had been before him, so full of the enthusiasm of possibility, even here in the Blue, even after her parents had gone. She had always seemed stuffed to bursting with her essential Claudia-ness, but she felt so thin now, as though the characteristics that had coloured her had been drained out. Her joy had gone, and it had been replaced with empty disillusionment and fear.

'It was all she ever talked about when we were growing up,' Julia said. 'She wanted to be a Candidate, really, but they take so few and, well, it didn't happen. But then she thought if she could be an Attendant that might be even better.'

Claudia had thought it would get her more time alone with the Noble, more time to seduce him. In the end, all it had got her was more exposure to Rufus's cruelty.

There had been bruises this past week, on her arms and hips. He took from whatever vein he wished, breaking her slowly, turning her pale skin into a marbled mess of blue and purple, green and yellow.

'But that didn't happen either?' Lucas prompted when Julia remained silent. 'They didn't make her an Attendant?'

'Oh no, they did. Of course they did. She's beautiful, you see. Very beautiful.' *Too beautiful*, she thought. *Too beautiful for Rufus to break.*

'So?'

'Things aren't working out as she hoped.'

'Ah. No fairytale?'

Julia shook her head, pushing down the tears. If she'd blinked then they would have spilled down her cheeks, so she stared wide-eyed at the grain of the wooden ceiling and waited for the feeling to pass.

She couldn't fall apart now. Not here, not in front of him.

She blinked away the remaining moisture from her eyes, but she could feel it sitting heavily on her lashes. There was no disguising it.

'Julia?'

'Claudia is assigned to Rufus,' she said.

He looked at her for a moment, and she could tell that he knew how Rufus would treat her. His expression melted into sympathy, but instead of gentling her, his reaction just hardened her resolve.

He was a Noble, the same as Rufus, and whatever the blood-taking did to her, whatever hold it had over her emotions, that didn't change the fact that he was one of them.

He'd still taken what he needed from her. He'd still cut her.

This was her fault. She should never have come back here.

She was as much of a fool as Claudia.

'There are no fairytales,' she said, her voice harsh with her anger and shame, 'not for Nobles and humans. It's just make believe.'

Julia had meant that to be the end of the conversation, but Lucas had other ideas.

'It's happened before, you know,' he said. 'It doesn't happen often, but when it does, people remember it. There's a reason the fairytales exist.'

'And there's a reason they call them fairytales,' Julia said, not willing to change her mind now that she was so firmly determined to think as she did.

'Have you ever been to the temple?' he asked.

'Of course. I met you there.'

'No,' Lucas said, 'not just the outside. Have you been inside the building?'

'No.' It was forbidden to Servers unless they were required to serve there, or unless they were summoned by the priesthood as Attendants. He should have known that, just as he should have known all the other things that were forbidden to her.

'Come on then.' He stood, leaving his empty bowl in the hut as he shrugged off the blankets and threw his cloak around his shoulders.

She was confused. Did he really want to go to the temple now?

'Well,' he said, 'are you coming?'

The square was empty as they crossed towards the wide steps that led up to the temple doors. Julia had expected their journey to feel clandestine, but Lucas's stride told her he was perfectly comfortable moving around the city. With the twinkling silver in the whites of his eyes, he probably only left his rooms in the darkness.

Julia had pulled up the hood of her cloak to hide her face, but there was no need. The only light came from the braziers set at the front of the palace and the temple, and from the soft glow filtering through the cracks of the doors and windows that bordered the square.

They moved quickly. Lucas took the steps two at a time, so Julia had to run to keep up. She was sweating by the time she reached the top, but whether it was from exertion or excitement, she didn't speculate.

Lucas beckoned her onwards.

The great wooden doors were so old and ill-fitting that they might as well have been made of stone, but he moved them aside as though they were no heavier than a curtain.

'Who is that?' came a voice from inside. It was wavering slightly, thin with age.

Lucas put out a hand towards Julia, palm up towards her, warning her to stay put as he slipped into the temple. 'It's just me, Alba,' he said.

'Oh, my boy. Thank the gods.'

They were strange words to hear, particularly given their location. The temple was, after all, dedicated to the Empress. No one believed in the old gods anymore.

'I wasn't expecting you to be here,' Lucas said, his voice muffled in a rustle of fabric that sounded like an embrace. 'I would have brought you some tomatoes. Are they treating you well?'

'Oh yes,' she said, 'no need to worry about that. Mistress Genevieve is a kind one. I'm just filling in for Vibiana. But what about you, my dear? What are you doing here? And are they looking after you? Have they given you a new Attendant?'

'Yes. Yes, they have,' Lucas said, but there was a pinch in his voice.

'What is it? Is she that terrible?'

Oh Empress. Julia didn't want to hear this.

'No,' he said. 'It's not that.'

'Then what is it?'

There was a frantic silence, then Lucas stepped back outside. He held his hand out to Julia again, this time in invitation. She didn't want to take it, not because she didn't want to touch him, but because she did, too much.

It was the kind of thing that Claudia would think.

Reminding herself that he was as much a Noble as Rufus was, she stoically allowed Lucas to take her hand and lead her through into a small atrium, separated from the temple itself by a further set of doors.

There was a woman waiting there with a lantern. The space was only about ten feet deep, but it was so wide and tall that the glow of the lantern was almost swallowed up before it reached the edges of the anteroom. The wandering light played on the furrows of the woman's skin and teased out the brilliant silvers that darted through her dark hair.

'Alba,' Lucas said, 'this is Julia, my new Attendant. Julia, this is Alba, my former Attendant.'

'You brought her here?' Alba asked, eyes flicking briefly over Julia before settling back on Lucas. 'What were you thinking?'

His fingers squeezed gently across the back of Julia's hand. They were interweaved with her own, twined together with an intimacy she didn't know how to interpret.

Control, she thought. *He just doesn't want me to run.*

'She won't say anything,' Lucas said to Alba, 'and you're not going to tell anyone we were here, are you?'

The woman blustered with affront. 'Of course not.'

'Well then?'

'I should have taught you better. You never did have any respect for the rules.'

Lucas raised an eyebrow at her. 'And you did?'

'Well.' Alba pretended indignation, but it was clear that she was quietly pleased. She reminded Julia of a chicken, all pride and impotence, fluffing up her feathers for the show of it.

Alba turned to look at Julia again, taking her time now, her eyes assessing her face, her hair, her clothes, before finally coming to rest on where her hand was cradled in Lucas's. Julia tried to slip away, but his grip didn't loosen.

He gave Julia a small smile, then turned back to Alba.

'You're here to tell her the story,' Alba said to him.

'Yes.'

'So soon?'

'Yes.'

'You're sure?'

'Baba, it's just a story. The world's not going to end if she hears it.'

Alba looked between the two of them for a moment, an unexpected twinge of uncertainty creeping into her expression. It didn't suit her.

'Go on,' Lucas said. 'I'll make sure all the lamps are extinguished before we leave.'

She hesitated for a moment longer, her eyes fixed on Lucas, then her shoulders relaxed into surrender.

'Alright then,' she said. 'But you two be careful.'

'We will, Baba. I promise.'

The woman rose onto her tiptoes to kiss Lucas on his cheek and then, to Julia's surprise, pulled Julia into her arms and held her warmly. One of Julia's hands was still claimed by Lucas, but she wrapped the other around the woman's back and patted her, feeling awkward and off balance.

'You'll take care of him, won't you?' Alba said, grasping Julia's shoulders in her hands so she could look her in the eye.

'Yes,' Julia said, although she wasn't sure exactly what the woman was asking her. She just wanted her to leave, so she would stop looking at the two of them with her sad eyes.

There was regret in them, and pain. She didn't want to leave Lucas, Julia realised. She had been taken from him to be another Noble's Attendant, but she hadn't wanted to go.

Was this envy, then?

With a final touch to Lucas's cheek, Alba left the two of them in the atrium and slipped out of the temple doors, taking her lantern with her.

They were left in the unlit gloom, listening to her quiet footsteps disappearing down towards the square.

'She was your last Attendant?' Julia whispered.

'My only one, before you.' Lucas said. 'She raised me.'

The woman only looked to be in her sixties, seventies at most, so Lucas couldn't be more than about fifty, though he looked younger. He had said he was younger than the others, too young to hide the silver in his eyes. How young exactly did that make him?

Julia didn't want to ask the question directly, so she hedged. 'She must have been young then,' she said.

'No, not really, and I've told you: you can ask me whatever you want.'

Julia turned to face him in the darkness, but it was still a few seconds before she spoke. In the chill that lingered between the doorways, she could feel the heat of him, not just from the hand that still held her own, but from his skin, from his breath. She could feel the brush of his cloak against her own.

It was dangerous to be this close to him in a place that felt so permissive; the darkness and solitude were too forgiving.

'So?' she said quietly.

'So what?' She could tell from his tone that he was being deliberately obtuse.

'So how old are you?'

'I'm twenty. Exactly as young as I look.' There was a hint of frustration in his voice, as though being so young were a bad thing.

'I'm only seventeen,' Julia said. 'You're still three years older than me.'

'Yes, but you're human.'

'I don't understand why that makes a difference.'

'Because humans only live into their seventies, maybe their eighties if they're lucky. You're maybe a fifth of the way through your life. I won't be old until I'm a thousand, and in the meantime, I'm the youngest.'

'Until the new baby comes.'

'The point is,' he said, 'that I won't be an adult in the eyes of the Nobles until I've lived a hundred years or more, and until then… Well, they think I don't know anything.'

Julia sympathised.

'It's not just Nobles that think that way,' she said. 'The older girls are the same with me, and some of them aren't even your age yet. But I'll never be older than them, so they'll always think they know more than I do. I imagine the Nobles are the same.'

'Maybe. Or maybe they do know more than me. I don't know. I just think my perspective is different. Unlike them, I still believe in fairytales.'

As he spoke, he finally released Julia's hand and pushed open the doors to the inner temple. They were smaller than the doors that led from the atrium to the square, and Julia could pick out ornate carvings across their surface as light started to leak through from the hundreds of lamps that lit the sanctum.

It dazzled her. The surfaces that weren't covered with gold were faced in white marble so translucent that the light seemed to shimmer inside it. The effect was made all the more striking for the fact that the entire, gaping space was completely empty except for the columns that trooped down its sides and a few rows of pews.

No, Julia realised, *not completely empty.*

At the very furthest point of the temple, at the end of the double row of pillars that processed towards it, there was a pedestal mounted on a stepped dais. A figure was laid out on top of it. For a moment, Julia froze, thinking it was a real person lying there, slumbering in the temple, but something didn't fit.

The figure wasn't breathing. It wasn't moving at all.

'Come on,' Lucas said, leading her down the aisle towards it.

'Is it a statue?' she asked.

'A tomb, really.'

As they walked, he snuffed out the lamps that lined the walls, until finally the only illumination came from the rounded alcove into which the dais rose. It was a bright island in the centre of the darkness, and in the middle of it the statue shone: a man, wearing fine clothing in an unfamiliar style, with a blanket of stone covering his body. His exposed skin was tinged with a sheen of gold that glowed like the walls of the temple.

'He looks so real,' she said, reaching out to touch the golden curls that crowned his head. They were slick under her fingers, so intricate they might have been moulded from a real person.

'They say he was.'

'You mean this is his coffin?' The pedestal certainly looked like a tomb. It was wide and deep enough to accommodate a body.

'No,' Lucas said, 'I mean that this is him, that this statue was once alive.'

Julia's hand had been tracing the lines of the face, but now she snatched it away. 'You're not serious.'

'I am.'

'This is why you brought me here,' she said.

'Of course. You want to hear the fairytale, don't you?' The smile he gave her was mischievous, teasing her into playing along.

'Alright,' she said, returning his smile with a tentative one of her own.

'Do you remember what I told you about the silver in our eyes?'

His company felt so easy that she might forget he wasn't human, but she could see the silver in the lamplight, glinting at her from the other side of the pedestal.

'Yes,' she said.

'Well, there's a reason we hide it, and there's a story that goes along with it.'

'His story?' Julia asked, nodding towards the figure stretched out between them.

'His story, but not just his story. It's a proper fairytale, so there's a girl too, and it doesn't have a happy ending.'

'Go on.'

'And no one can know I told you this, not even Claudia.'

'Alright.'

He fixed her with his dark eyes. 'You promise?'

'If you keep building it up then I'm just going to be disappointed.'

'Promise.'

'Fine, I promise.'

He smiled again, his eyes twinkling with the anticipation of confidences to be shared. 'Something happens when we fall in love,' he said.

Julia swallowed, then worried that he might have heard the sound.

The corner of his mouth twitched.

Damn.

'It doesn't happen often,' he went on, 'and it's not something they really talk about, but when the Nobles fall in love, something changes in their eyes. This silver,' he said, pointing to the whites of his own eyes, 'bleeds into the iris, leaving metallic lines in the colour, sort of bleeding in towards the pupil, circling it in the middle. They call it *silvering*.'

'You've seen it?' Julia asked.

'Only once. The Nobles don't exactly show it off. Now do you want to hear the story, or not?'

Julia shut up.

'So,' he continued, 'back when we didn't hide our eyes, our emotions were literally written in them for anyone to see. And that was a dangerous thing, because when one of us silvers, it forms a life bond with the person we silver for. If they were to die, we'd die too.

'Now, normally that wouldn't be a problem. Normally, if a Noble does silver - and it's pretty damn rare, by the way - then they silver for another Noble, which doesn't present much of a threat because we're hard to kill.

'But when a Noble silvers for a human, that's a different matter. Suddenly, they're vulnerable. They're weak, because all a rival has to do is kill the human the Noble loves, and the Noble will die too.'

'Is that true?' Julia interrupted. 'Or is this part of the fairytale?'

Lucas shrugged. 'Maybe. If it's happened in my lifetime, then I don't know about it.'

'It sounds made up to me.'

'You don't believe in magic, then?'

'Of course,' she said, 'but just because I believe in one kind of magic, it doesn't mean I have to believe in them all.'

She'd seen the Nobles move. She knew they had power in them, but there had to be limits to it. This *silvering* just sounded like fantasy.

'Well,' Lucas said, 'it may be made up, but not by me. So, if you'll allow me to continue?'

She nodded, suppressing a smile.

'Very gracious of you,' he said with a little bow. 'Now, our story takes place hundreds of years ago, long before the founding of the city. For thousands of years, our people had been ruled by a great king, a Noble who was as much a warrior as he was a statesman. He was kind and wise, but he had begun to tire of his responsibilities. His life seemed boring to him, and he could find no enjoyment in the world.

'In the depths of his apathy, a terrible army rose up against the land. People were dying, human and Noble, and it seemed like there would be no end to it. The people begged him to fight, to use his strength to stop the destruction that was ravaging through their cities, but he was so drained that he had no power left to offer them.

'Until one day-'

'I thought you said this story had an unhappy ending,' Julia interrupted.

'Empress's blood, Julia,' he said, but there was no real anger in it. 'Will you let me finish?'

'Fine,' she said, smirking a little. She was almost certain he returned the smile.

'Until one day,' he repeated deliberately, 'his closest advisors decided that what he was missing was purpose, and that he could find that purpose in love. They brought princesses to him from far and wide, hoping that there would be one he would deem worthy of fighting for. They were varied and accomplished and beautiful, each in her own exotic way, and yet none of them stirred his interest.

'But someone else did.

'The king was walking in the courtyard one day when he spotted a Server, the Attendant of one of the palace guards. She was beautiful, but not like the princesses. She was graceful, but not like the princesses. And, unlike the princesses, she refused his advances. The more she refused him, the more the king wished that she might one day come to love him as he grew to love her, because - of course - he had silvered for her.

'Now,' Lucas said, leaning over the statue towards Julia, 'if they're very lucky, a Noble who has silvered will have their love requited. When that happens, the bond between the couple seals, and they say the silver in their eyes turns gold.

'So, when the king woke one morning to find his eyes threaded with gold, he knew that the human woman loved him back. She had pined for him in secret, kept from his side by the guard she served, but when the king realised that she returned his feelings, there was no keeping them apart.

'But she was human, and even after the king's power returned to him and the war was won, the king was constantly under threat from those who wanted to kill him by killing his love. In the end, his advisors saw no other option: they stole her away and hid her from the world, hiding her so well that not even the king himself could find her.

'At first, he fought with them, threatening to kill them all, but there was nothing he could do, for only they knew the location of his love. They promised to return her to him when all his enemies were vanquished, and so he determined to make his way through all the lands he ruled, conquering his opposers to bring peace to his people.

'But there was always another enemy, always another battle to fight. For a time he fought on, but soon his joints began to grow stiff, and gold started to crawl across his skin, gilding him in the colour of his love. Eventually it covered him entirely and he lay down to rest, never to wake again, waiting in vain for the day his love would return to him.'

Julia was silent for a moment, looking down into the face of the statue. It looked so real that she could believe the story was true. There were tiny imperfections in the skin, and a slight asymmetry that bore more resemblance to life than art.

'So he was your king,' she said.

'No,' Lucas whispered, 'he was our god. They thought he would come back one day, that he'd wake up and purify the world for us, remove the contamination.'

'But his love was human.' Julia couldn't resist the logic. 'She'd be dead by now, so he must be too.'

'Hence the moral: Nobles and humans aren't meant to love each other, even if they sometimes do.'

Lucas's eyes were on Julia's, lingering so long that it made her wonder. But she could see the silver sitting firmly in the whites of his eyes. If silvering was as he described it, then she had nothing to fear from his emotions.

If only fear were what she felt.

'So this king,' she said, 'your god, was frozen into a statue because his love was taken from him?'

'That's how the story goes.'

'And is it true?'

'Does it matter?' Lucas's expression was quizzical. 'Wouldn't you like to believe it? And wouldn't you like to believe that he could wake up one day and free us from this place?'

'That's not what I asked.'

He held her gaze for a long moment before he replied. She'd probably been too direct, but she was beginning to understand that she could be, with him.

'No one believes it anymore,' he said. 'It's the story Baba told me when I was small, and she had it from the first Noble she was assigned to, so I'd like to think it's true.' He looked down into the face of his god. 'It feels true to me, but then they tell me I'm a fool. Maybe you shouldn't listen to what I think.'

Julia walked around the pedestal to stand next to him, tracing the letters carved on its side as she went.

'Solomon,' she read, breathing the name like a prayer. It felt powerful on her lips.

Lucas looked up at her, a half smile pushing some of the sorrow from his features.

'Maybe there is some truth in it,' she said, 'maybe not. Either way, I liked it.'

'Are you admitting that fairytales can be real?' His smile was full now, and quickly spreading into grinning territory.

'Not fairytales,' she chuckled softly. She couldn't believe in his story, but he needed to. He needed there to be something real beyond the Blue, just as much as she did.

'Maybe something like them could be real though,' she said with a smile. 'Maybe I could believe in more kinds of magic.'

8

The first thing Cam saw when he opened his eyes was the sky, blue and wide, and crisscrossed with leaf-laden branches. The rain had finally stopped, and the air was warm enough that he was willing to believe summer might soon be on its way.

His head was throbbing, but worst of all was the thirst. It wasn't just water he wanted either; he could smell blood on the air.

Blood and nutmeg.

He tried to sit up, but there was something wrong with his body. It wouldn't move, so he was stuck on his back like an upended tortoise. For a moment he thought he had been tied up, but slowly realisation dawned.

The fall.

Pain in his back and his head.

He couldn't feel anything below his neck.

But nor could he see the edges of the pit he had fallen into. All he could see were the branches and the sky, and he was too close to both.

Someone had moved him. Someone who had been following him. Someone whose skin smelled of nutmeg.

Shit.

It wasn't long before he heard footsteps - leather on wood - walking towards him.

'Got your blood,' a voice said; male and not friendly. 'Got some questions too.' The accent was unfamiliar. It wasn't foreign exactly, but nor was it speaking the same strain of Hungarian that Cam had grown familiar with in these forests. The vowels were wrong, just slightly flatter than he expected.

Cam opened his mouth to reply, but his voice was silent. There was a tight pain in his throat, a pain that had nothing to do with his thirst. He felt his head being lifted and, though he couldn't yet feel them, he saw that his shoulders were rising too. The back of his head was suddenly warm, and the nutmeg was pooling in his nostrils.

His head was resting in the man's lap. From this close, the nutmeg was overwhelmed by the other scents on his skin: the sharp smell of green things, grass stains and conkers, charcoal and tree sap. Beneath it all was the earth, a rich base note to the sunny spice.

A moment later, the full bottle of blood was pressed against his lower lip, and the smell of it eclipsed everything else.

Three precious mouthfuls of the curative ran into Cam's mouth. It was enough to heal his throat.

'You know,' he croaked, 'I don't usually do this on the first date.'

The man said nothing. It had been a stupid joke, incited by awkwardness, but the man's reaction told Cam nothing.

He still couldn't move his limbs, so for the moment he was entirely in the man's power. He decided it was probably a good idea to try to make friends.

'You had questions?' Cam asked him.

'You know the other Izcacus here?' He was so close that Cam could feel the pressure of the man's breath in his hair as he spoke, warm and green.

'No. I was passing through, travelling up from the south east, over the mountains.'

There was a pause before the next question, and in it Cam could feel the strength returning to his limbs. Just a little more blood, and he'd have his arms back. And then... well, he'd see.

'Why'd you kill the old man?'

It was the question that Cam had expected, and had dreaded.

'I didn't mean to,' he said. 'He startled me and I was, well... it was a mistake.'

But had it been? He couldn't seem to recall now.

He felt the crunch anew in his tingling palms, the grinding of the old man's bones beneath the skin, and a shudder raced along his spine. It made him twitch.

'You've never killed?' the man asked him.

'I've killed,' Cam said softly, 'but I like to think it's never been without cause, not before yesterday. Or whenever it was. How long have I been out? What happened?'

He could feel the tingles in his hands turning into sensation now. He was in the middle of planning how he would snatch the bottle from his captor when it was pressed to his lips once more, for good this time. After a couple more gulps he was able to hold it for himself, and by the time it was empty he was sitting up and feeling if not good, then at least functional.

It would have to be enough. That had been the last of his blood, and he'd find no more until his return to the Blue.

Belatedly, Cam realised they were sitting in a sort of treehouse settled high into the branches of a heavily-leafed beech tree. It was a platform about ten foot square, half of which was covered with a canopy of skins.

'You fell into one of my traps,' the man said from behind Cam's back.

'Izcacus traps?' Cam said as he turned to face him.

And stopped.

The man couldn't have been any older than Cam looked: perhaps twenty, twenty-two at the outside. His hair was brown, as was his rough-trimmed beard, but his eyes were an unusual ice blue. There was something familiar about him, but Cam couldn't put his finger on it.

'Hog traps,' he was saying.

'I guess you got unlucky, then. I'm Cameron,' Cam said, holding out his hand.

'Felix.'

He didn't seem the least bit concerned that Cam was Silver; there was no hesitation. He reached out almost lazily, as though he had so much strength in him that the movement expended none, and clasped Cam's hand.

His fingers were rough, rougher even than Cam's, and he'd been living out in the woods for centuries now. But then, he wasn't human.

Felix is human, Cam reminded himself. Why did that disappoint him?

'I feel like I should thank you,' Cam said, 'but then it was your trap that nearly killed me. I guess I should just be glad I'm not human, right?'

No reaction to Cam's attempt at levity.

'How long has it been?'

'Couple of days.' Felix reached behind him and picked up a pile of sticks, then drew a knife from his belt and started whittling them into stakes.

'That's a myth, you know,' Cam said.

No response.

'Stakes don't kill vampires. It takes more than that. Quite a lot more, actually.'

Felix still didn't look up from his work. 'I see that,' he said.

'Is this supposed to be an intimidation technique? Because I don't think it's working, my friend.'

'You broke a few. Gotta replace them.'

He was intent on his task, apparently completely disinterested in Cam. That shouldn't have bothered him - after all, he had a mission and should be leaving - and yet it did. He was reluctant to walk away.

'Strange that you live out here on your own,' Cam said, 'particularly when there's that big camp out on the plain. Not your kind of people?'

Felix just shrugged.

'You don't get out much, do you?'

'I live in a treehouse.' He finally looked up at Cam. 'I'm already out.'

'Fair point, fair point,' Cam said, nodding. He was getting nowhere.

'So,' he tried again, 'this is a pretty good shelter. I'm surprised no one sees it, though. Haven't the Izcacus noticed you up here?'

'When people are in a hurry, they don't look up.'

Now that *was* interesting.

'They're in a hurry when they come through here? You mean they're moving quicker than human speed?'

'Always seem to be.'

There must be uncontaminated blood to spare. They wouldn't waste it by regularly moving around at Silver speed unless they had more than they needed. Cam had assumed that the uncontaminated humans would be few and far between out here, and that had certainly been his own experience of the continent, but it looked like he had been wrong. Something had changed since he had last passed this way.

Where were they all coming from?

Felix tossed one pointed stick to the side and picked up the next, turning it quickly in his hand as he worked so the point was central. This was obviously something he did regularly.

'Catch a lot of hogs, do you?'

'Some.'

Cam cast around for something else to say, then gave up. It was obvious Felix didn't want to talk, and Cam had other places to be.

'Well,' he said, 'thanks for the save. I need to go find my horse, so…'

The bastard was *smiling*.

'What?' Cam asked.

'Where'd you think I got the blood?'

Felix reached behind himself and pulled a pack out from under the shelter, tossing it over to Cam. The saddlebags followed a moment later. Everything was just as he had left it, minus the blood.

'You found Hades?'

Felix laughed. He actually laughed. It was a deep rumbling in his chest, halfway between a chuckle and a purr.

'Hades?' he said. 'Well, that's fitting.'

'You know the name?' Cam asked.

There was no reason why this boy would have been familiar with Ancient Greek mythology. They were in the middle of what had once been Hungary, and no one remembered those scraps of history anymore.

But Felix didn't explain, he just said, 'He's tied to the tree. That took some doing.'

'I can imagine. The bastard's been trying to chew my feet for the past fortnight. He ate all the bloody apples, too.'

But the moment of camaraderie seemed to have passed, because Felix was already back at his whittling.

Cam rose awkwardly to his feet, ducking his head to avoid the overhanging branches. The platform was a good twenty feet off the ground. It must have taken Felix days of work climbing up and down to get enough logs up here to build it, and Cam couldn't imagine how the human had managed to haul his unconscious body up here.

Peering over the edge, he could see Hades tethered beneath him in undergrowth that was so thick that the horse was probably completely obscured from the outside.

'Well, thanks again,' he said, slinging the saddlebags and pack onto his shoulders.

Cam was about to step off the platform, one foot already peeling up from the wood, when the scratching rasp of the whittling stopped.

'Where're you headed?' Felix asked.

Cam felt an inexplicable sense of relief as he turned around. Why did this man's interest matter to him?

'Northwest, up to the coast,' he said. 'I'm looking for a friend, and news came through that there was a settlement up there, one where there are uncontaminated humans.'

'I know it.'

That was unexpected.

'You do?' Cam asked.

'Right up by the sea, where they keep the humans in the old jail?'

'Uncontaminated humans?'

'So they say.'

Cam couldn't believe his luck. It was enough of a coincidence to make him suspicious.

'That sounds like it might be the place.'

'Alright then.' With that, Felix dropped the stick he'd been carving and grabbed a rope from inside the shelter. Within a few short seconds he had secured the end and was using it to slide down to the forest floor.

'Alright what?' Cam shouted after him, before jumping down from the platform into the leaf litter. It was a small enough height that, with his strength, he barely noticed the impact.

'You need my help,' Felix said as he dropped the last few feet to the ground.

'I do? I mean, no, I don't, thank you, but if you could point me in the right direction then that'd be very helpful.'

'You won't find it without me,' Felix said, not breaking stride as he pushed his way into the undergrowth and released Hades. Cam could see now that there was another horse waiting amongst the bushes too, a piebald stallion, already loaded up with packs that looked as though they had been prepared for a long journey.

'Look,' Cam said, 'I appreciate the offer, but it's really not necessary. In case you've forgotten, I'm an Izcacus, and I can look after myself. I've been searching this continent for centuries, and I'm pretty sure I can find the settlement on my own if you give me the heading.'

But Felix had already mounted up. He sat astride the stallion, looking at Cam expectantly.

'Why?' Cam asked.

Half of him was screaming for him to shut up and stop trying to send the rugged woodsman away, but the other half was still suspicious. Why had his horse been ready? How had he anticipated when Cam was likely to recover? Why did he know about the settlement, and why was he so keen to take Cam to it?

He was so distracted that he only narrowly avoided getting his foot crushed beneath one of Hades's vengeful hooves. The horse clearly wasn't pleased that Cam had abandoned him.

Their reunion was not an emotional one. Well, that wasn't strictly true. Cam definitely had strong emotions directed at Hades, they just weren't pleasant ones.

'If we leave now,' Felix said, 'we'll make the river by sundown.'

'And why are you helping me?'

Felix shrugged, a gesture he seemed fond of. The breadth of his shoulders exaggerated even the tiniest movement. 'I don't like to stay in one place too long.'

Cam tried to think rationally, pushing away his apparent inclination towards this stranger.

There were weapons ranged around the blanket that served as Felix's saddle, in the same way that knives hung from Cam's, but it was difficult to see him as a threat. Even without his own weapons, Cam would have been more than a match for Felix and his hatchet. He had nothing to fear from the man.

There was clearly some duplicity in Felix's reasons for accompanying him, but his secrets would come out sooner or later. The best way to find out the truth was to stick with him, and stay alert. There were entirely too many mysteries in this forest, and Cam was willing to bet that Felix fitted into them somehow.

He hesitated for only a moment before mounting Hades, then with one last look at the treehouse, he kicked the horse into action and followed Felix through the trees.

* * *

Felix had been right about the river. They'd ridden hard, but light was still peeking through the trees when they heard the water. It was more of a stream really, but Cam wasn't in the mood to quibble.

It had been a peaceful day.

Cam was unsurprised to find that Felix was not a talkative man. After three or four attempts to engage him in conversation, Cam had given up and concentrated on memorising their route through the forest. So far, it was no different from the course he would have taken by himself.

The more the day had progressed, the more Cam was confirmed in his view that Felix had an ulterior motive for accompanying him on this journey. No one would come north just for the hell of it, not when the weather was so much better for outdoor living in the south, and no human would willingly walk into a vampire settlement.

Surely he didn't mean to take Cam all the way to the coast?

But whatever the truth of Felix's purpose, he wasn't prepared to talk about it.

Yet.

'I'll fetch some firewood,' Cam said as he dismounted onto the riverbank.

'I usually sleep in the trees.'

'You don't light a fire? What, because of the Izcacus? It's not like you have to worry about that with me here.'

'Yes,' Felix said wryly, 'I've seen what happens if your sleep is disturbed.'

The guilt roiled in Cam's stomach once more.

Had it been a crunch or a crack? Did the bones break, or had they been crushed in his hand?

It didn't matter, really. Neither one made old Peterke any less dead.

Maybe it wasn't such a good idea for Felix to be near him after all. Cam might not have anything to fear from Felix, but could Cam say for certain that Felix had nothing to fear from him?

'Well, I'm sleeping by the fire where it's warm,' Cam said, his voice a little unsteady. 'You sleep in the trees if you like. It might be better that way. Just in case.'

Felix unhitched a longbow and a hide quiver from his saddle.

'Going hunting?' Cam asked, trying to force some cheer into his tone.

'Making the most of the fire.'

With dusk falling, it was a bit late for the kind of marksmanship a bow and arrow required, so Cam was surprised when Felix returned in the full dark with a pheasant. The fire was roaring by that point. Cam put himself on the other side of it as Felix plucked the bird, partly as a precaution against the infected blood and partly because he was uncomfortable with their brief acquaintance.

The man had nursed him back to health, fed him blood for god's sake, and waited to take him on a journey he'd obviously been anticipating. But what did he want from Cam?

'How long have you been following me?' Cam asked.

Felix didn't reply at first. He was threading a stick through the pheasant's body to make a spit, which apparently took all of his attention.

'A few days.'

'Why? Did you know who I was?'

'What you were, yes.' He set the spit over the fire, balancing it across a couple of rocks he had salvaged from the stream.

'And you decided to follow me? You thought it would be sensible to follow an Izcacus? What, have you got some kind of death wish?'

But Felix's self-assurance spoke for itself. This wasn't a man who feared the woods, not because they weren't dangerous, but because he was competent enough to navigate them safely.

He lifted his gaze from the roasting meat, looking at Cam over the fire.

'You walked into that camp as a stranger.'

It was the first place Cam had caught the nutmeg scent of Felix's skin, that place where human bones were piled in the fire-pit ashes. But while Peterke had been close to the carnage, a victim of it, Felix had been on the outskirts looking in.

'You were watching them?' Cam said.

'I always watch the Izcacus.' He spoke lightly, as though it were just something he did for fun, but there was purpose beneath it. He was holding back the truth, and Cam had lost his patience. He was tired, he was salivating over the rich scent of the cooking pheasant that he couldn't eat, and he was starting to think he'd got himself tangled up in more trouble than he'd bargained for.

'What do you really want, Felix? You're wandering around on

your own out here, tracking the Izcacus, and now you're apparently leading me to them, and you expect me to believe there's nothing in it. Why do you want to go there? What are you planning, and what does it have to do with me?'

Felix's response was typically stoic. He leaned forwards to turn the spit, releasing new fat from the skin. It dripped down onto the logs, sizzling and bubbling into ash on their red-hot surface.

'You said you were looking for someone,' he said after a long moment.

'Yes.'

'They have someone I care about too.'

That would explain it: his behaviour, the foreign accent, his willingness to nurse Cam back to health. Felix needed Cam's strength.

'You want my help on the rescue mission.'

Felix shrugged. 'Since you're going anyway…'

'But you already knew that, didn't you? Even before I woke up, you knew exactly where I was going.'

'I always watch the Izcacus,' he repeated.

Cam wracked his memory and then it came to him: he had told Peterke's people about Emmy. There had been so many faces around the fire that night that they probably wouldn't have noticed an unexpected guest, or an eavesdropper in the trees. Felix had already proved how silently he could move through the forest.

'So you trapped me deliberately?'

Felix smiled. 'No, that was just good luck.'

'For you, maybe,' Cam snorted.

But in all honesty, he didn't mind the company. In fact, he rather liked sitting around the fire with Felix.

In those last few decades when he'd still had the other Solis Invicti searching for Emmy with him, he'd started to find their presence oppressive. He'd craved the solitude of the Red in the same way that he did when he was back in the Blue these days. They meant well, and he knew that, but being around them made his skin itch with agitation.

Felix was different.

Maybe it was because they were driven by the same goal. The fact that they shared a common purpose made Cam feel less isolated, and that was novel. But it still wasn't enough to explain Cam's ease around him; he was virtually a stranger.

There was just something about him.

A distant howl cut through the night, high and keening. It was picked up by others until the forests to the northwest seemed to be filling with its noise. It was coming from the direction in which they were heading, towards the settlement on the coast.

'Wolves,' Felix said.

Cam nodded. 'Right.'

But he knew it wasn't wolves. He knew the tone of that cry, and it was one he hadn't heard for hundreds of years. He had never expected to hear it again.

Weepers.

They found the first victim the next day.

'There's a wide beach,' Felix was saying, describing the coastal settlement, 'but there's no cover.'

They had been planning their route for most of the morning, talking quietly as they rode the horses through the trees at a walk. Hades was being mercifully well behaved. Cam wondered whether this was because the piebald was ever so slightly larger than him, so less of an easy target. Hades was a bully, after all, and he wouldn't pick on someone his own size.

'We'll have to come in from the south, straight down from the mountains,' Cam said. 'They haven't cut back the trees?'

'Not from the slopes.'

'Then that's our way in. Tell me about the place where they're keeping them.'

'There used to be a town up there. They dug out some of the ruins, and found the cells underneath it.'

'I remember it.' Cam had seen it the last time he had searched up this way, an old cellar or dungeon that people had turned into a cold store. There was only one way in, down a half-buried staircase, so unless they'd excavated further it would be difficult to approach without being seen.

'Guards?'

'Tens of them. There are Pijavica all over the place.'

Pijavica. It was the Czech word for vampire.

And from what Cam could remember, the settlement Felix was describing was on the old Czech border with Germany.

That was why his accented Hungarian was so odd.

'You came from there, didn't you?' he asked.

Felix looked away nonchalantly, but his eyes were too intense for the lack of emotion he was trying to convey.

'I lived nearby,' he said.

Apparently that was all he was willing to say on the matter.

Cam wondered who he was looking for, and how many others had been taken from him. If the Silver settlement was as big as Felix said, then it could easily have stripped the area clean of humans, contaminated or not.

For Cam, this was a rescue mission, but for Felix, it was a homecoming.

'You can speak your own language to me, if you like,' Cam said. 'I know them all.'

'So do I,' Felix said in German, at the same moment that Cam caught the scent on the breeze.

'*Scheisse*,' Cam muttered.

'What is it?'

'Blood. Stay here.'

Cam kicked Hades into a canter, weaving him through the thick oaks, but it was soon apparent that there would be nothing Cam could do. There was too much blood in the air, so much that it drowned out his other senses. He was piloting solely by scent, driven by the drag of it across his nerves.

The blood loss from his fall into Felix's trap had been too much for the single bottle to replenish. On top of the exhaustion caused by his weeks of trekking, Cam's need was sharp.

The blood was the only thing in the world.

He had only a second to worry that it might be a trap before he burst into the sun-drenched clearing where the bodies lay.

The sight was enough to quell his appetite.

It had been a trap after all, just not for him.

And it had worked.

Hoofbeats thudded up behind him as Felix reined in his stallion next to him. Cam had been so caught up in the scent that he hadn't even realised he was being followed.

As his thirst dissipated, it drew a cold line through his blood where previously there had only been desire. It widened his focus, so that now he smelled not just the blood, but the decay, and underneath it all the scent of violence.

One of the Silver had done this.

'I told you to stay behind,' Cam said, but he didn't look around.

The carnage drew his unwilling eye.

'You did,' Felix said. 'I didn't.'

Hades whinnied unhappily, baulking at the prospect of going any closer to the centre of the clearing, so Cam dismounted and hitched his reins to the nearest tree before he approached.

The clearing was only about fifty feet across, but a good half of the grassy surface was strewn with corpses. They were gathered into a mound in the middle of the space, where the tops of two wooden posts were just visible, poking out of the shoulder-high scrum.

'What-'

'Shh,' Cam said, holding up his hand.

If he concentrated, he could hear something. It was faint, but there was a noise coming from the centre of the pile.

He ran, climbing the unstable mass of bodies to reach its apex. Flesh slid under his feet, pulling away from the bones.

Some of these people had been dead a long time.

'What are you doing?' Felix called after him.

'There's someone alive in here!'

Cam was at the top now, pulling the bodies out from around the posts, digging down to the centre. His hands were slick with gore he didn't want to contemplate. Miscellaneous pockets of glutinous liquid burst open under the pressure of his fingers, releasing the sort of foul odours he hadn't smelled since the Revelation, but still he hauled the carcasses out.

The blood would be contaminated. Cam was covered with it, but all he could do was try to keep it away from his face. If it got inside him, then that would be the end of his immortality.

But he wouldn't give up. If he could save this person, then maybe he could one day forgive himself for Peterke.

By the time he reached living tissue, Felix was working at his side.

'You're sure?' Felix asked.

Fingers clasped around Cam's, reaching up through the hecatomb.

'I'm sure.'

They worked together to pull out three more corpses, finally revealing the sacrificial victim: a man of about forty, perhaps six feet tall, whose other features were entirely obscured with filth, blood, and raw, round wounds.

He had been tied to the posts and left as bait. The stench of Silver violence was thick on him, and the slash down his side was the origin. They'd opened him up, sweetening the trap.

It had obviously worked, because there must have been a hundred bodies in the clearing. A hundred Weepers after a single man.

One eye was gone. He opened the other a tiny crack, squinting up at where Cam and Felix knelt on the bloody charnel pile, but it was obvious that he wasn't going to walk away from this. There were bite marks over every part of his body, cutting into veins and through into his intestines. There was too much damage for him to be patched up.

'I'm sorry,' Cam said to him.

He didn't reply; he didn't seem to be able to. Instead, he just closed his eye and nodded shakily.

The skin of his neck was already so broken that Cam's knife slid in without resistance.

9

'Not like that,' Lucas said, taking the knife from Julia's hand. 'Here, let me show you.'

He reached around her waist to the bench that she was using as a chopping board, leaning over her shoulder as he knelt down next to her.

'You cut it in half first,' he said, 'top to bottom, then slice from side to side, leaving a bit of the edge intact like this, and then you can chop it top to bottom. Here, you try.'

He handed her back the knife and the onion, but he didn't move away.

'There's a reason they only ever let me wash the vegetables in the kitchen, you know,' she said, 'and my eyes are watering so much I can barely see what I'm doing.'

'Why do you think I want you to learn how to do it? I hate chopping onions.'

She elbowed him in the side, but somehow that just curved his body closer around hers. His hair was tangled in hers, his cheek brushing against her own, warming her skin as the sun went down.

He'd asked her to come early today, for the cooking lesson. It hadn't been dusk when they'd met this time, but afternoon, when the garden was rich with the smells of tomatoes basking in the heat, freshly watered earth and warm wood.

Lucas had let her see his home uncovered by the shadows of the night, unforgiven by the darkness. There were patched cracks in the pots, a leak in the water tank plugged with clay, and dirt everywhere. The few surfaces that were painted were peeling from exposure, and the surfaces that weren't painted had been so weathered that they looked ready to crumble away entirely.

But Julia didn't care. She loved every inch of it, because it felt nothing like the rest of the Blue.

And, of course, it was his.

His mouth was close to her ear, his breath tickling her skin as he whispered, 'Maybe you could use magic to turn it into a carriage to take us out of this place.'

'That was a pumpkin, actually, not an onion. If you're going to mock me with fairytales, at least get them right.'

'My apologies, your highness. Perhaps I should consult the book again?'

She smiled as he stood to retrieve it from his hut, the same book of fairytales they'd been reading together for the past few evenings. It was a hobby of his, to collect ancient folk tales, and although Julia knew it was silly, she had begun to share his interest. Some of the stories were familiar, some less so, but all of them called her away to a world outside of the Blue. Whole civilisations had existed before the contamination of the Red, and somehow the old fairytales, the ones before those of blood and poison on which she had been raised, gave her hope that those civilisations might one day exist again.

Besides which, Julia simply enjoyed the stories.

She could barely believe it, but she was actually happy here. It felt like freedom.

And yet every second she felt guilty, because she was cooking in the sunshine with Lucas while Claudia served Rufus in his cellar.

Lucas hadn't taken Julia's blood again since the night they'd gone to the temple, but Rufus drank from Claudia every day. Not much, she said, but every night she came back to their room a little paler, and with another mark on her skin.

Julia suspected it was the pattern that would appeal to a sadist. Why drink only once every ten days when instead you could take a sip every day, cutting into unmarked skin every day, every day a fresh thrill?

It wasn't about the sustenance for him. It was about the power.

Whereas Lucas seemed to view the process with a mixture of dread and nervousness.

Julia's cheeks still heated when she thought of the effect his proximity had on her; his lips on her fingertip, her wrist, her mouth.

But this quiet dalliance they danced on his rooftop, full of brushed touches and necessary closeness, was apparently permissible.

It felt so much like flirtation that it made Julia question everything that had come before it. She remembered his smiles and his lingering looks, his hand around hers in the temple, and the almost irresistible implication of the fairytale he'd chosen to tell her: that humans and Nobles could fall in love.

But then she'd be drawn unwillingly back to that night on the roof when she'd kissed him, and the words would echo in her mind.

Once is enough.

They made the smile twist from her lips.

'What's wrong?' he asked. 'You don't want to read tonight?'

A door slammed beneath them, so forcefully that Julia would have sworn it actually shook the building. She and Lucas shared a concerned glance, then walked in synchronised steps towards the side of the roof that looked out over the square. There was a cloaked figure striding away from them into the dusk, crossing the square towards the guardhouse. It was halfway across when the door on the bottom floor swung open, spilling an arc of light onto the pavement.

'Carmen!'

The figure turned and shouted back, '*Que te jodan*! You know what you are, *hijo te puta*? You're a child who doesn't even have the *cojones* of a dormouse.'

'Oh, come on, Car. Don't be like that.' Julia would have recognised the voice even if she hadn't known where he lived: Rufus.

'*Me cago en tus muertos*!'

Julia didn't understand the words, but from the tone she didn't think Rufus was going to be pleased.

The door slammed again a second later. They watched Carmen finish her journey back to the guardhouse, and then the square was silent once more.

'Well,' Lucas said, 'that was interesting.'

'What do you think that was about?'

Lucas grinned. 'I really, really hope it was a date, because then

I'd have it on good authority that Rufus has tiny *cojones*.'

'You know her?'

'I know of her. From what I've heard, she's about as ruthless as he is. They'd probably make a good couple, if it wasn't for the problem with his *cojones*. Poor old Rufus,' Lucas said, but he was stifling a smile.

No love lost there.

Julia returned to her inept chopping. 'She's one of the guards?'

'One of the first, apparently.' Lucas followed her back to the fire, sitting down on the bench next to where she worked. 'When they think we're not listening, they call themselves the *Invicti*.'

'Latin?'

'It means "the Invincibles". They're a modest bunch.'

Julia laughed, and a smile crept across Lucas's face. It was the same smile she had seen that first evening, pleasant and joyful as he pottered around his garden.

Content.

It was amazing that something so small could feel so significant. It was just a smile.

But he was a Noble, and she was human. Human, short-lived and breakable.

Julia turned her attention back to the blade, watching it as it sliced. It was the same knife Lucas had used to prick her finger, and to break the skin over her wrist.

She was human, and so she bled, like Claudia. Like Marcus.

'And the redhead?' Julia asked.

'You mean Lorelei?'

'I mean the one who was attended by Quintus.' She remembered the glinting light she had seen by the water tank from the square as she and Claudia had watched Marcus being sentenced. 'You saw what happened that day.'

He didn't argue. 'That was Lorelei.'

'And you think a human like Marcus would have walked out into the Red, on his own, to hide Quintus's body?'

'That's where they found him.'

'So she said.'

The silence hung between them, eyes locked together by the words neither of them would speak. The moment felt portentous, as though allegiances were being tested.

'She's a guard,' Lucas said. 'The law is what it is.'

But they both knew it only applied to humans. The Nobles had their own rules.

He leaned down towards her, his elbows resting on his knees, breaking the stalemate. 'Shall I tell you their legend?'

'The guards have a legend, and all your god gets is a fairytale?'

'He's not around anymore. They are.'

'So this isn't a story I should trust?'

'Probably not.'

'Alright then,' she said, scooping the chopped onion into a pan. 'I'm all ears.'

Claudia was outside Lucas's door when Julia finally walked out into the night. Julia nearly ran straight into her.

She was agitated, pacing and fretting in small, sharp motions.

'Thank the Empress,' she whispered, taking Julia's hands in her own.

'What's wrong? Why are you here?'

Claudia had never once climbed these stairs before. She'd waited at their foot for Julia before, but otherwise they just assumed they'd see each other back in their room at the end of each day.

'It's Marcella.'

'What about her?'

Marcella. The goddess. The Candidate with flint-black skin.

'She's in the kitchen,' Claudia said, hurrying Julia down the stairs to the square. 'She wants to talk to us.'

'Marcella's in *our* kitchen?'

The mental image was utterly incongruous. She was a girl made from precious gems, paint and fine cloth. Julia would be willing to bet that she hadn't touched an unwashed vegetable in her entire life. There was nothing for her in Livia's kitchen, where the dirt collected in cracks between the stones, and ash from the hearth stained the walls and ceiling.

'She's waiting,' Claudia said, chivying Julia along.

'But... why?'

'The Nomination's coming up.'

'And?'

It was the annual ceremony in which the Candidates were each claimed by a Noble sponsor. If all went well, then the sponsors would eventually present their Candidates to the Empress as potential new Nobles. The selection process was obscure, and Julia didn't pretend to understand it. She suspected it had a lot more to do with privilege and favours than it did with merit.

'What's wrong with you today?' Claudia muttered, frustration sharpening her tone. 'Why are you being so dense?'

'I'm sorry,' Julia said, 'but can you just tell me what's happening?'

'She wants to ask us about them, of course. Mine and yours. Rufus and Lucas.'

'You mean she wants to…' But something stopped Julia from putting the thought into words.

'I know! Why do you think I'm flapping so much?'

Before the Nomination, a sensible Candidate would ingratiate themselves with potential sponsors.

Marcella was targeting Rufus and Lucas.

'Well,' Julia said, 'she's probably talking to all of the Attendants.'

'All the ones who attend good-looking young men, anyway.'

'Is that a requirement, do you think?'

They were well across the square now, heading for the alley that led to their courtyard.

'Well, they'll be spending time together, I suppose,' Claudia said. 'I don't know. I know as much as you do.' She sounded irritated, but there was an hysterical edge to her voice that hinted at distress. It was unexpected.

'You don't want Marcella spending time with Rufus?' Julia asked.

'Of course not!'

As they arrived the kitchen was fully lit, the shutters still open, and warm light bled into the darkness. Julia could just make out the bruised signatures on the insides of Claudia's arms.

She told herself that Claudia simply wanted to protect Marcella from Rufus's violence, that it was the cause of her reluctance, but she suspected the truth was darker than that.

It was the same reason that Julia hadn't told Claudia about the afternoon in the alley when Rufus had touched her cheek, when his eyes had promised more, whether she wanted it or not.

However badly he treated her, Claudia still thought Rufus was hers. She wanted him to herself.

'Ah, here they are,' Livia said. 'I'll leave you to it.'

She was alone in the kitchen with Marcella, who was seated in Livia's chair in front of the fire. It was a surprising gesture of deference from Livia, who usually cared only for her own girls, but then it was difficult not to be overawed by the Candidate.

Her posture was regal even when seated, her chin tipped up in a way that might have been interpreted as supercilious had it not been accompanied by such a genuine smile.

'Julia?' she asked, in a voice that was lyrically rich.

'Yes, Mistress,' Julia said, surprised to find that her voice was a little unsteady. 'It's very nice to meet you.'

'And you.' Marcella's smile grew, spreading light across her face like the dawn breaking across the horizon.

Julia blushed.

Empress.

The fullness of her lips drew Julia's eye, making her think of mint and honey.

'I wanted to ask you both some questions if I could, about the Nobles you're each attending.'

Julia's discomfort increased.

Lucas had told her all sorts of things he shouldn't have, and she'd behaved in ways that no Attendant should. But she was less worried about that being discovered than she was about betraying the trust that it signified. The two of them had become almost friends, and that was a secret thing that she didn't want to jeopardise.

More than that, she didn't want to share it.

She was just as bad as Claudia.

'Ask whatever you like, Mistress,' she forced herself to say. 'I'll try to answer.'

Marcella looked at Claudia.

'Of course,' Claudia said, but she smiled as though there were something rotten under her tongue.

This was not going to go well.

Livia's chair was the only one in the kitchen, so they were left with the options of sitting on the floor or standing. Claudia leaned up against a nearby counter, keeping her distance, while Julia sat on the edge of the hearthstone. It was a warm night, but she liked the heat.

'So,' Marcella said once they were alone, 'how do you like your Nobles?'

'We are honoured to serve.' Claudia's tone was colder than Julia had expected it to be. A month ago she would have killed to meet Marcella and now she couldn't wait to be rid of her.

Julia blamed Rufus. She blamed him for all of the changes in her friend these past weeks.

Marcella's smile dimmed a little, but her eyes were sympathetic. They caught on the mark at Claudia's neck, tracing down her neck and along her bruised forearms, bared from her cloak where they crossed over her chest.

'Well, that is reassuring,' Marcella said gently. It was a tribute to her training that she spoke with no hint of sarcasm. 'And you, Julia? How are you finding your assignment?'

You can be yourself, and I won't complain.

Lucas's lips, but then Once Is Enough.

Are you admitting that fairytales can be real?

She could almost feel the touch of his hair on her cheek as he'd leaned over her that afternoon, his body wrapped around hers so carefully, a whisper away.

She cleared her throat. 'Yes,' she said. 'It's very, um, acceptable?'

How was she supposed to describe it?

'It's as I expected it to be,' she added, which was the sort of lie she thought Marcella would have anticipated.

'I'm glad to hear it. And Lucas,' Marcella said, 'how do you find him?'

Julia was sure her blush was back, and being so close to the fire wasn't helping. She could feel the heat in her cheeks.

'In what sense?' she asked, delaying as she tucked her hair behind her ears distractedly. After a second, she realised that the rearrangement would only make her blush more obvious, so she pulled it forwards again to hang loose over her face.

'Well, do you find him a kind master?'

Julia's gaze flicked unwillingly over to Claudia before returning to Marcella's face. 'Yes,' she said. 'I would say so.'

'And what does he like to do?'

'Um, he reads. And he grows plants.'

Marcella scribbled a note into a small book in her lap that Julia hadn't noticed before. The goddess could read and write, apparently, which wasn't a surprise. Julia was past being surprised by anything that she could do.

'Anything else?'

'Cooking,' Julia admitted. 'He likes cooking.'

'Hmm. Not a normal habit for a Noble.'

Julia was defending him before she could stop herself. 'He's not a normal Noble,' she said, then regretted it.

Marcella looked at Julia for a moment, then closed the book and leaned down towards her. The firelight gleamed off her skin, rich and smooth.

Julia could never be that beautiful.

'If you were me,' Marcella asked in a confidential tone, 'would you want Lucas for your sponsor?'

Julia looked down at her hands as she bit her lips, cracking dry from the fire's heat.

'I don't exactly know what a sponsor does,' she said.

'It's an important role,' Marcella said. 'I want to be sponsored by someone who will support me, who will protect me, and who is good enough company for me to enjoy spending time with them.'

It sounded a lot like Marcella was looking for a partner.

'So,' she said with a small smile. 'What of Lucas?'

Julia wanted so desperately to lie, but she couldn't do it. She couldn't sit in the ashes and lie to the goddess.

'Yes,' she said. 'If it were me, he's the one I'd pick.'

'Why didn't you tell me?' Claudia whisper-yelled as she closed their bedroom door behind her.

'Tell you what?' Julia said, feigning ignorance, but she knew very well what Claudia was angry about.

'You and Lucas! When did this happen?'

'Nothing happened.'

'Bollocks! You can't lie to me, Jules. You've never been able to, not even when we were children, so don't think you can start now. You've been coming back every night from seeing him, and I've not been asking because I thought you were miserable and I didn't want to make it worse, and all this time you and him-'

'Empress, Claud, why do you think I didn't say anything?'

She looked nonplussed. 'What do you mean?'

Julia dropped down onto the mattress, throwing her cloak from her shoulders. 'Every night *you* come back with another mark, pretending that everything's fine. You think I don't see the cuts, the bruises?'

Claudia pulled her cloak around her shoulders, trying to hide the marks that Julia had already seen. 'It's not that bad.'

'Isn't it?' Julia reached up and took Claudia's hand, leading her down to the mattress beside her. Running her hand along Claudia's arm, Julia moved back the sleeve to reveal the troop of bruises lining the inside of her friend's wrist, chasing the veins.

'Oh, you know me,' Claudia laughed, forced and harsh, and edged with tears. 'I bruise like a peach.'

'I had to sew you up, Claud,' Julia whispered, gently pushing the blonde strands away from Claudia's neck to bare the scar. 'Or have you already forgotten? You may not want to face it, but he's not a good man. I'm worried for you, and you won't talk to me.'

'I know what he is,' she whispered, and her tone held enough helplessness for the both of them. 'What good will it do to talk about it?' A tear slid quickly down her cheek, diving from her chin to bury itself in her lap with a quiet drop.

'Oh, Claud.' Julia wrapped her arms around her, holding her as she shook with silent sobs while tears wet her own cheeks.

She felt utterly impotent.

It only took a couple of minutes for Claudia's jag to run its course; she didn't have the energy for more. Julia stroked her hair, cradling Claudia's head on her shoulder.

'I'm sorry,' she mumbled soggily into Julia's dress. 'I'm tired. It really isn't as bad as it seems.'

'Oh?'

'He had some sort of injury,' Claudia said, sitting up as she wiped her face, 'but it's getting better. Once he's healed things will be better.' She sniffed hard and rubbed her nose against the back of her hand.

'I'm sure they will,' Julia said, smiling softly through the lie. It was a lie they both needed.

'But anyway,' Claudia said, blinking away the tears, 'you still haven't told me about Lucas. How long have you been in love with him, huh?' She jostled Julia gently, teasing her as she smiled through her misery.

And Julia let her, playing up to it because there was no alternative. 'I am *not* in love with him, Claud.'

'But?'

'But-'

'I knew there was a but.'

'*But* I do like him. And, well, we did kiss.'

'*What*?' Claudia's voice had risen in pitch and volume, until Julia was sure that Livia would have heard it, even though she'd be on the top floor by now.

She made frantic shushing motions with her hands. 'Will you keep it down?'

'He kissed you?' Claudia whispered.

'Well, yes, but it didn't really count because it was part of the ritual. Did they tell you in the temple that instead of marking you with their teeth, the Nobles can do it with a kiss?'

'What? No. The priestess didn't say anything about that.'

'Well,' Julia said, 'anyway, it was for the ritual, so it wasn't a real kiss.' She paused, then decided she may as well confess the whole thing. 'I did sort of kiss him though, afterwards.'

Her cheeks felt like they were on fire.

'Later afterwards, or right afterwards?' Claudia asked.

'Maybe a second later.'

'And he kissed you back?'

'Yes.' A tightness clenched in Julia's chest, the weight of the emotions she'd been struggling with piling up behind her teeth, and then they broke out into words of blissful relief.

'But then he was all "once is enough" and started being really distant, and then he took me to the temple and told me this fairytale, the moral of which is basically that humans and Nobles can fall in love, and now we're in this bizarre place where he touches me all the time on the hand or the arm, but it can't mean anything, and I'm just so *confused*.'

'Wait,' Claudia said, holding out her hand. 'Start at the beginning.'

So she did.

Julia told her about that first night, about the ritual, the temple and the dinners they made together on his rooftop. She told Claudia everything, up to and including the odd encounter they'd witnessed with Carmen and Rufus that evening.

With every word, the weight seemed to lift from her chest, until it was manageable again.

'They're not friends?' Claudia asked. 'I know Rufus doesn't think much of Lucas, but still. I mean, they live in the same building.'

They'd crawled under the covers as Julia rambled on, so they now lay side by side as they watched the moonlight filtering through the window. Occasionally there would be footsteps along the alley it opened onto, but at this time of night there weren't many people wasting lamp oil.

'I got the impression they hated each other, actually.' Julia said.

'Huh.' Claudia seemed surprised. 'I thought all the Nobles were friends.'

'Are we friends with all the humans?'

'There are more of us though.'

Julia smiled at her twisted logic. 'But we're not even friends with all the people who work in Livia's kitchen.'

'That's their fault, not ours.'

'You mean it's our parents' fault.'

If Julia's parents hadn't run, and if Claudia's father hadn't thrown his life away trying to save her mother, they might have had someone besides each other. They would have had their parents, for starters.

'I don't blame them, Jules.'

'Well,' Julia said, 'I blame mine.'

Laughter echoed out in the alley, rolling inside to bounce around their cell. The Nobles to whom it belonged didn't linger, though; no one paid attention to Julia and Claudia's little window, set at ankle height in the stucco.

The steps soon passed by, heading out towards the square.

'I heard something interesting about the Red today,' Claudia whispered when all was silent once more.

'Really?'

'The redhead came by. You know, the one with Quintus.'

That was two guards that had visited Rufus in the same day: Carmen and Lorelei. It couldn't just be a coincidence.

'Lucas said her name was Lorelei,' Julia said. 'What did she want with Rufus?'

'She said they might need him soon, because there was a problem in the Red that needed to be sorted out. I thought it had something to do with Marcus at first, but now I'm not so sure.'

'What sort of problem?'

'I didn't hear much else because they moved into the other room, but there was a latin-sounding word they kept using, something like "infinity". They were talking about how there was a traitor, and it wouldn't be long before the infinity realised what was going on.'

Julia rolled over to face Claudia, her mind filled with the stories Lucas had told her that evening.

'Invicti?' she whispered.

'Yes! That's it. Invicti. How did you know?'

'Lucas. He told me their stories. They're part of the guards, the oldest part.'

They had been soldiers. They were the elite, the best the god king could muster, tracing their existence all the way back to the Romans, fighting their way through the millennia.

No wonder the Nobles made such a fuss about their history, and about everyone born in the Blue having a Latin name; it was the origin of their heritage.

'So,' Claudia said, 'are the Invicti good or bad?'

'I don't know. I do know that Carmen's supposed to be one of them, so it doesn't look like they're on Rufus and Lorelei's side, does it? And given what happened to Marcus, I think Lorelei's conscience might not be entirely spotless.'

Claudia raised her hands to her face, pushing them through her hair then dropping them back onto the mattress above her head. 'I don't want to get stuck in the middle of this, Jules.'

'I know.'

'But there are people over at Rufus's all the time. There are loads of Noble girls, a few guys too, and they're always going off to discuss things. It's not like this was a one off.'

'Is Lorelei there a lot, though?'

'She's been a few times. And there's something else,' Claudia admitted. 'She mentioned humans.'

'And?'

'Humans out in the Red.'

'But humans can't survive in the Red,' Julia said stupidly. It was the cause of Marcus's broken arm, of her ostracism, of her own captivity. If it wasn't true, if people were living out in the Red, then every reason that had kept her in the Blue disappeared.

Except Lucas.

She squashed the treacherous voice. Lucas wasn't a reason to stay.

'I'm not sure if they did survive, Jules. I couldn't pick up enough to tell.'

Julia rolled onto her front and propped herself up on her elbows.

'We could leave, Claud. If it's true, we could go. We could get out of this place together, you and me.'

'And the poison in the earth? The poison in the blood? What if that's what's true?'

'I'm not suggesting that we go tomorrow.'

'Then what?'

'We watch. We listen.'

'You mean me,' Claudia said wryly. 'You mean you want me to spy on Rufus.'

'No more than you already do. But isn't it worth a little risk, Claud, if it means we might get out of this place? What would you give to get away from him?'

The pause was too long before her reply. 'I don't know,' she said, and Julia knew that she was wondering whether she wanted to get away at all. She was wondering whether she could leave him behind, even after all her bruises.

But at least she was wondering. If there were another option, then maybe she would finally risk the Red.

10

The Red seemed empty now, but Cam worried that it wouldn't last. They had heard no Weeper calls in the night, so he was starting to hope that all of them had been killed in the trap, but he knew how quickly the virus spread.

This wasn't his first encounter with zombies.

Felix was quiet as they rode through the trees. Well, even quieter than normal. Cam could almost see him turning the fact of the Weepers in his mind, trying to fit them into his understanding of the world. From the look of the frown on his face, it wasn't going well.

'Are you okay?' Cam asked him.

Felix's gaze jerked up from his contemplation of the piebald's mane. He seemed surprised at the question.

'Yes,' he said, but he didn't look okay. The anxious expression didn't suit him. It was out of place on a man usually so confident and self-contained.

He looked rattled. Cam couldn't blame him, not after yesterday.

Even Hades was subdued.

They'd picked through the bodies in the clearing together. They were undeniably eerie, arrayed so they all pointed towards the dead bait in a swirl of corruption, so deliberate that it seemed like dark art. Some of the corpses had been more decomposed than others, so decayed that they couldn't be new.

The implications were concerning.

There had been a hundred bodies in that clearing, a hundred bodies that had once not only been human, but uncontaminated as well. They hadn't carried the Weeper vaccine in their blood, which had made them susceptible to the virus itself.

They'd become infected.

But the moment they'd bitten the bait…

Felix had seen the results of that.

Cam had tried to explain. It wasn't the first time for him. It had been Emmy who'd discovered it, back when she had been newly turned Silver. She'd taken down a crowd as big as a city with that vaccine, turning one Weeper human, then watching the chain reaction as its neighbours bit it, then were bitten themselves, each one dying in turn as their human bodies were returned to them, unable to survive the transition from their Weeper selves.

And now it was happening again in miniature, only this time the vaccine had been contained in a living body. A contaminated human body. The bait.

Another death at Cam's hands.

If nothing else, the previous day's events confirmed what Felix had told Cam: there was, or at least there had been, a population of uncontaminated humans living out in the Red. It was the only way the Weepers could exist in these numbers. One of the uncontaminated humans must have turned, then infected the rest.

There was really only one conclusion Cam could draw: someone was trying to make more Silver, and failing.

That was what had started it all, centuries ago.

That was what had made the Weepers.

But unlike Felix, Cam had fought this battle before. He knew the weapon he could use against it.

Contaminated blood.

He'd been covered in it after the clearing, they both had. Although Cam had bathed with extreme care, he still worried about the residue now, even though he knew that any traces of it that remained would no longer be alive, even though he knew the cure degraded quickly without a host.

'You know you're safe, right?' Cam said to Felix. 'You know you can't turn into one of them.'

Felix was already contaminated with the vaccine. He'd have to be by now, with all the pheasants and rabbits he'd eaten. Cam had donated the jerky to him as well, which he'd been chewing his way through as they rode into the afternoon. He seemed to eat constantly, the movement of his jaw channelling his agitation.

'You said,' Felix replied.

It hadn't stopped Felix from washing just as thoroughly as Cam had washed himself.

Under fingernails, inside ears, between toes.

Once, twice, three times.

Even though Felix couldn't know that there was a danger to Cam from the traces of gore that had clung to them, because Cam hadn't told him that. He couldn't know that the vaccine was the cure, that the thing that had killed the Weepers could turn Cam human. He couldn't know what contaminated his own blood.

Nonetheless, by the time Felix had returned to their camp from the river, his skin looked like it had been scrubbed pink to the point of pain.

They'd burned their clothes while they sat in the trees and watched, feeling safer there than on the ground. Just in case.

But even now the fatty scent of decay clung to them. The water could wash away most of the stains, but the cloying stench didn't shift. It was stuck in Cam's nostrils, thick and pervasive.

The smell of dead things.

'So,' Cam said, 'you watch the Izcacus.'

'I do.'

'And what did you see? Did you happen to notice any of them trying to make more... erm, Izcacus?' He'd nearly said *Silver*. He needed to pull himself together.

Felix raised an eloquent eyebrow. 'You expect me to watch them in their tents?'

'No, that's not what I meant.' Cam could feel himself getting flustered. Was that really a blush he could feel creeping hotly up his cheeks? Jesus, he was all over the place. 'Look, there are two ways we reproduce. Mostly we're born in, er, the normal way.'

He saw the side of Felix's mouth twitching.

You're hundreds of years old, Cam reminded himself, *so stop behaving like a bloody schoolboy.*

'But,' he continued, clearing his throat, 'pregnancy is still rare so occasionally people try to supplement numbers by creating more Izcacus from humans.'

Felix nodded. These were the legends of the Izcacus and Pijavica that everyone knew.

'So, did you ever see them trying to turn humans?' Cam said.

Felix was quiet for a moment, contemplating the piebald's mane once more.

'No,' he said. 'In the caravans, they only bite to drink.'

'And outside the caravans?'

Felix's face darkened. 'I only watch them in the forest. But in the place where they're holding them...' He shrugged, but the movement was full of tension and anger.

'We'll find them both,' Cam said, with more confidence than he felt. Felix knew where they were keeping his own friend, but Cam had no assurance that Emmy would be there too.

Maybe Tommy and Viv were right. Maybe she was already dead.

'Do you have children?' Felix asked.

Cam was surprised into laughter. 'No,' he said. 'No, that's not really in the cards for me. I'm not often that way inclined.'

There was an empty pause in which Cam wondered why he'd made the revelation.

'So, what about you?' he continued, trying to cover the moment with conversation. 'You have a woman waiting for you somewhere?'

'No,' Felix said, his face closing down once more. 'Not a woman.'

'Ah.'

Well, that was worth knowing.

A few days' riding brought them into the thickly-wooded hills of what had once been Slovakia. The last time Cam had been this way, a small settlement by the Váh river had sheltered him for the night. They'd had a blacksmith's forge, where he'd hoped to trade for knives and needles for Ana and Vasile.

The place had been razed to the ground.

'What happened here?' Cam asked as they rode through the remains of the village.

Felix didn't have an answer, and in fact the smell of ash and blood was still fresh in the air. The destruction was recent.

'Did you ever see the caravan out this way?' Cam asked him.

'Sometimes.'

Cam had no other suspects.

He slid from Hades's saddle and followed a scent through the fallen buildings. Only the heavy rain of the past couple of days had saved the village from complete obliteration. The wood was charred and broken but still identifiable, darker than the mud and burned grass that surrounded it.

It was only after Cam had shifted a tumbledown pile of soggy charcoal aside that he finally found what he was looking for: blood pooled into the earth. The fire pit was nearby, and although the bones had been cracked in the heat of the flames, Cam could still make out the notches and scoring left behind as the flesh had been carved away.

'But why would they eat contaminated humans?' Cam thought aloud.

'They wouldn't,' Felix said. 'I've never seen them do this.'

Cam turned from where he was crouched on the ground, looking up at Felix. 'I've seen three of these Izcacus campsites now,' Cam said, 'and every one of them has had campfires filled with human bones like these. Look,' he picked up a femur, 'you can see where a knife has cut into the bone here, and scraped along it to strip the meat.'

Felix shook his head as Cam rose to his feet, chucking the bone back onto the pile. The rattle it made was too loud in the graveyard village.

'These people were butchered,' Cam said.

'The Izcacus wouldn't eat them.'

Cam couldn't make sense of it. 'Cannibalism then?' he said. 'Are they feeding them to other contaminated humans?'

But then he caught another scent, fainter this time, and muted by the chill of the evening.

'Or maybe to something else,' he said. 'Come on.'

They led their horses out of the village proper and into the grove of fruit trees that bordered its northern edge. On its far side, in amongst a bramble hedge, Cam finally ran the scent to ground.

Felix covered his nose with his sleeve as Cam turned the body over, revealing what was clasped in its hands.

'Shit,' Cam muttered.

The Weeper caught in the bramble thicket was only small, an old woman by the looks of her, although the level of decay made it difficult to be sure. The marks of her teeth were in the meat. The contaminated human meat. It had cured the virus and left the shell of her broken body behind, reanimation ceased, stopping her in her tracks.

'They were feeding contaminated humans to the Weepers,' Cam

said. 'Just like they did in the clearing, only this time with dead bait instead of live. They didn't want to attract them here, they just wanted to neutralise any Weepers that strayed towards their camp, as a defence.'

It had been effective.

Once they knew what they were looking for, it was easy to track the lumps of flesh scattered around the perimeter. They were small enough that the scent would have carried only far enough to distract a Weeper from the camp, not far enough to draw them from a distance. That was why they had cut them up small.

'They'd need to be fresh,' Cam said. 'So that it explains why there were more bones in the more permanent Izcacus camp. They would need to replenish their boundaries.'

Felix said nothing, he just looked at the meat on the ground.

'And you never saw them do this? I thought you said you watched the Izcacus.'

'Not all the time. This is new.'

'You're sure?'

'I'm sure.'

'Well,' Cam said, 'they're taking precautions against the Weepers, so they must have known they'd be here, right? And they must have a reason to protect the camps, so they have to be moving uncontaminated humans. So.'

Cam looked at Felix speculatively, trying to puzzle it through.

'You didn't know what the Weepers were, did you? Not until I told you. You'd never seen them before?'

'No,' Felix said.

Cam nodded to himself. 'Makes sense.'

'Does it?'

'I think so.' Cam paused for a moment, checking that the pieces fit. 'Yes, I think so. Look, the Weepers aren't much of a threat out here. All the people who live in these woods already have the vaccine in their blood, so the Weepers won't last long, because the first person they bite is going to bring them down. They're not much of a problem in small numbers, but then if they hit a group of uncontaminated humans…' Cam raked his fingers back through his hair, pushing it out of his eyes.

'You're going to tell me that story one day,' Felix said.

'What story?'

'The story of the Fall. That's what it is, isn't it?'

'What do you mean?'

'These Weepers, the stuff in our blood, the cities in the ground. It was the Fall, wasn't it?'

It was what they'd called it, that time after the Revelation when their triumph over the Weepers quickly turned into war, and then into a frantic search for the meagre stores of uncontaminated land and uncontaminated humans that remained. They hadn't realised then that they wouldn't be able to drink from vaccinated humans. They hadn't realised that vaccinated blood would turn the Silver human as surely as a direct dose of the vaccine itself. They'd poisoned their own food supply.

And then everything had fallen apart.

The Fall.

Cam took a step towards Felix, scrutinising the strange blue of his eyes. 'How do you know that name for it?'

'I watch the Izcacus,' Felix said, his answer for everything. He stood his ground as Cam stepped closer.

'And now you're watching me?'

Felix laughed, a rumble that was deep but somehow chilling. There was an edge to it, a break of despair in his tone. 'No, Cameron,' he said. 'I'm using you.'

One more step took Cam so close to him that he could feel the heat of Felix's body. The disparity in their height was more obvious from this distance; Cam had a couple of inches on Felix, but where Cam was all long limbs and awkwardness, Felix seemed like pure, concentrated power.

'Using me for what, exactly?' he asked.

'We both know you don't need me to show you the way,' Felix said softly. 'You know where you're going. But I'll need your help when we get there.'

Their eyes locked, brown on blue, blue on brown, and something passed between them. There was a tumbling free-fall moment, an unexpected second in which Cam's hands nearly reached out, in which he nearly closed the few inches that separated them.

But then he broke the connection, pushing his hair out of his eyes again as he stepped back.

'Alright then,' he said. 'I can live with that.'

'You don't mind me using you?' Felix said, following Cam as he walked back to the tree where they had left the horses.

'As long as we want the same thing,' Cam said, not entirely sure whether they were talking about the rescue mission or something else entirely.

But then Felix had someone waiting for him, didn't he?

He caught Cam's wrist, turning him back around.

'What do you want, Cameron?'

Cam searched his eyes, but there was no invitation in them. Even if there had been, Cam would have hesitated.

Something was wrong here. There was an intensity about Felix that was new. Cam could feel a significance underneath the woodsman's words, a secret hinted at then not divulged, but he didn't know what it was. All he could see was the blue of his eyes, the sunshine playing in the rugged strands of his cropped beard, and the determination in his expression.

'I want to find Emmy,' he said.

'I want to find Otho,' Felix replied, then he let go of Cam's wrist and held out his hand.

A bargain.

Cam contemplated it for only a second before they clasped each other's wrists, sealing the accord. There would be no breaking it until their task was completed.

Cam was too distracted by the thud of Felix's pulse under his fingertips to wonder how the woodsman knew the meaning of the Silver gesture.

The further north they travelled, the less it felt like spring. Flowers that had been blooming for months further south were only now starting to break their buds in this part of the continent, leaving the woods dank and without accent colours.

Three days out from the blacksmith's settlement, there were fewer people too. It was as though the ten-day approach to the northern coast had been cleared out, sucked dry of habitation.

At least Cam had found what he needed for Ana and Vasile. The items he sought had been buried under the ruins of the forge, dirty but not destroyed. He rode with ten more knives on his saddle now, and with a thick roll of needle-studded fabric in his pack. Just the salt now, and his duty would be fulfilled.

Well, one of his duties, at least.

He and Felix had a pact.

'It's nearly dark,' Felix observed. They'd been riding hard all day, and Cam could hear the impatience in his clipped consonants.

'We're nearly there. I'm sure it was somewhere around here, but it never was very easy to find. It'll be worth it, I promise.'

He was starting to doubt his memory when they crested a rise and finally saw it, nestled in a tiny hidden valley among the trees.

'There,' he announced. 'Didn't I say it would be worth it?'

It had been a swimming pool once, a thermal bath attached to a grand hotel. The hotel was mostly gone now, as was the architecture of the pool, but the hot spring was still there, bubbling water that steamed into the darkness of the hills.

Felix didn't reply, but he didn't hang around either. He vaulted smoothly from the saddle and led his piebald stallion, whom Cam had learned was called Sandor, down into the basin where the remains of the resort nestled in a cocoon of trees.

Unwilling to be left behind, Hades scrambled down the slope after them without giving Cam a chance to dismount.

'Hades…' Cam groaned, pulling pointlessly on the reins.

There was no stopping the creature. A strange sort of rivalrous affection had sprung up between him and Sandor over the past few days, and it had become impossible to separate the two horses. He and Felix had given up trying.

'No tracks,' Felix said as Cam finally escaped the saddle at the bottom of the bank. 'No campfires, no traces.'

'Good. We won't be disturbed then.'

Felix caught Cam's eye in the dusk, and Cam had to look away. He hadn't meant it like that, and he didn't want Felix to think that he had.

But he only worried about it because he felt the tension in the space between them, always now, in the way Felix's eyes seemed to light as he smiled, in the way his gaze lingered, and in each casual touch.

There was a closeness there that felt transgressive, despite its innocence.

'It's been a long time since I had any blood,' Cam continued, hoping the shatter the mood, 'and I'm not sure I could handle an ambush right now.'

'They have uncontaminated humans in the caravans,' Felix suggested.

'Yes, but when was the last time we even saw their tracks? Two days ago? Three? Maybe they don't come this far north. Maybe there's something keeping them away.'

There had once been a pool house of sorts next to the hot springs, a two-storey construction of concrete, stone and glass. The glass was long gone, and so was a lot of the concrete, but the framework of the stone building that had supported it was still fairly solid. There were three walls left to support the ceiling, the open side leading out to the pool. It would all have been glass once, Cam thought. There were traces of it still in the soil, broken but durable.

Just as Lorelei had said.

Metal corroded, but the glass, like humanity, remained.

They stabled Sandor and Hades together in the pool house, clearing a corner of the wide room for their camp. The roof had fallen away a little towards the front of the building, so that was the spot they chose for the fire. It wasn't hard to find dry wood in the bones of the hotel, where blown branches congregated under the cover of overgrown ruins. Barely recognisable as a building, the symbiosis of foliage and masonry was still elegant, in its own way.

'How hot is it?' Felix asked once the fire was roaring.

'The water? I don't know. Hot, but not too hot.'

Felix eyed the bubbling centre of the pool and raised an eyebrow sceptically.

'I promise you,' Cam said. 'I've been here before, and it's fine, but if it makes you happy then I'll test the water. If I boil like a lobster, then you'll know I was wrong. Alright?'

'Fine.' He didn't seem overly concerned at the prospect of Cam's possible demise, but neither did he look away as Cam stripped himself of his grubby riding clothes and sank gratefully into the water. He had to negotiate cracked rocks and jagged paving slabs to reach it, but it was worth it for the release the heat granted to his tired muscles.

'Oh god,' he murmured.

'Are you dying?'

'Maybe. I could die happy right now.'

Cam had closed his eyes to enjoy the heat, so it wasn't until he heard the splashing that he realised Felix was joining him.

'Watch your step,' he said, keeping his eyes firmly closed. 'There's debris under the water.'

A loud splash heralded a wave that washed over Cam's head. By the time he'd wiped the water from his eyes, Felix had already clawed his way back up to the surface.

'That was your foot,' he spluttered.

'Yes it was,' Cam said, squinting at him through the steam, 'but it wasn't deliberate, so I still owe you one.'

'One what?'

'Attempt on your life. You know, to pay you back for when you tried to kill me in your wild boar pit.'

Felix looked at him sternly, or tried to at least. It didn't work very well when he was soaking wet, his too-long hair pushed haphazardly back from his face. 'I saved your life,' he said.

'After you put it in danger. I'm surprised I even allow myself to sleep with you around.'

Felix laughed, his eyes bright in the darkness. 'I couldn't throttle you in your sleep even if I wanted to.'

Peterke's neck snapping in his hand.

Bones breaking.

The shock on his face.

Cam felt the heat drain out of him, then rush back too fast, nauseatingly fast, and suddenly the pool was too hot for his skin.

'Cameron?'

He didn't realise. Cam could see it written in his expression, the confusion. He hadn't meant to make the connection; only Cam's mind had made the jump.

But it was too late for Cam to reclaim his cheer.

He forced a rueful smile, ducking his head under the water one last time before moving to leave, but Felix caught his arm before he could turn away.

'Stay,' he said. There was a promise there, the shadow of an invitation. Not for now, but for later, maybe.

Cam's fingers curled themselves around Felix's wrist, unconsciously mimicking the shape of their bargain.

He allowed himself to be drawn back into the water.

'A little longer,' he said.

They rode on early the next day. The departure felt almost guilty, as though they were creeping away before the daylight could find their refuge.

But it had been… nothing.

There was nothing for Cam to regret. There was nothing in

Felix's clasped wrist over which to reproach himself. There was no need for him to be ashamed.

It wasn't like the slide of the knife into the live bait's neck, or the crunch of Peterke's vertebrae in his fist.

The bones grinding against each other as they broke.

'Do you still have family out this way?' Cam asked, just so there would be something to interrupt the noise in his head and in his hand. 'Friends, or anything?'

'No family. Just Otho.'

The elusive Otho. They hadn't spoken about him, and Cam didn't pry. Romance seemed to be a fenced subject between the two of them, although it was difficult for Cam to tell whether that was deliberate or not on Felix's part. He was hardly talkative at the best of times.

'So you don't have any friends out here? You've just been living on your own for, what, years?'

Felix said nothing, which Cam took as an affirmative.

'Don't you get lonely?'

'Don't you?'

'It's different for me,' Cam said. 'I'm just passing through. I don't plan on staying here.'

'Well, then.' Felix shrugged, as if to say that there was no difference between the two of them. But a year alone for a human and a year alone for a Silver were two very different things. One could turn a man mad, but the other was just part of immortality.

You learned to be alone.

Cam had learned.

A howl cut through the forest, even though the sun was high.

Shit.

The Weepers were still out there. They must have been hiding in the shade of the trees, because they usually never came out in the sunlight.

'Wolves,' Felix said.

'No. Not wolves,' Cam said. 'Weepers.'

They found them around the next corner. The path veered into the shade around the carcass of a fallen tree, and that was where they had congregated.

Hades skittered backwards, whinnying frantically as he pulled his head away.

There were about thirty of them, barely venturing out from the cover of a laurel hedge. Their eyes dripped blood, trailing down their faces as the sunlight crept through the canopy.

Cam had forgotten the way they moved. They crowded under the trees in a rolling dance, never stationary, always in motion, flowing up and down like waves on a sea of putrescence.

'Get into the light!' Cam yelled at Felix. 'They won't follow.' At least, Cam hoped they wouldn't. In the last days of the Fall, even the sunlight hadn't been enough to keep them contained, but these Weepers were new. There was no calculation in their movements, not yet.

Sandor was frantic. The horse took two stuttering steps backwards then reared, throwing Felix from his back. Felix hit the ground with a thud on the opposite side of the path, away from the Weepers but still under the cover of the trees.

Still unsafe.

There was a point a hundred metres up the path where the shade closed over it, a dark crossing place from one side of the forest to the other. The Weepers could use it to reach Felix under the cover of the trees.

The Weepers started to move. Felix didn't.

'Shit,' Cam muttered, dismounting. 'Felix!'

Still nothing.

The horses were circling each other skittishly around the fallen tree, instinctively keeping away from the shadows, so Cam left them where they were and rushed to Felix's side.

'Get up, Felix,' he said, slapping his cheeks gently.

His eyes remained closed. When Cam cupped the back of Felix's head his fingers came away bloody, but the pain must have got through because Cam could hear him groaning faintly.

But there was no time to wait for him to recover. The Weepers were moving closer, already across to this side of the path, running now, feet scuffing quietly but efficiently through the leaf litter.

'Fine,' Cam said, hauling Felix over his shoulder, 'I'll do all the heavy lifting.'

He stepped back into the sunlight just as they came into view, careening determinedly through the tree trunks towards the divide. For a moment Cam worried that they wouldn't stop. It wasn't that there was any risk of infection - Felix was vaccinated and Cam was Silver, so he had nothing to fear from their bite - but the sheer weight of their numbers had the potential to harm Felix. Cam was understrength, unsure of his capacity for violence, and he was quickly becoming overly protective of the woodsman he carried in his arms.

He was already bleeding.

Cam propped Felix, semi-conscious, in full sun against the trunk of the fallen tree and squared up to meet the Weepers.

They would stop at the edge of the shade.

He flexed his fingers then rolled them into fists.

They had to stop.

Stop.

As the first one hit the sunlight, a tall but almost skeletal creature of indeterminate sex, it rolled backwards as though it had hit a wall, but the Weepers behind it were still coming. They piled into it, forcing it over the line and out into the open.

It fell to the ground and screamed, clawing at its eyes. The others stopped in their tracks.

'*Kurva!*' A Czech profanity. Felix was awake, then.

The lead Weeper turned and crawled back between the legs of its fellows, losing itself in the shadows of their bodies. There was no more movement forwards, but the rhythmic swaying of the living mass resumed between the trees, sending faint wafts of gore and dirt out into the sunlit clearing.

'It's alright,' Cam said. 'I don't think they're coming any closer. There are more of them though, I think. About fifty now.'

'Can we get through?' Felix asked, looking over his shoulder to where the shade covered the path.

'We can't just leave. They'll track us through the woods, all day if they need to, then find us in the dark. We have to put them down.'

Felix said nothing, but his expression betrayed his reluctance.

'They're not people anymore,' Cam said. 'I know some of them look it, the newer ones, but whoever they were is gone. There's nothing inside them now except hunger. All we can do is put them out of their misery so they don't infect more.'

'They're dead?' Felix said.

'As good as. They might be walking around, but they're not human. They aren't thinking, they're just reacting.'

Felix got to his feet and took an unsteady step towards Cam. 'How do we do this?'

Cam turned to him, reaching out a hand towards Felix's head.

'May I?'

At Felix's nod, Cam wet his fingers in the fresh blood in Felix's hair, carefully avoiding the wound itself, then held up his fingers. The attention of the Weepers snapped to them, following the bright flash of colour.

'It'll be quick,' he said.

He stepped towards the nearest Weeper, putting himself just out of reach, then in one quick movement leaned forwards and wiped his bloody fingers across the creature's lips. It took less than a second for the vaccine to work its magic, for the Weeper's eyes to clear from blood to blue, and in that tiny window of time humanity washed briefly across its face then died, dragging it down to the ground.

Its companions caught the body with their teeth.

The dominoes started to topple. One by one the successive rings of the Weeper crowd were revealed as those in front of them fell, biting into the bodies of the fallen, then falling, fallen.

'Wait!' Felix shouted, stepping towards the trees. 'It's…'

But by the time Cam had identified the figure Felix was looking at, it was already down. A young man, with red hair and once-white clothing, the last of the Weepers to drop.

Felix dropped too, his knees sinking into the spring flowers at the edge of the path.

'Otho,' he said. 'It was Otho.'

11

Lucas was already making dinner when Julia arrived that evening, but not for her.

The goddess had finally made her appearance.

Marcella was perched gracefully on Julia's usual seat, her back to the hatch as Julia climbed out onto the roof, so Lucas saw her first.

His face fell momentarily into an incongruous expression of dismay, but he made a good recovery, plastering on a smile. Still, he was clearly uncomfortable with the situation.

Julia could hardly blame him; she was uncomfortable too.

'Good evening, Julia,' he said.

'Good evening, Master.'

For the first time, he didn't correct her. He was probably just keeping up appearances for Marcella's sake, but it still stung.

The goddess turned to greet her, and although Julia wanted to feel resentful that she had been usurped, she found herself smiling instead. Marcella's face was filled with such pure joy that it was impossible to bear her any ill will. In any case, it wasn't in Julia's nature.

'Julia,' she said, standing to take Julia's hands in her own. 'I'm so pleased you're here.'

At least one of them was.

'I wanted to thank you,' she continued, her voice lower. 'You were right, and I'm very grateful for your advice.'

She could see Lucas tensing over Marcella's shoulder. He'd be able to hear every word.

'You're welcome,' Julia murmured, trying vainly to smile. 'I'm glad it worked out.'

Lucas turned his back to them then, chopping vegetables on the bench. The bench where, last week, he had wrapped his arms around her as he taught her how to do the same.

She needed to get out of here, now.

'Well, don't let me interrupt your dinner,' she said, raising her voice so it was clear she was speaking to Lucas too. 'I'll leave you two to get to know each other.'

Lucas continued to chop without pausing.

'Oh no, please stay, Julia. Lucas,' she called over her shoulder, 'there's enough for three, isn't there?'

She already called him by his name.

'I can certainly make enough,' he turned, smiling at Marcella.

Julia could see it in a flash: their future stretching out in front of them. Marcella, newly immortal, and Lucas by her side. They'd be beautiful together forever. That smile of Lucas's, his pure contented smile, would point at the goddess and Julia would be lost in the background, watching and serving until she aged into nothingness.

'Wonderful,' Marcella said, smiling warmly back at Lucas.

It was the longest dinner of Julia's life.

Marcella and Lucas sat side by side as they ate, talking about poetry and music and history. Unlike Julia, Marcella had been educated. She could read. She could make interesting conversation.

Julia just sat on the other side of the fire and watched, swallowing her food without tasting its flavour.

The warm light burnished Marcella's skin so she seemed gilded by the flame.

They drank a bottle of wine, which Julia was prohibited from sharing, so she was all the more aware when the alcohol started to encourage their proximity. Lucas touched the goddess on her hand, her waist, her thigh. Her *thigh*.

Julia wished herself away, back to the kitchen, back to the courtyard, back to the edge of the Red: anywhere that was away from this fracturing paradise. In all her wishing, she lost track of the conversation.

'Julia?' Marcella said.

'I'm sorry?'

'Marcella asked where your parents are working,' said Lucas.

'Mine work in the vineyards,' Marcella said with a smile. Other Candidates might have tried to hide their heritage. They might have been ashamed to have parents who still worked as Servers, but not Marcella. She was glorious, down-to-earth perfection. 'I was just curious where yours worked. I wondered whether we might have friends in common.'

Julia scrutinised her for a moment, but she seemed genuine. 'Do you not know about them?'

'Should I?'

'I suppose not. They walked out into the Red when I was a baby. They left me on the temple steps.'

Marcella looked down at her hands for a second before meeting Julia's eye. 'I'm so sorry,' she said. 'I didn't realise that was you.'

'It was.'

Even Marcella, the epitome of tact and good grace, couldn't find a way to bring the conversation back to life after that revelation. Julia was *that* girl, the one whose parents had scorned the protection of the Nobles with their betrayal.

The silence grew.

Lucas finished his wine. Taking his cue, Marcella did the same.

Julia was about to take her leave of them both when Lucas spoke.

'I hope you don't mind, Marcella, but I do need some time with my Attendant this evening.'

'Of course,' she said, rising to her feet. 'Thank you so much for a wonderful evening. It has truly been a pleasure.'

'You're welcome.' The smile he gave Marcella broke Julia's heart, just a little. Just enough that she had to control a wince.

It was *that* smile. His contented smile. The one that made his eyes soften and crease.

'We must do this again some time,' Marcella said, and her own smile was no less genuine.

'We must. Let me see you to the door.'

He handed Marcella down through the hatch then followed her onto the ladder and out of sight.

Would they kiss? Julia wondered. Was that why he was walking her to the door, a courtesy he'd never extended to Julia, so they'd be away from her prying eyes as they said their goodbyes?

She had long enough to imagine it. When Lucas finally returned, Julia was wishing she hadn't come at all.

One look at his expression only cemented that wish.

'You told her to come?' he said as he strode across the roof towards her, his jaw so tense that he was biting out the words.

'I didn't know she'd come here,' Julia said.

'Well you said something to her. So what was it?'

'You don't like her?'

He paced between the benches on the other side of the fire, his image oscillating in the heat haze. 'That's not the point.'

'Isn't it?' Julia's whisper was sucked away into the night, but she knew he had heard it.

'What did you tell her?'

She pulled her cloak tighter around her shoulders, needing the comfort despite the warmth of the fire. 'She asked me about you,' she said. 'I told her the truth.'

'Really? And what was it you *advised* her to do? Don't think I didn't hear that.'

Julia sighed. It was the question she had expected from the moment the words came out of Marcella's mouth. 'She asked me who I would pick as my sponsor if I were her.'

Lucas stilled and turned towards her. The fire stood between them, snapping with heat, a barrier of flame. It reflected from the silver in his eyes so they seemed to glow with it.

'And?' he asked.

'I said you.' Her voice broke on the last word, cracking in the back of her throat.

He sat down on the bench across from her, dropping as though the weight of the words was too heavy for him to bear. 'Julia,' he whispered. 'What have you done?'

'I haven't done anything.'

'You've set her sights on me. Do you even know what sponsorship takes, what kind of bond you have to make to someone if you're going to make them into a Noble? It's forever, Julia. Is that what you want?'

Her heart sank, but she'd half-suspected the truth. She'd known when she sent Marcella to him that she was giving him up.

She'd never wanted to be an Attendant, she reminded herself. All she wanted was to find a way to get out of the Blue. Lucas, Marcella… they were just a distraction.

'Isn't it what *you* want?' she said quietly. 'You won't find a more perfect human girl.'

'Perfect? Or perfect for me?'

'Who doesn't want perfect? She's perfect for anyone.'

He shook his head, but the gesture wasn't a denial, not really. It was something he did when he was thinking, concentrating, his focus fixed on his hands as they rested between his knees.

'This is what you think I should do, then?' he said. It wasn't exactly a question, so Julia didn't exactly give an answer.

'She's kind,' she said. 'She's intelligent. She's beautiful.'

Lucas said nothing, his eyes still cast down at his hands, fingers entwined, thumbs rubbing against each other.

It was too late for her, she knew. She just wanted it to be over now, a done deal, so she could stop agonising over it.

'If I were you,' she said, 'she's the one I'd choose.'

Lucas didn't take her blood that night, or the next day, or the day after that. It had been so long now that Julia was starting to wonder whether he had already made an arrangement with Marcella, despite the scandal. She knew it happened, that the Nobles sometimes took blood from those they were... romantically involved with, but a Candidate wouldn't normally sully their good name with that sort of behaviour, particularly not this close to the Nomination.

Marcella didn't seem like the type.

No, Lucas wasn't getting his blood elsewhere. The only possible conclusion was that he was avoiding taking it from Julia.

She intended to force the issue tonight. He couldn't carry on like this. She didn't want him putting himself in danger just to spare her his proximity, not when she missed it so much her hands itched for him, even though she knew it was a bad idea.

It was full dark by the time she started her walk along the square, skirting its edges to avoid the feeling of vulnerability she felt crossing its centre with so many windows looking down on her. The shadows hid her around its rim.

But she wasn't the only visitor to his building that night. At first she thought the cloaked figure was Marcella, coming to interrupt her evening with Lucas again, but it stopped at the main door, the door to the ground floor apartments. Rufus's door.

Julia stopped, tucking herself into the cover of a nearby clump of wisteria. The last thing she wanted was hassle from Rufus, particularly now things were so difficult between her and Lucas.

She wasn't sure he'd protect her a second time.

'Lorelei,' Rufus said, greeting her on the doorstep.

'Not here, idiot,' she hissed, just loud enough for Julia to catch the words.

Rufus was silhouetted for a moment in the light of the doorway before he stepped aside to let Lorelei in, then he closed the door.

Claudia wasn't in there, Julia knew. She'd just left her in the kitchen with Livia. There was no one there to overhear Rufus and Lorelei's meeting.

She hurried quietly over the remaining distance to the building, her bare feet silent on the paving stones, then ducked into the alley where the staircase rose to Lucas's room. She didn't climb it, though. Instead, she followed the alley past it to where colour spilled through the cracks of Rufus's wooden shutters at the back of the building, spotting the ground with yellow light. There were new weeds here, but few enough that Julia could crouch close beneath the window with her back to the wall.

A door slammed inside.

'Be more careful,' Lorelei said. 'It's bad enough I have to come to the front door without you shouting my name out for any passing bloody Server to hear.'

Julia hoped they couldn't hear her racing heartbeat. She could, at the back of her throat and in her ears. Her breath was a hurricane in the silent darkness.

'I'm sorry,' Rufus said, but he just sounded irritated.

'You will be if you ruin this for me. For us.'

'It's under control.'

One of them was pacing. There was the sound of boots on floorboards, creaking and thudding softly, but quickly enough to betray some agitation.

'And Carmen?' Lorelei asked.

A pause before Rufus replied. 'She's loyal. She won't come over.'

Silence.

When she finally responded, Lorelei was not happy. 'That's the best you can do?' she said. 'A month, I gave you, and so far you've given me nothing. Do I have to be concerned about your motives here? You know what'll happen if you try to play me, Rufus. You're out of your fucking league. I hope you realise that.'

'I know where I stand,' he said, as though through gritted teeth.

'What you should be worried about is where *I* think you stand, and at the moment it looks to me like you're standing on a whole heap of bullshit.'

'There's Priscilla.'

Lorelei snorted. 'You think you get points for her? You're kidding, right?'

'There'll be more. Soon,' he promised.

'Just stay away from the fucking Invicti, alright? You've made it abundantly clear that you're too fucking juvenile to handle them. I mean, Jesus. You couldn't even manage Carmen, for fuck's sake, and she's been praying for this for centuries. She hates the bitch.'

'Fine,' Rufus muttered.

'Oh, don't bloody sulk. Just do better. And get me a drink.'

There was a squeaking noise, a chair being dragged across the floorboards. The glugging of wine from a bottle.

'Lucas?' Lorelei asked.

For a terrible moment Julia thought he might be in the room with them, that Lorelei was addressing him, but Rufus was the one who answered.

'Still a sanctimonious prick,' he said. 'He asked about Marcus.'

'And you told him…'

'Nothing, obviously.'

'You did something right for once. Well done. Have a fucking biscuit.'

'Well, it would have been difficult for me to tell him what's going on, wouldn't it, since you won't actually tell me.' There was anger pinching his voice, but he was muttering too much for his tone to be anything more than petulant.

'You'll get my trust when you've earned it,' Lorelei said.

'And when will I get the rest?'

Lorelei laughed, full-throated and mocking. 'So that's what this is about? Still thinking with the wrong fucking head, Rufus. That's your problem.'

'You said-'

'You'll get what I promised. After you give me what I want.'

More squeaking of chair legs, followed by a soft thump.

'When?' he said, and there was a new liquid quality to his voice. The frustration was gone, replaced with a whispering impatience.

'After the Nomination. You know what to do.'

'You know I do.'

Another snort from Lorelei. 'I'll believe *that* when I see it. After all your cock-swinging, you'd better not be a disappointment.'

There was a creak above Julia's head. Lucas's door, opening and shutting.

'Julia?'

His voice was gentle, but not gentle enough that it didn't reach Lorelei and Rufus. They stilled in the room behind her as she tiptoed as quietly as possible to the base of the stairs. She prayed they wouldn't have heard her move.

'Sorry I'm late,' she said when she reached the edge of the square again. 'I got held up in the kitchen.' She was speaking too loudly, too brightly, particularly given the awkwardness of their last few evenings, but she was trying to give the impression that she had just arrived. It didn't matter what Lucas thought, so long as Rufus and Lorelei didn't realise she'd been eavesdropping.

'Well, come up,' he said, a puzzled look crossing his face.

It doesn't matter what Lucas thinks.

She hurried up the stairs, desperately resisting the temptation to check the alley beneath her. For a moment, she contemplated telling him about what she had overheard, but she couldn't. The point was to escape this place, if it was possible for her and Claud to live out in the Red, and that wasn't something Lucas would support.

She couldn't tell him.

'Have you eaten?' Lucas asked.

'Have you?' she said as he closed the door behind them, sealing them in the darkness of his room together. 'What I mean to say is, it's been a long time since you had any of my blood. I wondered…'

'You wondered whether I had another source?' he asked.

As he spoke she felt rather than saw him step closer to her. It was in the movement of the air, in the scent of his skin, and in her sudden awareness of the warm plane of his body in front of her.

'That's none of my business,' she said.

'My blood supply is none of your business? I'm your Noble,' he said, in a way that made her stomach clench.

If only that were true. She crushed the thought down.

'I just wanted to offer,' she said.

'It's appreciated.' His fingers were somehow tangling with hers, teasing their way into her grip as his thumb stroked up the inside of her palm. 'I am a little in need.'

The room was closing around her like a warm embrace.

His other hand was at her neck now, brushing the hair away from her throat, then running so lightly over the skin that Julia almost didn't feel it at all. He used the two points of contact, one hand at her neck and the other in her own, to spin her around so when he started inching forwards she moved backwards until her shoulders were braced against the door.

Still he didn't seem to be close enough. His leg slid between hers, pinning her in place with a hairsbreadth of space between their bodies. If she moved a fraction further forwards, her hips would be flush against his.

'You didn't want to be an Attendant,' he said softly.

She wanted to deny it, because she didn't want him to step away, but they both knew it was true.

'No,' she whispered.

'And now?' His fingers had moved from her throat to the nape of her neck, twisting teasingly around the soft hairs there.

'Where is your knife?'

He leaned forwards, his cheek so close to hers that she could feel the gentle graze of his stubble against her skin.

'I'm afraid I don't have it with me,' he said, his lips at her ear. 'But perhaps we can find another solution.'

Julia's pulse thudded in her throat as he lowered his mouth to her neck, warm on her skin. It was almost as though the blood in her veins were rushing up to meet him, anticipating the touch of his lips.

But he didn't bite.

Instead, he drew a hot line of breath from the top of her collarbone to her earlobe. There he paused, drawing it into his mouth, and Julia could barely catch her breath for the anticipation swirling in her stomach.

He bit.

A single tooth pierced the centre of her earlobe.

She hadn't had time to imagine how it would feel, to anticipate the pain, but there was none. Instead she felt only a rush of dizziness, drunk on the sweet mint of Lucas's scent and the stroke of his tongue on her flesh as he replaced his teeth with his lips, with the heat of his mouth.

Her legs weakened while the room began to spin. In the

darkness there was nothing to pin her eyes on, and she suddenly felt as though she'd been knocking back too much of Livia's home-brew.

But before she could fall, Lucas's arm was around her waist, cradling her against him. His leg was pressed between hers, trapping her against the door, and finally pushing her hips to his.

Her breath stuttered in her throat until his lips left her skin.

'My mark,' he said, reaching up to his ear to release one of his silver studs. She was too distracted by the press of his body against hers to feel the pain as he slid the scrap of metal through her earlobe and fastened it there.

'A gift for a gift,' he said.

'But I'm your Attendant,' she whispered. 'You don't have to give me anything.'

He pushed away from her a little as though suddenly awkward.

The moment slipped. A cold wave washed away the crush of their bodies, the press of skin into skin, and whatever impulse had pushed him to give her his earring. It was all gone now, along with his touch.

Julia straightened. He pulled away.

'Well, what I'd like to do is give you dinner,' he said with a laugh that sounded forced, brushing at his clothes as though pressing up against her had dirtied him. 'Your cooking skills could still use some improvement. So let's go up to the roof, shall we?'

She followed him, quiet and unobtrusive, just as an Attendant should be.

Marcella was waiting for her in Livia's kitchen when she rose the next day.

'Are you ready to go?' she said to a startled Julia.

'What?' Julia had only been awake for ten minutes. Her head was foggy, and she was fairly certain that the tightness she could feel on her cheek was dried sleep drool. She wasn't feeling up to an encounter with the goddess who, despite the early hour, was looking her usual radiant self.

'Didn't Livia say? You're my sponsor's Attendant, so I thought we could spend the day together, if that's alright.'

'Oh.'

He'd said yes, then. He'd agreed to sponsor Marcella.

It wasn't a surprise.

It was the right thing. It was the best thing, she knew. And yet it crushed a little spark she'd been nurturing in her chest.

'Only if you want to. I know it might seem strange to do it this early, but since we've already met...'

'No, it's fine. Just let me wash my face,' Julia said, trailing outside to the pump. When she reached it, she contemplated filling a bucket, but instead just put her whole head under it. She needed the sharpening effect the cold water provided.

It was a tradition of the Blue, this day of bonding. It was advertised as an opportunity for Attendants and Candidates to get to know each other, to smooth relationships before they were tested by the process of the Casting, but it usually didn't take place until after the Nomination, and it was generally viewed as nothing more than a formality. Marcella was that rare kind of person who took it seriously.

Feelings mattered to her.

She stood at a discreet distance while Julia rinsed out her hair and rubbed her cheeks clean. When she was happy enough, she squeezed the excess water from the length of her hair and plaited it away over her shoulder.

'You have Servers of your own, I guess,' Julia said, taking in the elaborate hairstyle Marcella was modelling.

'Since the Inauguration,' Marcella admitted, but her voice was quiet, as though she were ashamed of the fact. It would have been easier had she been prideful, because then Julia would have had a reason to dislike her. But the goddess was perfect.

What rankled most was that Julia wasn't sure she would have been so gracious in Marcella's place. Would she have gloated? Would she have let the privilege make her feel superior?

Probably. Julia often suspected she wasn't a very good person.

Marcella, however, was.

Julia followed her north through the city and out into the fields, listening to her talk gently of what it had been like to grow up surrounded by their greenery. The vineyards were laid out on the slopes ahead, tilting their south-facing crops at the sunshine that made the day too warm for a cloak. Flower buds clustered among the leaves like verdant beads, the vines offering up the harbingers of their fruit.

It was a long way from the paved centre of the Blue that had birthed Julia.

If only Claud were here. She'd understand how it felt to walk out of the arms of the buildings and the trees into this open space, into the green.

Had she been ambushed by a Candidate today too? Julia wondered. Would Rufus be sponsoring his own Candidate? Given what she'd overheard of his conversation with Lorelei the previous night, he probably had other things on his mind.

After the Nomination, she'd said.

But what? What happened then?

'Julia?'

'Sorry,' she said, turning her attention back to the girl at her side. 'I didn't sleep well.'

Because she'd been dreaming of mint-sweet lips in the darkness, and of another life where she was the Candidate and not the Attendant.

She fingered the earring Lucas had given her, turning the shaft in the wound.

'That's pretty,' Marcella said, noticing the movement.

Julia smiled reluctantly. Marcella's own ears were adorned with precious stones of every colour, marching in loops of gold up and around their outside edges. The plain silver stud in Julia's earlobe was nothing by comparison, except that it was so much more, because he had given it to her. Lucas had given it to her, and he still wore its twin.

That had to mean something, and she didn't want to share it with Marcella.

There was a group of Servers clustered by the gateway to the vineyard as they approached, circled around a figure that stood under a wide, rose-laden arch. His voice intoned loudly into the calm air of the morning: the priest.

It was a child's naming ceremony.

'What name do you give her, my lady?' the priest said to the Noble standing next to him, a woman Julia half recognised.

The child was in the Noble's arms, squalling as it pushed its little fists impotently into the air. Its parents would be somewhere in the crowd that Julia and Marcella joined, but this ceremony was not for them. It was for the Nobles, for the continuation of their blood crop.

Every crop in the Blue was plucked for them.

'I name her Tullia,' the woman said, then she slipped a knife from her pocket and cut the baby's palm.

The child's scream rose and broke, twisting a visceral instinct in Julia that she hadn't known she possessed. She wanted to snatch the bundle away and hold it to her chest, to wipe away the cries with warmth and contact, but not even its mother would dare to do that. It wasn't the way of the Blue.

The Noble shook the child's wrist carelessly, scattering blood on the dry dirt.

'Blood for the earth,' she said, 'and blood for the Empress.'

Julia knew what was coming, so she watched her feet as the Noble touched her lips to the baby's tiny hand.

'They'll do it to me,' Marcella whispered, her unexpected tone drawing Julia's gaze up from the ground. 'They do it at the Nomination, you know, but there'll be so much more blood.'

It wasn't reverence that made her whisper. This was not the dutiful, respectful, perfect goddess that Julia had come to know. Instead, there was emptiness in her tone, resignation to a future from which there was no escape.

'I watched a girl die last year,' she continued, her eyes fixed forwards on the ceremony as she spoke, her voice so quiet that she might have been speaking to the breeze. 'She fell after the Nomination, on her way back to her home. Her sponsor had been feeding from her, and on top of the blood loss at the threshold ceremony…'

'I remember.' The kitchen had been alive with the scandal for weeks afterwards. It was the girl's fault, of course. It was her shame to have allowed her sponsor to feed from her.

'But the Nobles must wash the world clean with blood,' Marcella continued. As she spoke, her tone shifted almost imperceptibly, tinging with fear, until anger started nibbling into it. 'Always our blood. Never theirs.'

'Every threshold,' Julia murmured.

'Every threshold.'

Every threshold purified in blood.

12

There was less blood to clear away after burying Otho than there had been after the carnage in the clearing, but the memory of it was thicker. It sat heavily on Felix's shoulder like one of the crows they had left pecking at the other corpses, a shadow on his mood so palpable that Cam could almost see its shape.

He didn't weep.

He didn't speak unless absolutely necessary.

He didn't look at Cam, not directly.

On the first day, Cam worried that something was wrong beyond his grief, that the head wound had knocked something out of him. He'd always been laconic, but now he was pushing it to extremes. They hadn't discussed what would happen now that there was no one left at the end of this journey for Felix to save, they'd just travelled on as though everything remained the same. Everything except Felix.

On the second day Cam rode up closer, once touching Felix's thigh to try to get him to listen, to focus on something other than the piebald's mane, but the accusatory look he received in return made it clear that Cam's comfort was not welcome. More than that: Cam was the problem.

Then he understood.

He had kept company with guilt long enough to recognise it in Felix.

They travelled in silence then, for enough days that they were almost on top of the old Czech-German border before Felix broke his peace about Otho.

'He was alive,' Felix said as they sat by their campfire, and he didn't need to say the name. Cam knew.

'He was a Weeper. Otho was already gone.'

There was no point in softening the blow. It would have been more unkind to lie, to let Felix torture himself with possibilities that had never existed.

'He was walking.'

'The virus was making his body walk. He was *gone*, Felix. There was nothing either of us could have done for him except what we did. We put him to rest, and that was the best we could do. It was too late.'

The fire cracked and hissed, and in it Cam felt the spitting of Felix's coiled frustration. There was nowhere for it to go, and the cold would only push it further into his bones. He was withdrawing again.

The mountains towered over them here, some still tipped with snow. In the ruins of the old tram station where they were camping, in amongst the broken cars, there were bones. Human bones, wrapped in scraps, so profuse that there was no avoiding them. If there had been any other shelter on these wind-scoured slopes then they would have taken it in a heartbeat to escape this graveyard.

The bones were too close.

'How did you meet?' Cam asked.

Felix said nothing.

He'd thought that maybe, if he gave him a chance to talk about Otho, he might find the space to mourn instead of rolling it all up inside of himself and crushing it down. Cam had always been a talker, but then Felix was clearly not.

The silence lasted so long that Cam was startled when he finally did reply.

'I hunted to feed the others, that was my job. I found him in the woods one day. They assigned him to help me and after that...' He shrugged.

'They?'

'Charlestown. The Pijavica who run it.'

'*Charles*town?'

Charles. It was a common enough name, even now, so it wouldn't necessarily be the same person. But still.

Charles had been there that day in Delphi. He'd always been an egomaniac, and apparently the chance to play god had been too much for him to pass up. When it all fell down, while the shantytown burned around them, Charles and Emmy had both disappeared in the smoke.

'Charlestown?' Cam repeated. 'That's what you call it? Please tell me the Pijavica in charge isn't a dark-haired waste of space called Charles.'

Felix looked at Cam. 'Not anymore,' he said.

'*Shit.*'

Cam rose to his feet, throwing the apple core he'd been picking at into the fire. Sparks flew out the other side, dying quickly in the dirt.

'Friend of yours?'

'He's the bastard who took Emmy. He's a fucking psychopath.'

'Good news, then.'

'He's very fucking bad news. If he's still got her after all these years, if she's been trapped with him doing god knows what to her...' Cam raked both hands through his hair, clasping handfuls against his scalp. It had grown long as he travelled.

'Good news that you're on the right track,' Felix said.

Cam looked down at him, dropping his hands to his sides. 'You're right. You're absolutely right. This is the best lead I've had in centuries.'

It was the thought of it, though. He'd suspected it, but to know that it had been Charles...

Sitting down again, he put a pan on the fire and took a handkerchief-wrapped loaf from his pack. It was set solid like concrete, but it was nothing a little hot water couldn't fix. Bread soup was a depressing staple of his travelling diet.

'Centuries?' Felix said.

'Yeah,' Cam laughed, 'I've been searching a long time.'

When Felix exhaled, the sound of his breath formed words that Cam wasn't supposed to have heard.

Me too.

The wind took them, whistling through the cracked corners of the building.

'You don't need to carry on,' Cam said. 'There's no reason for you to cross these mountains with me. I don't want to drag you into this when, well...'

You've already lost so much.

'I just don't want to drag you into this.'

'I'm coming with you.' His voice was quiet but determined.

'This isn't your fight, Felix. I know where I'm going, and I'm strong enough to manage alone. Trust me, I've been doing this for fucking centuries.'

He didn't want to do it on his own though, not anymore, but he wouldn't ask Felix to come with him either, not when there was no one waiting for him on the other side of the mountains.

Better that Cam did this alone.

'I didn't know Otho long,' Felix said, the unsolicited confession spilling quickly from his lips. 'A year at most, but it was enough to *know* him. He didn't have that darkness in him that you and I share. He didn't deserve to end up in a shallow grave wearing a rotting body that spent days walking around without him before we put it down. Do you understand that?'

Unwillingly, Cam thought of Ed, a man so gentle that he would have lost a brawl with a human just so he didn't have to hit anyone. He couldn't even fight to save his own life when the time came, because he hadn't known how.

'What do you want, Cameron?'

'I want to find Emmy.'

Felix met his eye. 'And I want my revenge.'

A beat passed, their eyes fixed on each other's as they sat side by side in the firelight and took the measure of their wills. Cam was the first to reach out, offering his arm.

They clasped each other's wrists, and the bargain was sealed.

The horses struggled with the crossing. Cam knew that he could trust Hades in the snow after their trek through the Carpathians, but Sandor's feet were less sure. The crossing point was on the eastern edge of the Ore Mountains, so they traversed slopes and plateaux rather than soaring peaks, and the snow coverage was comparatively light amongst the pines, but nonetheless Sandor's hooves seemed to stick.

They could just about trace the path of the old road, where the going was easier, but the landscape had changed beyond recognition since Cam's first visit to the area. There were sharp trees everywhere now, often so thickly clustered that it was difficult to pick a route between them on horseback, and he would swear that even the land itself had moved. The climb seemed higher and steeper than the image he held in his memory, but it had been summer then. In the snow, everything felt sheer.

'We're not going to make it by nightfall,' Cam said. 'We'll have to find a place to camp.'

'There's no shelter here.'

Soon there was more than enough.

They must have taken a wrong turning somewhere, because the mountains had started to close in on them from either side until they were walking through a tight valley that was carved out of the rocks. They teetered in piles a hundred feet tall, layered haphazardly in fused slices so that they looked like nothing so much as unstable stacks of gigantic books covered in deep, snow-white dust.

There were footprints in the gorge, Silver or human or Weeper, and the tracks of something else too. Something with claws. Too small to be a bear, too big to be a wolf.

'Lynx,' Felix said, following Cam's eyes to the pitted snow.

'Shit. We can't leave the horses standing around outside, not at this end of the winter. The cats are probably hungry enough to try for one of them.'

'Do we have a choice?'

Which was the problem, of course. There was no choice. The darkness sucked the warmth out of the landscape as shadows lengthened under the trees, and with every step into the snowy canyon it became more urgent that they built a fire and a shelter. They could survive the frostbite, but Felix's toes wouldn't grow back like Cam's did.

But they couldn't camp on the path - it would be asking for trouble - and the valley had quickly narrowed until it was barely twenty feet wide. There was no space to hide them.

It was full dark now. They were navigating only by Cam's vision, resigning themselves to settling in for the night on the track that would lead the lynx straight to them, when Cam spotted it.

'There,' he said, pointing off ahead to where one of the rock stacks stood proud of the others. It was a pointless gesture; the night was so perfectly black in the still embrace of the mountain that Felix wouldn't have seen his hand in front of his own face.

'Is that an alcove?' Cam said.

Sure enough, a tributary of the canyon split off in front of the outcropping, so narrow that Cam had to raise his knees to fit through on horseback, leading to a small dead-end clearing surrounded on all sides by towering stone. It was just large enough for a fire, the horses, and a small snow shelter.

There was no wood, just a pile of snow so deep that it must have tumbled down from the rocky shelves above.

'Well,' Cam said, 'that'll make building the shelter easier at least.'

'What will?' Felix was right behind him on Sandor, crowding the tight space.

'It's a space about twenty feet square, filled with snow about as deep as I am tall. You've still got those branches?'

Felix felt behind himself blindly to where Sandor's rear end was concealed in the tunnel that led into the hollow. They'd brought the branches up from the tram station, light enough to carry because they were tinder dry from sitting under cover. They wouldn't feed the flames for long, but they'd be good enough until Cam had the shelter dug out, until he could backtrack to where they'd seen the last trees.

'Got them.'

'Good. Stay in the saddle while I get us sorted.'

The horses took up most of the space even before they lay down to sleep, but once Cam cleared the ground and got him pointed in the right direction, Felix managed to build a decent fire.

The shelter proved to be more of a problem. Three feet down, Cam hit a hard surface of curved ice that felt like steel in comparison with the hard-packed snow he'd already dug away. With his strength diminished by tiredness and lack of blood, it took him three tries to punch through it to the space below.

He wished he hadn't.

There was no smell; it was too cold for that, and in any case the bodies hadn't had a chance to rot because they were frozen solid.

They'd made their own ice cave here, better crafted than Cam's best efforts had ever been, but it hadn't saved them.

The ice of the walls was red, blood frozen in rich drips along its surface.

'Shit,' Cam muttered. He didn't want to tell Felix, but there was no way to cover it up, not when he was crouched barely ten feet away. The bodies would have to come out.

Then he saw the shape of the bites. He'd assumed that the damage had been caused by a lynx, which would have been bad enough in the circumstances, but these marks hadn't been made by a cat. The two men whose meagre remains were preserved in the ice cave had been dismembered by teeth that looked remarkably human, which could mean only one thing: Weepers.

They didn't just have to worry about the wild cats. There were Weepers out here too, and they'd found this spot before.

Shit shit shit.

Cam backed out of the cave and roused the horses.

'We're not stopping here,' he said. 'We'll eat, get some hot food in ourselves, but then we're leaving.'

'You're not serious. It's pitch dark.'

'Weepers have been here. There are bodies. We can't stay here, blocked in a corner like this. What if there are hundreds of them? What if they all pile in here? They'd crush you before your blood could turn them. Look, I know it's dark, but I can see well enough. We can ride together on Hades and I'll just tie Sandor behind.'

Felix wasn't easily convinced. He took a half-burned branch from the fire and used it as a torch to scout out the broken igloo for himself, despite Cam's protestations. After Otho, he didn't want to subject Felix to it. He didn't want to make him wonder.

When Felix emerged, his expression was starkly unemotional, but clearly marked with exhaustion. He needed this night's sleep.

'We can just put the meat out for them,' he said.

'Like the caravan did at the forge? It wouldn't work. The, er, meat is frozen solid. I don't know what freezing does to the vaccine, but I'm pretty sure it wouldn't do it any good. I mean, I don't see any Weeper bodies here. And anyway, it doesn't scent right. They'll ignore it as long as they can smell you.'

Felix sighed, a visceral dirge for the sleep he would miss. 'I'd better eat quickly then.'

They left the moment they heard the first howl, scrambling to secure their bundles to Sandor's back. As soon as the horse had been tied to Hades's saddle, Cam leapt into his seat and, pulling Felix up in front of him, kicked Hades into a trot, then a canter, and finally a gallop, until they were racing through the gorge like a bullet down the barrel of a gun.

'How far away?' Felix shouted over the stamping of hooves.

'I'm not sure. It's difficult to tell with these cliffs all over the place, but they're definitely behind us.'

The howls multiplied in the darkness, but whether it was because the Weepers heard their movement or because they'd found the camp, with its fire and frozen corpses, Cam wasn't sure. Either way, they needed to press on, but the horses couldn't sustain a gallop for long, particularly at the end of an already difficult day. It took only five minutes for Hades to drop into a trot, with Sandor trailing reluctantly behind, and within another half hour they were both walking. It didn't help that the snow was getting thicker as the walls of the valley finally widened around them. It stood in drifts that were higher than Cam's head, even though Hades added a good three feet to his height.

But the Weepers didn't seem to be following. When the howls came now they were distant, on the other side of the wall of rock that separated them from what had once been Czechia, and they weren't moving any closer.

'Are you alright?' Cam asked Felix.

'Fine,' he said, but he sounded uncomfortable.

There had been no time until that moment to contemplate anything but their escape, and that urgency had made things like Cam's hand around Felix's waist seem like an irrelevance. Now, calm descended like a shock of cold water to the face, and self-consciousness asserted itself.

Cam moved his arm away, putting one hand in front of Felix on the reins and resting the other on his own thigh. It was the best he could do to minimise their contact.

After a little while, Felix began to shiver.

Cam thought about it. He thought about pulling Felix back against him to share his heat, but instead he drew Hades to a stop and called Sandor alongside so he could rummage in their packs for blankets.

It was easier to see now that they were out of the shade of the rocks, even though the trees were thickly distributed. The light of the thin crescent moon reflected off the snow, giving the world a cold, blue tinge. Cam wouldn't have been surprised if Felix were able to see for himself now, although neither of them suggested that they separate onto their own horses.

When Felix was bundled up warm, Cam made a frame of his arms around him, but it was still an awkward embrace. It was wide and tense, touching the other man's body only to the extent absolutely necessary.

Cam had always been such a tactile person before. He wasn't sure exactly when that had changed, but his aversion to contact was now so ingrained that he avoided it even when his body wanted to lean into it.

It wanted to now. It wanted him to wrap Felix close against his chest and hold him, to tuck his chin into the side of Felix's neck and smell his hair.

But his arms had forgotten how.

Even as he remembered his head cradled in Felix's lap in the treehouse, he wondered at it. Had it ever been so easy for him to reach out to someone else like that, to feel the warmth of their touch without rebounding from it?

It seemed so foreign.

Proximity had become threat, calculation and reaction, an assault, not an expression of tenderness.

Proximity made the seconds stretch.

It was Felix who spoke eventually. His voice and the crunch of snow under hooves were the only noises in the night.

'You're certain that he took her, your friend?' he said abruptly, as though he'd been wanting to ask for some time. 'How do you know she didn't just leave?'

'She wouldn't. She's bonded to one of the other Pijavica. She never would have left if she'd had a choice about it.'

'You mean she silvered?'

That gave Cam pause. 'How do you know about that?'

'Charlestown,' Felix said, but there'd been a beat of hesitation before he spoke.

Still, what did it matter out here? There was no harm in him knowing.

'More than silvering,' Cam said. 'She silvered for someone who had already silvered for her. So the bond sealed.'

'I've never heard of that.'

'It's rare. But anyway, the point is that she would never have left him. She loved him, he loved her, and they were bonded together. She wouldn't have walked away from that. The only way she would have left him is if she had been taken away by force.' *Or if she were dead,* Cam added silently in the privacy of his own head. They were words he didn't want to acknowledge aloud.

Apparently the awkwardness of the ride was making Felix talkative, because he wanted to know more. 'What happened to the other silvered Pijavica?'

'Nothing good.'

'He still alive?'

'I think so. Look, it's complicated, and it's late, and you haven't had any sleep, so why don't you rest? I'll wake you if anything exciting happens.'

All there was after that was the crunch of the snow and the whisper of breath.

In the end, increasing their proximity wasn't Cam's decision. It wasn't anyone's.

As they rode out of the forest of snowy peaks, the dawn at their backs, exhaustion finally got the better of Felix. His body slumped back into Cam's, tipping from side to side with the motion of Hades's steps so Cam had no choice but to press his limbs in more closely, bracing Felix in the cocoon of his arms, of his thighs.

His head tipped back on Cam's shoulder and slowly, stride by rolling stride, Felix's slumbering body fit itself against Cam's until it didn't seem so unnatural after all, this contact.

This closeness.

This comfort.

Dresden, like so many other ancient cities, had fallen into the sea. It had been gradual, but no less destructive for the time it took the water to creep into the streets and wash the buildings down from their foundations.

On the bright side, there was no snow here.

They left the horses in the forest and came in along the shoreline, through the salt ponds. The evaporation pools had been fields once, but the banks that marked their edges now contained only the sea, spread thin across the ruined soil.

At least Cam would be able to gather the salt he needed for Ana and Vasile here. Or Ana, rather. Cam suspected that Vasile might have found his end by now.

The settlement itself was hard to miss. In a landscape of beaches and fields, it crouched in the rocks like a barnacled crab.

'Shit,' Cam whispered. 'I didn't think there would be so many of them.'

From their vantage point behind a tumbledown wall, there was an uninterrupted view of the buildings on the slope above them. Most of them were no more than two storeys, although some still had the remains of higher floors piled on top of them. All of them were busy with activity even this early in the morning, particularly in the central area that seemed to be used as a combined meeting place, trading hub and rubbish dump. Unfortunately, that was also the location of the doorway that led down into the cells.

'I don't think I have the strength for a fight,' Cam said. 'It's been too long since I had any blood.'

'And mine's no good to you,' Felix said, a statement but also an offer.

That was… unexpected. Waking up to find himself in Cam's arms had obviously had as much of an effect on Felix as it had on Cam. Things were definitely changing between them, but Cam wasn't sure that was a good thing. Not now, not when he needed to focus on his mission.

'I'm afraid I need uncontaminated blood,' he said.

Turning human would make him less than useless to Emmy. He had a promise to keep to her, to Laila, and to himself.

'They keep blood in there,' Felix said, nodding towards the squat internment building that was more underground than over, if Cam's memory could be trusted.

He could make out the darkness of the doorway, but it was difficult to see clearly because there were guards to either side of it, and at least one on the stairs beyond. The market place was alive with bustle, but that doorway was a point of frozen stillness in the stream. Unnatural stillness. Either the guards were incredibly well trained, or they were Silver.

'So,' Cam said, 'to recap: the uncontaminated blood that I need in order to fight the guards is inside the building that's being heavily guarded by the guards I need to fight. Is that right?'

'There are other ways in.'

'It's the only door, you said.'

'We don't have to fight, though.'

Cam looked over at him, assessing his intent. 'What are you suggesting?'

'A distraction.'

'What kind of a distraction?'

Felix shrugged lightly. 'They know me.'

The words were ominous, but Cam was reluctant to debate it while they were exposed in the salt ponds.

'Well,' he said, 'neither of us is going to be in a fit state to walk in a straight line, let alone infiltrate a Pijavica compound, unless we get some proper sleep first. Let's go back up to where we left the horses and camp there today, then we can make a move when it's dark. Agreed?'

'Agreed.'

They kept low as they picked their way back around to the trees where they had left the horses. It was a laborious process when they were both already so exhausted; Felix wouldn't have slept well while they rode, and Cam couldn't remember the last time he'd managed more than a few hours at a time.

If they tried to sneak into Charlestown now, Cam was so impaired that he'd probably get them both killed.

They'd just ducked into the tree line when Cam heard it: horses approaching. The sound was coming in from the southwest, but a straight line to the settlement on the water would take the newcomers right past the place where Cam had intended that they would camp for the night. Right past where they had left their own horses.

'*Shit*,' he said. 'Is nothing going to go right today?'

'What?'

'There are riders in the forest, and they're coming this way. We need to get the horses under cover, and quickly.'

'Just riders?'

Cam was already on the move, but the tone of Felix's words stopped him. It wasn't just speculation; he already knew the answer to his question.

Cam listened again, and now he could hear what he had missed before. 'Carts too,' he said. 'The caravan?'

Felix nodded, as though his expectation had been confirmed. 'They'll veer north along the path till they hit the edge of the trees, then circle east to Charlestown. They'll miss our camp.'

The pronouncement was so definite that there was no room for Cam to doubt its truth.

'Come on,' Felix said, pushing through the shallow undergrowth. 'I know a place where we can watch.'

'I bet you do. You watch the Izcacus, right?'

'Right.'

But as he turned to meet Cam's eye, Felix's expression betrayed him. There was more to it than that, and he was still holding back. The pause hung between them, the unanswered questions silently acknowledged, but that was as far as it went.

Felix turned and ducked his way through the low branches,

heading west, and Cam had little choice but to follow him.

The path was a mile or so from where they had started, a wide avenue of dirt between the dense pines. The carts were still some way off, but the track was already well-rutted. This was a regular thoroughfare, suggesting a level of organisation and routine that Cam hadn't expected from the caravan.

Felix clearly had.

He tapped Cam on the shoulder to get his attention and pointed upwards into the canopy.

When people are in a hurry, they don't look up.

The height would give them a better view, and if they picked their tree carefully, it would also keep them out of sight.

Cam nodded and started to climb as quickly and quietly as he could. When he looked down after reaching a suitable perch, he expected to see Felix trailing far below him, but he was right on Cam's heels.

He had underestimated him.

The first of the riders came into view then, and they both fell still.

There were a lot of them in the convoy. First came a few riders who must have been the scouts - their horses were the best of the bunch - and behind them rolled five separate wagons. Two carried luggage and three carried passengers, but only one of those three was uncaged. In the other two, people sat crammed along benches with their hands and feet bound, surrounded by a frame of metal and wood.

The uncontaminated, Cam guessed. So Charlestown was where they had come from after all, and now they were returning.

But why? What was the point of taking them out into the forests of the continent?

More riders followed the caravan behind the huge column of people that brought up the rear on foot. The walkers were mostly human, probably contaminated, but there was the odd Silver mixed in with them. Cam didn't need to look at the riders' eyes to know that all of them were Silver. This part of the world was not one in which the humans would be in charge.

They were all quiet.

Even though they were in motion, the Silver were possessed of the characteristic stillness that marked them out, but it had settled over the humans too. Those in the caged carriages looked as though they had been drained into apathy, their few movements listless and faint, but it was in the walkers that the exhaustion was most evident. There were so many that it must have been a struggle to keep them all fed, which might have accounted for it in part, but there was a general air of defeat about the caravan that sat heavily around it. Wherever these humans had travelled from, whether they'd set out with the caravan or been collected on the way, there was no more fight in them. The only sounds were of hooves, footsteps, creaking wheels and the rub of filthy cloth against skin and wood.

'He should arrive within the next few days,' a voice said, quiet in volume but unexpected enough that it made a few of the humans on the ground jump. Or flinch, more accurately.

People were crowded together so tightly on the track that Cam struggled to zero in on the source.

'He'll come across the mountains,' the voice continued, feminine but hard, 'because he's a *tonto del culo*, but he'll be weak by the time he gets here, so you can take him with three, maybe four to be on the safe side.'

The voice that replied was male and brash with youth. 'Four?' he said. 'That seems excessive.'

'He's one of the Invicti, but if you want to be a *hijo de puta* about it then be my guest. You can clear up your own mess.'

And then Cam saw her, walking near the riders at the very back of the procession: Carmen, here, nearly nine hundred miles from the Blue.

The Invicti had a traitor in their midst, and she'd betrayed him.

13

Julia watched for Rufus on the morning of the Nomination, but she could hear no noise from within his rooms as she weeded the alley outside his window.

'He's not there.'

She turned to see Claudia silhouetted against the dawn at the edge of the square.

'He hasn't been there all night,' she continued. 'I stayed late just in case, then came back early, but I don't think he's been here.'

'I was worried about you,' Julia said, wiping her muddy hands on her dress as she got to her feet. 'I didn't hear you come home.'

'I didn't want to wake you, not with today being, well, you know.'

She'd told Claudia about the overheard conversation between Lorelei and Rufus, and now they were both on the look out for anything strange. It would happen today, or some time after today, but the truth was that they had no idea what they were waiting for. Lorelei's words had been weighty, as though it were something important, but they had nothing else to go on.

After the Nomination. You know what to do.

The problem was that Julia and Claudia didn't.

'I'm not sure this is worth it,' Julia whispered. 'All this risk, and for what? So far we know nothing more than we did a fortnight ago.'

'You're the one who wanted to do this, Jules.'

'I know.' Julia sighed as she stooped to collect her trug, twisting her hair over one shoulder as she leaned down. The gesture brushed her hand against the stud in her ear, reminding her that today was not only the day for which Lorelei and Rufus had planned… something, but it was also the day on which Lucas would tie himself to his Candidate as her sponsor.

It would be a threshold day like no other, and Marcella would be the one to bleed for it.

'I haven't changed my mind about leaving,' Julia said, 'but I don't want to put you in danger. Or me. I just want better than this.'

'Better than hot meals, a roof over our heads, and protection from whatever's out there in the Red?'

'Yes, better than that!' Julia's voice had risen, but she carefully controlled it back down to a whisper. 'I want to be able to choose the price we pay for our lives. I don't want to buy mine in blood anymore, Claud. Do you?'

Julia reached over and tucked Claudia's hair over her shoulder, baring the scar at her neck. It was less obvious than it had been when it was fresh, but it would always be there, raw pink on the alabaster skin of her throat.

'And if there's no other choice,' Claudia said, dropping her chin, 'what will you do then? If there really is no way to live out in the Red, would you go anyway?'

'There has to be a way.'

Claudia shook her head. 'No there doesn't. Just because you want there to be something better than this doesn't mean it exists. You can't just wish it into being. I know you want there to be another way, I know you want your parents to be alive out there, but what if there isn't, and what if they're not? Do you really think the Blue would have lasted this long if it was as simple as just… leaving? All those people they've thrown out - Balbina, Septimus, Marcus - you know that was a death sentence. You know this is a long shot.'

Julia's shoulders slumped a little in the wake of Claudia's quiet tirade. 'So you've just been humouring me,' she said. 'You were never planning to come with me at all.'

'That's not what I said, Jules.' Claudia twisted her fingers in Julia's and pulled her closer until they were face to face. 'Look, we'll keep listening, and if we find something…' She shrugged. 'I just don't have your faith, that's all. I don't want you to go running out there because you've convinced yourself it's safe when there's no evidence that it is, when you just want it to be. I don't want to lose you.'

'You won't.'

'Alright then. So, are we going to the Nomination, or are you going to hang around in this alley all day waiting for Lucas to turn up?'

'I wasn't-'

But then the man himself appeared, his door opening and closing above them.

'Morning, ladies,' he said, leaning over the balustrade. 'Going to the Nomination?'

'Yes,' Julia said, at the same time as Claudia said, 'Yes, Master,' and bowed her head.

'No need for that,' Julia said under her breath as Lucas came down the stairs. 'He doesn't like it.'

'Really?' Claudia whispered.

'Really,' Lucas said with a gentle smile, joining them. 'You must be Claudia.'

She pulled herself together more quickly than Julia had managed when she'd first met him. 'Yes,' she said. 'Pleased to meet you.'

'Likewise. So, you're coming?' he asked them both, but his eyes lingered on Julia's. She couldn't tell whether he was hoping she'd say yes or no.

'We were planning to,' she said.

'Ah.'

No, then.

'I can stay away if you prefer,' she offered, modulating her tone so it was half a statement and half a question.

'No, no. It's just, you know.' He ran his hand over the back of his neck. 'Marcella.'

She squinted at him, not quite sure what the problem was. She'd attended Nominations before. She knew about the blood, and about the rituals. There was nothing to shock her there.

'Well,' he said, giving up any attempt to articulate his unease, 'shall we go then?'

'I have to return my trug first,' Julia said, hefting it onto her arm. 'I'll see you there, or this evening. Usual time?'

'No, not tonight.' His eyes told her what he was dancing around: things were going to change. Once he was sponsoring Marcella, everything would shift focus. He would shift focus. From the moment of the Nomination, Julia would be on the periphery, and Marcella would be in the centre.

She hadn't expected it to happen so quickly.

'Of course,' she said, wishing Claudia wasn't here to witness this. If she could have had just a few minutes alone with him to understand what it meant... But they didn't have that time. 'Perhaps it would be best if you just sent word from the temple when you next need me.'

His eyes were fixed on hers, and she couldn't have escaped them if she wanted to. There was a long moment before he looked away, nodding to acknowledge her words.

'Nice to meet you, Claudia,' he said. His eyes flicked back to Julia for a second, to the earring of his that she wore, then slid over her face and away.

Julia reached up to her ear. 'Did you want-'

'No,' he said with the smallest of smiles. 'No, it's yours. Goodbye, Claudia, Julia,' he said, and then he was gone, blending into the crowds clustered around the temple.

Claudia fell back against the alley wall and fanned herself with her hand. 'Wow,' she said. 'That was intense.'

'Don't you start. It's bad enough that I sort of like him without you making it any worse. He's sponsoring Marcella. We have to be sensible about this.'

'You might have to be, but I don't. And why didn't you tell me about his eyes?'

Julia's stomach plummeted for a moment, thinking that Claudia had noticed the silver. It was harder to see in the daylight, but it explained why Lucas had kept his distance from them in the alley. He wouldn't have wanted Claudia to see.

But in the end, she needn't have worried.

'They're so *dark*,' Claudia continued, 'and gorgeous. Just like the rest of him.'

'You're not helping.'

'I wasn't trying to help. Come on, we'd better hurry or we'll miss all the good bits.'

The streets were so blocked by the time Julia had returned her trug to the yard that they had to circle around to the other side of the square to get anywhere close to the temple. They ended up down an alley behind the palace and the guardhouse, where there were far fewer people. It was the more prestigious side of the Blue, the side that was populated sparsely with Nobles rather than densely with Servers, so the streets were practically empty.

They were concentrating on mapping a route back to the square through buildings that were unfamiliar to them, so they only just avoided stumbling into the middle of a hushed dispute that was taking place in one of the temple alcoves. Julia noticed at the last minute and hurried them past, but as soon as they turned the next corner she tucked in close to the building and tried to listen in.

'What?' Claudia asked.

Julia made frantic shushing motions with her hands. 'Didn't you see?' she said, her whisper so quiet that she was doing little more than moving her lips. 'That was Lorelei.'

'Well, I can't hear a thing from here. What do you want me to do about it?'

But Lorelei was already on the move, walking towards the corner where Claudia and Julia were hidden.

'Don't fuck this up, alright?' she said, her voice just loud enough for Julia to hear over the noise of the crowd in the square. 'Just keep him secure in the Red until it's time.'

There was a masculine murmur in response, but the low tone rendered the words indecipherable.

'Because I say when we're ready,' Lorelei replied, 'and we're not. Fucking. Ready. Yet.' She didn't sound happy. 'Why is it that you all seem to think you should be in charge when you're hundreds of fucking years younger than me? You think just because you have a cock you're imbued with some kind of magical, penis-powered omniscience?'

More murmurs, from more than one source this time.

'I swear to god, the Fall changed nothing. Fucking *men*. Always looking for an excuse to swing your dicks around.'

She walked straight past the corner, paying no attention to the alley where Claudia and Julia were huddled, but they still watched her out of sight before they moved again.

'She's an angry woman,' Claudia said when they were sure the coast was clear.

'Does she always talk like that?'

'From what I've heard. Who do you think they were talking about?'

'Hello, girls.'

Julia nearly jumped out of her skin. One minute they had been alone, and the next thing she knew Rufus was standing closer than she would have liked, leaning over them with one hand propped against the wall.

'Master,' Claudia said, bobbing her head. It took Julia a moment to realise that she should do the same, but by then it was too late.

'Hello, Julia,' he said to her. 'How nice to see you again. I take it you're both on your way to the Nomination?'

'That's right,' Julia said. Claudia remained pointedly silent.

'Then you should come with me.'

Julia hesitated, reluctant to say yes, but unable to say no. Rufus was a Noble, after all.

'Come on,' he said. 'I promise you a great view. You won't get that if you have to push through the crush with the others. A little thing like you will be lost in the crowd.'

Julia wanted to protest that she wasn't that little, even though everyone did seem to be taller than her, but she'd be damned if she'd give Rufus a glimpse inside her head. The less he understood about her the better.

Suddenly she wished she'd had the Attendant training that Claudia was relying on. If she knew how to be blank, to be obedient, then he would see nothing of who she was, only what she was. The priestess's rules weren't just meaninglessly oppressive, they were protective.

She'd been a fool, and he already knew her too well.

'Indulge me,' he said, offering Julia his arm. There was no way to refuse, not now that the people at the other end of the alley had noticed them. They were crammed in tight at the entrance to the square, craning to get a look at what was going on there, but apparently Julia and Rufus were now providing better entertainment.

She slipped her arm reluctantly into his, but proximity to him wasn't actually all that bad. His cloak was warm, finely woven from soft wool, and it was clean. The smell of him was clean too, with a slight hint of something masculine but botanical. Beneath it all, though, was the threat.

He offered his other arm to Claudia, who took it without hesitation or expression, as Julia should have done.

She was getting this all wrong.

Densely packed though the crowds were, they parted in front of the three of them as though the people were afraid to dirty their clothes. They took care to avoid brushing against even Julia and Claudia, despite the fact that they were human, just like them. Rufus made them different, and not in a positive way; the looks they received were filled with veiled anger.

Large banks of covered seating had been built up to either side of the temple steps as usual, reserved for the Nobles, and that was where they were now heading.

'I bet you've never sat in the boxes before, am I right?' Rufus said, apparently speaking to Julia, but pitching his voice loud enough for everyone to overhear, even over the noise of the gaggle.

'I'm a Server,' she said, which was answer enough.

'Well, today you're my guest. You can have a front row seat.' The smile that split his face seemed perfectly pleasant, but Julia doubted Rufus's intentions were. He could only mean to unsettle them with his attention, and with his offer to show them the ritual of the Nomination close up. It was bad enough from the other side of the square.

Meanwhile, Claudia was silent on the other side of the Noble, burrowed deep into the shell of her projected self. She'd need that, when the blood started to pour. Julia wished she had that kind of composure.

She could feel the eyes of the people on her back as she climbed the temple steps on Rufus's arm. Their hatred was in the silence she left in her wake, and in the hissing susurration of returning conversation once they thought she was out of range. She couldn't tell whether it was directed at Rufus or at her, whether it was anger or envy, but it didn't matter in the circumstances. All she felt was the heat of their scrutiny.

The entrance to the seating was about halfway up the temple stairs, leading off at a right angle into tiers of temporary wooden seating. Somehow Rufus had sufficient standing to oust a group of Nobles from the front row in order to make space for the three of them. She'd had no idea that his rank was that high.

It was then that Julia began to feel concerned. She caught Claudia's eye, but there was no reaction there.

Her friend was good at this.

'Here,' Rufus said as he led them into the row. 'You go next to me, Julia, and Claudia can go on your other side.'

Trapping her in the middle. As they turned to take their seats, she got a glimpse of Lucas sitting in the back row. He didn't look happy to see her here.

'Oh, yes,' Rufus said, seeing the direction of Julia's glance. 'I forgot that you were assigned to Lucas.' He spoke with such disdain for him that Julia opened her mouth to defend Lucas before remembering that she would do better to imitate Claudia's silence. She fixed her eyes on the ground.

'So you have been trained after all,' he continued. 'I was starting to wonder, but then I imagine Lucas would be a demanding master. We're not all so difficult, you know. Not usually, anyway. I know I myself have been rather demanding over the past month, as I'm sure Claudia has told you.'

Julia clamped down her expression, trying not to show her distaste. Perhaps she succeeded, because Rufus said nothing further. Minutes passed without conversation as they waited in the swell of the crowd's uproar for the ceremony to begin.

She wondered why she was here. It could only be a power play, a chance for Rufus to rub his superiority in Lucas's face. After all, Lucas had invited Julia and Claudia to accompany him this morning. She regretted saying no now, although it was doubtless cooler in her seat than it was at the back of the box where Lucas sat. Even in the front row, where the breeze wafted in from the square, the midday heat made the atmosphere thick under the cover of the tarpaulin above their heads. Julia could feel the sweat collecting at the nape of her neck, sticking her hair to her skin.

She gathered her hair in her hand and twisted it, exposing the damp patch as she pulled it over her shoulder.

'Why, Julia,' Rufus said, 'what is that piece of tat you're wearing in your ear?'

Idiot! Why had she let him see it?

She'd been concentrating more on her comfort than on playing the game, this obfuscatory dance at which Claudia apparently excelled.

Julia kept her eyes downcast and said nothing.

'I recognise it, you know,' Rufus said lightly, looking over his shoulder as he spoke so that Julia would know that he had connected the dots. He knew the stud belonged to Lucas.

'So why,' he continued, 'are you wearing it?'

She said nothing.

'You can answer me.'

'It was a gift,' she said softly.

'Is that what he told you?' Rufus laughed, the tone almost sweet. 'How naive you are. That's nothing less than a mark.'

Julia tried to control her irritation when she spoke. Everything she said and did, and everything she failed to say and do, revealed more about her. And about her relationship with Lucas.

She had to tread carefully.

'He told me,' she said. Her tone was calm because she made it so, and because Lucas *had* told her, and she knew exactly what the stud was. There was nothing duplicitous in it, nothing sordid of the kind that Rufus seemed to be implying.

'A mark that won't heal,' Rufus continued, as though Julia hadn't spoken, 'because it's held open with silver. He means to own you.'

'I'm his Attendant,' she replied, feeling that she must be missing something. They were all owned, every single one of the Servers, and she could see nothing in Lucas's gesture that should concern her.

'Is that all you are, though? I wonder.'

To Julia's relief, the unsettling conversation was interrupted as hush flowed over the crowd in response to some visual cue that she couldn't see. Everyone was staring intently at the front of the temple, where the columns obscured her view of the door.

It was starting.

A few moments later the priest and priestess processed out, each leading their Candidates until they were lined up along the width of the temple on one of the lower steps, on a level with where Julia was now sitting.

There were perhaps forty Candidates in total, some from this year's Inauguration like Marcella, but the majority were leftovers from previous years. They wouldn't be given many chances before they were relegated back to being Servers.

Marcella was close, only three Candidates between her and the box, conspicuous for her bearing, for her beauty, and for the colour of her skin. Skin tones varied wildly across the Candidates, almost as though they had been chosen to represent the entire palette, but there was so much interbreeding in the Blue that the majority were neither dark nor pale. That made Marcella exceptional for the extreme she represented in the same way that Claudia was for her paleness, only more so because she was also the goddess.

It was in every movement she made, standing in front of the crowd that filled the square as though she were a queen, comfortable with their attention. None of the other Candidates stood as she did, with easy confidence. She outshone her jewels.

Rufus perked up at the sight of her, like a dog pricking up his ears at the sound of his name.

'I present your Candidates,' the priest said to the box opposite them, on the other side of the temple steps. Looking around herself, Julia realised for the first time that the boxes were divided: the one in which she sat was for Nobles who preferred a female Candidate, so the girls were lined up closest to it, and the box on the other side was for those who preferred a male Candidate. In previous years she had been too far away to mark the division.

The priest wasn't talking to the Nobles around her, and he took his time. He presented each male Candidate by name, gave a brief précis of their skills then asked the Nobles to demonstrate their interest. On a couple of occasions a Noble in the opposite box stood to offer their sponsorship, but it seemed that most were reluctant this year. Usually at least a quarter of the Candidates would find themselves a sponsor, but apparently this Nomination was going to be an exception to the rule.

Finally, the priest moved aside and ceded to the priestess. She started at the centre of the steps, so it would be some time before she reached Marcella.

That was the moment Julia was waiting for. That was the moment when Lucas would declare himself. She wished it would never happen, but at the same time longed for it to be over.

She spun the stud in her earlobe, fiddling with it until it caught Rufus's attention and she forced herself to stop. He was looking at her too closely. She could feel the heat rising in her cheeks, prickling around her jaw with her anxiety and the warmth of the box.

Three down so far, and no sponsors had stepped forwards. Four more passed with no offer, their faces falling into disappointed resignation, before there was any movement in the box.

'Diana,' the priestess announced. Julia recognised her: a friend of Claudia's, the girl who'd had her hair done up like a spray of carrot leaves on the day of the Inauguration.

Julia flicked her gaze sideways to Claudia and saw the tension in her posture. She wanted to take her hand, to soothe away her worry, but she didn't want to give anything away to Rufus. Instead, she sat silently and watched as the priestess narrated the girl's virtues.

There was a scuffing of feet in the row of seats behind them.

'This one is mine,' a voice said, a woman's, quiet enough that it was almost under her breath. Julia only heard because she was so close to the speaker, but of course the woman didn't need to raise her voice to be heard by the rest of the Nobles. She could have whispered and her claim would still have reached them.

A few moments passed in silence. Julia didn't turn around to look at the woman, but she did glance once more at Claudia's face. She was smiling, a smile so faint that Julia only noticed it because she could map her friend's face in her head without a second thought. She could see the smile in the minute squinting of her eyes, in the slight tightening of her cheeks where she suppressed her joy.

Diana had got what she wanted, then.

After a couple more seconds, the priestess nodded at the Noble behind Julia, who took her seat again, and then proceeded along the line. The priestess extolled the skills of the young women paraded in front of the temple between Diana and Marcella, one by one, in detail and with a tinge of desperation as more and more passed unclaimed, but still no Nobles stood.

And then it was time.

'Marcella,' the priestess announced. 'Our most intelligent girl, skilled at reading and writing with excellent numerical ability and recall. She is-'

'I claim her.' Lucas, from the back row.

Julia had known to expect it, but she hadn't understood until that moment how it would feel to hear him say the words. It was like someone had gathered together the muscles of her chest in a fist, gripping them tightly in a sharp squeeze of pain before releasing them in an ache that felt almost like relief, until it turned into its own kind of torture.

A beat passed in silence, and then there was something she didn't expect: a rustle of movement from beside her. For a moment Julia was too wrapped up in her own emotions to understand it, but then Rufus added words to his actions.

'No,' he said. 'I claim her.'

There were gasps from the crowd outside in the square, but inside the box there was only a leaden silence.

Was this a reprieve, or something worse?

'The girl has already been claimed,' said a man on the far side of the box, also in the front row.

'I outrank him,' Rufus argued.

'But he claimed her first,' the man insisted.

Rufus smiled, a vulpine grin that filled Julia with apprehension. 'He's already claimed another,' he said, and as he spoke he wrapped his fingers around Julia's arm, pulling her up beside him. 'This is his Attendant,' he said, spinning her sideways as he stroked her hair away from her ear, 'and this is his silver in her flesh.'

Eyes raked over her. If she had felt exposed climbing the temple steps with the crowd at her back then it was nothing compared with the skin-crawling scrutiny of the hundreds of Nobles who were now staring at the stud in her ear.

Damn Lucas. She hadn't understood what it meant at all.

But... he'd *claimed* her?

'Is this true?' a woman in the front row asked Lucas.

He looked for a moment as though he might fight it, but then he simply shrugged. 'It's my silver.'

The Nobles' eyes were on him now, but the open curiosity they had shown when examining Julia had turned from suspicion to disgust as they rested on Lucas. *What had he done?*

'Very well,' said the man in the front row. 'Precedence goes to Rufus's claim. You, boy,' he said to Lucas, 'should remove your Attendant to your own rank.'

Rufus interrupted. 'If you don't mind, Gallus, she's my guest for the ceremony.'

'Well perhaps you should have thought of that before you revealed her base connections for your ploy.'

'But Gallus-'

'She goes to the back, Rufus. You've had your little spectacle and won your prize. Don't deprive him of his, and don't try my patience.'

Rufus sat abruptly, his face flushed with indignation, leaving Julia standing alone.

Gallus smiled at her kindly. 'Go on, my dear,' he said, nodding towards the back of the box where Lucas stood.

His expression was locked down, but there was frustration in his eyes. Whatever was going on here, it was not what he had intended.

Julia could have withered away from mortification. She looked to Claudia for support, but her friend was still wearing her mask of detachment. Julia was on her own.

The Nobles in the rows behind her made sufficient space for her to climb the benches towards Lucas. In fact, they made rather more space than was necessary. In the same way that their proximity to Rufus had caused the crowd to avoid her and Claudia, Lucas had apparently now tainted her in the eyes of the other Nobles.

He offered his hand as she finally scaled to the top of the tiered benches, seating her closely beside him, but he said nothing. She could understand that, when they were surrounded by so many eavesdroppers, but he didn't so much as look at her. No smile, no nod, just a hand offered and reclaimed at the earliest opportunity.

She would have questions for him later, and by the Empress he would answer them.

The last couple of Candidates were presented quickly and uneventfully. All the while, the cramped conditions in the back row pressed the length of Julia's thigh against Lucas's, so warm in the top of the structure that she could feel her sweat soaking into the fabric of her dress between them.

The quality of the silence changed, then. For a few moments Julia could see nothing from her new seat because the canopy above them obscured much of the view, but then she saw the crowd parting, unzipping itself as the Empress walked from the temple to the palace, then sealing up again behind her. She was escorted by two guards, including a familiar face: Lorelei.

They were just for show. Empress Laila could have taken the entire crowd down on her own, Julia had no doubt.

She saw Rufus lean forwards in the front row, resting his elbows on the top of the wooden bar that marked the edge of the box as he looked up towards the temple's pediment. Julia ducked her head to follow his gaze, trying to work out what had caught his attention.

The Empress was directly opposite the temple doors now as she approached the steps, perhaps twenty feet distant from the first one. That was when it happened, the thing that Rufus had been waiting for.

There was a rush of air, the sensation of a tiny whirlwind rolling through the box. It pulled Julia's hair loose and pushed her hood up and into her face, and more than one Noble was struggling with her skirts by the time it settled once more. When it did, the white stone of the pediment was red with lettering, but Julia could only see its edge.

The Nobles in the box around them stiffened.

'Blood,' one murmured, then the others took up the refrain. Soon they were standing, clamouring to push out onto the steps and see for themselves the message that was hidden from all but the front row by the tarpaulin above them. Julia was shoved back into her seat, her legs crushed against the bench until she managed to gather them up to her chest while the Nobles streamed out around her.

All she knew for a few seconds was the heat and the scramble and the frame of Lucas's arms protecting her curled-up form.

They were the last to step out of the box.

She saw the bodies, then. They were sitting propped up against the temple pillars, almost comical in their doll-like positioning. There were six that she could see, discarded there as though they had been plucked from the crowd and drained to write the message on the pediment, all within the few brief seconds it had taken the whirlwind to arise and recede.

It was impossible though. They must have been drained earlier and simply arranged in the moment, to create the tableau. There was art in the presentation, and the impact was in its perfect execution.

Of course the whirlwind hadn't been a wind at all. It had been a Noble moving at the speed only they could track, writing a message for the Empress in the blood of her citizens.

Make no more Silver.

14

They were making more Silver in Charlestown. It was the only way that Cam could explain the Weepers.

He'd seen the proof now: the bodies clustered in the space between the buildings and the trees. The Silver had been laying traps here, dead bait that attracted the Weepers, who then became the bait themselves.

But they weren't just baiting the perimeter. There was an enclosure to the west, a short but carefully respected distance from the settlement, where the Silver of Charlestown took their humans. Cam had watched that afternoon while the head-high fences that marked the edge of the arena had been loaded up with hunks of flesh. When the job was done, two Silver had each led a human through the gates and into the building within. A few minutes later, the doors had crashed open and the transformed creatures were disgorged. They didn't last long before they found the bait, but what had transpired inside the building was obvious.

The Silver of Charlestown clearly weren't very good at making more Silver, but of course that was the point. They were not only trying, but they were failing. They were making Weepers instead.

Laila was going to be livid.

Cam noted the set-up, mentally recording the details that the Empress would want to hear on his return, but right now he had other things to attend to. He had to concentrate on avoiding whatever Carmen had planned and on finding Emmy.

'They'll be keeping her in the cellar with the uncontaminated,' Felix said.

'But she's a Pijavica. She could break out in a second flat.'

'They'll have drained her.'

Cam winced at the thought, but Felix spoke with the kind of authority that suggested he'd seen this sort of thing before in Charlestown. Cam wondered for a moment how many other Silver had been incarcerated there over the years, but he didn't ask. He found that he didn't want to know the answer.

They'd spent the day in their camp, watching the settlement below as they took it in turns to eat and sleep. They couldn't risk a fire, but the day was warm enough that unheated food didn't feel like a hardship. It was approaching dusk now, and they still hadn't made a plan they could agree on.

'We go for the cellar.'

'They know I'm coming, Felix. Not only do they know you, but they'll know me too thanks to bloody Carmen. She'll be on the look out. Hell, they'll all be on the look out for me. One glimpse of an unfamiliar Pijavica and that'll be the end of it, so we can't just walk up to the doors and talk our way inside. We've been over this. They'll be expecting us.'

'They'll be expecting *you*.'

'And they'll all recognise *you*. You lived here for how long, exactly?'

Felix didn't answer, turning his attention deliberately to the jerky he was laboriously chewing.

He remained cagey on the details of his time in Charlestown. Cam should have been suspicious of that, and he was, but not enough to make him challenge Felix's privacy. After all, this was the place he and Otho had in common. Cam could understand why those memories might be painful to share.

'We just can't go for the cellar door,' Cam said. 'It's too dangerous.'

'Then the window.'

'It's too dangerous. Even if we manage to creep up to the back of the building, even if no one sees us, even if they're not guarding it, which they'd be stupid not to, we still probably wouldn't be able to get inside because I don't think I have the strength for a break in right now.'

'Do you have a better plan?'

Cam raked his fingers through his hair and pushed his hands against his skull, as though that might magic an answer out of thin air. There was no way of getting around it: they needed to get a look inside that building, and the window was their best bet. In the absence of a workable plan, the least awful option would have to be good enough.

'Fine,' he said, 'but you're staying here.'

Felix raised a single, bronze-streaked eyebrow.

'You're human,' Cam went on. 'The Pijavica will be able to hear you running around after me, and I can't be worrying about you when I need to concentrate on not getting caught myself.'

'The Pijavica never hear me,' Felix said.

'Still, you'll just be a distraction out there. I need to have my mind on the mission, not split between that and trying to keep an eye on you.'

'You find me distracting, Cameron?'

Cam could cope with the jibe, but not the smile. It twitched at the corner of Felix's mouth, but his lips were pressed too tightly together and there was no mischief in his eyes. The incongruity wiped away the playfulness in the gesture and rendered it bleak, as though flirtation were a thing pursued simply to drive away the pain of his loss. There was no intention in it.

At least, that's what Cam told himself. It was easier that way.

He sighed. 'Fine, we'll both go. After dark, from the west. We can use the enclosure as cover on the approach, but from here to there we'll just have to hope that no one's paying attention.'

'They never were before.'

'They might be today. Bloody Carmen. What I don't understand is why.'

Cam had been agonising over it for most of the day. Why would Carmen betray Cam, betray Laila and the Blue? What could possibly bring her here? Yes, this settlement had uncontaminated humans, and yes, they seemed to be in the process of making more Silver, but that didn't make them any more advanced than the Blue. In fact, it put them several hundred years behind.

The connection had to be personal. There had to be someone in Charlestown who meant something to her. It was the only thing that made sense.

'Maybe she just doesn't like you.'

Cam shook his head. 'Things were never like that between us. I mean, we've never been particularly close, but we've been working together for centuries. If she had something against me,

I'd know about it. No, she just wants me out of the picture. So either Emmy is here and she doesn't want me to find her, or there's something else here they want to hide from me.'

'Does it matter?' Felix seemed supremely unconcerned. His nihilism was understandable; he didn't care about any of this. All he wanted was to make a mess of the people who had killed Otho. He'd zeroed in on the enclosure the moment they'd set camp, and now his eyes kept sliding back in that direction, tracing its vanishing shape in the dusk.

That was going to be a problem.

'This isn't a revenge kick,' Cam said. 'We're scoping the place out, and that's it, alright? We're not going tearing through. At least, not until we've found me some blood.'

'I know that.' But Felix's eyes didn't budge from the enclosure.

'We can't, Felix. We just can't. Not yet.'

The determination still lined his face, tinged with despair. For a moment Cam wondered whether this would be a suicide mission, but then Felix blinked quickly, twice, and the tension in his expression dissipated.

'I know,' he said.

Cam clapped a hand on his shoulder, but he didn't let it linger. 'Come on then,' he said, glancing at the sky, 'it's time.'

The evening was dry and cold, perfect weather to avoid being scented by the Silver guards, although they saw none as they tracked along the tree line to the west.

They crossed the forest paths carefully, listening long and hard before stepping out from their cover, but they saw no more travellers. It seemed like they were the only ones out that night, which worried Cam. Charlestown had cleared the way for them, leading them into the settlement. They might as well have rolled out a bloody red carpet for all the subtlety with which they were communicating *we know you're coming.*

He considered abandoning their mission and turning back to camp, but without more blood, he'd never be stronger than he was right now. They wouldn't get a better chance.

When they reached the part of the forest closest to the enclosure, Felix held up his hand in a fist. They stopped.

The gesture was strangely anachronistic; Cam remembered it, mostly from watching spy films back when television still existed, but he hadn't seen it for centuries. Charlestown must have been teaching its citizens some worrying things for Felix to be familiar enough with it not only to use it, but to assume that Cam would know it too.

'Those are new,' Felix whispered, pointing towards the western edge of the settlement. There were a few pools of light there spilling down from lanterns suspended along the outside of the ramshackle buildings, beyond the enclosure. After only four such illuminated spots, the outskirts of Charlestown were once again bathed in darkness, but Cam could see that it wasn't for lack of equipment. The lanterns were spaced at regular intervals all around the perimeter, and although the curve of the buildings made it difficult to be certain, a faint glow at the eastern edge of the settlement suggested that the lanterns were lit on the other side too. The lanterns in the middle of the south perimeter had been deliberately extinguished.

'They're trying to push us to the centre,' Cam whispered back. 'They want us to come in through that dark space.'

'Do we have a choice?'

Before he could think too hard about it, Cam struck out towards the enclosure, keeping it between him and the settlement. It was unlit, but the haze of the lanterns picked out its edges from the darkness.

It was larger than it had seemed from a distance, and the smell of blood was strong. It was contaminated of course, but that didn't stop Cam's body from contracting with need. It felt as though his veins were squeezing shut, pushing heat into his cheeks as the deficiency raged through his muscles.

'Cameron?' Felix was beside him, so close that he felt the faint rasp as their clothing touched. Cam could almost believe that he smelled the warm blood beneath Felix's skin.

'I'm fine,' he whispered, clamping down on the desire as he curled it into a manageable ball in his stomach. It would hold there for a while, but he could already feel it starting to unravel. He'd pushed himself too hard these past few weeks.

They crept along the fence line, cloaks catching on the rough new wood, until they reached the far end. They'd have to make a break for the settlement from here, a hundred yards of rubble-strewn grass from the fence to the first of the buildings.

A movement caught his attention then in the darkest section of the perimeter, slow and deliberate, too measured to have been caused by the wind, and too assured to be an animal.

They were waiting for him.

'We go to the light,' he whispered. If he could muster up a tiny bit of strength, just enough to let him speed through the illumination with Felix, then they might get by unseen. With all of the guards looking outwards, it could give them the time they needed.

Felix just nodded. The stiffness was back in his jaw. He was spoiling for a fight, but if it came to that then neither of them would make it out alive. Maybe this would be a suicide mission after all.

'Stay close,' Cam murmured, and then he moved.

They crouched low, stepping wide and slow to negotiate the grass-covered hummocks of buried ruins that stretched between the enclosure and the city. Cam could only hope that the guards were human. Even if they were Silver, Cam was avoiding the path, so in the dark night his and Felix's figures blended in with the obstacles amongst which they clambered.

He didn't tell Felix what he was planning.

When they reached the outer corona of the nearest lantern, Cam caught Felix's hand to keep him in the darkness. He whispered, 'Stay quiet,' and then they were in motion, Cam's arms scooping under Felix's shoulders and legs as he rushed them through the light in a blur of bleached colours until they stood side by side in an alley that was only just wide enough to accommodate them.

'Fuck,' Felix breathed as he bent over with his hands braced on his thighs. The expletive was strange on his lips.

But Cam was in worse shape. As soon as they stopped, he fell back against the crumbling brickwork and slid slowly to the ground. It had been too much energy for him to expend, and he could almost feel his body cannibalising itself to make up the deficit. It was acid burning in his muscles.

'That was a stupid risk,' Felix said, looking sideways at him.

When Cam could gather the strength to speak, the words came out in a gasping wheeze. 'Stupider... to just... walk under... the lantern.'

It was coal dark in the alley, the light creeping into it from either end so faint as to be practically useless, but Cam could feel and smell that the floor was just sandy dirt, piled up higher towards its sides in soggy slopes of mud. Everything smelled of salt, fish and rotting weed. It was soaking through his trousers.

He really should get up. If they were going to get out of here alive, he needed to get up.

But the only thing he could feel was the gritty cold of the water sinking into the cloth beneath him. His eyes had closed at some point, though he hadn't noticed it happening. The unconsciousness that pulled him down was like drunkenness in the way it spun him out, twisting through him until it felt as though his limbs were all turning in different directions, drifting away from him as his blood ate the strength from his muscles.

He almost vomited when Felix shook him awake.

'Cameron!' His voice was hushed but urgent.

'M'okay,' he mumbled back.

Then Felix was in the dirt next to him, pulling Cam into his arms. 'Told you it was stupid,' he said. 'Do you think you can walk?'

He could, after a few false starts. He was like a foal finding its legs for the first time, deprived of the superhuman balance that his Silver abilities normally afforded him. They were all compromised now, every part of his body was. He couldn't see as well, or hear as well, or smell as well. Now that the blood craving was so deeply ingrained in him, the latter was probably a blessing.

He didn't have long left.

'This way.'

They weren't far from the cellar, but the layout of the streets made navigating practically impossible. The alley they'd stopped in wasn't an anomaly; half of the settlement's streets were similarly narrow and twisting, and completely deserted. The ruins of old Dresden had been used as a starting point in places, mud brick and wood piled on top of ancient masonry, but the density of the buildings made it impossible to pick out landmarks, if any of them had been preserved.

Without Felix, Cam might never have found his way through, but the further they walked, the more worried he looked.

'Where is everyone?' Cam said.

'I don't know.'

It didn't make any sense. It was dark, but at this time of year darkness came early. People should still be out and about, or at least moving around in their houses, but Cam could hear nothing except the gentle squelch of their footsteps in the mud.

'It might be a cull,' Felix said.

'A *what*?'

'The caravan brought new contams. Charlestown can't sustain them, not with the number of noncontams in the carts.'

Being back in Charlestown was bringing out a different side of Felix. His stride was different, more confident even as they crept their way through the streets, and the way he spoke...

Contams, noncontams, the shorthand unfamiliar to Cam but its origin obvious: these must be the names the Charlestown Silver gave to their humans. There was too much disdain in them for the words to be names the humans had given to themselves, but Felix spoke without rancour or sardonicism, as though contams and noncontams weren't both his kin. As though he wasn't a contam himself.

'You've seen this before,' Cam said.

'Yes.'

'So, what, they evict the contaminated humans to make room for the uncontaminated?' Even as Cam spoke, he knew his interpretation was optimistic. If the Silver of Charlestown were as protective of their little kingdom as they appeared to be, then they wouldn't want to let people loose after they'd been part of it. They would be a liability.

'They take them to the beach,' Felix said.

'And they don't come back, I guess.'

'They all go. Most come back.'

'But some don't.'

A beat of silence. 'No.'

Cam stopped, leaning up against a wall to catch his breath. He was starting to wonder if he'd make it back to the forest, but he pushed the thought away. It wouldn't help him.

'Then what about you?' he asked. 'If they kill the contams rather than let them leave, then how are you still alive? How did you get out?'

Felix leaned up against the wall opposite. Just as he opened his mouth to reply, there was a faint sound from the wider street that transected the alley they stood in, a scuffing noise coming from perhaps twenty feet away.

Felix's eyes went wide in the scant moonlight. They both froze.

Cam had expected a patrol, or maybe a solitary person walking through the settlement, but he hadn't expected the figure that shuffled into view in the narrow mouth of the alley, just for a second, before it passed them by as it continued its journey down the street.

A Weeper. Here, in the heart of Charlestown.

Cam scrutinised Felix's reaction, but it betrayed nothing except shock. His eyes were still intent on the end of the alley, either watching for more Weepers or still unable to believe the presence of the first.

It explained why the streets were empty, at least. The question now was whether it had been deliberate or accidental.

'Come on,' Cam whispered when a couple of minutes had passed in silence. 'We need to find the cellar.'

The back window to the cellar was in the worst location possible: the dead end at the terminus of three passageways that followed on one from the other at right angles, with no tributaries. The way was so narrow that at times Cam had to turn sideways to fit through.

If someone found them here, they'd be trapped, and with Cam so weak, they'd be dead. One Silver, or a few Weepers, and it would all be over.

This dank cul-de-sac would make a good killing floor. It already smelled like death.

The window was flush with the ground, but someone had nailed a plank across the bottom half, presumably to stop the alley floor's slop from draining through when it rained. There was still a foot of the glassless window open to the air, and the bars across it were ornamental wood, not metal. A human could have broken them, and he did now, Felix, on his hands and knees at the end of the alley.

'It's clear,' he whispered over his shoulder.

Cam was supposed to be watching the exit, keeping his senses alert for any incursions, but he kept losing concentration. His eyes drifted to where Felix was crouched in front of the window, his neck craning out to give him a view inside the building. It must have been Cam's imagination, but for a second he thought he could see Felix's pulse throbbing beneath his skin.

'Take a look,' Felix said, beckoning Cam over.

They switched places, which meant sliding past each other sideways in the confines of the passageway. It wasn't an easy fit;

the manoeuvre pressed their chests against each other, flattening their backs into the muddy bricks. Cam had a second to be grateful for his enfeeblement, because otherwise he wasn't sure what he might have done with that proximity. The feeling disappeared in the next moment as Felix's body released his from the wall, and he had to put a hand against the opposite side of the alley to stop himself from toppling headfirst into it.

'Better hope there's some blood in there,' Cam muttered to himself.

Miraculously, there was. It was bottled and racked against the wall in which the window was set. Most of the closest alcoves were empty, but there was one bottle on the very top, its contents glimmering like a glutinous jewel. There wasn't enough light for Cam to discern its colour, but he imagined it nonetheless, the ruby red rolling around the inside of the glass.

He could reach it.

But despite his desperation, he wasn't stupid enough to just stick his arm in and grab it. Instead, he lay on his stomach in the dirt, prying away the plank that barred the bottom part of the window. It let him see the whole of the room beyond, including a hatch in the floor.

That was where they would be. If Emmy was here, she'd be beneath that hatch.

There was no way Cam could fit through the window though. It was about a foot and a half tall, but less that a foot wide. However he manipulated his shoulders, they weren't going to fit through that hole. They would have to come back and go in through the door. It was the only way.

Cam could see the door from here, but there were no guards in view. That alone was enough to make him suspicious, so suspicious that he spent a moment checking the view through the door to reassure himself that this was indeed the building he remembered from his ancient visit and their recent scouting, but there was no mistaking it. Although he hadn't noticed the hatch the last time he had seen the room, its vaulted roof was the same, crumbling brick arches providing shelved alcoves around its space in an irregular cross shape.

Perhaps it had been a church, once. Perhaps the space beneath was comprised of catacombs. Either way, whatever was under the hatch, twice underground, would be secure. It was the perfect location for the holding cells.

But all he could do from here was take the nearest bottle of blood, so that's what he did.

He was about to move away from the window when he was distracted by a creaking sound from within. Turning back, he saw a tiny hand reach out into the darkness, followed by a tiny arm, and the rest of a tiny person. When the hatch slammed closed, a little boy was standing in the room beneath him. He didn't look more than five years old, but then it was difficult to tell these days. So many children were malnourished, particularly the uncontaminated.

The boy stared up at him wide-eyed, apparently unafraid despite the darkness.

'Are you Cam'ron?' he said.

Cam turned and looked over his shoulder at Felix. He was still watching the alley and didn't seem to have heard.

'Yes,' Cam whispered back. 'Who are you?'

'My mum said to tell you she's not here, and not to drink that blood.' He pointed at the bottle still clasped in Cam's hand.

'Who's not here?'

'The sleepy lady.'

'And who's the sleepy lady?'

The child shrugged, a gesture so exaggerated that his whole body seemed to sigh when he released it.

'Cameron,' Felix hissed from the other end of the alley, 'someone's coming.'

'Here y'go,' the little boy said, dragging a bottle of blood from one of the far racks. He was so small that the weight unbalanced him, making his steps skew wildly as he tottered back towards the window. He lifted it above his head, his face fierce with concentration, until Cam could pluck it from his outstretched hands.

'Thank you.'

The boy's expression became stern. 'I have to go now,' he said, and then he was running up the unguarded stairs and out into the night.

'Cameron!' Felix's whisper was more urgent now, and despite his deficient state Cam could hear them too.

He looked at the two bottles of blood in his hands: one the bottle the boy had handed him, and the other the one that had been on the top rack, suspiciously within reach, now that he thought about it. The one the boy had warned him not to drink.

Shit.

He couldn't remember which was which.

He stared at them for a moment in mute horror, dark spots crowding his vision, then pulled the corks from them both.

'Cameron, what are you doing?'

'Just give me a minute,' he said, sniffing at the bottles.

'We don't have a minute.'

Yes, they were different. One smelled a little saltier than the other, a little more appetising. Without thinking too hard about it, he downed the whole bottle and waited.

The pain hit quickly. It raged through his body, screaming along the drained veins as it plumped them out and sent its tendrils out into his muscles, bunching them tight. When they released, the ache came with them, and the need.

It was the right bottle, but it hadn't been enough. He wanted more. He *needed* more.

It took only seconds to punch away the wall so the window was big enough to accommodate him, his muscles finally starting to reclaim their strength, but in those seconds their pursuers had closed on them.

'Felix!' Cam cried, waving him towards the enlarged window.

Felix ran down the alley, dropping into a slide as he neared the gap so his speed and the muddy ground conspired to drop him neatly through the window, feet-first.

If their pursuers had been rushing, they would have arrived minutes ago, but they were either reluctant or cocky, and by the time the four Silver rounded the corner Cam was ready for them. He sprayed the other bottle of blood, the contaminated blood, into their surprised faces and watched the silver strip from their eyes as the cure found purchase in the membranes of their mouths, eyes and nostrils.

They spent the next few seconds in shock, when they should have been looking at Cam. They hadn't been trained as Invicti. He had them all knocked out and laid in a neat line along the passageway before Felix's feet hit the cellar floor.

Cam followed him.

Always prepared, Felix had brought an empty saddlebag with him and started to fill it with bottles while Cam slugged back five from the rack in quick succession.

'What next?' Felix asked.

But Cam already had his hand on the ring that would pull up the floor hatch. The wooden cover was heavy, so heavy that Cam was surprised the little boy had managed it on his own, but it was nothing to him now that he had his power back.

There were concrete steps leading down, turning sharply right as they met the foundations of the building, faintly illuminated by light that seeped up from somewhere in the basement.

'Are you coming?' he said to Felix.

'You go,' he said, his eyes flicking over to the door that led to the outside world. 'I'll keep watch.'

Cam propped the hatch open and stepped down carefully, stopping regularly to listen. There was probably no way out of the basement except this set of stairs, and he didn't want to get stuck down there like they had nearly been in the alley.

The musty scent of the cellar was stronger here, and as he descended it started to take on a sour odour, heavy and unpleasant. When the stairs turned, Cam could see that the room they opened onto was indeed a dead end, but there was nothing here to threaten him. Instead, the squat, long walls were lined with metal-barred cells filled with people. Humans, hundreds of them, mired here together, unwashed and broken.

'Cameron?' a voice said, female, from one of the middle cells.

She was petite, dark-skinned and elven-eyed. He didn't recognise her, but then it would be difficult to recognise anyone in these circumstances.

'Chloe,' she said.

His expression must have betrayed his horror at the conditions of their captivity, because as she spoke she pointed to herself as though he might be unable to process the information without her gesture. She wasn't far wrong.

'Chloe?'

The people around her stirred with interest, but they remained silent. The attention they gave to Cam suggested that this was what passed for entertainment around here, but their posture made it clear that the Silver were not trusted. He was one of them, and they feared him, some with open hostility, but others with diverted gazes. None of them saw him as a saviour, except Chloe.

'From London,' she said. 'Remember? With Benedict and, erm,

that whole thing.'

'The thing where you betrayed Emmy?'

She looked away. 'Yeah. That thing. I'm trying to make up for that thing.'

His eyes raked over her, but he could see no trace of silver in her eyes. 'You're human now?'

'Have been for a while.'

'So that was your little boy?' He could see the resemblance now. They had the same eyes, and their skin colour was similar, although the boy had been a little darker. But then Chloe was so covered with dirt that it was difficult to remember what she had looked like without it.

Except on her arms. When he looked closer, Cam could see that her skin was cleaned to a shine in circles along her veins, where darker marks spotted and spread into her flesh.

'Did he get out alright?' she asked.

'Ran out the door before it all kicked off. I thought it was just the uncontaminated down here?' If Chloe was human now then her own blood would be contaminated.

'All except us,' she said, gesturing around at the people in her cell, mostly women. 'We all used to be Silver. They like to test us, you know.'

'And Emmy?'

'Charles took her away. I can show you which direction, if you'll get me out of here.'

'I was going to do that anyway,' he said, horrified at the thought of walking away from this foetid place without freeing them all. 'You'll have to make sure everyone's careful, though. I saw a Weeper out in the street, and for the people who are uncontaminated...'

Chloe grinned, an evil expression on a pixie-sweet face. 'I can deal with that.'

They drank from her.

It took an hour or so to empty the basement, each uncontaminated human pressing their lips against an open wound on Chloe's arm in a strange, vampiric reversal before they ran up the stairs and out. A drop each was enough, the tiniest taste of blood, but Cam was still surprised that they didn't baulk at the process.

They were complacent enough about it to impress upon him how different things were here from in the Blue. Here, the uncontaminated knew their value, and so they were locked away to prevent them from contaminating themselves into freedom. In the Blue, the Silver kept them subjugated by ignorance.

The more Cam thought about it, the more he failed to see any moral difference between the two.

He intended to do something about that. He needed to find Emmy, and get her back where she belonged, with Sol.

He'd sort all of this out.

Despite the grim circumstances, Cam was feeling optimistic. He hadn't found Emmy, but at least he knew where to look next. Chloe would show him the way, and then they'd slip away tonight, he and Felix, and they'd find her together.

But when he finally got to the top of the stairs, Chloe by his side, the bag of blood had been discarded by the hatch, a single bottle rolling free.

Felix was gone.

15

It had only taken seconds for the guards to erase the display at the temple, washing out the bloody words and tidying the bodies away to some unmarked mass grave in the Red, but by then the damage had already been done.

The words might have gone, but they had been seen, and Julia was no longer the only human who felt that the Blue might not be such a safe place after all. People were congregating now, in each others' rooms, while they worked, and in Livia's kitchen, as though they were any safer together than they were apart.

'Ten dead, they're saying.'

'Who's saying?'

'Ten? I only saw four.'

'It was ten. I had it from the priestess.' This was one of the older Attendants, a girl whom Julia rarely saw in the kitchen these days. She'd come back to bring gossip and, perhaps, because this was the place where she had been raised. A lot of the girls in the Blue had been brought up by Livia, and now that the world felt dangerous they were all coming home to hide. There was barely any room for Claudia and Julia in the cellars now, and they actually lived there.

'How long is this going to go on?' Claudia murmured to Julia.

'Maybe forever. It'll get worse before it gets better.'

Claudia nodded at that. They could all feel it, the pressure bottled up in the city like a jar of meat that no one had realised was rotten until it smashed itself open in a miasmic detonation.

The incident at the Nomination had only increased everyone's antipathy towards Julia. If she had been *persona non grata* before, then now she was a true pariah. No one spoke to her except Claudia and Livia, although they all spoke about her. Sometimes without bothering to make sure that she was out of earshot first.

A group of girls was eyeing her from across the room while she and Claudia sat on the hearth as they made some herbal tea. They didn't hide their stares, however much Julia glared back, but at least she couldn't hear their words.

'They're just jealous,' Claudia said, noticing Julia's distraction.

'No, Claud, I really don't think they are.'

'Well, they should be. A Noble's claimed you.'

Whatever that means.

'It's not as if he meant to do it,' Julia said, 'and because of that Marcella's stuck with Rufus. I don't think I'd be jealous either, in their position. I think I'd probably hate me too.'

There'd been so much blood. Even after they'd washed it off the pediment, the new sponsors still had to bleed their Candidates, to purify the threshold. Marcella and the other three had stood in front of the Empress as their sponsors cut their skin, three releasing just a little, the other far too much. Marcella had swayed on her way down the steps on Rufus's arm, her face a perfect mask of control like the one that Claudia showed to the Nobles, but her dark skin had been shining with pebbles of sweat.

Julia had waited no longer than was absolutely necessary before collecting Claudia and leaving Lucas behind in the box. They'd run home, but not fast enough to beat the others.

'They don't know what happened in the box,' Claudia said. 'They couldn't have heard it, and I didn't tell them.'

'The closest Candidates heard it. They've probably told the whole temple by now.'

'Well, they still don't know what it means.'

'*I* don't know what it means, Claud.'

And she hadn't wanted to ask. She'd needed to get away from Lucas, as though remaining in his company made her an accomplice to the embarrassment of the Nomination. It was partly that, at least. But it was also that she couldn't face his explanation, because she knew he hadn't meant the earring to symbolise what Rufus chose to make it.

It had been a gift for a gift, that's all. It didn't make her his.

But Rufus had a plan, and apparently they'd played right into it.

'Are you seeing Rufus tonight?' Julia asked Claudia.

'I hope not.'

'I hope so,' Julia countered. 'I'm worried about Marcella being alone with him.'

Claudia dropped her eyes. 'He really isn't all that bad, Jules.'

'How can you say that?'

'Look, he said it himself this morning at the ceremony: He's not been well, and he's been more demanding than normal. He's not a complete monster.'

'You saw what he did to Marcella with the threshold cutting.'

Claudia shrugged. 'Mistakes happen. She was fine.'

'When she left.'

'Jules, she was fine. He'll look after her. Didn't you see the way he looked at her?'

Julia snorted. 'Like he was hungry.'

'Like he was *smitten*. She's the goddess. Of course he'll look after her.'

'I hope you're right.'

But Julia couldn't shake the suspicion. It was all too convenient, that he would choose to sponsor the Candidate whom Lucas had intended to support. Maybe Rufus had always planned to oust him by rank alone, but when he'd seen the stud in Julia's ear...

Well, it was the perfect excuse to take Marcella from Lucas.

Perhaps Rufus really had just fallen for her. He'd certainly paid attention when she'd turned up.

Maybe he'd just wanted to irritate Lucas.

But Julia knew that if she accepted either of those explanations she would just be avoiding the possibility that worried her most: maybe it was all tied in to that moment before the whirlwind, those few seconds in which Rufus had looked for the writing on the pediment before it appeared.

So many deaths and so much blood, and in the middle of it all: Rufus.

Lucas walked into the kitchen that evening.

Julia had half expected to hear from him, but she hadn't let herself hope, precisely because it was a hope that she wanted to nurture. She had enough self-awareness to know that, and to hate herself for it.

She'd expected a messenger though, or perhaps simply a

message. She hadn't expected him to come in person, and in the end she wished he hadn't.

He came through the courtyard door as though he had every right to be there, bypassing the main entrance at the front of the building, where the bell pull would have rung to summon Livia.

With so many of them packed in the kitchen, it took a few seconds for his presence to register. When it did, the silence came fast and thick.

'I'm looking for Julia,' he said.

Livia bustled forwards like a mother hen, moving the girls out of the way with a proprietary touch on the arm, on the shoulder, on the waist, because these were *her* girls.

'Of course you are,' she said. 'Can I get you some tea?'

'No, thank you.' Lucas seemed surprised by the offer, but his expression was no less serious. 'I'm just looking for Julia.'

'I'm here,' Julia said, standing from the place she had reclaimed on the hearth.

'We'll give you some privacy,' said Livia, looking pointedly at the girls around her. They began trooping out into the corridor, but Julia couldn't imagine where they would all go. They'd never fit in the cellar, and Livia didn't usually invite the girls up to her own rooms.

'You didn't come,' Lucas said once they were alone, somewhere between angry and offended. He hadn't moved from his place by the door, and Julia made no attempt to close the gap.

'You were expecting me?' she said.

It was clear from his expression that her words did nothing to quell his anger.

'I mean,' Julia went on, 'that I thought you would send for me if you wanted me. That's what we agreed this morning.'

'Yes,' he conceded, 'but that was before.'

Again Julia had the impression that she was missing something important. He was looking at her as though she had insulted him, and as though he thought it had been intentional.

'Maybe you should just tell me what's going on,' she said, taking a single, small step closer. 'If I've done something wrong, then I don't understand what it is. If I'm supposed to know, then I'm sorry, but I don't, so maybe you could just tell me.'

'You don't understand,' he said to himself, as if he were considering the possibility for the first time.

'That's right.'

He looked at her for a moment, scanning her face as though it would let him read her thoughts, then he opened the door to the courtyard and stood to one side of it, holding it open for her.

'Come on then,' he said.

'Where?'

'My place. I'll explain, I promise.'

She hesitated, but in the end her curiosity won out.

The night felt uncomfortable around them as they walked. The streets were empty, which wasn't unusual for the evening of the Nomination, when the Nobles celebrated the potential of the next crop of Candidates, but the city was also silent. The walls should have been reverberating with ribald laughter, bouncing out of windows and along alleys, but instead all Julia could hear were the distant howls of animals in the Red.

'May I ask a question?' Julia said.

Lucas turned to her. As they walked past lamplit windows, the glow from within caught the silver in his eyes, so they seemed to flash with animation.

'Go on,' he said.

'You and Rufus. What happened?'

Lucas said, 'We grew up together,' as though that alone explained the animosity between them.

'And?'

'He's the Empress's son.' This was news to Julia. 'He gets what he wants because of who he is, and I don't, for the same reason.'

'And who are you?' It was an impertinent question, and she didn't really expect him to respond to it.

'I'm trying to work that out,' he said.

They crossed the square in silence, Lucas hurrying her up the staircase and into his room, slamming the door closed behind them as though the darkness were chasing them in.

He leaned back against the doorframe, a smudgy silhouette in the unlit room.

'Is everything alright?' Julia asked.

'No, not really,' he said, pushing away from the door. 'Everything's starting to fall apart. Can't you tell?'

'I heard something,' Julia confessed.

He looked from side to side, misunderstanding her words, apparently on the alert for intruders.

'No,' she went on, 'I mean I heard something the other day, downstairs, while I was working outside Rufus's window.'

There might have been a significant look on Lucas's face in the pause that followed, but it was practically impossible for Julia to tell because he was standing in shadow.

'Sit,' he said, ushering her onto the bed. She'd never sat there before, but it didn't look slept in. It didn't feel like an intrusion or a threat, so she did as she was told.

'Now tell me,' he said.

'Lorelei was there,' she said, hesitantly. 'They were talking about something that was going to happen after the Nomination. They mentioned Carmen, and how she was loyal, and then I saw Lorelei again this morning, talking to some men outside the temple. She said it wasn't time yet. And she swore a lot.'

'You think they're responsible for this morning?'

Julia thought back through what she could remember of her eavesdropping, but she couldn't make it add up. 'I don't know,' she said, 'but I do know that Rufus was expecting it. I saw him look up at the temple a moment before it happened, like he was waiting for it to happen.'

Lucas put his hands on his hips, looking down at the floor with a sigh that sounded like irritation.

'I didn't think they were going to make a move so soon,' he said.

'You know about this?'

'No details, but I know they want Laila gone.'

'His own mother?'

Lucas laughed bitterly. 'Noble families are a bit different from human ones. I think Rufus's main ambition in life is to supplant the Empress. He wants it so much that he even tried to recruit me to the cause, despite how much he hates me.'

Julia remembered the conversation she had overheard between Rufus and Lorelei, when they were talking about Carmen: *She's loyal. She won't come over.*

'And you refused,' Julia said.

'That's not what I want. If I'm honest, I couldn't care less about the politics of this place. I don't really care who's in charge, because I'm not planning on hanging around.'

'Oh?'

He turned to look at her, his face picked out in grayscale by the moonlight from the open ceiling hatch. 'As soon as I can hide this stupid silver,' he said, pointing to his eyes, 'then I'm gone. There's nothing to keep me here.'

'Oh.'

That shouldn't have hurt. It was really perfectly reasonable. After all, wasn't it exactly what she was planning to do herself? If Julia had been a Noble, if she'd had the strength to survive the Red, then she would have left years ago.

'Shall we go upstairs?' he said. 'I've got the fire lit, and if you're hungry-'

'I've eaten, thank you.'

'Well, for the heat then.'

Part of Julia wanted to stay here in the dark with him, close to the place where something like a promise had passed between them in the exchange of gifts. But that was just silliness. She pushed it away.

So up they went. He found her a blanket and they abandoned the benches, sitting on the ground close to the fire with their backs to the wooden slats that formed the base of the seats.

He was close.

'We should talk about it,' he said after they'd watched the fire for a few minutes.

'Talk about what?' she said, although she suspected she knew what he meant.

Lifting his hand to her face, he brushed her hair away behind her ear and trailed his fingertips along its edge until he reached the silver stud.

'This,' he said. 'There are things I should have told you, I suppose, but I didn't expect it to come up. I didn't expect Rufus to take you to the Nomination, or for him to see it. I didn't expect anyone to see it. I thought I'd be sitting here with Marcella now, and instead she's downstairs with him.'

Julia ducked her head, drawing away from Lucas's touch so her hair fell back over the offending piece of jewellery.

'I offered it back to you,' she said. 'You should have taken it.'

'It was a gift, Julia.'

'One that I don't understand, and that you didn't want anyone to know about.'

He opened his mouth then shut it again, grasping for the right words. 'I'm not unhappy,' he said eventually, but then his expression soured. 'Except that you smell like him. That, I'm not thrilled about.'

'I don't understand.'

'You smell like Rufus.'

'No, I understand that.' She resisted the urge to roll her eyes. 'But I don't understand what you mean. You're not unhappy? What, that I'm here instead of Marcella, about the scene Rufus made earlier?'

'I'm not unhappy about any of it, really. I would have preferred that Rufus hadn't made a scene. I'm used to him trying to humiliate me, but I didn't want you dragged into it.'

He stopped, looking away for a moment.

'I would have done it, Julia, don't get me wrong. I would have sponsored Marcella, because she asked me to, and because I think you wanted me to as well, but I'm not upset that things turned out this way. I'm just sorry that you got stuck in the middle of it.'

She didn't know what to say. So many questions were still unanswered.

I'm not unhappy.

How was she supposed to feel about that? He still wasn't actually *happy*, but then happiness wasn't something to which anyone she knew had ever aspired. Survival, yes. Happiness was something the Nobles pursued, something out of her reach.

'Lucas…'

The corners of his eyes twitched. 'You said my name.'

'Well, yes.' Julia was caught off balance by the softening of his eyes, his mouth. Tension was unravelling from his expression.

'That's the first time you've called me by my name,' he said.

She looked away, but he gently pulled her chin around so she faced him again. 'I suppose it is,' she conceded.

There was a quiet second while his eyes darkened. 'Do it again.'

'Lucas?'

He reached for her once more, his fingertips brushing along her cheek to cup her jaw as he leaned in. 'Julia,' he whispered.

'Lucas.' The word was a breath, a prayer and an invitation, and it drew his lips to hers.

It was nothing like the kisses they had shared on that night when he had first taken her blood. This time it was magnetic, neither leading the other, but each of them pulled closer by a force simpler and yet more complex than that initial chemistry. It was irresistible, but entirely in Julia's control. She was strong in its power, not helpless as she had always felt in the drag of her blood to his mouth.

This she chose.

She chose to run her hands through his hair and feel its silken blackness. She chose to push closer, crawling to her knees as he did the same, pressing their bodies against one another in a rush of warm desire.

She chose this kiss.

When their lips broke apart, Lucas held her face in his hands. Their foreheads bumped against each other and he smiled, then laughed softly while Julia mirrored every emotion.

'This is what it means,' he said, his fingers finding the stud in her ear.

'That you claim me?' she said, surprised by the teasing note in her own voice.

'No,' he said. 'That you're the one I would choose.'

Julia didn't go back to the kitchen that night. Instead, she lay with Lucas side by side next to the fire, arms entwined, fingers entwined, faces close enough to kiss, wrapped in blankets as they stared up at the stars together.

'The world feels bigger here,' Julia whispered. 'Normally the city feels so small. Too small.'

He turned his head to look at her. 'You think about leaving?'

'I did, but with Claudia... You know, it's not safe for us. If it were just me I might take the risk, even though I'd likely die.'

'I know how that feels,' he said, turning his head to look at her. 'I'd take you with me if I could.'

'If it were safe, you mean?'

'If it were.'

Julia rolled over to face him. 'Did you ever wonder, though, if it might be? After all, the fact that it's dangerous is the only thing that keeps us humans here.'

'And the city needs its humans.'

'Exactly.'

The silence that followed was thoughtful and comfortable, but heavy with the possibility that hung between their words.

What if...

What if there was another life out there, in the Red? What if there was some way for humans to survive out there, a way that no one had tried, or a way that the Nobles knew and kept secret from them? What if they could find a way?

But it was fairytales again, just more fairytales.

In that respect, the evening felt no different from any other they had spent together, quietly existing in restful company, surrounded by fantasies, but at the same time it was like no other night of Julia's life. She'd never felt this elation, so potent that it was almost as though she could finally breathe for the first time.

But it was tainted by the knowledge that it couldn't last.

'So you're leaving,' she said.

'It could be decades yet. There's no way out of here for me until I can hide the silver. That's the rule.'

'And after that?'

'I try to join the guard, I guess. See if they'll take me. They're the only ones who go outside the boundary.'

Julia rolled onto her back again and let her head fall to the side, pillowed on the mousy tangle of her hair. All she could see now was the silver, glinting in the whites of his eyes, the only thing that was keeping him here with her.

Decades. So there might be time.

'I don't want to leave you behind,' he said.

'But you will.'

He didn't need to answer. She could see the determination in his eyes, and she couldn't blame him for it. She knew that in his position she would do the same. She'd want to see it for herself, even more so if it meant finding a way for her and Claudia to be free.

'I've always wondered whether it's what my parents did,' she said.

'What, watched the stars together?'

'No.' She shook her head, the gesture awkward with her cheek pressed against the ground. 'If they left me behind because they intended to come back for me. Claud thinks... Well, every time I want her to be a dreamer like she usually is, she comes out with an annoyingly sensible opinion instead.'

'She doesn't think they're coming back?'

'I don't either, not anymore. But I wonder if they meant to and just, I don't know, got lost on the way. I'd rather believe that than, you know, the alternative.'

Dead three steps into the Red, bodies cleared away, burned.

He was quiet for a long time. She expected him to change the subject when he spoke again, but apparently he'd just been lost in thought.

'Just because one fairytale is real,' he said, reaching out to stroke her cheek, 'it doesn't mean they all are.'

She smiled, but ruefully. 'I want to believe this,' she said, taking his hand in her own. 'I want to believe that this is real, but that doesn't make it true.'

'You need me to prove it to you?'

She shook her head, trying to dig down to the root of the unease that was shifting in her chest. 'I think I'd rather you didn't,' she whispered.

'You don't trust me,' he said, his expression concealing his hurt, almost.

'You're a Noble.'

'I'm your Noble.'

'No,' she said, 'you're not.' She didn't want to break the moment, to shatter the illusion of the paradise around them, but there was no way to shut off the speeding anxiety that chased logic into her heart.

This wasn't a fairytale. She wasn't a princess, Lucas wasn't a prince, and fairytales were stupid anyway. They only existed to mollify people, and to make them wish for the unattainable.

'You're not my Noble,' she said. 'I'm your human.'

'Can't both be true?' He looked genuinely hopeful.

Her laugh was quiet, and too old for her years.

'Alright,' he said. 'Maybe not yet, but soon. We could change things in the Blue.'

'Now you sound like Rufus.'

'We want different changes.'

'Really?' Julia said, propping herself up on her elbow. 'Because it sounds to me like you both just want to be in charge. That might change things for you, but it won't make the slightest bit of difference to me or mine. I'll still be working for you, giving you my blood, trapped here in this city.'

'And if I find a way to get you out of here?'

It was tempting. She imagined another rooftop, somewhere far away in the trees of the Red, sun-dappled and truly quiet, where they could lie like this together. An oasis in a sea of contamination.

But it wouldn't work.

Where would Claud be, and Livia, and all the other girls from the kitchen? They might shun her, but that didn't mean she wanted them left behind.

And if she could get them all out then maybe, just maybe, they might stop hating her.

'It can't just be me,' she said, settling back down into the blankets. 'That would make me no better than my parents. I don't want to be someone who would just abandon everyone I love.'

There was a long pause. 'I don't know if I can do that,' he said. 'If it's possible at all, I don't know…'

'Then there's no point talking about it. I won't worry about the impossible,' she said, but that was a lie. She had been worrying about it all her life: whether she could find somewhere to live in the Red, whether she could escape this place, whether her parents might still be alive.

But then the inevitable corollary: if they were still alive, then they hadn't cared enough to come for her. She wouldn't cry about that, not here.

Perhaps Claud was right: it was better to think they were dead.

'My parents are gone too,' Lucas said.

'They left you?'

'Apparently.'

Julia could hear in his voice the bitterness that she felt when she spoke of her own parents, and it made her suspicious. It seemed like a strange coincidence that they would both have been abandoned, particularly when orphans were so rare amongst the Nobles.

Noble babies were special. They weren't ever unwanted or discarded, not like humans. They were to be cherished, not used up and thrown away.

Her face must have betrayed her thoughts, because he exhaled heavily and looked back up at the stars, saying, 'No one ever believes me.'

'Are you surprised? It's sort of far-fetched.'

'It's what Baba told me.' His tone was almost surly now. 'It's all I know.'

'Alright,' she said, 'alright. I'm sorry. It's just… Everyone knows what happened with my parents. I've never heard of an orphan Noble, that's all.'

'All the Nobles have, sadly.'

A few more pieces of the Lucas puzzle slid into place. Of course he'd hate the son of the Empress, with his lineage, and of course Rufus would hate him back, with Lucas's lack of the same. Of course he'd want to get out of this place, where he'd never be anything more than a child no one wanted, for a century of adolescence.

No wonder he seemed to understand Julia so well.

'It *sounds* like a fairytale, doesn't it?' Julia whispered. She waited for him to turn back towards her before she spoke again. 'Two orphaned children, a boy and a girl…'

He smiled at that, and although it wasn't the contented smile she'd hoped for, there was a little shadow of it playing around his lips.

'Happily ever after?' he said.

She could have laughed. She *wanted* to laugh, at the absurdity of it all, and because she would never believe it, but instead she smiled at him and turned her attention back to the sky, and to the endless stars.

Julia must have dropped off to sleep, because she hadn't heard the door to Lucas's rooms opening. Instead, she was woken by the sound she could now hear, rasping gently like sandpaper across soft wood, the dragging of grit.

The fire was low but still flaming, so it must have been closer to dusk than dawn. Maybe these were the revellers she'd expected to hear earlier, now finally hauling themselves home.

But that's not what the noise sounded like.

She rolled gently to her feet, taking care not to disturb Lucas, and crept over to the side of the roof. Following the dragging sound below her as it curved around the corner of the building, she found herself looking down into the alley.

The noise stopped at the same time she did, silent in the darkness.

Nothing.

She was about to go back to the fire when the shutters of Rufus's window opened below her, throwing a sharp trapezium of light across the paving slabs. There was a figure there, and something else too, partially blocked from Julia's view by the staircase on the side of the building.

Just remember,' a hushed voice said, 'it can't go beyond the water. The last thing we want is for the caravan to find it.'

Julia wasn't sure, but the voice could have been Rufus.

The figure lit by the window's glow nodded its head, but the angle was too steep for Julia to identify who it was. Probably a man.

'Well, go on, then,' maybe-Rufus said, and the figure started to walk away down the alley, dragging the half-hidden object behind him, into the light.

It was a sack. A big sack.

Big enough for a person, if she was small.

Two names sprang unwillingly to mind, but Julia had only one prayer: *please not Claud.*

16

There was no sign of a struggle. None of the bottles of blood were broken, as though Felix had put the bag down rather than dropped it. It was as if he had just walked away.

Shit.

When Chloe returned a few minutes later with her little boy in tow, Cam was still trying to make a plan.

'You should really get out of here,' she said. 'They're a bit disorganised, sure, but they're not totally stupid.'

'I can look after myself. You should worry about him,' Cam said, nodding towards Chloe's son. He was standing by her side, one hand in hers and the other wrapped around her leg.

She laughed, stroking the little boy's hair. 'Oh no. Alex looks after me, don't you, baby?'

He grinned up at his mother, then turned an earnest gaze on Cam. 'I'm strong like Daddy.' His eyes twinkled with childlike intensity, and with something else too.

'He's Silver?' Cam asked Chloe.

She nodded. 'They don't know it though, haven't bothered to look close enough, so keep it to yourself. Are we going?'

Cam sighed. 'Not yet. I've got a friend to find first.'

He picked up the bag and slung it over his shoulder, praying he wouldn't need to use too many bottles to get Felix out of whatever trouble he'd got himself into.

Now, where would he go?

Cam left Chloe and Alex in the streets outside the cellar, promising to find them in the woods to the south of the settlement. Better that they get out into the trees than that they hang around in Charlestown trying to avoid the Weepers. Cam found that enough of a challenge on his own as he tracked Felix through the twisting alleys.

He was expecting to find him in the enclosure, wreaking his own brand of revenge, but the green nutmeg scent of his skin led in the opposite direction, dead-ending in an alley by the shore. The smell of salt and seaweed was so strong in this part of the settlement that it almost eclipsed the forest scent of Felix, but Cam could follow the trail, just barely.

He could smell the blood, too, and hear their voices from behind the wall at the end of the alley.

What he couldn't seem to do was find a way in.

'Where is he, Felix?'

'I told you, I don't know.' Felix's voice was slurred and distorted, as though he were talking around a broken nose.

'And I told you I don't believe you.'

There was a cracking sound that quickly slid into a familiar, wet crunch. Felix cried out, and Cam could have broken down the wall itself in that moment, but that would have been stupid. He didn't know how many Silver there were, or how they were distributed. If he rushed in, they could kill Felix before he got to him. Instead, he leapt from the alley up to the half-tumbledown second storey wall, hid his bag there and searched for a way in.

Below him at ground level, Felix was spitting liquid and something solid that hit the floor with a muffled rattle.

'Even if I did know,' Felix said, 'I wouldn't tell you. You know that. Not after what you did to Otho.'

'So that's what this is about?'

Cam found a hatch buried under some masonry and cleared off the detritus at Silver speed, taking care not to make a sound. The wood was rotten but still sturdy enough to lift away silently in a single piece, and then he could see the stairwell leading from the first floor beneath him to the ground floor where Felix was.

Felix and... two others. Cam could hear them now, their heartbeats thudding slowly in the manner of the Silver.

Just two.

'You turned him into one of those things,' Felix said. His voice was tight with rage, despite the thickness of his words.

'I didn't think you'd care. You left him here.'

'Because you didn't give me a choice.'

Cam lowered his long body carefully through the hatch, unfolding until he hung by his fingertips so he had only inches to drop to the top of the stairwell. He fell straight into a crouch, trying to absorb the impact as best he could, but the Silver beneath him weren't even listening.

Poor training, Cam thought. Not the kind of opposition he had expected, and not the kind to worry him. He could take them down in his sleep.

'Oh, you made your choice alright,' Felix's tormentor was saying. 'It was us or them, and you chose them.'

'And I've paid for that choice,' Felix spat through gritted teeth.

'Not enough. Not until we find him.'

'You don't want him. You want *her*.'

The man laughed. Cam used the noise to cover his progress down the stairs, step by step, until he could see the whole room spread out before him.

Just two, a man and a woman. The man was familiar, but Cam couldn't place him. He didn't recognise the woman. They should have seen him by now in their peripheral vision, but they still weren't paying attention.

Amateurs.

There was no more need for caution. In a single rush of movement, Cam sped down the stairs and punched his fist into the woman's skull. She'd recover, but not for a day or so. The man had less than a second to react, enough time to raise his fist but not enough to deflect Cam's as it rushed towards him and crushed in his face.

A second was all it took.

'You alright?' Cam asked, turning to face Felix with blood and brain matter oozing between his fingers.

Perhaps he should have felt like a liberator, but his mind just repeated those two, quick crunches. He knew they'd get up again, that this was nothing like Peterke, but his memory made the connection nonetheless.

Crack. Crunch.

The knife in the throat of the bait, hot blood on his hands.

And now his fingers were sticky and warm.

'I'm fine,' Felix mumbled through a bloody mouth. 'Thanks.'

One eye was swollen, his nose was clearly broken and he slumped awkwardly to the side. He'd been tied to a chair, and as Cam released the knots with his gore-drenched fingers it became apparent that the ropes were as much to keep Felix upright as they were to keep him captive.

'Shit,' Cam said, catching him as he slid out of the chair. 'What did they do?'

'They don't like me much.'

'Yeah, I can see that. I recognise the guy, though. Who is he?'

Felix spat on the ground, a gob of blood and mucus to join the mess that was there already. There was a shard of tooth sticking up from it.

'Name's Richard,' Felix said as Cam helped him to his feet, one arm slung over Cam's shoulder. 'We call him Lestat though,' Felix grinned, revealing a snapped premolar, 'which he hates.'

Now Cam remembered him.

'Wait… Lestat, who's friends with Charles? That Lestat?'

'That's him.'

It was Emmy's nickname for him, because of some old book about vampires. Apparently he'd dressed and acted like a pretentious jerk. It gave Cam a perverse joy to know that the name had stuck.

'He thinks he's in charge since Charles left,' Felix went on, staring down at the man's collapsed face.

'It doesn't look to me like anyone's in charge here,' Cam said. 'No one seems to have a fucking clue what they're doing. No military training, Weepers out on the streets, culling people on the beaches…'

As Cam spoke, Felix reached one arm out to the side until his lacerated hand was hovering a few feet over Lestat's face and then, slowly and deliberately, he squeezed. Blood dropped from his fist onto the mess that remained of the body on the ground, contamination seeping into the corpse.

A corpse now, not just a body, because Lestat wouldn't be getting up again. He had been cured, hallelujah, by Felix's blood.

Cam didn't stop him. He could have, but he didn't.

'Who was he looking for?' Cam asked.

'You,' Felix said, and then his legs buckled beneath him.

'Shit.' Cam scooped Felix up into his arms. 'We need to get you out of here.'

He sped up to the roof, but as he paused to collect the bag of blood, Felix stopped him with a clumsy hand on the back of his head. Cam turned to follow his line of sight and for the first time noticed the clear view of the moonlit beach, spread out below them beyond the salted fields. The sea moved like treacle, rolling up the sand to submerge the dark heaps that lay here and there along the shoreline, merging and retreating, merging and dragging. Some of the heaps were sucked away as the tide rose gently, rolling them out to sea.

The cull.

They hadn't gone far from Charlestown before Felix passed out with the pain. There was too much blood as well, contaminated blood, all over Cam's hands and clothes, and they had to stop.

While Felix was out, Cam gently explored the damage. It was mostly confined to Felix's face, but reddening of the skin over his ribs suggested they might be broken. It was difficult to be sure while Felix was unconscious and unable to tell him what hurt.

Better that he stayed out of it for the moment, until Cam had done what needed to be done.

He had to steel himself for it first, because he knew what he would feel when the cartilage slid back into place over the bone. It would grate in his hands, like the grind of vertebra on vertebra, as he reset Felix's nose. He did it quickly and cleanly, because it was something he had done a hundred times before, back when there were different ghosts in his head.

Crunch.

He also removed the remains of the broken premolar, which had splintered with the force of whatever blow had snapped the top off. There wasn't much else he could do but wash away the blood, and for that he would have to move Felix again, back towards the mountains and the place he had left the horses, where a spring bubbled up through the rocks.

In the meantime, he concentrated on making sure he didn't touch his own face. He didn't want to administer himself the cure unwittingly. That would be a let down, after they'd come this far. He'd have a bag full of blood bottles and no use for them, and a lead that he probably wouldn't be strong enough to follow up.

He needed to find Chloe.

There was a crunch in the undergrowth, too heavy to be an

animal, and accompanied by a pulse too slow to be human.

Cam didn't have a very clear grasp of Chloe's scent, but Alex's was strong enough for Cam to track: faintly aniseed, with an edge of salt. That wasn't the scent he could smell on the breeze now, playing among the midnight pines. Instead, he smelled decay and soil, and blood too old to be coming from either Felix or him.

But he wouldn't risk moving Felix, not until the howl went up, not until they were spotted, because they might still get lucky.

He didn't have to wait long. He always had shitty luck these days.

One Weeper, Cam could have managed, but he could already hear more moving through the forest towards them, converging on the call of the first, who was now stepping out of the trees and into the small clearing where he had laid Felix. He didn't know how many were in the forest, and he couldn't fight them at the same time as protecting Felix.

He didn't hesitate.

Within a fraction of a second, he'd scooped Felix back up into his arms and started flying eastward through the trees, weaving a path around foliage and grasping hands, gone before some had even realised he was passing. And they were everywhere, crowded so densely in places that Cam had to jump over their heads because there was no space in which to move between them.

He could only hope that there had always been this many of them, and that he and Felix had simply missed them on their approach to Charlestown earlier that evening. The alternative was that these were new Weepers, and that there had been another group of uncontaminated humans in the settlement, one that he had failed to save.

He picked up on Alex's scent then, sharp amongst the richness of the pines. It took him a little further south, and a little deeper into the crowds of Weepers. They were silent here, no need to howl because they could all see the meat.

Chloe was backed up against a tree while Alex ran in circles around her, physically pushing the Weepers away from his mother. She was screaming at him to stop, begging him to let one of them bite her so they would turn, as though she thought she could survive the crush.

He was just a little boy, even if he was Silver. He couldn't keep going forever. He'd kill himself trying to protect Chloe, like Cam had nearly killed himself infiltrating Charlestown.

Chloe knew it, too.

'Baby, no!' Her voice was beyond cracking, so destroyed that the words squeezed breathlessly from her throat.

There was no time to do this properly, so Cam made a choice. He moved to the back of the wave of surging Weepers, hundreds deep, and let them see him. He let them see the burden in his arms too, Felix's bleeding, contaminated body, and it was a moment of surrender. From that point onwards, events were beyond his control.

This wasn't like the stand off with Otho's Weepers, that now seemed so long ago. There was no sunlight in the night forest to hold them back, and there were so many of them that he was soon inundated.

He covered Felix's body with his own when he saw the first bite, but it wasn't the only one. He couldn't stop them.

They piled on.

The driving weight of the horde pushed down on him, until all he could do was brace his body over Felix's to keep them from crushing him, and try to minimise the bites. They sank into Cam as well, as though the Silver could provide the Weepers any sustenance, littering his back and limbs with self-healing punctures before they registered the taste and looked for better meat.

They dug.

They bit.

They turned.

They were dug out and bitten.

Soon the only movement Cam could hear seemed far away, tens of feet above them at the apex of the pile. The bodies on top of him muffled the sounds of the forest, and eventually there was nothing at all but the beating of his and Felix's hearts in the foetid cocoon of silent Weepers. Everything else was still.

'Cameron?' the sound was faint, even to Cam's ears.

'Cameron!' So faint, despite the grating edge that told him Chloe was shouting for all she was worth.

He could move. He should move, but everything hurt.

The sack of blood bottles was beneath him, beside Felix's still unconscious body. He manoeuvred his hand into it and tried his best to swig back a bottleful quickly, but the space was so tight that it proved a challenge.

The air was close.

Cam drained the bottle and moved, heaving up to shift the Weepers' deadweight aside, digging his way up with Felix held close to his side.

The air was close because there *was* no air.

He pushed up, fighting to slip between the awkward sagging shapes without hurting Felix, and without infecting himself with their contaminated blood.

There was no air.

Felix couldn't breathe.

Cam swam up, kicking his legs to propel them to the surface, until he finally felt the breeze on his skin. One last push and the bodies at the top of the heap scattered, flung out and away until Cam lay on his back in the night air with Felix cradled to his chest.

Part of him was surprised to burst from the darkness of the pile into the darkness of the forest. It felt strange, because for some reason he had expected sunshine. That would have felt right, but it was enough that he could feel Felix's heartbeat against his ribs, ten beats for every one of Cam's, and Felix's breath running hot across the blood-slicked fabric of his shirt.

More clothes for the fire.

'Cameron, please,' Chloe said, and he registered for the first time that she was still calling for him.

He blinked blearily down at her, twenty feet below him on the forest floor with Alex collapsed in her arms.

'Shit,' he said, because he'd left the sack of blood at the bottom of the Weeper dog pile.

He pushed himself to his feet on the unsteady surface, Felix in his arms, and joined her. Once Felix was safe beside her, Cam waded back into the pile to retrieve the blood. It was quicker this time without his burden, but it was still a few seconds before he was holding a bottle to the boy's lips.

'Come on,' he murmured.

Chloe's expression was almost blank, cloaked with disconnection, but there was horror under the surface of it. Her eyes were wide but empty, and her head shook almost imperceptibly from side to side, disbelief laid over certainty.

Cam lifted the boy's head, cradling it in the crook of his elbow as he tipped the bottle up, filling his mouth so full of blood that it began to overflow, slopping down his cheeks in thick runs.

'Come on, Alex,' he said.

There was a new thud, faint and close, in Alex's chest.

The boy swallowed.

'He's okay,' Cam whispered, and Chloe broke, life flooding back into her body as she lifted Alex's hands to her face, pressing her forehead against them as she wept.

But something was wrong.

Alex's pulse started slowly enough, but then it picked up speed, gathering momentum until it was the Silver equivalent of a drumroll in his tiny body.

No, not wrong. Different. *Changed.*

It was a human heartbeat, strong and quick.

Somewhere in the rush to get the bottled blood into his mouth, Alex had been cured.

Chloe wasn't upset. After all, she was human now, so her son probably should be as well, but there was regret in her eyes and a sigh in her voice as she told Cam this.

Silver children were special. Now Alex was just like all the other contaminated children in the Red: free, but normal. Chloe would have to protect him now, rather than the other way around.

Maybe that was why she chose to go with Cam when he went to collect the horses from the campsite, despite the fact that she'd already given him the directions he needed.

Charles was south of here, she'd heard, on the western side of the Ore Mountains.

'So,' she said as they walked, 'who's your friend?'

She was hand in hand with Alex, who seemed entirely recovered from his ordeal, and Cam was carrying Felix once again. He still hadn't woken up, and Cam was starting to become concerned.

'Someone I met on the way here.'

'Human?'

'If he were Silver, I wouldn't be carrying him.'

That wasn't the only thing that gave Felix away. His face was swollen, bloody and bruised. Cam barely recognised him. The sooner he could fetch the horses and get both Felix and himself cleaned up at the spring, the happier he'd be.

'Contam?' Chloe asked.

'That's right.'

'Shame. For you, I mean.'

Cam shook his head. 'Not for him, though. Better that you're all contaminated. Things would be easier.'

'Is that what Laila's preaching down in your Silver mecca now? *Death to all Silver?*'

Cam ducked his head and looked away. That wasn't Laila's way. 'You've heard about us?' he said instead.

Chloe laughed bitterly. 'The model society? Richard salivates over it, only he thinks he can do it better, of course, arrogant twat that he is.'

Richard, Lestat, now cured and dead.

'Mummy,' Alex complained. 'You said a bad word.'

'Sorry, baby.'

'But none of this was here when I last came up this way,' Cam said. 'It was all villages and farmland, and now it's just... empty. What the hell happened?'

'Cam'ron...' Alex said, his little voice full of censure.

'Sorry, Alex.'

'You can guess what happened, can't you?' Chloe said. 'I mean, you don't really need me to tell you.'

'They started making Weepers?'

'They started trying to make more Silver. They found a bunch of noncontams up in the mountains who'd been living there for centuries, seems like, and when they'd used half of them up on meals and failed turnings, they brought the rest down here to breed. They thought they could get away from the Weepers, that they'd all just die out, or go off and bite contams and get changed. Idiots.'

Cam laughed. 'As if Weepers die.'

'They'd all forgotten that. The only ones left from back then either got cured, got driven off, or were too damn - sorry, baby - stupid and arrogant to think it'd be a problem.'

'So the Weepers followed them.'

'They followed them, alright.' The fear in Chloe's voice was real as she spoke, and Cam wondered whether it was a good idea to make her talk about this here, in the darkness, after everything that had just happened. But she didn't seem inclined to stop. 'They multiplied,' she went on, 'until there were hundreds more of them than the noncontams. That's when they started bringing the contams into Charlestown, so they could defend themselves.'

'They didn't learn, though, did they?' Cam said, thinking of the enclosure, and of the people who went into it as humans and left as Weepers.

'They never do,' Chloe said, 'not that sort. Charles did, eventually.'

'So they chucked him out?'

'No. He was cleverer than that. He ran, and he took with him the one thing they really wanted, the thing they've been searching for ever since.' Chloe turned towards him in the moonlight. 'The thing you've been searching for too.'

'Emmy?' he said.

She nodded. 'Emmy.'

Cam couldn't make the dots connect. 'But why?'

'Because she's got the Primus's blood in her veins.'

'So?'

Chloe stopped walking. 'You haven't heard this?' she asked, her tone incredulous. 'You really don't know the legend?'

Cam simply shrugged.

'The sleepy lady?' Alex said. 'She's going to save us all, isn't she, Mummy?'

'You don't have to worry about that anymore, baby, because you're already safe. You're just like me now.'

He grinned at her, a genuine grin, so wide that Cam could count all his teeth. It was enough to wipe away the last vestiges of regret from Chloe's face and earn Alex a carry from his mum.

'You know why Charles took her?' Chloe asked.

'Sure. He wanted to take Sol down, but I did wonder if that was the only reason. He always had a weird thing for Emmy.'

'Right. But then Charles gets turned a few years back-'

'Charles is *human*?' Cam said. 'How long ago?'

'Couple of decades.' Chloe shrugged, although the gesture was a little awkward with Alex on her hip. 'You lose track of time, you know. So he decides she'll be human too-'

'*Emmy's* human?'

Chloe stopped walking again, whirling to face Cam. 'Will you let me finish? So he decides she should be human too-'

'Such a fucking nut job,' Cam murmured.

Chloe and Alex both glared at him.

'Fine,' he said, 'I'm sorry. Carry on.'

'So,' Chloe said, walking on, 'he decides to inject her with contam blood, but it doesn't work. She stays Silver.'

'She's immune?'

'Or something. So they try using her blood on other people, and it does nothing, then they use it on other Silver, but they still get turned with contam blood. So newly-human Charles decides the only way to make it work is the old-fashioned way.'

'No,' Cam said, dread and disbelief heavy in his tone. 'He can't think that'll work.'

'It's his only hope, so yeah, that was his plan. Last I heard, he was still trying.'

The old-fashioned way. There was only one way to interpret that.

The crazy bastard was trying to make Emmy fall in love with him.

It was dawn by the time they'd collected the horses and made their way up towards the spring. They camped there, far enough away from Charlestown to risk a fire, but not a big one.

Hades had made his displeasure at Cam's abandonment perfectly clear, head-butting him as soon as he got close, but the misbehaviour had stopped as soon as Hades noticed Alex in his mother's arms. The little boy had fallen asleep there, and Chloe hadn't had the heart to disturb him. Apparently the horse had some latent protective instinct, because from that moment on he wouldn't leave their side. He even refused his nosebag so he could give Alex his full attention, which for Hades was pretty serious.

In the end, Cam had just tied Alex into a sling around Chloe's shoulders then helped her into the saddle, where she stayed until they made camp. He'd opted to travel by foot himself while he carried Felix, not wanting to defile Sandor's saddle with the gore that still coated his clothing.

He burned it as soon as they got the fire going, then got himself clean in a pool beneath the spring: once, twice, three times, even though he knew the blood was dead now. Still, he was grateful that the Weeper bite marks on his own body had healed as they were made. The thought of the water sluicing contaminated blood into them was too much to contemplate.

When he was clean, he rummaged in the saddlebags Sandor had carried, now augmented by the bag of blood bottles, and found enough food to make a pretty decent stew for them all. Felix wouldn't have approved, because there was no meat in it, but he could have some jerky if he wanted.

If he ever woke up, because through all of this, Felix still didn't move.

Cam had laid him on the ground for the time being, convinced that at any second he would open his eyes. He'd want to wash the gore from himself, in the same way that Cam had just done, and criticise Cam's cooking, like he usually did.

He was not a fan of bread soup.

But still he didn't stir, and Cam couldn't let his wounds fester, so he left Chloe and Alex slumbering by the fire and took Felix to the spring.

Not even the cold water woke him. Not even the cleaning of his lacerated face, or the careful rinsing of his mouth.

His clothes needed burning too, so Cam stripped him, in circumstances starkly different from the ones he had hoped for on their journey to this place. It had been an idle hope, he told himself, for just a little while, from time to time. He stripped out of his own clothes to wash Felix in the pool, and that reminded him of another pool, and another spring.

They'd made a vow, half-fulfilled now, Cam supposed.

But Felix had been present then, and now he was just gone, his body an empty cipher that was waiting for him to return.

Once Felix was clean, there was nothing Cam could do but bandage his ribs, dress him in clean clothes and wait for him to awaken.

But still he slept on.

Cam could hear his heartbeat in the brightening of the day, strong and regular. He could hear his breath, light and shallow with sleep, but otherwise just as it should be. Most of all, he could smell the nutmeg freshness of Felix's skin as Cam cradled his head in his lap beside the fire, stroking his hair away from his forehead.

And then, finally, when it was already late into the morning, Felix's ice-blue eyes blinked open like a second dawn.

17

Lucas didn't stir when Julia slipped out of the blankets that morning. He'd tired himself out tracking through the dark city, following the figure with the sack, for Julia, because he wouldn't let her risk it herself. When he'd eventually returned with the news, she'd already bitten her nails down to the quick.

A man he hadn't recognised was in the sack, he'd said, dead and dumped out beyond the boundary by one of Rufus's lackeys.

Not Marcella.

Not Claudia.

A dead man. Sad, but… just some man.

Seconds later Lucas had fallen asleep, apparently exhausted. It had been a while since he'd had her blood. She'd cried her own exhaustion out in silent tears before settling down next to him, both relieved and horrified by her relief.

So when she rose in the dawn, she didn't wake him. Instead, she slid from the blankets and into her cloak, stepping lightly on bare feet across the roof, down the ladder, through his room and out.

It was a dry day, which was just as well since she and Lucas hadn't thought to shelter in the hut before falling asleep in front of the fire, but it meant the streets still bore the memory of the previous evening. The marks were clear as she walked down the staircase: a smear of darkness running from the front of the building around into the alley and away towards the edge of the city. She could probably have followed it if she'd wanted, a trail of gore leading straight from Rufus to the Red.

Rufus's door swung open as she reached the bottom of the

227

stairs, and there was the man himself, with Marcella on his arm. Both of them were smiling with every appearance of genuine cheerfulness.

'Well, good morning, Julia,' Rufus said.

She nodded at him, not willing to trust her words. She could smell it, that heavy odour of butchery and incontinence, rising as the sun hit the ground.

'You probably heard our sad news, I suppose,' he continued, following her eyes to the stains dried onto the paving. 'Such a shame, but Paulus was an old man, after all. In the family his whole life. You're such short-lived creatures, aren't you?'

'Such a shame,' Marcella murmured, patting Rufus's arm.

'Would you mind, Julia?' he said, pointing to the stains. 'Only my Servers are all busy cleaning up inside, and I think this is your patch, isn't it?'

She nodded, wishing she could say no.

'Lovely.' Just like that, his cheerfulness returned. 'Now, my Candidate,' he said, turning to Marcella, 'I shall see you this evening.'

'I shall look forward to it,' she said, with a curtsey. A *curtsey*. As she rose, she cut a look sideways at Julia, a tiny gesture to undermine her deference. A message: this is not surrender.

Rufus didn't notice, because he was already kissing her cheek in dismissal. The door shut behind him a second later, and Marcella and Julia were abruptly left alone on his doorstep.

They didn't speak until they were halfway across the square, Marcella on her way to wherever she lived and Julia on her way to the kitchen to fetch a bucket.

She knew it was rude, but Julia couldn't stop her eyes from drifting over the other girl's skin, searching for signs of violence. There was the cut at her wrist from the Nomination, but it was already healing, even without stitches. Now that she looked, Julia could see that it was actually very small, less than an inch long.

Perhaps it had been an accident after all, the blood that had poured onto the temple steps.

Marcella smiled. 'I'm fine,' she said.

Julia realised belatedly that she had been staring. 'Sorry. I didn't mean to-'

'It's alright.' She took Julia's hand for a second, squeezing it briefly, just hard enough for her to feel the strength in Marcella's dry fingers. 'I'm fine,' she said. 'He's really not that bad.'

Julia snorted. 'You sound like Claud.'

'He's better than most. Not as gentle as Lucas, perhaps, but he's kind in his own way.'

'I don't think I'd describe what he did yesterday as kind.'

Marcella tilted her head from side to side, equivocating. 'It may have been embarrassing for you in that moment, but didn't it get both you and Lucas what you wanted in the end? I wouldn't call that unkind.'

'That wasn't what I was talking about,' Julia said, her cheeks heating with the memory, and with shame, because it felt as though she had betrayed Marcella. She'd recommended Lucas to her, then taken him for herself, unwittingly or not.

'I meant disposing of a life-long Server by dragging his body out to the Red in a sack,' she continued.

A twitch at the edge of Marcella's mouth was the only hint that Julia's words had upset her composure. 'He did have him buried, in his own grave. It's better than having him drained and dumped, as most of us are.'

Which was true, but hardly enough to merit praise.

'You're showing your scepticism,' Marcella said, circling her finger at Julia's face, but she was smiling kindly as she spoke. 'Hide it better, my friend.'

Julia grimaced. 'I'll try.'

'Lucas will forgive you it. The others... Well, some of them think it's a game. You need to learn to play it.'

But as Julia trudged back to the courtyard, she was decidedly not in the mood for playing.

Listening at windows was a habit bound to get Julia into trouble, but she just couldn't seem to give it up. In her defence, it wasn't intentional, on this occasion at least.

Rufus must have known she was there because she wasn't making any attempt to hide the sound of her work as she scrubbed away at the paving slabs, but it didn't make him moderate the volume of his voice, or close the shutters to the alley. Either he didn't realise that she could hear every word, or he didn't care.

After all, she was only a Server. Being Lucas's Attendant didn't seem to count for much.

'It's done?' A man's voice.

Rufus: 'Yes.'

'Tonight, then.'

There was a high clinking sound, like the chiming of the fine glassware Livia reserved for special visitors. Julia moved back into the shadow of the staircase and stood up, slipping her foot into one of her gloves so she could move the scrubbing brush with her toes, maintaining the aural illusion that she was still distracted by her work.

There was no question of touching the blood with her bare skin. Even though she had never left the Blue, Julia was always careful.

She peered carefully into the room.

'You've kept enough for your humans?' the man asked. He had his back to the window, and all Julia could see from her vantage point was a wide slice of dark cloak.

'Should I have?' Rufus asked.

'Well, it's up to you.' The voice stopped just short of derisive, and Julia wondered whether the man was holding back in the face of Rufus's rank. 'But if you give it to your Attendant, you'd better not drink from her after, is all.'

Poison, Julia thought. *They were talking about poisoning Claud.*

'I'll think about it,' Rufus said.

'Question is: do you care if she lives or dies? If not...' A shoulder raised quickly into a shrug, then released. There was a snort, then Rufus walked into view, reaching a hand out to the man.

The tinkling noise again, and Julia could see the source now: a box of tiny glass vials filled with dark liquid. The man handed five to Rufus then secured the remainder in a large leather satchel that dropped out of sight below the window frame as he lowered it to the ground.

Julia missed something, soft words lost in the hollow ring of Rufus's heels as he walked away from the window. She strained to listen, but when his footsteps stopped she could hear nothing at all.

She'd stopped scrubbing, she realised, so she returned quickly to her knees. If there was one thing guaranteed to get her bled dry, it was spying on Nobles. She had to be more careful.

'What happens tonight?' Rufus asked, his voice louder now that he had turned back to the window.

'You'll see.'

Footsteps were followed by the sound of the front door opening and closing, and Julia gathered that Rufus's visitor had left.

She heard nothing else before her task was finished. The gloves the tanner had given her from his discards were now so thoroughly impregnated with dark gore that she suspected they would never be clean. It was a small loss, the defilement of a possession that had been special for the pure rarity of possessions.

Perhaps she could wash them clean.

But not now. Now, she had to find Claudia.

With one last glance up to the roof, looking for Lucas but knowing he would still be asleep, she picked up her bucket and walked quickly back across the square, hoping that Claudia would be home.

The kitchen was empty.

It was so unexpected that Julia found herself looking out of the doorway back into the courtyard, making sure she hadn't walked into the wrong house, but there was no mistaking Livia's kitchen.

Except there were no pots boiling over the fire, no bread proving on the hearth, and no pans soaking in the sink. The countertops were clear from vegetables and flour, clean like Julia had never seen them before.

'Livia?' she called out as she walked into the hall, stowing her empty bucket and brush in the cupboard under the stairs.

There was no response but the slight ticking of the brickwork in the fireplace as the embers cooled. The flames should have been roaring at this time of day, getting the coals heated so they could cook the Nobles' midday meal, but instead there was only the slipping warmth of breakfast's ashes.

The place felt cold.

Julia walked down the stone steps to the cellar, calling for Claud, but their room was empty too, as were all the other rooms that had so recently been packed with newly-returned girls. Nothing was out of place; in fact everything was beautifully neat, as though the house had been tidied and sealed up in anticipation of an extended absence.

Julia had only been gone for a few hours, but something had changed. She told herself it must have been something drastic for them all to up and leave without finding her first, but perhaps they simply hadn't missed her. Perhaps they had been glad to leave her behind.

She trailed back into the kitchen, wondering what she was

supposed to do now. Would Claudia come back here? Should she be out looking? Or should she wait here, and start trying to make lunch on her own?

The doorbell rang, strident in the empty building.

Julia hesitated, waiting to hear steps from the upper floors.

Livia was the only person who ever answered the door, and she was always home. Always. If she wasn't in her kitchen then she would be in her rooms. Even on the rare occasions when she was unwell, she would wrap herself in her fine-spun woollen cloak to come to the door.

Of course she'd be home, Julia told herself, upstairs somewhere, and the swinging ring of the bell would bring her to the door.

But by the time the bell rang again, Julia could feel the anxiety creeping up her shoulders and pricking her upper lip with the tingling presages of sweat.

Upstairs, there was only silence.

Julia wiped her face on her sleeve and walked to the heavy door, palm slick on the bronze doorknob. It swung open silently, its weight lending an ominous smoothness to the motion.

It took her a moment to place the wizened figure that blinked up at her from the doorstep, before she realised that it was Lucas's baba. What was her name again?

'Alba,' Julia said with relief as the memory returned.

The older woman blinked at her, obviously as surprised to see Julia as Julia was to see her, before breaking into a smile.

'You're Lucas's girl, aren't you?' she said.

'I'm his Attendant, yes.' Julia nodded her head deferentially as she spoke.

Alba gave her a canny look, then bustled past her into the hall.

'I was looking for Livia,' she said. Of course they would know each other, the two mother hens.

'I don't think she's here,' Julia said. 'I only just got back, but no one seems to be here.'

'Checked upstairs, have you?'

'No. I mean, we don't-'

'Well, let's see, then,' Alba said, already halfway up the ancient wooden steps.

'I'm really not sure that you should... I mean, we don't tend to go upstairs.'

'Oh, don't you worry about that, dear,' she said as she continued up the stairs, disappearing onto the landing above. 'Livy won't mind. It's only me.'

More anxious moments passed as Julia waited at the bottom of the staircase, twisting the end of her braid in her fingers as she contemplated following Alba. Perhaps she should have gone herself, or stopped Alba from going. After all, Julia was the one who lived here, and she had a sense that Livia would blame her for this.

It was less than a minute before Alba's footsteps made their way back to the head of the stairs.

'Mm-hmm,' she grumbled as she descended. 'It's true then.'

'What's true?'

'Come on.' Alba walked straight past Julia and into the kitchen. 'I think we could both do with a cup of tea.'

'But shouldn't we look for her?'

'Oh, I know very well where she is. And no need to worry; she'll be safe. It's us we need to be worried about.'

'But the other girls-'

'They'll be safe too.' Alba stoked up the fire, adding more logs, then fell back heavily into Livia's hearthside chair. 'No, come on now, and let's have a think. You make the tea.'

Julia crossed her arms over her chest. 'Where are they?'

There was a beat of silence while the two women tested their wills against each other, but nothing was going to deter Julia. Claudia was in danger and missing, and she needed answers.

Alba lifted her chin, pausing for a moment before she spoke to make it clear that Julia had not won the battle, but that Alba had decided to be beneficent nonetheless.

'They'll be with the Empress,' she said.

'What? Why?'

'Get the kettle boiling, girl,' Alba said with an imperious wave, settling down further into Livia's chair. 'Now, you know that Livia used to be an Attendant of the Empress?'

'Yes.' Julia filled the kettle and hurried back to hang it over the fire.

'Well, she's called them all back to the palace, I heard. All of the ones who've served her. I didn't think Livia would go too, but if she's left her kitchen...'

Alba didn't need to finish the sentence. If Livia had abandoned her hearth, then it had to be something serious.

And they'd left Julia behind.

'But why would she take the girls with her?' she asked, hoping for an explanation that would stop it from hurting.

'To protect them, of course.'

'From what?'

'Whatever's got the Empress in such a flap, something to do with the scene at the Nomination, I imagine. She would have taken all the girls she could with her.'

Julia couldn't go after them, not to the palace. She was alone.

Alba turned a sharp look on Julia, apparently noticing her despondency for the first time.

'Don't be glum,' she said. 'She wouldn't have been given the time to fetch you, and you have Lucas to look after you, don't you? Now, how about that tea?'

At least Claudia was safe.

That was the only thing that comforted Julia through the long afternoon in the kitchen, sitting on the hearth next to Alba as they waited for night to fall so she could go back to Lucas. Alba wouldn't let her leave until then, not wanting her to risk the journey until they were sure Lucas would be there waiting for her.

He'd expect her at dusk.

Claudia was at the palace. By all accounts, Rufus wouldn't follow her there. She was safe from his poison.

'You're sure it was tonight?' Alba asked for the third time as they sipped on their illicit tea.

'That's what they said: Tonight. Then the little glass bottles, that they said were for the humans, if you didn't care whether they lived or died.'

'Hmmm,' Alba murmured to herself as she had twice already, propping her chin in her hand, her elbow braced on the arm of the chair.

Julia had never felt so impotent. They should be doing something: warning people, or trying to find a way to stop whatever was going to happen, but they had too little information and no power here. Alba had already sent a runner to the temple, and there was nothing else to be done.

But Julia could feel the itching under her skin, begging her to get to her feet and do something, to go somewhere, anywhere, just so she could feel as though she wasn't sitting and waiting for the worst to happen. She'd already cleaned the kitchen, so now she watched the sky through the courtyard door, waiting for dusk, and while she waited she fidgeted, tapping her feet, shifting her shoulders, and spinning the fine china tea cup in her fingers until Alba took it away from her.

'Patience,' she said. Alba hadn't moved from Livia's chair all afternoon. In fact, her eyes had slipped closed, and not for the first time.

'How can you be so calm?' Julia said.

'And what good would panicking do us?'

'But you're not doing *anything*.'

'Aren't I indeed?' Alba's grey eyes cracked open so quickly that the colour startled Julia. 'And here I thought I was planning the night's work, all the while keeping you safe and conserving my energy for this evening, wondering why you didn't have the sense to do the same. But I'm just a silly old woman, so I must've been mistaken, mustn't I?'

'I didn't mean it like that.'

Alba sighed and leaned down towards Julia, reminding her of Livia in a way that squeezed her heart. 'This isn't the first time this has happened,' she said. 'Every now and then, one of them gets out of hand. It'll blow over, once they track him down.'

'Rufus?'

'You'd credit him with this?' Alba laughed. 'The boy doesn't even know what initiative is. No, I reckon it's someone else, this time at least. Anyway, that's not for you to worry about. All you need to worry about is staying out of their way, and keeping yourself safe.'

'But what about the vials?'

'Well, that's the mischief, isn't it?' Alba replied cryptically, but before Julia could ask her to clarify, a pale figure came barrelling in through the courtyard door.

'Claudia?' Julia rose to her feet.

'Hi,' Claudia smiled. 'Where's everyone else?'

'We thought you were with them,' Julia said. She tried to catch Alba's eye, but the woman looked away into the fire. 'Weren't you with them?'

'No. I've been with Rufus all day.'

'What?'

'What's gotten into you, Jules? Where else would I have been?'

Claudia walked further into the kitchen, her eyes alighting on the teapot set on the hearthstone. 'Have you been drinking *tea*?' she said. 'Livia's going to kill you.'

'Livia's not here,' Alba said, murmuring against the teacup pressed to her lip.

'Er, Claud, this is Alba. She's Lucas's... Well, she raised him.' Julia looked to Alba for confirmation, but the woman's eyes remained fixed on the fire. 'Alba, this is Claudia.'

'Pleased to meet you,' Claudia said, the response automatic.

Alba assessed her briefly, then flicked her gaze back to Julia. 'I suppose it makes sense, that the two of you would be friends, with your parents.'

'Did you know them?' Claudia asked, shedding her cloak as she went to crouch by the fire in front of Alba.

'A little. Yours too,' she said to Julia. 'That was the last time the Empress called her Servers back.'

'She what?' said Claudia.

'It's where we thought you were,' Julia said. 'Livia's gone to the palace and taken the others with her. We thought you'd gone with them.'

Claudia just shook her head, and Julia noticed for the first time that she wasn't looking well.

In her relief at seeing Claudia alive, Julia had forgotten why she had wanted to find her so badly: to warn her about Rufus and the vials of poison, and to keep her away from him. But she'd been with him all along, the entire day, and in that time...

Julia sat beside Claudia and grasped her friend's hands in her own. 'Did he give you anything, Claud?'

'What do you mean?'

'Rufus. Did he give you anything? A drink, or something to eat?'

'Jules, what are you talking about?'

Julia shook Claudia's hands, desperate to get her to answer the question. 'I was there this morning,' she said. 'He had me clear up the blood from the slave that died overnight-'

'Oh yes,' Claudia interrupted, 'poor Paulus.'

'Yes, poor Paulus,' Julia said irritably. 'But Rufus was talking to someone, and he had these vials of liquid, and something's happening tonight, Claud. I think they're going to use the vials to poison their humans. So did he give you anything?'

'What? No! Of course he didn't!'

'Claud, please,' Julia begged her to focus. 'He could have put it in something. Did he give you anything at all to eat or drink?'

Claudia paused to consider the question this time instead of answering on impulse, but still she shook her head.

'Nothing,' Claudia said. 'I didn't eat or drink anything while I was there, except water that I fetched from the pump myself.'

'Thank the Empress,' Julia said, resting her head back against the wall in what felt like a whole-body exhalation.

But Claudia didn't share her relief.

'You think he's poisoning his humans?' she said.

'It's what the man he met with said: that the vials were for his humans, but it was up to Rufus whether he used them. He said it depended whether he cared if they lived or not.'

'But why?' Claudia asked. 'Rufus wouldn't hurt me, not really, and why would the Nobles want to kill humans?'

Julia shrugged, and they both looked at Alba. Her eyes were closed again, and the deep slowness of her breathing suggested she really was asleep this time.

'Alba?' Julia said softly.

'Two clever girls like you,' she said, her eyes still closed, 'and you can't think of a single reason the son of the Empress might want to cause trouble for her?'

'The son of the Empress?' Claudia said.

'Your Noble,' Alba said, finally opening her eyes. 'Rufus. You didn't know?'

'No one told me.' Claudia glared at Julia.

'Lucas only told me last night. I was going to tell you.'

'Well, he doesn't like to,' Alba said. 'You wouldn't, would you, if she were your mother, but that's beside the point. Now, the question is: what are we going to do with you two? You can't stay here on your own, and I can't take you back to the temple with me, so I think you'd both better go to Lucas, don't you?'

'What?' Claudia said, still one step behind.

'Something's happening tonight, Claud,' Julia said again.

Alba finally stood from her chair. 'And you don't want to be here when it does.'

They used the scant remaining time before dusk to bundle up a few supplies: food, skins of water and warm clothing.

Julia wished for shoes. None of the Servers wore them in the Blue, their feet toughened by use and rarely exposed to any surface more demanding than flat paving and soft fields, but on that evening it felt as though the city itself might shatter. She would have welcomed a barrier between her skin and the crack of glass, the flow of blood, and every other obstacle she imagined might attend the wrath of the Nobles.

Nothing felt predictable that evening, when the air was heavy with heat, dread and silence.

Alba took the opportunity to help herself to a couple of bottles of Livia's home-brew, and the girls didn't begrudge her it. Julia snagged a bottle herself, not knowing when, if ever, they might be able to return.

It had been a month last time, Alba had told them. A month closeted in tight corners, hiding from the appetites of the Nobles as the city broke on top of the humans, smashed apart with the force of Noble insurgency. A month to break the square, a decade to rebuild. A month to avoid the searching hands of the Nobles, so desperate for blood to fuel their fighting that they wouldn't notice when your heart stopped.

Julia had never wondered about the cracks. She'd seen them, of course. She'd pulled weeds from between the broken slabs of concrete every day, but she'd never stopped to question why the cracks were there, or why some of the buildings seemed to be nothing but a patchwork of repairs.

She'd just assumed that was what happened when things got old, but now all she could see were the shattering impacts of bodies and fists in the stone of the courtyard.

'I'll take you as far as the square,' Alba said, her voice quieter than a whisper, 'and don't dawdle or detour. Go straight to Lucas.'

Claudia and Julia each nodded, their heads bobbing under their dark hoods. Despite the heat, all three of them were wrapped from head to toe in black, hoping they might become shadows in the night.

But they were the only people on the streets, and there was no hiding their movement. Julia wished they could have just stayed in their cellar room, but Alba had insisted it wasn't safe.

Walking the dark alleys felt far less safe, and too soon they were waving goodbye to Alba as they reached the square. She pulled them both into her arms and, with a brisk but thorough hug, she was bustling off towards the temple.

They were on their own.

Claudia slipped her hand into Julia's, huddling closer as they skirted the edge of the square towards Lucas's building. Julia would have felt more secure had it not also been Rufus's building. She couldn't shake the suspicion that Paulus's death had been less than natural, and that somehow Rufus was at the centre of everything.

They didn't make it far enough to find out.

There was a noise up ahead, a soft sound, but the city was so quiet that it reverberated through the empty streets, making the grating shuffle into a crashing roar.

It was coming from one of the alleys to their right, an alley they would have to pass to reach Lucas's building.

Julia pulled Claudia around to her other side, putting herself between the alley and her friend, and moved their course away from the edge of the square.

The noise kept coming, like bare feet scuffing on the ground.

Was someone else out in the city too, doing as they were? Had someone else been left behind?

When they drew level with the alley, there was no way to hide themselves. They were silhouetted against its end no doubt, in the same way that the bundled figure was silhouetted in its mouth, the details hard to discern in the shadows.

Their footsteps faltered.

The figure was stooped, hunched over one of its arms as though it were injured, and now that they were closer Julia could hear its keening: a soft whine no louder than a breath.

Against every urge in her body, that sound of pain made Julia stop.

'Are you alright?' Claudia asked the figure.

Its head jerked up, and two ragged footsteps brought it into the dimming sunset light.

Its clothes were filthy, clumped together and matted where something had congealed over their surface. From the smell of it, it was nothing pleasant. The clothes hung from a skeletal frame, a body so starved that Julia was surprised the creature was managing to walk at all. Its limbs were nothing but bone and skin, and there wasn't much of the latter on its bare wrists and ankles, where ligature marks sank black into the joints.

Julia took an involuntary step backwards before she noticed the face: sunken, crusted with grime and weeping blood from the eyes.

It was a face Julia recognised.

'Marcus?'

He lifted his head to the sky and howled.

18

'Felix?'

He blinked, his head pillowed in Cam's lap, and then his eyes found Cam's.

'Is he dead?' Felix croaked.

'Lestat? Yeah, he's dead.' *You made sure of that.*

'Good,' Felix said, pushing himself up onto his elbows so he pulled away from Cam's embrace.

That was the end of that, then. It would make what he had to do next a little easier, or at least it ought to have done.

Cam got to his feet slowly. 'I'm going on alone,' he said.

Felix looked over his shoulder, flinching as he registered the pain in his ribs. 'To find your friend?'

'To find Emmy, yes.'

'You know where she is?'

'Chloe told me.' Cam looked over towards where Chloe and Alex were playing in a nearby meadow. Alex was sitting on Hades's back, while Chloe led the horse in figures of eight amongst the waist-high flowers. She probably needn't have bothered supervising; Hades treated Alex like his favourite foal.

Temperamental old bastard.

'Found her yesterday in Charlestown,' Cam went on. 'She's an old friend. Sort of.'

Felix probed the site of his missing tooth with a cautious finger. 'You trust her?'

'It doesn't matter much either way. I have to go and look, at least.'

241

Felix nodded and, with some manoeuvring, sat up by the fire. 'I'm coming with you,' he said.

'You're injured.'

The marks of the previous night littered Felix's face in protrusions of purple and crimson, but he wouldn't be deterred.

'This is nothing,' he said.

'I need to travel at speed.'

'Well, I didn't walk here, did I? I assume you can carry me.'

Cam paused. There was a playful edge in Felix's voice that he was determined to ignore.

'It's not safe,' he said eventually.

'Cameron,' Felix said, reaching up to wrap his hand around Cam's wrist, 'I have nothing left to lose.'

His fingers trailed over Cam's pulse, following the line of the vein to the bone in a touch that was so light it might have been accidental had it not been so slowly drawn.

'No.'

'We had a vow,' Felix reminded him with a squeeze to his wrist. *A blood vow.* 'I've got what I wanted. Let me help you find her.'

Cam would have refused had it not been for the bare entreaty in Felix's eyes. He needed this, Cam realised. Perhaps to take his mind off Otho's death, or to give him some purpose, but for whatever reason, Felix was desperate to come with him.

'Alright then,' he said, clasping Felix's wrist in return, 'but first we eat.'

Cam gave Hades to Alex. The horse had made up his mind and broadcast his decision with hooves and teeth aimed at Cam's tender spots, so he didn't really have a choice in the matter.

'You're sure?' Chloe asked for the third time.

'Look at the two of them,' Cam said. Hades had lain down in the grass to let Alex clamber up onto his back. If Cam hadn't seen it, he wouldn't have believed it.

'Plus,' he went on, 'it's not like I can carry him as well as Felix.'

'Here,' Felix said, handing Chloe Sandor's reins.

'No,' she said, pushing Felix's hands away, 'I can't take both of them.'

'Look after him for me,' Felix said, wrapping her fingers around the leather.

They'd be travelling on foot from this point, tracking along the edge of the mountains until they found Emmy. Cam would have to carry everything himself, including Felix.

They had to leave the horses behind.

'He'll be waiting for you when you get back,' Chloe said, leaning forwards to press a quick kiss against Felix's stubbled cheek.

A twinge of unwanted jealousy surged through Cam's chest. He ignored it, but it was becoming more and more difficult to fool himself that there was nothing between him and the woodsman. It hung thickly over every word, look and touch, a potential that made Cam's ears tingle.

It didn't help that Felix was just as ruggedly handsome without the beard as he had been with it. They'd had to cut it back to tend to the cuts on his face, but now that Cam could see his chin... Cam almost wished he'd just persisted with cleaning the blood from between the hairs.

'Where will you go?' Felix asked Chloe.

'I don't know. Over the mountains I guess, southeast, back the way you came. Away from this place,' she said, looking at Cam, 'maybe as far as your island.'

Cam grimaced. 'Laila wouldn't have you.'

'Really?'

'It's nothing personal, they just don't let contams into the Blue.'

'Oh. Well, I don't know then.'

Cam had a thought.

'How well do you know the Carpathian mountains?' he asked.

The sun was high when they waved Chloe and Alex off.

Chloe had agreed to lead the horses through the pass and back along the route Cam had followed on his way to Charlestown, which meant they'd reach the mountain lake in a few weeks' time. Cam's name, along with the gifts he had collected for Ana, should secure Chloe and Alex a berth in the community, at least until Cam could find his way back there.

In the meantime, he and Felix had work to do.

'How many bottles do we have left in that bag?' Cam asked.

They'd had to take only the most essential supplies: two days' worth of food, and all the blood.

'Twenty,' Felix said. 'One water.'

'That's all yours. Do you know this area at all?'

'Nope.'

Cam narrowed his eyes at him. 'Fat lot of use you are. I'm literally carrying you on this mission. Remind me again why you're here?'

Felix smiled. 'You like having me around.'

That had Cam blushing again, his eyes drifting to the ground as he cleared his throat. 'Right, then we'll follow the mountains south and try to pick up a scent. Anything else you know that might help?'

'They'd stay away from the caravan route if they didn't want to be found.' The bastard was still smiling.

'Right. Uh. Right.'

'So,' Felix said.

The problem was that carrying Felix when he was awake was an entirely different proposition from carrying him when he was unconscious. The latter was one-sided, the former decidedly not. They'd be touching, and every point of contact Cam felt, Felix would feel too.

The thought made Cam's palms sweat, despite the cold.

'Piggyback?' he suggested, his voice too high.

Felix just carried on smiling, so Cam loaded him up with the bag of supplies in the hope that its weight might distract him from the tension. Unfortunately, Felix was stronger than he looked. Even with the bag, and even with his bruised ribs, he was still able to jump onto Cam's back with the grace of a consummate climber.

His limbs snaked around Cam's body with an intimacy that made him want to groan.

Instead, he ran.

The world streamed past, strobing away behind them as he leapt from rock to rock, between trees, and over streams. They covered miles in minutes, moving so quickly that they could see the shape of the landscape changing as they moved south into the mountains, crossing the snow line as they climbed, but still Cam could track the movement of every living thing whose path they crossed. The trails were loaded with scents, lynx and deer, and something bigger and darker.

Humans.

Silver.

But they moved in circles.

Shit,' Cam said, slowing to a halt after they'd passed the same tree for the fifth time. 'All the tracks are mixed up here.'

Felix slid down from Cam's back, apparently unruffled by the experience of moving at Silver speed. He teased a bit of foliage from his hair and asked, 'What are you looking for?'

I don't know. Anything. Or a conspicuous amount of nothing. Someone's been messing with these tracks, probably trying to throw people off. That's suspicious in itself; there can't be many people who bother to trek out this far into the mountains. There're no passes here, so if you want to go to the other side then up and over is the only way.'

Cam knelt in the new snow, scraping it away so he could see the ground underneath.

Snow's thinner here,' he said. 'Thinner than it should be. Thinner than it is anywhere else.'

Then he saw it: a single drop of blood, frozen in the snow. If it had been fresh, he would have smelled it from a mile away.

Are you bleeding?' he asked Felix.

'No.'

No. And anyway, he already knew that it wasn't fresh. It was alone too, that single drop of blood. There were no other traces in the area - Cam looked - and that just wasn't natural, not when the blood was Silver.

He picked it out of the snow and rubbed it between his fingers until it melted.

Yep. Definitely Silver.

This way,' Cam said, pointing up the blood-marked path towards the mountain.

'You're sure?'

'It's a blood sign,' Cam said. 'It can't be a coincidence.'

Sure enough, he found three more drops as they travelled on, each isolated, each hidden beneath the foliage, and each marking a single path at what would otherwise have been a crossroads.

They followed the blood straight to the cave.

A mine?' Felix whispered, his breath warm on Cam's ear.

Maybe,' Cam said, trying to concentrate, which was a challenge with Felix pressed against his back. 'Maybe a bunker.'

The aperture was set into the side of the rock, a rectangular hole too regular to be natural and too irregular to have been created by industry before the Fall. Either this was something new, or it was something ancient.

'What do they mine around here?' Cam asked.

'Marble, I think.'

'No metal?'

'I don't know.' Felix's lips were too close to Cam's ear.

'I'm leaving you here,' Cam said abruptly, setting his shoulders back so Felix's feet unwrapped from his body and swung to the ground.

He had expected a protest, but instead Felix nodded quickly then hoisted himself into a nearby tree, dragging the bag of supplies up behind him. He was ensconced in a leafy hideout, tearing into a strip of jerky, before Cam had even decided how he was going to approach the mine.

'Toss me one of those,' he whispered up at Felix.

A bottle of blood dropped silently from the branches of the conifer, and Cam downed it just as efficiently. No telling what he'd come up against when he got inside, but he knew there'd be other Silver around.

He could smell them.

Despite the chill, the ground was saturated in the scent of Silver violence. There were individual scents here and there, tendrils of aroma that were tantalisingly familiar, but none that he could place.

Except one.

Rich and sweet, like dark chocolate, buried beneath the rest, but so desperately precious that he could have found it under a thousand other smells.

He prowled until he located its source under the snow: a scrap of material the size of a coin, faded and pale, but loaded with scent.

Emmy.

She was here.

He had found her.

Unfortunately, there were the scents of a lot of other Silver here too, more than he could take on alone.

Shit.

A noise escaped from the mouth of the cave: a door shutting, footsteps and conversation, all echoing enough to suggest a large cavern behind the small opening in the rock.

Cam ducked behind the foliage gathered at the base of Felix's tree.

'Did they say how long?' The voice sounded male and young, an impression confirmed when it was followed through the rock door by a skinny teenaged figure dressed in ill-fitting clothes that could have been inherited from an older brother.

'You never listen, do you? You were there too. Or were you too busy eyeing up your girlfriend to pay attention?'

'She's not my girlfriend,' the boy mumbled back through the door.

He was followed into the midday sunshine by a bigger figure, more a man than a boy, although still young enough to retain a slight crack in his voice.

'You want her to be, though, don't you?' he said. 'Moritz told me he saw you giving her flowers yesterday. Like she'd be interested in you.'

'You don't have to be a dick about it.'

'Wouldn't you rather hear it from me than from her?' the older boy said, putting his arm around his small companion. 'Better to just give up, mate. Find someone who isn't so far out of your league. I'm just looking out for you.'

From the resentful look on the younger boy's face, it didn't appear as though he appreciated this kindness.

'Did you hear what they said or not?'

'Of course I did. *I* was actually listening.'

'And?' The younger boy was visibly struggling to keep himself restrained, his fists clenching at his sides. Cam could separate his scent now, and it didn't seem human. Were they turning them this young, or was there really a big enough population of Silver hidden within the mountain that they were breeding?

That would mean hundreds of Silver beyond the rock wall.

'They said it would be tonight,' the older boy said.

'So how soon can we leave?'

'Impatient, are we?'

The younger boy finally lost his patience, punching the other's arm so hard that Cam heard the bone shatter.

The older boy laughed, shaking out his arm as it healed.

Both Silver, then.

'Alright, alright,' he relented. 'Any day now, they said. We're to wait for word from the island. It's going down tonight, and if all goes well, we should hear from them tomorrow. Then it'll be ours.'

The older boy grinned while the other stared off over his

shoulder, apparently lost in his imagination.

'Wow,' he said eventually. 'I mean, wow.'

'I know, right?' the older boy said, returning the punch, but softly. 'This time next month, we'll be in the Blue.'

Cam didn't wait to hear more. Snatching Felix from his perch in the tree, he spirited them both away towards the mountains, and his home beyond.

He just hoped he'd make it in time.

They weren't dressed for the cold. That wasn't a problem for Cam, but Felix was already shivering when they were halfway up the peaks of the Ore Mountains.

'What are you doing?' Felix shouted, the flirtation in his voice gone as he clung on grimly to Cam's shoulders. They were high now, probably high enough that Cam should have thought to secure Felix to his body properly.

'I'm taking you to Chloe, then I'm going on alone.'

The wind took Cam's voice and whipped his hair into his eyes, but he didn't miss his footing. Somehow, Felix didn't miss his words either.

'Like hell you are,' he shouted.

Ten more minutes' strobing travel and one stomach-churning plummet took them over the mountains and down into the familiar wooded slopes of Czechia, where Felix demanded a halt.

'What are you doing?' he demanded as he regained his feet.

'I'm going home. I'll take you back to Chloe.'

Felix studied his face suspiciously. 'Was Emmy not there?' he said.

'No, she was there.'

'Well then?'

Cam wanted to explain, but the tension was churning him apart. His fist thudded into the nearest pine before he could stop it.

'Cameron,' Felix said, grappling with his hands until, despite Cam's superior strength, he had them secured in his own. 'Cam, please.'

Cam's eyes locked onto Felix's - one swollen in the socket, the other ice blue beneath the lashes - and trailed down to his lips. He couldn't seem to look away.

Felix raised his hand to Cam's cheek, rough fingertips on stubble, and in any other circumstances that might have been the breaking point. That might have been the moment when Cam let himself fall apart, because he could feel his resolve stretching.

But he had to snap it back into place.

Not now.

'My people are in danger,' he said, struggling to make his voice more than a whisper. 'I have to go, and I have to go now.'

'Then I'll come with you.'

There was still that point of contact between them, hand to cheek, and it was enough to make him sway.

'I can't take you there,' Cam said eventually.

'No contams, right?'

'No,' Cam said, and this time it truly was a whisper, because he realised what it meant. This man, this strange green-scented support who had somehow eased his way into Cam's life, had Silver poison running through his veins. He was contaminated by the cure.

Even if this was something Cam wanted, it would never be safe. It would never work.

'Then take me as far as you can. I'll wait for you there,' Felix said, in a tone that made it sound like he was offering more.

How could Cam accept that?

'I might never come back,' he said.

Felix shrugged with one shoulder. 'Then at least I'll know. Now, I'm guessing you need to drink all this,' he said, hefting the bag.

Cam eyed the remaining bottles, trying to calculate the distance he had to travel and the weight he'd be carrying.

'I don't think it'll be enough.'

Felix looked at him strangely. 'What do you think the caravans are for?'

There was a beat of silence as Cam tried to understand what Felix was saying.

Caravans shunting uncontaminated humans around the Red, between the Blue and Charlestown.

It was so obvious.

'No,' he said.

'Yes,' Felix replied. 'They're Pijavica way stations.'

Cam could see the connections now.

It was a blood supply to speed travel from Charlestown to the Blue. Any Silver travelling between the two points would need to stop to refuel multiple times on the journey, using more blood than they could carry. The Charlestown Silver, or perhaps the ones who were keeping Emmy captive, had set up stores of uncontaminated humans so they could cross the distance in hours on foot rather than in weeks on horseback.

They would never run out of blood.

No wonder Cam had seen evidence of so many caravans on his journey; he'd been following their route.

That was what they'd use, to attack the Blue: their blood expressway.

They made it through Slovakia on the remaining blood bottles, but by the time they crossed the old border into Romania, Cam could feel his strength starting to ebb again. He'd needed to drink more and more bottles at every stop, the blood required for each mile increasing exponentially as his exhaustion increased, until finally the last bottle was empty.

He could go maybe fifty miles more on what he had left in the tank, and then he'd have to stop for good.

'We'll need to find them soon,' he shouted over his shoulder to Felix.

They'd passed through several old camps on their journey, but they hadn't seen a single resident caravan. Cam was starting to get concerned. Maybe they'd moved them all in anticipation of this evening's attack.

'They won't go over the mountains,' Felix yelled back. 'They'll go south instead.'

Cam knew that. He'd realised it himself when he'd followed the caravan north from the shores of the Blue, but exhaustion was taking over. He had already taken the path up into the Carpathians by the time Felix spoke, so they lost valuable time tracking down the side of the slopes into the valleys to the south.

In the end, the mistake was their saving grace, because they never would have found the caravan otherwise.

It was huddled up close in the lee of the mountain, tucked in a deep valley whose treetops were so uniformly level that Cam mistook them for grass until he was already mid-jump from the rocks hundreds of feet above.

More evidence of his exhaustion.

Reaching out, he tried desperately to find a purchase on the rock face, but only succeeded in pulling a load of boulders down with them. They dropped amongst the stones to the forest below. Cam barely had time to pull Felix into his arms before they hit, crashing through the canopy like a lead weight dropping into water.

The impact smashed his ribs, which meant that most of the remaining blood in his system went into healing, but at least Felix was safe, lying close along Cam's side with a finger pressed against his lips.

'Another fucking rockfall,' someone said. 'Seriously, why can't we move the camp, just a little bit?'

'Scared, are you?' someone else replied, a man this time. The first voice had been female.

'Of being crushed to death in a rockfall? Of course I fucking am, and if you're not then you're either an idiot or you're lying.'

A third voice: 'You talking about Dumitru? Because if so, it's definitely both.'

Laughter followed, mean-spirited and more fulsome than the joke merited. Dumitru was clearly not well-liked.

When he was able to push himself up onto his elbows, Cam saw that the boulders had fallen around him and Felix, effectively shielding them from the camp on the other side. Of that, there wasn't much to see from their vantage point except a line of empty carts stowed beneath the trees off to one side.

Cam rolled silently to his knees and peered over the top of the nearest boulder, Felix close to his side.

Then they saw the fires. The camp must have been waiting here for weeks, maybe ever since Cam had lost the trail on his way out to Charlestown, and the flesh-stripped and burned bones had been emptied from the fires and piled around them in grotesque heaps. They represented tens of dead people.

'Better refresh the boundary,' the woman said. 'Rockfall might have shifted things.' She was standing by the nearest fire, accompanied by five others, all Silver. Three more fires burned a little further off, but those were sparsely populated.

Where were all the others?

'I did it last time,' said the man the others had called Dumitru.

'Well, you're the expert then, aren't you? Go on. There's some leftover meat by that fire.'

Cam and Felix exchanged a glance. They needed to move before Dumitru came to investigate the rockfall, and they needed to keep Felix out of sight so his body didn't become the next boundary ward.

They crept around the boulders towards the line of carts, where the ground cover was thickest. After one breathless moment of open space between the trees, they settled behind the nearest axle while they scanned the carts and campsite for blood.

There was none, of course. At least, not visible, and not conveniently bottled in the way Cam had become accustomed to drinking it. Out here, the Silver drank straight from the vein. What they were looking for, then, were people.

'And here he is,' the woman said, turning away from Cam and Felix's hiding spot. 'What bloody time d'you call this?'

'Yes, yes, I know.' The voice came from the other side of the trees, and there was the cart, being drawn awkwardly through the trees by four horses. It was filled with humans, perhaps thirty in total, guarded by three Silver, including a familiar face.

'No,' Cam breathed.

Felix turned to him, but Cam couldn't drag his eyes away. They were glued on the boy walking at the head of the cart, the youngest member of the Invicti, a boy he had helped to train: Tiberius.

'You know we've only got a couple of humans left,' the woman said.

Tiberius threw his bag to the ground by the fire. 'Yes, I said I know.'

'The Empress won't be pleased if-'

'The Empress is much less pleased with your lot right now, so I wouldn't push your luck if I were you.'

'It's not our fault he escaped,' Dumitru said. 'We weren't even in Charlestown when it happened.'

'You think that's going to save you?' Tiberius said. 'The only thing the Empress cares about is that Cameron's still alive. If your people had done your job, then we wouldn't have to worry about him anymore.'

Cam was so shocked that when Felix's hand slid into his, he didn't even stop to agonise over it. It was a well-meant gesture, but Cam could barely feel it in the horror of the moment.

Carmen hadn't been acting alone in Charlestown. She hadn't been the lone renegade traitor that Cam had assumed her to be. She'd been acting with Laila's authorisation, at her request.

Laila had tried to have Cam killed, and she was using the Invicti, his brothers and sisters, to help her do it.

Cam couldn't feel his skin. He couldn't feel his almost-healed ribs. He couldn't feel anything at all.

While he sat in emotional paralysis, the cart containing the uncontaminated humans backed into line next to their hiding place. This time it was Felix who curled Cam in his arms, pulling him underneath the axle as the horses were freed from their traces and the Silver wandered over to inspect the new meat.

'You're not to touch them,' Tiberius said. 'You'll let them out during the day so they don't sicken, but lock them up again at night, and if we find a single unauthorised mark on them, you're all going in concrete. Those were the Empress's words: in concrete.'

'We've never touched them yet,' the woman said. 'We're not going to start now.'

'Good. Then they're all yours.'

In the next moment, Tiberius had disappeared, no doubt racing back to the Blue in preparation for whatever was happening tonight.

But it didn't fit. If the caravans were working with Laila, then why would they want to attack the Blue? It was already in her power.

'What a prick,' Dumitru said.

The woman slapped him around the head. 'Sort out the boundary. The rest of you, get the humans out for some food, and you heard the man: hands off.'

Felix tightened his hold around Cam's body as the humans started to file down from the cart and into the undergrowth.

'Not yet,' he whispered, so close to Cam's ear that the sound needed to be no more than a breath. 'When they're all out. Do you have the strength for some speed?'

Cam tested the potential in his muscles, feeling for the fizzing power that could fuel him.

It sparked in his legs, just a flicker, but enough to get where he needed to go.

'Hang onto me,' he breathed back.

Felix wrapped his arms around Cam's shoulders, and the moment the three Silver turned away from the humans, Cam snatched one of the noncontams from the back of the clutch. He didn't hang around to see whether or not the Silver noticed the loss.

* * *

It wasn't until Cam was standing in the next valley with Felix at his back and a half-naked human in front of him that he realised the full import of what he was doing. He couldn't remember the last time he'd drunk blood from a living donor.

Years.

Decades.

Centuries.

Teeth to skin was just... intimate, and a knife in his hand felt like brutality. It felt like putting the bait out of its misery, the blade sliding into the flesh like butter while blood poured hot over his hands. Squeezing between his fingers like the sticky softness of Felix's revenge.

'Er, hi,' he said to the young man, trying - and failing - to cover his discomfort. 'I'm Cameron. This is Felix.'

'You saved me,' the man whispered. He couldn't have been more than twenty.

'Well, not really,' Cam said, rubbing at the back of his neck.

Felix raised his eyebrows at Cam.

How did one go about this kind of transaction? In the old days, back before the Revelation, there had been rules. Customs, really. But now, in the days of contamination, Cam had forgotten how to ask someone to feed him.

'We need your help,' Felix interjected. 'My friend needs some of your blood, and then you can have some of mine. It's contaminated.'

'Oh,' the man said. He took a second to think, but there was only one sensible choice. 'I accept.'

In the end, there was nothing for Cam to do. Felix made it easy, using an adapted needle from his pack to drain the young man's blood into a bottle, so practised that it was almost as though he were performing a familiar task.

Cam didn't ask where Felix had found the equipment or the skills. It wasn't something he wanted to dwell on.

When the bottle was full, Felix rubbed some of his own blood into the needle cut, rendering the man useless to the Silver, and sent him happily on his way towards the mountain lake settlement where they were apparently sending all their strays.

One bottle wasn't much blood, but there was power in its freshness. It would be enough to fuel Cam until the end of their journey.

'Thank you,' Cam said as Felix handed it to him, a small gesture filled with so much meaning.

Felix smiled. 'I can't feed you,' he said, 'but I can make sure you're fed.'

And that was it. That was the sentiment exactly. It was precisely what Cam would have wanted him to feel about an act that held a significance that was difficult to communicate to anyone human.

Felix understood it without being told.

'One day we're going to talk about what you did in Charlestown,' Cam said as he lifted the bottle to his lips.

'We'll talk about a lot of things, one day.'

Cam found himself hoping that was true, that one day they'd have the time for talking.

They were on their way again too soon, racing towards the shore of the Blue and towards the point at which he and Felix would have to part. Cam was no longer sure what he would find in his home, why he was rushing there, or if he even wanted to return.

They couldn't all be against him. His friends: Tommy, Viv, Lorelei... they couldn't all have wanted him dead. Could they?

There had to be something worth saving in the Blue. Even if there wasn't, he had to know. He had to look into their faces and understand why they'd betrayed him.

The silence was thick over the water when they arrived at the shore. Their journey had taken hours of hard running, but the fresh blood still lent an effervescent edge to Cam's exhaustion. He could be strong for a while longer.

'This is it?' Felix asked.

'This is it.'

Cam could still smell the rotten, earthy scent of the blood spilled into the ground by the caravan, and he could still trace the shapes of Hades's giant hooves in the dried mud by the water. It was familiar to him, this act of returning, and yet this time it was so different from every other homecoming of the past centuries.

He was coming back to a home that wanted him dead, so that might have had something to do with it.

But that wasn't all that was bothering him.

He had found Emmy.

For the first time, he was bringing good news with him into the

Blue, so why did it feel as though he had lost a part of himself in the Red?

'I'll wait here,' Felix said.

'They're trying to kill me, Felix. You know I might not come back.'

The woodsman took Cam's face in his hands. The dimming light made the familiar ice-blue of Felix's eyes even more striking, a single sharp colour in a sea of orange and yellow, and Cam couldn't look away. That breaking moment threatened again in the tension of their fixed gaze, a softening of Cam's resolve, and this time Felix didn't let it pass. He kept his eyes on Cam's, letting him know exactly what he intended to do, and Cam didn't pull away.

It didn't even occur to him that he should.

When their lips met, it was with a chasteness that Cam hadn't expected. Through all these weeks of proximity, of resisting, the quick, gentle press of Felix's lips against his own was not what he had anticipated.

It was the tiniest taste of what he craved, the barest whisper of a promise of what Cam had tried to deny he wanted.

And Felix knew it.

'I'll wait here,' he said again.

Cam might have abandoned the Blue there and then, chucking it all in for more of Felix, if it hadn't been for the howl. It rolled out over the water, shattering the silence of the dusk with a sound that Cam had never heard from the island before.

He must have been mistaken, he told himself. It couldn't be right. There couldn't be Weepers in the Blue.

But then he heard the screams.

19

Julia and Claudia backed up into the square.

'Marcus?' Julia said again, but he didn't respond to the name. He just fixed his bloodstained eyes on her and matched their every footstep with one of his own.

'What's wrong with him?' Claudia said.

'I don't know. Marcus? Are you alright?'

'Jules, I think that's blood on his hands.'

It wasn't coming from his wrists. Despite the depth of the lacerations, the wounds seemed dry. Instead, the gore looked like it had been spread up from his fingers.

His arms hung carelessly at his sides, his broken limb twisted in a way that made Julia wonder whether his shoulder was dislocated as well, but it was clear now that he wasn't in any pain. His posture was stooped because his body was broken, not because he was trying to protect it from further harm.

The damage didn't seem to affect its function. In fact, the fist of his injured arm was clasped tightly around something that dripped darkly onto the paving slabs.

As they watched, he slowly opened his fingers and the object fell to the ground, rolling across the stone to stop at their feet.

It was an eyeball, and it was the right size to be human.

Claudia stifled a shriek, but it was nothing compared with the screams that cut into the night from the alley.

'Claud, run,' Julia said.

There were already more figures piling out into the street behind Marcus. They were pouring from doors and windows, battering their way into every doorway they passed, pulling screaming bodies out with them as they emerged.

They didn't scream for long.

'Julia!' Claudia called back to her. She was already ten yards away, racing across the square towards Lucas's building, while Julia stood stupidly watching the crush of blood-soaked people rolling towards Marcus.

The moment she turned to run, he followed. His arm might have been broken, but there was nothing wrong with his legs. Within ten paces he was on her heels, his hands reaching out, pinching towards her.

She stopped looking back and just ran.

'Go, Claud!'

Claudia had been waiting for Julia when she should have been putting distance between herself and the mob. By the time she got herself turned the right way around, she and Julia were running side by side, pelting as fast as they could towards the staircase that climbed up the side of Lucas's building.

Julia was yanked backwards, falling halfway to the ground. Her cloak had been caught by someone or something. She scrabbled at the ties around her neck, pulling the cord away from her throat as she struggled to stop herself from choking. No sooner had she released the knot than a hand wrapped itself around her shoulder. She shrugged it off with a blind elbow jab aimed at head height, connecting wetly but with enough force to push her out of her cloak and back to her feet.

She stumbled for a second, but then she was up and running once more, sprinting towards where Claudia now waited at the base of the stairs.

'Just go!' Julia screamed at her.

Julia snatched a quick look behind herself and wished she hadn't. A writhing flash of blood-spattered faces confirmed her fear that the whole crowd was right behind her now, tens of people chasing her down.

'Lucas!' Claudia was yelling, pounding at his door as Julia finally reached his building.

A hand latched around her ankle as she slowed for the steps, but she stamped it away with the other foot and took the remaining stairs two at a time, leaning so far forwards that she was nearly touching them.

The door finally opened as she reached it, and a startled Lucas stood aside to let them in.

'What in- *Shit!*' He slammed the door closed on the grasping fingers. 'Get up to the roof, now.'

Julia was already halfway up the ladder, dragging Claudia behind her. When Lucas had followed them up onto the terrace, he kicked the ladder loose and slammed the hatch closed.

'Do you think we're safe up here?' Claudia asked.

'I doubt it,' Lucas said. 'They'll work it out sooner or later. Do you know what happened to them?'

'No. I was hoping you would,' said Julia.

'No.'

'They were killing people,' Claudia said. 'They were pulling them out of their houses and *eating* them. Not biting them to drink their blood, not like the Nobles, but actually *eating them*.'

There was a cracking sound below them as their pursuers forced their way through the rotten door. Their footsteps were loud and ungainly on the floorboards. A thud followed, together with the singing crash of ceramic.

'There go the mushrooms,' Lucas said.

The thudding continued for another few seconds, but then they heard the footsteps again, scrambling messily out of the room.

'Where are they going?' Claudia whispered.

Julia wished the thought hadn't come to her, but once it was in her mind she couldn't shake it. She was thinking about that staircase, and about how it ended just a single storey beneath the roof on which they now stood.

It wasn't an insurmountable height.

She edged towards the ledge over Lucas's door, not wanting to look, but knowing she couldn't stop herself.

'Julia?' Lucas whispered as she peeked over the edge and found herself face to face with Marcus.

She shrieked and staggered backwards into Lucas's arms.

'They're coming up the wall,' she said, her words nearly drowned out by the sound of the howl that had just left Marcus's lips. He was hoisting himself over the lip of the roof, bolstered by his fellows from below, although he was struggling to pull himself up with his broken arm.

'Empress,' Claudia breathed, huddling close behind Lucas as the three of them backed away from the edge. He'd put himself between the girls and their attackers, but the fear in his face told Julia he didn't think it was going to be enough.

'I hate to ask,' he said to Julia over his shoulder, 'but I could probably use a little extra strength right now.'

'Where are the guards?' Claudia said. 'Isn't it their job to protect us?'

Julia stretched her arm over Lucas's shoulder to offer him her wrist, saying, 'Take it.'

He groaned. 'I really wish I had you alone right now, because in other circumstances-'

'Just hurry up and bite her!' Claudia interrupted.

His lips touched Julia's skin like the softest kiss, but his teeth had her knees buckling, and not with pain. If she hadn't been watching Marcus rolling to his feet at the edge of the roof with four more people following close behind, it might have been something she savoured. As it was, her arm was soon returned to her, the line of Lucas's teeth imprinted in her flesh. The sight gave Julia an irrational kick of pride.

She was his, and she didn't mind.

'Get over by the hut and give me some space,' he said to her and Claudia, rubbing his hands together as Marcus started to move their way.

'What are you doing?' Julia asked.

Incongruously, he smiled.

'Don't worry,' he said. 'There's just something I've always wanted to try.'

The square was already full of Weepers when Cam reached the city, having used most of his remaining strength to speed through the forests that rimmed the Blue.

The creatures were multiplying freely here, because nearly every human in the Blue was uncontaminated. At this rate, they'd wipe out the whole place within the hour.

The doors had already been pulled off the hinges of the first house he reached. The lower two storeys had been emptied, but there were screams from somewhere above him. He found five Weepers on the third floor, obviously just turned, and three humans trying to fight them off with a fire iron.

'Thank the Empress,' one of the women said as she saw him. 'Help us, please!'

But that distraction was all the nearest Weeper needed to let him duck under her guard and sink his teeth into her thigh.

Six Weepers, two humans.

Cam managed to bundle the Weepers out of the window before they caused any more damage. They thudded sickeningly into the concrete, but they made no other sound. Seconds later, they were already crawling or dragging their way back towards the building.

'Get to the palace,' Cam said to the two remaining humans as another howl sounded out in the square.

'The palace?' The man looked horrified, as though it were blasphemy even to suggest seeking refuge with the Empress.

'It's either that or the temple, but you're not safe here. Make your choice, but go now, and go quickly.'

There were eleven more humans huddled in the upper floors of the building, and after Cam had ushered them out safely with the others he turned his attention to the bunkhouse.

Where were the rest of the bloody Invicti? Why was Cam, who was exhausted from spending the day trekking across the continent, the only one here?

He needed blood, and he needed backup.

Time to regroup.

He was just turning towards the bunkhouse at the northern edge of the square when something on the other side of the city caught his eye. There was a building there, four storeys high with foliage covering its roof. Cam would have sworn that he'd just seen something falling from the top. It seemed that the Weepers had noticed it too, because all of them were congregating around that building, leaving off their fruitless searches in exchange for the promise of whatever was within it.

As he squinted into the darkness, he saw it again: a body hurled backwards through the stands of bushes and out into nothingness, describing a graceful arc in the air before it plummeted down into the stone that paved the square.

Someone was kicking Weepers off the roof.

'Fucking hell,' Lorelei said from beside him. 'Who's up there?'

'Don't know. Where the hell have you been?'

'Dealing with the ones round the other side of the city. They were trying to get in the temple from the back.'

She'd brought her whole squad with her: twenty guards pumped up on blood and adrenaline. As soon as she gave the order, they dove into the fray, incapacitating Weeper after Weeper with blows that broke their bones.

But they wouldn't die. They wouldn't be neutralised until they'd been given the Weeper vaccine, the cure.

He needed to contaminate them.

'It's not going to work,' Cam said to Lorelei.

'What?'

'You know this, Lorelei. You remember the Fall. We have to get some contaminated blood in them or we won't have any humans left alive.'

'You can't bring contaminated blood into the Blue,' she said, her expression broadcasting her horror.

'Why not? It's either that or we watch all our humans turn Weeper. That's not much of a solution either.'

'Nor's yours. Where are you going to find the blood? You can't just go running around the Red with a bloody bow and arrow, hoping to come across an infected rabbit.'

'That wasn't my plan.'

Cam grimaced. He knew exactly where there was a cache of contaminated blood. It was waiting just outside the Blue for him, by the salt lake shore, inside Felix's veins.

'Can you take care of things here?' he went on. 'I just need to load up on blood, then I'll be out and back here in a flash.'

'Shit. Fine. Go.'

Cam hadn't expected her to give in that easily, but he wasn't going to question it.

'In the meantime, you need to get up there,' Cam said, pointing towards the roof at the south edge of the square. 'That's where the action is.'

That wrested a laugh from her, low and joyful. 'It'll be my absolute pleasure,' she said.

'This place isn't looking so boring now, is it?' he said.

She slapped him on the back as she sighed happily.

'Welcome home, Cam.'

Cam found the bunkhouse empty, but the bottles of blood were where they always were: stacked neatly in row upon row of chilled racks in the cellar. After a month of scraping by on what he could carry, steal or extract from willing humans, he felt like a starving man at an all-you-can-eat buffet.

He drank as many bottles as he could, and stashed two more into his belt, just in case.

The journey through the forests was shorter this time, but it hurt more. He could feel the exhaustion ramping up against the back of his eyes as though it were just waiting for one moment of inattention to flood him into unconsciousness.

Just a little further.

He just had to get to Felix and back into the city, and then he would be able to do what he came here to do.

'Miss me already?' Felix said as Cam appeared beside him.

Just the sight of him made Cam grin, and that was a dangerous thing. The tousled hair, the ice-blue eyes, and that smile playing around his lips like a promise of mischief.

'You don't seem surprised to see me,' Cam said.

'I'm not, though you might have washed first.'

Felix had put the short time to good use, starting a fire and washing the grime of their journey from his skin. Cam, on the other hand, was soaked up to the elbows in the gore of Weepers.

'No point, I'm afraid,' Cam said. 'It's only going to get worse.'

'Trouble?' Felix asked, suddenly alert.

'Weepers.'

Felix looked around, peering into the darkness under the trees. 'Here?' he said.

Cam shook his head. He almost took Felix's hand to reassure him, but then he remembered the blood on his own hands.

There always seemed to be blood on his hands these days.

'They're on the island,' Cam said. 'You'll be safe here, but I need a favour.'

'Ah. You need my blood.'

'Yes. I need your blood.'

Felix sighed as he pulled a knife from his belt and drew it across the meat of his palm.

'Never thought I'd hear you say that to me,' Felix said as blood beaded the wound, and there was a wistful edge to his tone.

'Felix…'

'I know.'

And he did seem to know. He knew what his blood would do to Cam, and what Cam would be risking if this went any further, this nascent connection between the two of them.

He'd be risking his eternal life, his strength, and every part of him that was Silver. Right now, with Emmy so close to being returned to them, it was too much to surrender for an emotion that hadn't yet defined itself.

Not yet.

Cam cupped his hand under Felix's as the drips began to fall, those deadly drops, and with that he had what he needed to save the Blue.

Or destroy it utterly; he wasn't sure which it would be.

'Will you wait?' Cam asked.

Felix smiled. 'I'll always wait.'

Lucas had kicked Marcus from the roof first. He was the first one to come at them, so he was the first one to fall, sailing into the night through a curtain of greenery.

Lucas kept up a steady pace after that, one body after another pitching out over the edge while Julia and Claudia watched from the safety of his sleeping hut and waited for it to end.

But it seemed as though there might never be an end to it. For every broken person Lucas ejected from the roof, three more climbed up from the far corner. They were coming thickly, first two at a time, then three, then four, until they rushed Lucas so continuously that there was no point in counting. He couldn't deal with them one by one anymore, so instead he was trying to push them all off the wall as they climbed up.

The problem was they never hit the ground, so they just climbed right back up again.

Pretty soon, Lucas was going to lose this fight.

'Are you alright?' he called over his shoulder.

'We're fine,' Julia shouted back. 'It's you I'm worried about.'

'Don't be. I could do this all night.'

It was false bravado. Lucas knew it. Julia knew it. Claudia was the only one who seemed comforted by the empty statement.

It didn't matter what they did. Julia knew they were all going to die on this rooftop.

She should have been devastated for the lives that had been lost here today, and for the lives that she and Claudia were about to lose, but all she could think about was how irritated she was that she was being cheated out of the future she might have had with Lucas.

Yes, it was a fairytale, and yes, it probably wouldn't have

worked because he would have abandoned her eventually, but she didn't *know* that because they hadn't had a chance to try.

And that was just unfair.

She didn't want to die without kissing him again. She couldn't die without seeing what he looked like naked, and finding out what other things they might enjoy doing together while she was similarly unencumbered.

They'd only had last night, and everything had been so new.

It had only been a kiss.

'No,' she said to herself. She rooted around in the junk at the back of the shelter.

'No what?' Claudia said. 'What are you looking for?'

'No, I'm not giving up. I'm not giving in without a fight, and I'm not letting him go.'

Her fingers closed around some bamboo stakes and a length of twine. With the addition of her pocket knife and a few judicious knots, it only took her a couple of minutes to build a makeshift pike.

'You're not going out there,' Claudia said.

'I am.'

'Well, then you're not going out there without me.'

'Claud-'

'No.' She grabbed her own fistful of bamboo and tied the tubes into a tight bundle, then looked over at Julia and nodded. 'Alright then,' she said. 'Together.'

Julia took her hand. 'I love you, Claud.'

'Don't go getting soppy on me now, Jules. I'm a bit busy.'

And with that, Claudia dragged her out of the shack towards the opposite edge of the roof, where Lucas was kicking at faces and fingers.

'What are you doing here? Get back to the shelter!'

'You can't deal with them all,' Julia said, jabbing her knife into the hand of a man whom she only recognised as one of the latest Candidates when he was already falling to the paving below.

'It's not safe,' Lucas insisted, kicking the priestess in the jaw. 'We don't know what's wrong with them.'

'We're helping,' Claudia said.

Lucas might have argued, but Claudia demonstrated her point by dispatching five of the rabid mob with precision hits to the skull, tumbling them backwards off the roof.

But they were still going to lose.

Lucas was visibly tiring, his movements slower and less controlled.

Then Claudia lost her pole. It was wrenched from her hands to fall clattering down the staircase, and she held on to it so stubbornly that she nearly followed it over the edge. Julia lost hers seconds later, and after that they were no use at all.

All they were was bait.

They backed up towards the shelter, pulling Lucas with them. He had scratches and bites the length of his arms, and he'd lost his cloak somewhere along the way. He might be a Noble, but he'd taken so many hits.

'Alright, children, get out of the way. The grown ups have arrived.'

Five figures ran up onto the roof so quickly that they might as well have materialised from thin air. The one who had spoken was a familiar, red-headed fighter: Lorelei.

They made Julia and Claudia's efforts seem completely pitiful. If Julia was honest about it, they put Lucas to shame as well.

It was over in a blink.

The roof was cleared in seconds, the climbers tumbled from their perches leaving behind only smears of blood to mark their passage. As the other four walked the walls, kicking back the stragglers, Lorelei turned to where Julia, Lucas and Claudia stood.

'You look familiar,' she said, pointing at Claudia. 'Rufus's Attendant, right?'

'That's right.'

'Then you must be Julia.'

'Julia's my Attendant,' Lucas said, shifting his stance so Julia was tucked behind his shoulder.

Lorelei watched the possessive gesture with obvious amusement. 'I see,' she said. 'Well, aren't you lucky we turned up when we did? You're welcome, by the way.'

'How many are dead?' Lucas asked pointedly.

'Not many, so far.'

'So far?'

'He's back,' one of Lorelei's companions called from the edge of the roof that overlooked the square.

Lorelei surveyed the three of them for a moment, two scruffy human girls and one blood-drenched Silver boy, then she seemed to reach a decision.

'There's something you ought to see,' she said.

So they watched.

They watched while a man pushed his way into the torch-lit square, moving so fast that his passage through the bodies was like a breeze rippling through a field of wheat. He was taller than the others; that's what made him stand out to Julia. When he stopped in the centre, dead centre, there was something correct about his placement, standing so tall and still in the midst of a field of movement.

Then the stillness started to spread. It started from his hand, a palm placed almost reverentially on the face of the nearest person, and when that body dropped, the others followed it down. They were flattened, detonating from the centre, wheat in a gale, straight to the ground.

They didn't get up again.

'You asked how many dead,' Lorelei said, waving her hand towards the square as though she were presenting a gift. 'Well, there's your answer.'

Cam didn't wait around to help the other guards clean up the mess. He didn't stop to clean himself up either, because there was something else he had to do first.

He left bloody handprints on the door to the palace as he forced it open, pushing back the flimsy barricade piled up against the inside. It might have kept the Weepers out, but it wasn't enough to discourage a determined member of the Invicti.

He had a score to settle.

The corridors were empty, as were Laila's usual rooms. Cam took perverse delight in tramping across her cushions in his gore-streaked boots. The fizzy feeling he gathered to himself as he trailed his bloody fingers along her tapestries was one of indescribable malice.

He took joy in these petty revenges, because he knew that confronting Laila would give him no satisfaction. It couldn't change what she had done, or the trust that she had broken, and it wouldn't change what he was going to do next. She would twist his words and bend them back at him until they brought him no pleasure.

Still, it had to be done.

He finally found her at the back of the palace, sealed up in a jewelled bedchamber while her favourites whispered together anxiously in the surrounding rooms.

There were no guards here, and her acolytes didn't try to stop him.

His entrance was loud. He slammed the doors open so wide that they knocked chunks of plaster from the walls.

'I know we've never exactly been friends,' he said, 'but I didn't think you'd actually try to kill me.'

'Oh, Cameron. Must you be so melodramatic?'

She was sitting cross-legged on the bed, a platter of fruit at her side and a glass of wine in her hand, apparently unconcerned with the Weepers that had until recently been threatening the entire human population of her city.

'We both know I had good reasons for wanting you dead,' she went on. 'If you didn't see it coming then you only have yourself to blame.'

Cam sighed. It was as he had anticipated. There was no satisfaction to be had in this, only more pain.

'Just tell me why, Laila.'

'Because of Emmy, of course,' she said, unfolding her neat legs from beneath herself so she could slide off the end of the bed and onto her feet.

'But you said you wanted to find her,' Cam said.

'And that's true. I never lied to you. I'm as eager to find her as you are, although for different reasons, obviously.'

'You don't want the Primus back?'

'Of course I don't.' She spat the words. 'You had it right to start with: I might not have much here, but I'm not giving it up, particularly not to that cheating bastard.'

Cam kicked nonchalantly at one of the doors, sending more plaster dust scattering over the floor. 'You always have liked your things.'

'Yes,' she said, raising an eyebrow with surprising tolerance. 'Now why don't you take a seat before you break anything else?'

Laila indicated a low chaise with a graceful gesture. Cam eyed the spindly piece of furniture with suspicion.

'No thanks,' he said, imagining his ungainly limbs spread awkwardly across the floor. 'I think I'll stand.' Laila probably chose her furniture deliberately, designing each piece to make everyone else look like a clumsy giant next to her petite poise.

'I don't want Emmy here,' Laila said. 'You know I wasn't... unfond of her, but the last thing I want is Solomon returning. No, I can't allow that to happen.'

'Then what *do* you want, Laila?'

The Empress sat back on the edge of the bed, crossing her feet neatly at the ankle.

'Do you remember the attack on Athens?' she asked. 'The one just before Emmy was taken from Delphi, when we were trying to cure the Weepers in the harbour at Piraeus?'

'You were there that day?' Cam asked.

He could remember it well, fighting alongside Emmy and Tommy, half in and half out of the water, but he didn't remember seeing Laila. The Weepers had bobbed like buoys, moving so naturally with the waves that you could almost have believed they were inanimate, until you got close enough for them to drag you under.

'I was there,' she said. 'I came with the Invicti, because Emmy asked me to. I was right beside her when she waded into the water, so I saw when she stabbed the vaccine into the first one. Did you see it, Cameron?'

He shook his head. 'I just saw them go down.'

'They went down,' Laila said. 'She went down too, though, because another of them already had a grip around her leg, and when she fell, the first one fell on top of her. She had her eyes open, and her mouth, when his blood, his *vaccinated blood*, dropped into her face.'

'What are you saying?'

Laila's gaze locked with his. 'I'm saying there's no way she should have walked away from that still Silver. She should have been cured.'

'It doesn't mean the blood got inside her. If you'd seen the amount of contaminated blood I've been swimming through this past week-'

'No, Cameron,' she interrupted. 'I was two feet away from her when it happened. I wasn't mistaken.'

Cam tried to digest the implications of this. If Emmy was immune to the cure, then that meant a shortage of uncontaminated humans wouldn't be a problem for her. She'd be able to drink from anyone, contaminated or not.

If they could pass that ability on to other Silver, then the boundaries of the Blue would be a thing of the past.

'My tests confirmed it,' Laila went on.

'Excuse me?'

'*I* found her, Cameron. And we were close to a solution, so close, before she was taken away.'

'You *found* her?' Cam's fists clenched at his sides, his muscles itching for impact. 'You found her, and you didn't tell anyone?'

'Yes. But apparently Charles wanted her to himself. He took her away, we don't know where.'

Cam laughed in disbelief, and the bitterness of it raked his throat. She had let Emmy slip away to keep her grip on a kingdom that was pulling itself apart at the seams.

But Laila wouldn't have the chance to get to Emmy again, because now Cam had a head start. He was going to get there first.

'Well,' he said, 'you'd better find her again quickly, because I just filled your city with contamination to deal with our little Weeper problem.'

'It doesn't matter,' Laila replied, reaching into the folds of her tunic to pull out a handful of blood-stained vials. 'Someone beat you to it. Whoever set the Weepers loose took the time to administer contaminated blood to some of our humans first. We think they might have been trying to vaccinate their own, to protect them from the Weeper virus.'

'Either that or they were hoping you wouldn't notice that your Attendants were contaminated. You could've ended up curing yourself when you drank from them. That would have been ironic.'

Laila looked down at the vials, rolling them in her fist. 'Indeed.'

It was the pause before she answered that gave her away. If it hadn't been for that, Cam wouldn't have listened for the beat of her heart, or scented the air to find the humanity beneath the lingering shine of Silver.

'Oh,' he said.

She put the vials back into her pocket, her eyes unfocused as she looked beyond Cam.

'Do you remember what he used to say?' she asked. '*We are not moral creatures*. He knew it, your Primus.'

'You can be loyal to someone without believing everything they say.'

'Perhaps,' she said, 'but I think he was right about that, if nothing else. I am not a moral creature, Cameron. I'm not sure I even remember how to be human.'

Cam almost gave in to the urge to comfort her, but after all she had done, she didn't deserve his sympathy.

'I expect you'll work it out,' he said, then he turned and left her there, sitting alone in the shell of her broken palace.

20

'So,' Tommy said as they piled back into the bunkhouse, 'you're home.'

'I am,' said Cam.

'Looks like you caught us at a bad time.'

'Looks a lot like that, Tommy. What the hell did I miss?'

Cam eyed him as they walked into the lounge with the rest of the guards, trying to see him as anything other than a friend, but he couldn't separate the Secundus from the man he'd fought beside for centuries. If Tommy had betrayed him, he couldn't see it in his face. He wasn't sure why he'd ever thought he might, because if there was one thing everyone knew about Cam, it was that he trusted too easily.

At least, the old Cam had.

Was he still that gullible?

'There are always malcontents, Cam.'

'Yeah, sure, but there are never Weepers in the Blue. There were never Weepers in the Red for that matter, not until this last trip.'

'They're in the Red too?'

'You're telling me you didn't know?'

Tommy looked genuinely shocked. 'What exactly are you accusing me of?'

The room fell silent around them, the other guards alerted by Tommy's tone.

'You're missing a couple of Invicti,' Cam said. 'You know where they are?'

Tommy looked around the room, searching for the missing

faces. 'Yeah, they come and go on assignment. You know that.'

'I know that yesterday, Tiberius was handing over uncontaminated humans to a caravan of feral Silver roaming around the Red. I know that a few days ago, Carmen was up by old Dresden in a place they call Charlestown, selling me out to the locals. And I know that Laila was the one who decided to use the Invicti to have me killed. So, do you want to tell me whose side you're on, Tommy?'

There was a moment of staggered silence, and Cam could have believed that all of this might have been a surprise to his comrades in arms, if there hadn't been so many people trying to avoid his eyes.

'What?' Tommy said.

He followed Cam's gaze around the room, alighting on the faces of each of his soldiers, every one of them sworn to follow his orders and none other. When he spoke again, to them now, his voice was so loud it shook the floor.

'What? Am I supposed to accept this? Did you think I'd forgive insubordination, that I'd forgive an attempt to kill one of our own?'

Most of his audience seemed as outraged as Tommy was, but there were so many wearing masks of shame or defiance. How had they not realised that they'd become so divided?

'I want you out of here,' Tommy said to them. 'Every single one of you who had something to do with this, or who even knew about it and said nothing, you're gone. Go to the palace if the bloody Empress wants you, go to the Red for all I care, but get the hell out of my sight.'

There was a scramble as people moved towards the door, and a scuffle as a few of their former comrades helped them on their way.

'And you lot,' Tommy said to the remaining crowd, 'you mark my words: I'll be looking into this, and if you were involved and you're not gone by the time I find out, then you're going to wish the Weepers had got you. Are we clear?'

Apparently satisfied for the moment, Tommy released them back to their bunks, leaving just him and Cam behind.

'You didn't know, then,' Cam said.

Tommy looked at him, the hurt evident on his face. 'Of course I didn't know.' As he spoke, he clasped his hand around the back of Cam's neck and pulled him close until they stood forehead to forehead, Tommy's eyes staring as though they could burn the truth into Cam's brain. 'You're my brother. I'd protect you with my life.'

'Even if Laila ordered you to kill me?'

'She knows what would happen if she tried.'

Cam closed his eyes, the tension finally slipping from his jaw as Tommy pulled him into a rough hug.

'You're my brother, you fool,' he said, 'and if you want to spend the next millennium searching for Emmy, then I'm behind you.'

'Oh, yeah,' Cam said as Tommy released him, 'that actually won't be necessary.'

Tommy smiled a little. 'You've been dedicated, man. No one would fault you for that, but I've got to say it's a relief to hear you're coming back to us. It's time we all laid Emmy to rest.'

'I've found her.'

Tommy stared. 'What?'

'I've found Emmy.'

'You're kidding.'

'Nope.' It was Cam's turn to smile. 'She's up close to Charlestown, the place I mentioned, a bit further south against the mountains. There's a passage carved into the rock with a load of Silver guarding it. I didn't get inside, but her scent's all over the place.'

'You're sure?'

'Seriously? After this many centuries, you ask me that?'

Tommy took a breath. 'Okay, you're sure. Holy shit.'

'We can get her back, Tommy.'

Tommy was smiling too, properly now. 'And then we can get *him* back.'

'And then everything changes.'

They said it was contamination.

The guards had come back to Julia and the others after the dramatic collapse of their attackers, to take away the bodies and destroy the smears of gore that littered the rooftop.

The guards told them not to touch the blood. They told them that Marcus had walked it in from the Red and then infected everything he touched with its taint.

The guards told them it was what was waiting for them out there, if they ever tried to leave.

So now there was nothing to do but hide while they waited for normality to return, if it ever would.

'You can stay here,' Lucas said to Julia and Claudia, 'if you want.'

But there was no magic left on the rooftop. Lucas's plants had all been flattened or pulled by the scrabbling hands of the infected, and those that had escaped the fight had been cleansed by the guards.

There was nothing left of his garden, not even the soil in the pots.

It would never be the same again.

'I don't think we should,' Julia said, looking around at the remnants of Lucas's home. It had all been utterly destroyed.

'I'm so sorry,' she added, but he just shrugged.

'It'll grow again, eventually. I can always plant more.'

It wouldn't be the same, though. The evening had smashed apart their paradise, this little slice of isolation that had been just theirs, if only for a short time. With the place gone, Julia felt a precarious sense of unease, as though its loss would change what had started between them.

'It was so beautiful,' Julia said.

Lucas looked at her and smiled. 'It was.'

'So,' Claudia said, 'what now?'

'What do you think?' Julia said to her. 'Back home?'

'At least then we'd be warm, and we could wait for Livia and the others.'

'Alright then. You can come with us if you like,' Julia said to Lucas. 'I can't promise you'll be able to stay, but while the others are away…'

She avoided his eyes while she spoke, because she didn't want to assume. They had been close before tonight, she could accept that, but the evening's events felt as though they would be life-changing.

The Red had come into the Blue, and now the whole world was contaminated.

But she could still feel the zing of his teeth in her wrist.

'Thank you,' he said. 'I'd like that.'

His smile settled the sprinting of her heart. When he took her hand, entwining his fingers with hers, it cemented her conviction that nothing would ever be the same again.

Whatever happened now, this was more than just a fairytale.

'Okay then,' she said. 'Let's go home.'

'Laila didn't do this, Tommy,' Cam said.

'I know,' he said. 'It doesn't make sense that she'd attack herself.'

'So you know you've still got a traitor on your hands?'

'I know.'

'You've got someone else in this city who's working for Charles, who decided to soften us up for him with a good old-fashioned Weeper attack.'

'I *know*, Cam. But it doesn't change anything, because I'm still coming with you.'

They'd been arguing for at least an hour now, monopolising the bunkhouse lounge, but Tommy wouldn't give in. The other Invicti had got bored of listening in and wandered off.

They were all Invicti now, even those who hadn't been before tonight. If they were with Laila then they were just guards, but if they were with Tommy, fighting for their king, then there was only one name he could give them.

'What about Viv?' Cam said. 'Are you really going to leave her behind, pregnant, to fend for herself?'

'Of course not. She's coming with us.'

'*What?*'

'Well, I'm not leaving her here while the Blue self-destructs. Do you have any idea how dangerous it's going to be?'

'Yes!' Cam yelled, his exasperation cracking his voice. 'That's exactly why you should be staying behind. You have to keep the peace while everything settles down.'

'Why? For Laila? We don't work for her anymore, Cam. We've got a different mission now, and that's where I need to be: bringing Emmy back.'

It was difficult to absorb the change. Cam had seen empires rise and fall in his lifetime, but Laila had been ruling in the Blue for centuries, ever since the Fall. The thought of having to deconstruct their civilisation and rebuild it again, all whilst dealing with the new threat of contamination, was enough to give Cam a headache.

'What about the humans?' he said. 'And what about the Primus? Charles's people are on their way, and we might not be able to stop them. We can't just abandon the Blue.'

'We're not going to. We'll leave a contingent behind.'

'Led by Lorelei?' Cam asked.

Tommy nodded. 'That's what I was thinking. Her people are well-trained, and she remembers the time before the Fall. She remembers Emmy and Sol, too. She knows what we're fighting for.'

'She's fierce,' Cam agreed, 'and she was a real help tonight. Saved a lot of lives.'

Tommy looked down at his hands. 'You're sure you don't want the title?'

Cam smiled. 'I'm sure. I just want to find Emmy and put an end to this. I'm not a leader, Tommy, and I don't want to be.'

'Alright then, if you're sure. Lorelei!' he yelled.

'Yeah?' she said, poking her head around the corner from the kitchen.

'You want to come in here a sec?'

She said, 'Sure,' and took a seat on the chair opposite Tommy's, but she didn't look comfortable. She looked like she'd rather be anywhere else.

'You alright?' Tommy asked as she fidgeted.

'Fine,' she said, 'just antsy. It seems like a pretty fucking exciting time out there right now, and I can't help but feel like we should be doing something about it.'

'Clean up's done,' Cam said.

'Well, the bodies have gone, yeah, and the blood's been washed away. I wouldn't say things were clean, though. We're a long fucking way from clean. In fact, everything feels messy as hell.'

'And it will for a while,' said Tommy. 'Which is why I need you to stay here and keep an eye on things while we go after Emmy.'

'Why can't I come with you? I mean, that's where the fight's going to be, right? Busting her out of a mountainside fortress. A fucking fortress. You can't leave me behind for that.'

'I need you here, Tertius,' Tommy said, emphasising the title.

'What?' Lorelei gaped.

'I want you to be my second-in-command, and I need you here, because Charles is bringing the fight to us as surely as we're taking it to him. So will you do it?'

Cam could track the emotions across her face: disappointment, reluctance, happiness, and underneath it all: a ripple of gentle self-satisfaction. She wouldn't be Lorelei without it.

'Alright then,' she said. 'But you'd better bring her home.'

'You know we will. And in the meantime, you'd better get ready, because they're coming.'

'Don't worry,' Lorelei said. 'I'll be waiting for them.'

Rufus visited Claudia a little after they'd returned to the kitchen. He came to the front door, ringing the bell like a proper gentleman despite the late hour, and Julia found herself listening again for the thump of Livia's footsteps upstairs.

But the kitchen had been cold when they'd got back, the coals burned out in the grate. It was exactly as they'd left it when they'd set out for Lucas's that evening, a memory that felt years old rather than hours.

Livia didn't answer the door. She hadn't returned, and neither had any of the others.

They were on their own.

Claudia answered instead, and Julia tried not to eavesdrop as Rufus spoke to her in the hall.

'You have tea here?' Lucas said in surprise. He was rooting through the cupboards, looking for interesting herbs and spices.

'Not for us,' Julia replied. 'For the Nobles. Livia provides it to them, along with their meals. Or to you, rather,' she corrected herself, remembering that Lucas was not like her and Claudia. He was one of them.

'I never get tea,' Lucas said. 'I never get honey either, and I have to steal my wine from the temple. You've got everything here.'

The fire was roaring now, crackling wildly with its first taste of fresh wood. It went some way towards erasing the cold of the night, but there was a bone-deep chill that Julia was struggling to shift.

She turned from her seat by the hearth when she heard the front door closing, praying that she wouldn't have to deal with Rufus at this time of the morning. Claudia wouldn't invite him in, would she?

'He's gone,' she said, laughing at Julia's expression. 'He just wanted to check that I was alright, and apologise for not being there to help us. He got stuck on the other side of the city, making sure Marcella was safe.'

'Really?' Julia asked. 'So he didn't have anything to do with what happened tonight?'

'Oh, don't start. He really isn't that bad.'

'He really is,' Lucas said, scowling as he slammed the cupboard door.

'Is that a genuine opinion,' Claudia asked, 'or are you just jealous that he keeps flirting with Julia?'

'Claud!' Julia was horrified. She never expected Claudia, of all people, to speak to a Noble like that.

But Lucas was laughing.

'Yes,' he said, 'I'm jealous.' His eyes settled on Julia's, then drifted sideways towards the silver stud she still wore in her ear. 'Giving you that earring was the best decision I ever made.'

Their eyes met again, and Julia never wanted to look away.

'Alright,' Claudia said, 'I'm going to bed. Long day, you know, running from crazy infected people. See you both in the morning.'

'Night, Claud,' Julia said, but she didn't break her gaze with Lucas.

'Night, Claudia,' Lucas said, similarly distracted.

'Goodnight, you two.'

Julia could hear her laughing quietly to herself as she walked down the stairs to the cellar.

Lucas's mouth was on Julia's the moment they heard the door close. It wasn't gentle, the bruising crush of lips, but it was so vital that Julia couldn't bring herself to rein it in. She needed to lose herself in the sugary addiction of his kisses and know that whatever else might change around them, they still had this.

They had survived this night, and despite everything that stood in their way, they still had each other.

They still wanted each other.

Lucas wrapped his arms around her, one hand pushing up through her hair and the other clasping her waist as he lifted her onto the counter. She slipped her hands down his sides and pulled his hips towards her, dragging him closer as she spread her legs to either side.

He groaned as their bodies pressed against each other through the fabric of her dress.

'You have no idea,' he said, kissing his way down her throat, 'how long I've dreamt about this.' His hand found the back of her calf and started sliding upwards, pushing her dress up with it. 'I can't remember a time,' he whispered against her ear, 'when I didn't want you.'

Her hands were under his shirt now, and he shivered as her fingertips traced the ridges of his chest. She followed them upwards, then ran her hands around to his back.

They leaned out of the embrace for a second, just enough time to let Julia pull Lucas's shirt over his head, but in that second she got a glimpse of his eyes, and realised that something had changed.

'Lucas,' she said as he kissed her.

'Say it again.'

'No, Lucas,' she said, her palms flat on his stomach as she pushed him away. 'Wait.'

'What's wrong? Did I do something wrong?'

'No, it's not…' She could see it then, the thing that was missing. 'Lucas, what happened to your eyes?'

'Nothing,' he said, and his confusion was evident. 'Why?'

Julia reached behind her to the knife block and pulled out the cleaver.

'Woah,' Lucas said, catching her wrist in his hand. 'What are you doing?'

'Just look,' she said, turning the blade sideways so its flat edge faced him like a mirror. 'Look at your eyes.'

He looked at Julia, then tilted the reflective edge towards himself. It was dim in the fire-lit kitchen, but still bright enough for him to see the reflection that was missing, the silver that was no longer in his eyes.

'It's gone,' she said.

'It's gone,' he repeated.

'When did you learn to hide the silver?'

He shook his head. 'I didn't know that I had. Tonight, I suppose.'

'Oh.' Julia pulled the skirt of her dress back down.

When their eyes met again, the heat had disappeared.

For the first time since she had met him, Lucas appeared entirely human. There was nothing to mark him out as what he was, and that sent a chill through Julia's veins, because they both knew what it meant.

He looked back at his face in the cleaver as irritation suffused his features, then he threw it hard into the kitchen door, where it embedded itself with a dull ring.

He was going into the Red, and he was leaving her behind.

* * *

In the bunkhouse, the Invicti were getting ready to leave, but Cam had nothing of his own to pack. Instead, he went to the temple to see his king.

It was empty now, because the Weepers had broken their way in through the doors. They hung askew from their hinges, so twisted that there was no way to keep them closed. The people who had sheltered here were secure in the palace with the rest of the survivors, and with Laila, the imposter Empress.

That wouldn't last for long.

Cam didn't mind the quiet of the sanctuary, but with the inside of it cleared of blood-soaked seating and other detritus, there was nothing for him to do. He couldn't sit, or read, or even light a candle. He wasn't sure why he had come at all, only that it felt like the right thing to do. It was the end of a journey, and the beginning of one that would usher in a new age.

That felt as though it warranted some kind of ceremony.

He waited a while, looking at the dais, then sighed to himself. He wasn't going to start talking to a statue, so he may as well go and help the other Invicti with their packing.

He was halfway to the door when an impulse struck him, so irresistible that it felt almost necessary, so he strode back to the statue and left a little token behind on its chest: a tiny piece of material, the size of a coin.

Then he went to find his queen.

Outside the Blue, beyond the water, on the shore where the caravan had soaked the ground with blood, Felix waited. The trees were short and wide-branched here, too low for there to be any point in climbing them, and in any case he wanted to be seen.

He had been told to wait.

When he heard the footsteps, loud and deliberate, he knew that the noise was a courtesy. His friend could move as silently and quickly as she wished.

'Otho's dead,' he said as the redhead appeared between the trees. 'Richard too.'

'You think I give a shit about Richard? You let the Invicti find the bloody queen!'

'I didn't have a choice.'

'Didn't you?' She crossed her arms and leaned her hip against a beech trunk, staring Felix down, but he didn't baulk.

'Cameron rescued a cured woman. She told him where to go. What did you expect me to do?'

'He shouldn't have got that far.'

'And whose fault is that?'

The redhead's mouth puckered, as though she were biting her cheeks to keep herself in check, but her mouth twitched as she surveyed his lumpen face. Perhaps his injuries mollified her. Perhaps she thought he'd tried.

'Well,' she said, 'you'd better make sure he doesn't manage to get her free. Stay with him.'

'Didn't you hear me?' Felix said, stepping towards the woman.

She pushed away from the tree, taking a more defensive stance, as though a human could ever hurt her.

'Otho's dead,' he said. 'You can't save him now. You have nothing to offer me, and I have no reason to help you.'

'Is that what you think?' She was mocking him, a tinkling edge of laughter in her tone.

'I'm leaving, Lorelei,' he said, stooping to collect the bag at his feet. He swung it over his shoulder.

'So you don't want to be Silver again?' Her voice was soft, a whisper on the breeze, but the words were so heavy that even Felix's human hearing had no trouble picking them up.

'We're close,' she said. 'We can do it, as long as we have her.'

He paused for a moment, then dropped the bag back to the ground.

'What do you need me to do?'

Epilogue

In the mountains of the Red, Charles was becoming impatient.

He'd never wanted to be a kidnapper, but then he'd never wanted to be human either.

If only her blood had worked. If only they hadn't lost the child. If only he had never gone near her in the first place.

This was all her fault.

How he wished he could close his fingers around her throat and choke the air from her lungs, but she was still one of them, one of the creatures he had once been: Silver. She was hundreds of times stronger than he was now, in his decaying body. Even as she lay helpless before him, paralysed by the concoction flowing in her veins and the blood flowing out, he was still the helpless one. He could strangle her, stab her, drain her dry, and still she'd live. She was immortal, while he was being killed by every tick of the clock.

The door to the cell opened behind him.

'They're not happy,' the newcomer said.

Charles didn't shift his attention from the notebook in his hand. 'I don't care.'

'You should.' The man wore an apron, bright and clean, as a doctor's clothes should be. He looked as though he belonged in the room, more than Charles did, anyway. While the doctor was slight and neat, Charles stood wide in a way that took up space. It wasn't that he was particularly large, but his aggression filled the corners of the cell.

'Tell me you have something,' he said.

The doctor wrapped his fingers around the woman's wrist,

feeling for her pulse. She was perfectly still, except for the occasional rise of her chest, too infrequent to sustain a human.

'She's been asleep too long,' he said. 'Her blood's too weak. We needed the child.'

Charles flung the notebook at the wall. It ricocheted across the corner of the room before coming to rest with a soft thump on the stone floor. The doctor raised an eyebrow, then returned to his examination.

'Tell me something that's actually helpful,' Charles hissed.

'I told you: we need the child.'

'The child's gone.'

'Then I can't help you.'

Charles gritted his teeth, working the muscles at the sides of his jaw.

'Wake her up.'

In the temple of the Blue, everything was silent.

There was a scent in the air, a lingering touch of rich sweetness rising from the scrap of material Cam had left behind, so faint that it might have been a memory. It drifted around the dais alcove, threads of it wafting across the statue of the king in the convection of the candles that surrounded the space.

It stroked the marble skin and tickled its way into the nostrils, then hung there for a second, building its concentration in the olfactory receptors.

The pressure around the alcove dropped, just slightly.

If there had been anyone in the temple, they might have turned to see whether the door had been opened, or if a draught was creeping in through an unsealed shutter, but there was no one there to detect the change. The statue was the closest thing to a living being in the room.

And, if there had been anyone in the temple, they might have thought it seemed just a little bit more alive in that moment than it had previously. Previously, the golden sheen that covered the statue had seemed sunk in the stone, an integral part of the structure, but now it was as though it had been expelled to the surface.

Then the gilding started to retreat. It began at the statue's feet, where marble-white pushed golden waves of colour away from it, leaving light folds of soft cottons in its wake. By the time it reached the face, a dense foil of precious metal had gathered under the skin, slipping from hair and chin as it crept inwards towards the eyes, where it disappeared beneath the lashes.

Then the air pressure returned, a gentle thud of sensation, although again there was no one in the temple to feel it.

Or so it might have seemed a few moments previously, but now the surface of the statue looked distinctly different. It was minutely variegated in uneven colours, the weave of the fabric pitted with imperfections, the skin appearing pliable with its blue-tinged veins, the cheeks so subtly pinked.

A finger twitched.

When he opened his ice-blue eyes, they were threaded with gold.

If you've enjoyed this book, please do consider reviewing it on Amazon.

Book reviews can make a huge difference to the success of a novel, particularly those of self-published authors like me. If you have time to leave a review, even if it's just a couple of lines, then I would be very grateful.

If you would like to join my mailing list to receive details of new releases, you can do so on my website:

www.josiejaffrey.com